Shad

CW00506599

By A C

This novel is a work of fiction. Names, characters and events are products of the author's imagination. Any resemblance to actual persons, living or dead is entirely coincidental.

Copyright © 2016 by A.C. Salter

1

Dedication

For my loving wife, who puts up with my odd ways
and my children, who make up the rest of team Salter.

Shadojak

Chapter 1

Earth Bound

"I can't come; I wish I could," Bray sighed, shaking his head at the injustice of the fact. He stood erect, scowling at his feet then kicked a broken piece of masonry across the blackened church hall. It skittered against the ruined font before falling into the Well of Redemption.

Elora squeezed his hand, recognising the hurt in those moss-green eyes and feeling empathy for her boyfriend and for herself.

Bray had tried to dissuade her from returning to Earth without him. Pleading that they should find a way to take the journey together and cross the barrier into the world with help from the Emperor and with the strength of his armies. But, she wouldn't take the longer route or wait for the Emperor to make a decision. This was her mess, her actions that released the Dark Army upon the Earth and it was her job to put it right.

"I'll be fine," Elora said, glancing away from his concern etched face and staring out of the ruined wall of the church, taking in the city of Aslania that stretched out below them.

An entire division of the Emperor's army was down there. She could make out the ranks of scarlet and gold along the streets and buildings waiting to escort her to Rona, the Empire's capital.

They'd be waiting a long time because she wasn't going with them.

Elora and Bray were in the Minuan church that was carved out of the mountain, high upon a rock face above the city she was born in and smuggled from as a child. The immense hole in the wall was created by her father, the God of Chaos. A legacy left behind along with death and destruction before she had killed him, ending a song that had been sung without pause for thousands of years. Eversong had died upon her lips when she released her father.

Elora leaned against the upturned font and gazed at the carnage. The granite scorched black in the very place she had ended her father's life, along with the Shadojak's. Both killed by the same sword. The Soul Reaver which was her father's before becoming the property of the Shadojaks. Now it was hers. Hidden within her smuggler's pouch, invisible and unreachable by others; she felt its weight, sensed its power and accepted the burden of responsibility that came with it. Elora was now the Shadojak. Judge, balancer and protector of both realms.

The silence between herself and Bray was broken only by the breeze that buffeted past the broken wall, whistling as it passed over the fallen masonry and smashed rock. The church in ruin, its last song sung was now replaced by the haunting tones of the wind.

They had both known this was their final moment together, the last time they would be with each other until Bray found a way to cross over to the other side, yet she couldn't think of anything to say. What could she say?

Words wouldn't keep them together, wouldn't cleanse the world of the Dark Army and couldn't bring the dead back. It would be her actions and her energies that would unpick the chaos left by her father.

A figure stepped into the large broken chamber. Delicately he weaved between the debris on the rubble-strewn floor, careful not to lose his footing and break the lute he carried.

"He's ready for you Elora," Otholo said. His usual sing-song voice taking on a sombre quality. He gave them both a sad smile before returning the way he came, gently plucking a melancholy tune on his beloved instrument.

"This is it then," Bray said, rising from the font and brushing dust from his cloak before offering her his hand.

"This is it," Elora replied, taking his hand and pulling him into an embrace and not bothering to brush the dust from her own black cloak; a gift from the Minuan people for ridding them of the curse that tied them to Eversong and to her father.

She put on a brave face as they followed the bard through the anti-chamber and up a stone staircase that led out into the open. A small garden lay behind the church; a glade that was hidden from below. A secret place, away from the Imperial Guards and hidden from those who wished to meet her. Only the peaks of the mountains bared witness to her departure, the snow from their sentinel points dusted off by the wind to drift across the blue sky.

They approached the fairy circle hand in hand, wild grass wet with mountain dew clinging to her boots as a yellow lotus tree infused its sweet aroma to the secret garden. The few friends and family that came to see her off parted as they neared.

Elora nodded towards the three elderly ladies. The Sisters Devine; Aslania's Elders and Council. They smiled back, bowing as she passed and giving the respect shown to a Shadojak. Elora didn't think she'd ever get used to that. Her uncle Nathaniel stood next to the circle of moon daisies, his arm around her mother. Athena's tears running freely down her face. Elora's heart ached to spend more time with her, the last three weeks spent at her mother's home had passed by in a blur, giving her only a taste of what she had been missing out of her life.

They hugged each other, mother and daughter, Nathaniel's arm giving her a squeeze as he placed a kiss upon her head.

Everything that needed to be said had been said earlier, before they left and Elora was thankful for it. She doubted her own cheeks would have been dry if they hadn't. All the goodbyes had been done at her mother's house. The plans for the future, the decisions of how to handle the Emperor who demanded that she come to him. How they would handle the Shadojak Supreme, who would need to grant her the official title of Shadojak - if he didn't her life would end on the point of her sword. Ejan wanted them all to return to Rams Keep, everyone had different ideas of what was for the best, but it was guilt that set her on the path to return to Earth.

Ejan stood before her now, the Fist of the North resting against her shoulders and seeming far too heavy for the Norsewoman to lift. As Elora approached she lowered the great war hammer, its shaft resting in the grass.

Elora grasped the weapon, her own hand print embedded in the steel head and hoisted it upon her shoulder. The sheer weight of it forced her to bend over to the side to compensate for the burden. Yet she carried it with pride. It belonged to Ejan's late husband Ragna. A Viking warrior who gave his own life to save her and the small group they travelled with. This had happened only a few weeks ago and his passing had left an emptiness in her heart. It was her job to give the hammer to his son Jaygen, who had yet to learn of his father's death.

Ejan gave her a quick kiss on the cheek and wished her luck as she stepped through the crackling moon daisies and into the fairy circle, leaving the world of Thea behind.

She had only been in a fairy circle once before, in a cellar at a London town-house. This one was much the same; a raised dais of grass with pretty flowers in various colours and sizes, fairies busily flying amongst them. The outside world beyond the circle was a blue and green blur, the oscillating air shimmering before her forming a dome. It was like standing inside a huge snow globe.

Bray had followed her into the fairy circle but could go no further. Apart from the fairies themselves, only gods or god-created creatures could travel through them. It was a risk she was taking going through herself. She was only part god and that being the deity of Chaos, yet it was a risk she was determined to take.

Prince Dylap was sat atop his black falcon, perched on a fallen log with two other fairies flanking him on smaller grey-coloured birds. He was god-created himself, a weapon to serve a forgotten god for a war that had long ago been fought and also forgotten. The small Farrosian was now Prince of the fairies that lived in the Farrosian Forest.

He gave her a nod and kicking his heels into the flank of his bird, rose into the air and flew through the shimmering wall, his bird-riders following.

"It's not too late to change your mind," Bray said, pulling Elora around so she was facing him.

She leaned into his body, a final embrace before she departed.

"You know I can't do that."

"I know," he said, resignation making his words sound thick with emotion. He placed a kiss on her lips and stood back, allowing her to leave and letting go. "I love you."

"Love you too, Elf boy," Elora replied.

The days spent together in each other's company and in his arms had been heaven. She'd known it was going to end and it could be weeks or months before they were together again.

She willed herself to move, to make this departing as brief as possible. Elora stepped through the crackling air blinking back tears.

Pain exploded within her chest as the world collapsed. A crushing weight pressed in on all sides, a pressure that forced her eyes into the back of her head and the air to squeeze from her lungs. The blood in her veins began to boil. If she'd had the ability to scream, Elora would have scoured the sky with a banshee's siren.

A disorienting feeling washed through her brain as stars rushed towards her inner vision; millions of sparkling needle points passing through her as if she had no more substance than a ghost.

Then she thumped down hard against solid ground.

Elora slowly opened her eyes, fighting down the nausea that threatened to empty her belly, but felt reassurance that she was in one piece.

She was still in a blurring dome, although the colours were now different shades of green and the ground was smooth stone cobbles with strands of yellow grass poking between the cracks. She waited a moment for the dizziness to pass before stepping out of the fairy circle and into the ruins of Rams Keep.

Evening had set in. What light she had filtered through the forest canopy, casting dark shadows over the ancient ruins. The maze of fallen walls and towers lay about in broken piles, the footings of staircases and partial archways were covered in creeping ivy and shrubs as the forest tried to claim it back. Rams Keep had a haunting, mournful edge about it, her memories of her last visit only adding to its mystery. Elora had been here before, been in its dungeons, the place where she had been re-born as that other person - the Queen of Darkness.

Prince Dylap waited for her by a fallen doorway, rusty iron bands were the only remnants left from the door itself. He was perched upon a branch of a twisted birch tree that had grown through the wall. His bird-riders either side of him. He raised his silver javelin, pointing in the direction of a deer-track and spoke in a high-pitched voice.

She quickly put her tinker's tongue charm in her ear; the magical device which Bray had given to her when she first arrived in Thea. The small coin-shaped charm allowed her to understand the unfamiliar languages spoken to her.

9

"The protective ward that surrounds the keep still works," explained the fairy Prince, the spines of his wings flexing as he spoke. Tiny forks of lighting sparked between them, different to the delicate butterfly-like wings of his bird-riding companions.

"It would be best that you remained within its protection. Although the main body of the Dark Army are marching east into Europe, there remains pockets of Solarius's force in all areas."

"It's Silk I want. Has he gone into Europe?" Elora asked. She didn't think Prince Dylap understood English, but he knew the name Silk.

"I don't know. He was in the capital, maybe he's still there or has followed his army. Either way I will find him. My bird-riders have already scattered to the far reaches of his host and we three," the fairy spread his arms out to his companions, "will leave for London after the birds have rested."

"Good," Elora said, nodding gratefully. "I will wait for your return."

She left them on the wall as she began the slow walk to Rams Keep Inn, a little over a mile away.

As she took the first step it began to rain, heavy tears falling through the trees. Elora pulled her hood over her head and heaved the war hammer onto her shoulders as the sky turned black. It was going to be a dark evening - as dark as the words she had for Jaygen.

Warm light spilled out from the inn's leaded windows. The old thatched building was a welcome sight as Elora trudged through the courtyard, passing a stone well while her boots spattered mud up her ankles and shins.

The heavy door creaked inwards when she put her shoulder to it. The thought of putting the Fist of the

North down so she could knock had occurred to her, but once that heavy weapon was on your back the momentum just carried you forwards.

Warmth from the open fire greeted her, as did the smell of freshly baked bread, yet there was nobody in the bar room. The large oak table was polished, its chairs neatly pushed underneath, the old bar was also clean and void of life. Surely they were not to bed already.

She was about to shout out when an elderly man sauntered into the room.

"There you are Jaygen. I've been...Elora?" asked Norgie, a grin spreading across his weathered face. His eyes became alight with excitement as he rushed across the room and crushed her in a tight hug.

"Hello Norgie," Elora replied. "I take it Jaygen isn't here then?" She lowered the huge hammer from her shoulders, her body suddenly feeling feather light.

"No, he's still in the stables. Spends most of his time with the horses." He scratched the grey stubble on his chin, making a scraping sound while glancing down at the hammer. "Where are the others?"

Elora tightened her lips, giving herself a moment before replying. It was all still too raw. "I better wait for Jaygen, he should hear it first."

"Right you are lass," Norgie said, a sad smile playing across his aged lips. Once he was satisfied that she was safe he leaned over the bar and took a bottle of wine and two glasses from a shelf. After pouring himself a drink he offered Elora one. She shook her head.

"Did you do it then? Sing that song to bind Solarius?" Norgie asked.

"Yes, I sang the Eversong but it was a trap. I ended up releasing him and he released his Dark Army onto

11

Earth." She pulled a chair from under the table and slouched into it. "I guess you can't see what's happened beyond the protection that surrounds Rams Keep."

Norgie nodded, the news giving him a sombre expression.

"I killed him," she continued. "My father and Diagus both. I drove a blade straight through their hearts." She studied him, expecting the old man to flinch away from her, to call her a killer, a monster - she deserved it. Instead he pulled out the chair next to her, sat down and poured her a drink.

"It's the deeds that makes a person evil. What you did, killing your father; that wasn't evil. And if the Shadojak needed to die, then I'm damn sure it was his decision."

She swallowed a mouthful of wine, tasting blackberries and cherries, the sweet flavours in stark contrast to her bitter mood.

"I'm the Shadojak now."

Norgie's glass paused halfway to his mouth, his hand trembling with age as his brow deepened.

"That explains the black cloak then. So you're here to do what? Judge? Avenge? Balance?" He drained the remainder of his glass. "Alone?"

"I'm here to do whatever it takes." She finished off the wine. "And it would be safer for all involved if I do work alone."

The door suddenly swung open and Jaygen stepped onto the polished floor. His boots were as muddy as hers and half the night's rain dripped from his matted hair and clothes. He took one look at her, his hazel eyes widening as they swung to his father's hammer which she had left leaning against the table.

12

"I'll go see what Gurple's up to, leave you two to talk," Norgie said as he excused himself, closing the door behind him.

Elora took in the tall boy, a couple of years her junior, fourteen, maybe fifteen years of age. His usual shy demeanour changing from shock to anger as he approached her, his wet fingers reaching for the hammer.

"Are they both..."

"No, your mother is alive. She's making her way home with Bray," Elora said, watching him grasp the Fist's shaft and lift it from the floor.

"How did my father die? Was it in battle?" Jaygen asked, sadly. "He always said that's how he wanted to go. Fire in his blood and steel in his hand."

Elora nodded. "Your father saved our lives. He held the pass by himself, holding back the Imperial Army."

"Yeah," Jaygen said, his voice dropping to a whisper as he lifted the hammer onto the hooks on the wall beside the fire. "That's how he wanted it."

"The Fist belongs to you now. Ragna wanted you to have it."

Jaygen stared up at his father's weapon, the dull steel glowing red in the firelight.

"I don't want it. Big clumsy lump of metal," he said.

Elora rose and took a step towards him and placed a hand on his arm; a pathetic attempt at consoling but she didn't know enough about the boy to help. In the end he flinched from her touch and without saying a word marched outside into the storm.

She made to go after him but Norgie called her back.

"The lad's best left alone. He'll come around in his own time."

Elora paused, her hand on the door handle. "I don't know how much time we have. This world's already fallen, the longer we leave it before retaliating, the deeper the hold the Dark Army will have."

She pushed out into the night in search of Jaygen.

The stables were dark, yet warm. A musky smell of horse and hay reached her nose as she pushed the gate open and stepped inside.

"Jaygen?" Her only answer were the snickers from her own horse, Daisy.

The Gypsy Vanna nuzzled her before nipping at her cloak. Elora stroked her nose as she stepped passed, brushing her hand down the mare's slender neck and feeling the soft skin. Jaygen had done a good job of looking after her and a great deal of time grooming. But he wasn't here now. Maybe he found somewhere in the forge or inn to run to. He knew this place a lot better than she did.

She left the stables, snapping the gate shut behind her when something hit her legs hard and almost drove her to her knees.

Elora kicked out. Reflexes already moving to her smuggler's pouch where she drew out her sword; the blade arcing around as she grasped her attacker and shoved it against the stable wall. Her fingers found a furry throat as she squeezed and lifted upwards.

The body of her attacker was small and squat. An overly large head was now level with her own as sharp pointy teeth reflected the inn's lamps, beneath a short stubby muzzle. Small paws grasped her wrist that was pushing into him.

"Gurple?" Elora asked, hastily withdrawing her sword from his neck, his large frightened eyes focusing on the red glow of her blade. "I'm sorry Gurple, you startled me."

She lowered the wood troll to the ground and placed her sword away. The little furry creature immediately stepped away from her, wringing his paws together, ears standing tall and erect.

Elora held a hand out to him and he flinched from it before hastily retreating.

"It's ok Gurple, I won't hurt you," she said, but the little wood troll was already running towards the inn with his little feet thumping into the wet mud.

She wasn't doing well, she thought and let out a heavy sigh. Less than an hour at Rams Keep Inn and she had already upset two out of the three inhabitants. Poor little Gurple, she must have frightened the life out of him and all he meant to do was greet her with a hug. What was she turning into?

The last few weeks had changed her, toughened her up, hammered the softness away and shaped the once quiet girl into a hardened killer. A demigod, the Shadojak.

Gurple gave her a final glance, his child-like body silhouetted in the inn's doorway before he slammed it shut. She would try to be more like her old self around the wood troll, he wouldn't understand. That is, if she could. Her reactions were now that of a swords master. The blade in her pouch giving her the reflexes of all that had wielded it since her father first created the sword thousands of years ago. Add to that her lineage, being the daughter of Chaos, the Queen of Darkness and you had an evil combination. Something which she needed to control. Her temper could cost the lives of innocents.

The rain lulled, the wind dropped and the only sound came from the water running from the inn's gutters. She glanced over the shadows of the outbuildings, into the blackened windows and crevices, seeking out Jaygen, but the boy was long gone. Maybe Norgie was right, he needed time alone.

Resigning to the fact he wouldn't be found unless he wanted to be, she crossed the muddy courtyard for the third time that night and went into the warmth of the inn.

Norgie had heated water for a bath and made a simple supper of cheese and biscuits. She was hungrier than she thought and ate until she was full before soaking in the bath. Not quite on the same level as the steam baths in Aslania, but very welcome all the same.

Gurple stayed hidden for the remainder of the night avoiding her, most probably still fearing her. She felt guilt at that, what a monster she must have appeared. She resolved to make things up to him in the morning.

It was almost midnight before Jaygen returned. Letting himself in through a back door he attempted to creep through to the kitchens but Elora had sat herself on a chair positioned half in the bar, half in the corridor with a view into the kitchen.

Jaygen's shirt clung to him. It was wet from the rain and stuck to his slim frame. Sweat shone from his brow and his cheeks were ruddy as if he had just been running. When he noticed her, his hands paused midway to a plate of food that Norgie had left out.

"I'm sorry I ran out like that," Jaygen said.

"It's ok, don't worry about it," Elora said, offering him a reassuring smile. "Truth is; I probably would have done the same."

He timidly reached for the food, his eyes glancing to the door again as if he wanted to make a hasty retreat.

"Thank you for taking care of my horse," she said, willing him to talk.

He grunted a reply, she thought it might have been, you're welcome. It was plain he had no intention of making conversation.

"Do you want to talk about it?" Elora offered.

Rain dripped from the ends of his long hair when he shook his head.

As he lurched passed to the corridor, Elora glimpsed a deep cut along the side of his neck and the back of his shirt was torn along one side, the pink welts of a scratch lay beneath on his pale skin. She wanted to ask him what had happened but he had already closed the door, leaving her alone. The injuries he had, didn't seem to bother him, maybe she would enquire about them in the morning.

Her legs felt weary as she made her way to her bed chamber. Norgie had kept it aired and clean sheets were spread on the comfortable four poster bed. A loneliness crept over her as she climbed into it. This was the first night she would spend alone. Bray had shared her bed whilst in Aslania and she had slept alongside the others as she journeyed through Thea to reach God's Peak.

She closed her eyes and sought sleep, hoping that Bray didn't take too long in finding a way back to her.

Chapter 2

Survivors

Elora awoke to a grey morning, the remnants of a nightmare still lingering at the edges of her memory. The panicked feeling of being chased down, being beaten, being prey. Flashes of another's life, another's death long ago recorded in the blade and fed to her while she slept. The blade's quickening; an ordeal that fresh Shadojaks accepted along with the title. They would haunt her dreams for years and maybe for all her remaining years.

Unwrapping the sheets which had tightened around her legs she sat up and stretched her neck. The loneliness from the previous night creeping back with the emptiness of the chamber. She was used to Bray being there when she woke. His warm body pressing against hers, his arm draped protectively over her shoulders. But he could be weeks away - months even.

The inn was quiet before she descended the creaking staircase, she guessed Norgie and Jaygen were still asleep and so crept outside to walk off the clinging thoughts of being hunted. The sun had yet to make an appearance, the pre-dawn light turning the scattered clouds pink as she trudged through the damp courtyard to the stone well. She turned the wheel that reeled the bucket up from the underground spring and splashed icy water on her face.

Rams Keep was so peaceful, the gentle swaying of the surrounding forest, a breeze sighing through the green canopy interlacing with the snickers from the stables and the occasional bleating from the goats. She wondered what life was like outside the fairy protection that surrounded the area. If there were any people still alive, still striving to make life or forming a resistance for themselves.

Elora meandered along a track towards the lake as the cockerel broke the peace, letting the inn know that morning had arrived.

The last time she had been at the lake was with her uncle Nat, when she had manipulated the wind element making a blade of grass hover and spin above her palm. She smiled at the memory, yet it fell from her lips as she realised that he hadn't been her uncle then, but a spliceck. A creature similar to the takwich; a weapon of her father's creation that would possess the host body of whomever it sunk its teeth into. In the end it was Ejan that had killed it, saving herself from being bitten and saving Nat with the same crushing blow.

Ducks broke away from their hiding place beneath a willow as Elora approached the water's edge. Their wings flapping wildly and catching the lake's smooth surface as they half flew, half paddled away. Elora watched the ripples left in their wake, felt the rhythm of the white crests upon the dark water and cocked her head. The pattern of the flowing element found her so naturally even though water was one of the harder elements to manipulate. Biting nervously on her lip she reached for that rhythm and teased at its edges.

In her mind's eye she pictured the ripples turning the crests of the small waves to fall in a different way and swirl into circles. Coalescing into one another as they formed rings within rings. Yet in front of her, the water hadn't altered.

When Nat had manipulated the elements, he hummed or sung to the rhythms, matching the beat before changing it. Elora knew the tune for wind, she had already changed the dance of that element and if she wanted to she could reach out and touch the rhythm easily. She recalled the song her uncle had sung back on the Molly.

The words wouldn't come but the tune was a flowing melody with high notes swinging into low before rising again in a steady flow. The moment her mind began to run through the tune the water before her changed.

She meant for it to be a subtle shift upon the surface. Something small, but before she could reel the rhythm back in, the swirls and waves became deep troughs and peaks slapping together as the body of the lake became a broiling mass of turbulence, a maelstrom of dark water causing a wind to whip at the willow's limbs.

Elora let go of the thread completely and was rewarded with a rogue wave crashing over the bank and slapping her across the face.

Anger sparked within her, fuelled by the mocking touch of the water. She scowled at the lake as its white foaming surface began to settle down and searched for the element of fire. She would flash boil the water and send it into the sky in a violent cloud of steam - see then who mocked who.

Her hand was at the water's edge, fingers dipping below the surface and the rhythm of fire at the forefront of her mind. All she need do was think it and the lake would be no more.

Elora hesitated.

Taking a deep breath, she rocked back on her heels and stood, flicking the water from her finger tips.

Getting slapped by the lake was her own fault, her foolish actions and nothing better than she deserved. The anger was that other her, the Queen of Darkness that resided within her own mind waiting for a chance to release chaos. That realisation would have brought on another wave of anger if she let it.

A little further away within the forest she had once released her anger, allowing the darkness to creep into her heart. That had been before she travelled to Thea, before she had control over the whispers that enticed her to kill. Afterwards, when she had become her true self again she was surrounded in white ash, the surrounding trees reduced to smouldering black stumps.

She shuddered at the memory. If she couldn't control her inner darkness, then only destruction would will-out and Bray wasn't here to put an end to it. He had once made a promise that if she ever lost control and put others in danger he would kill her. He hadn't liked it but had no choice.

Elora turned and made her way back to the inn, putting the lake behind her and vowing not to practice her elemental manipulation until Bray was with her.

Norgie was in the kitchen when she returned. Frying eggs and bacon, hash browns and mushrooms. She had had one of his breakfasts before when she was in London. She was unable to finish her plate then and doubted she would now.

Gurple was helping him. Stirring baked beans in a saucepan but the wood troll scuttled away when he saw her enter.

Norgie laughed, "I think you really put the frighteners up him last night. He'll come round, don't worry none," he said in his broad Yorkshire accent. "Can you set the table?"

Elora began to collect plates and cutlery to set down on a table in the bar room. "Will Jaygen be joining us?" she asked, setting the silverware upon the highly polished oak.

"Not presently, no, he's got jobs around the yard to do. Feed the animals, put the horses in the paddock, muck the stables out, collect eggs; that kind of thing. I've tried to get him to eat breakfast but the lad always rushes about his chores, comes in about mid-morning and shoves whatever I've made into his belly then goes back out."

"Where to?"

Norgie shrugged. "Maybe the keep or the lake, I don't know. He's usually back for supper, looking tired and worn out though, so whatever he's doing it's keeping him busy."

"You never thought to ask?" Elora didn't mean for her words to sound as a rebuke but couldn't call them back after they were said. Luckily the ex-marine didn't react as if had taken it as such.

"Never, the lad likes his own company. I expect he'll be back to himself once his mother returns."

They ate breakfast, Gurple timidly joining them once Norgie plated out the sausages, which were his favourite. They washed the food down with mugs of tea as Elora talked about the journey she had taken through the Shadowlands with the small fellowship. Norgie didn't interrupt, his concentration showing in his weathered face, as expressions turned from shock to pity, to awe and disbelief before returning to shock.

"That's a hell of a journey," he remarked as Gurple finally plucked up the courage to lean his head against the back of her hand. She stroked the fur behind his tall ears and he grinned, his huge tongue flopping loose from his widening mouth. It was good to have him back in her confidence.

After helping clean up the breakfast plates Elora strolled out to find Jaygen. She found him in the stables mucking out the old straw into a wheelbarrow, his clothes thick with the dust that floated about the building catching the morning sun. Sweat stuck strands of his hair to his brow. The boy seemed taller than she remembered, or was that because he was usually standing close to his father who dwarfed everybody?

"Morning," she greeted him as she picked up another fork and began to help, the prongs scraping along the stone floor as she heaved the damp straw onto the wheelbarrow.

"Morning," he grunted back as he pulled his shirt collar up, attempting to hide the scratch on his neck. Elora acted as though she hadn't noticed - if he didn't want her to know then she had no business interfering.

"Don't need any help, I can manage this," Jaygen said, sweeping an arm about the stables.

Elora stuck the fork into the straw, hands resting atop the shaft.

"I know. You've done a good job at looking after the animals, the farm, the land. Norgie told me that you're out early and don't finish until late."

She rested her chin upon her hands as she gazed at the boy. He seemed less bashful around her than he did before she left for the Shadowlands. And it also seemed that he stood straighter, his shoulders appearing a little wider.

"It's what my Da told me to do," he said.

"Yep, but I'm here now and so I can help."

Jaygen stared at her, hazel eyes accusing. "I thought you were the Shadojak. Shouldn't you be out there, sorting the bulworgs, grumpkins and other nasties out?"

The words hit her like a thump to the gut. He was right, she was the Shadojak. She should be re-balancing the world, judging the Dark Army instead of remaining within the safety of Rams Keep while her father's army spread across the continent. Then another realisation hit her.

"What do you know of the world outside the Keep? Have you gone beyond the fairy protection?" She knew he had from the guilty look he tried to mask by staring out of the barn door. "What's out there? What's happening?" she asked, desperate for something more concrete than the vague descriptions she'd had from Prince Dylap.

"Death, mainly, there are some survivors. Young children, the elderly and the crippled, left behind by the takwiches, deemed too weak to fight, too frail to supply the Dark Army."

The hairs on Elora's arms pricked up, a flash of anger pulsing through her body. Her knuckles turned white as she gripped the shaft of the fork.

The wood splintered between her fingers as shadows weaved towards her from the corners of the building. Tendrils of blackness, curling in fine wisps as the darkness reached for her. She gritted her teeth and willed herself to calm down. Taking a deep breath, she ignored the voices whispering for her to kill, to destruct.

24

"How many survivors?" she asked when she regained control.

Jaygen shrugged. "I don't know, around fifty about the local area. Maybe more, maybe less. I don't get too close, there's still a few bulworgs and the odd takwich roaming the towns and villages. They leave the weak and elderly alone, they're not worth the effort, but I think they still search for anybody left who's strong enough to fight."

Elora left the fork sticking up from the straw as she crossed the stables, she paused at the door. "Can you help me saddle my horse? I'm going to town."

Jaygen's fork clattered to the floor.

"Yep, I'll saddle mine too. I'm going with you."

Elora was about to deny him that request, but reasoned that he knew where to find these people and would save her precious time.

"Fine. But if we bump into any nasties, stay out of my way."

Averton had not changed much since she was last in the town with Bray some few weeks ago. The chemist from which they had taken the dye to turn her black hair blonde and the contact lenses to make her violet eyes blue, was much the same. The windows smashed, front door kicked in, just like the other shops along the narrow town centre. Empty, fire scorched and ruined.

Jaygen led her through the quiet street, the clopping of their horses' hooves the only sound as they struck the tarmac. Cars lay abandoned, parked haphazardly at odd angles along the roads. The owners leaving the vehicles that had failed to work once the leviathans had sung to rid the world of all electrical power, including the stored energy of batteries. A van lay on its side, doors wrenched open and the remains of food wrappings left to swirl about inside at the mercy of the wind. The only life around the town were the pigeons, happily pecking along the main road now void of people.

They rode through other roads and lanes, passing a row of terraced houses - all quiet. The houses and dwellings of an estate were much the same. Empty, some with doors left open, hinges creaking as they moved in the breeze, curtains flapping through open or smashed windows. A cottage on the edge of town had furniture strewn across an unkempt lawn, the signs of a struggle or fight showed in the smashed chairs, the upturned table and the dried blood which stained the wall. A body lay half buried under a rose bush, legs sticking out - one of which was twisted at a wrong angle.

Those that put up too much resistance would have been killed. Innocent civilians wouldn't have stood a chance against trained and armoured soldiers that had spent thousands of years waiting for the chance to let their weapons sing. The Dark Army would have swept through the town in moments, taking the healthy, killing those that opposed and leaving nothing but the weak and the dead. Was this what the rest of the country looked like? The rest of Europe?

Her father had the numbers, his army was big enough already – she had witnessed that with her own eyes in the Shadowlands. If the takwiches stole bodies along the way, the army would be swelling to an even greater number. How was she to turn such a tide and return Earth to how it was?

They turned onto a narrow lane, high privet hedges to either side and followed it to a large three-story building that sat raised upon a small hillock, surrounded by once manicured lawns and gardens. The grass was now yellow and gone to hay, burying the flowers that edged the property. A wooden sign with black scrollwork read: Averton Lodge. Elora guessed it was an old people's home.

As they approached a hooded figure stepped from behind a thick birch tree, levelling a shotgun on them. Two Staffordshire bull terriers were at his heel, mouths pulled tight to reveal sharp teeth.

"That's far enough," he said. The voice sounding young, yet tired. The face hidden under a dark hoody, the peak of a baseball cap poking out.

"Mayor?" enquired Elora, recognising the voice and the gun both.

The youth's fingers gripped his weapon tighter as he sucked air through his teeth.

"It's you," he said, taking a cautious step back. His dogs whimpering as they also backed away, tails hiding beneath their legs.

The last time Elora had met this boy was at the chemist in town. He had aimed the same gun at her then, demanding payment in kind for the things they needed, stating that he was the Mayor of Averton. She had almost torn his friend's arm off as Bray disarmed him and took care of the other thugs. The memory had haunted her since; she had come within a gnat's whisker of killing them all.

"Yeah, it's me," she said, resting her hands on her saddle horn.

The Mayor lowered his gun, then lowered his hood. "I did what you told me," he said, fear edging his voice.

Elora climbed down from her horse.

"Show me," she said, giving her reins to Jaygen.

The Mayor nodded and gestured for her to follow him into the home.

Bolts slid back from the inside and the door was pulled open by the same thug she had hurt in their last encounter. His eyes widened as he recognised her, his hand resting against the arm covered in a plaster cast. A small girl of maybe three or four clung to his legs, large blue eyes staring through untidy blond curls.

Elora smiled at the child, disarming the fear that she saw in her young features.

"Don't worry bruv," said the Mayor. "She's just here to check." Then he turned to her. "Come on I'll show you around."

He led her around the ground floor introducing her to the elderly who were sat in the common room, an aged man on a stool at the centre reading stories to a crowd of children that sat before him on the floor; faces gawping up in fascination. Another young hoody, one which she recognised as having a baseball bat that he swung violently at Bray the last time she had seen him, was now crouched in front of an old lady in a wheelchair, spoon feeding her porridge with a gentleness that belied his appearance. Rocking a baby in his arms by the window, was another one of the Mayor's crew, the baby appearing tiny in his huge hands.

"They left the oldies," explained the Mayor. "The monsters which came to town. There were these spider insect things that jumped around biting people and sending them crazy. Everyone changed and began to walk off, marching like soldiers out of town. They just appeared out of nowhere, them and the dog monsters.

Huge stinking things that sniffed out anyone hiding and dragged them to the spiders."

"Bulworgs and takwiches," explained Elora. "How did you get away?"

"We did what you told us to do. I was here with my crew, bringing in food for the oldies, making sure they had water and stuff, you know, helping. Been here for a few days, even brought them medicines from the chemist. Then a couple of weeks ago these creatures appear and began to attack. We hid in the attic, me and my boys." He looked down in shame, his voice becoming softer. "We stayed up there for a few days, like scared kittens."

Elora laid a hand on his shoulder. "There was nothing you could have done."

"No, I guess not. They took everyone, the entire town, anybody that was here after the electricity stopped working. Even my boys that were out foraging never came back. I think they got what the rest had - bitten or something. When we eventually went back out to search for food we found a bunch of kids. Little children, loads of em. Last count we had forty-seven and each time we go out we find at least another toddler, hungry and alone."

"You've done a brilliant job. What's your real name? I can't keep calling you Mayor."

"Melvin," he answered. "Not so gangsterly, is it?" He smiled sheepishly, most probably unused to the compliment. Then his face hardened once again. "What's happened? Why has the country gone completely nuts?"

It's all my fault, I set the Dark Army loose. I'm responsible for the deaths of thousands, maybe millions. All for the price of just one single song - Elora wanted to tell him, wanted to tell him the truth, he deserved it they all did. But she was the Shadojak, the balancer. Telling them would make enemies of the very people she was trying to save.

"Who's this?" came a female voice from behind. Elora turned to see a woman in her mid-thirties, hands on hips and heavily pregnant. She stepped carefully out of a kitchen, her hands supporting herself while gripping the door frame.

"She's, actually I don't know," admitted Melvin.

"My name's Elora, I'm the Shadojak," she said and watched the puzzled looks written in both the faces of Melvin and the woman. "I'm kind of a protector, judge and executioner all in one."

"Really?" asked the woman. "You've not done a good job of it."

"You're right, I haven't. But I'm here now," Elora replied, realising the words sounded pathetic.

"And what good is that now? We have a protector already," argued the woman, her belly appearing incredibly big as if she was about to go into labour at any moment.

"I know. Melvin and his friends have done a great job, but it isn't over, those things, the bulworg and takwiches will be back."

"Not them, some wolf-man killed a dog monster just last night. Cut the ugly thing down with a huge sword. If it wasn't for him, I wouldn't have made it back here."

This new information intrigued Elora. Was there somebody other than herself willing to fight?

"Who? What wolf-man?" Elora asked as Jaygen stepped into the corridor.

"I don't know," continued the woman. "He wore a huge helmet and visor in the shape of a snarling wolf. It covered his face so you could only see his eyes."

"Damn right, Cathy," said Melvin. "We've seen him a couple of times gutting them bullbars down, his sword's got a wolf's head on the handle. Looks cool."

"It's bulworgs," corrected Elora. "Who was he?"

"He doesn't say much. But he did tell me his name when we caught up with him a few days back. He had found two babies left in a house. Turns out we found almost twenty little ones throughout the town, poor little things. We did a house search after that, checking every single home. He said his name was Darkwolf, no Greywolf, err...It was something wolf."

"Grimwolf?" offered Jaygen, his face appearing concerned.

"Yep, that's it, do you know him?" asked Melvin.

Jaygen shook his head. "I've heard stories about him. Didn't think he was real, though."

"Oh, he's real enough. Scares the hell out of me and my boys. He looks so mean in that wolf mask, but he's done us more good than harm."

Elora glanced at Jaygen. "We need to find this Grimwolf. Maybe he would help us."

Jaygen shrugged. "If he exists, Grimwolf is a legend, a myth. My Da used to tell me bedtime tales about him when I was young."

"But the tales were of somebody good, right?" Elora asked.

"Well...kind of. He was a Viking originally until his family was killed by a neighbouring clan and he was left for dead, but his body was never discovered. Some say a witch took him in, shaped his soul into doing grisly tasks.

Others say it was the God of Winter giving him special powers and a suit of armour shaped like a wolf. My Da said he was most probably less dead than his attackers realised and crawled off somewhere quiet to lick his wounds. Whatever happened, the clan that attacked him died the next full moon. All the menfolk hacked to bits, the women sent raving mad and the children left with night terrors about a man-wolf. The story spread, people forgetting the man's real name and replacing it with Grimwolf, on account of his suit and sword. Over the years that had passed, he was sighted up in the mountains, his wolf armour silhouetted against the night sky. And every so often when the moon was full the bodies of men were discovered, mutilated, torn and hacked through. If no true killer was found the deed was blamed on Grimwolf."

"It can't be the same guy, can it?" asked Melvin. "The man we saw was in broad daylight and nowhere near a full moon. His suit and sword sounded pretty similar though."

Either way, Elora thought, this Grimwolf would make a good ally if she could find him.

Elora turned her attention back to the woman. "Cathy, is it?" She waited for her to nod, brows knitting together. "How long before, you know?" She glanced down at the swelling bump pressing tight against the woman's dress.

Cathy's hand slipped below the bump. "Any day, now, with everything that's been going on, I'm surprised I've not popped already."

"And you're planning on having your baby here, at the home?"

Cathy nodded. "There's nowhere else to go. No doctors, nurses, nothing."

Elora turned to Jaygen. "How many rooms does the inn have?"

"It's got twenty-two guest rooms as well as Ma's bedroom, mine, yours and the one Norgie's sharing with Gurple."

"I'm not leaving. These boys have got good intentions, Lord knows they helped me, but I can't abandon them here leaving them to take care of all these babies, children and the elderly."

"You won't be leaving them; I'm taking you all back with me. Everyone. This place isn't safe," Elora said.

Melvin sucked air between his teeth before he spoke. "Been safe enough so far. Running a bit low on food, but we've managed."

"The Dark Army is huge, massive. At some point they're going to run out of food. The takwiches will find you eventually, they maybe in the town already watching, waiting. You boys would make good hosts and Cathy, when you've given birth you will be a target too. The rest of the survivors will be food for the bulworgs and whatever other beasts have come through the barrier." She glanced again at the pregnant woman as she thought things over. "We've got fresh spring-water, a well and a small farm. We've food enough for everybody and the inn is self-sufficient. It's also safe from the Dark Army. Nothing can reach you there without being shown the way."

Cathy exchanged a look with Melvin. "How are we going to get there? Some of these people can't walk and we've barely enough people to carry the babies."

Jaygen cleared his throat. "There's a trap back at the inn. An old cart too and we've more horses for those that can ride."

33

"What do you think?" Cathy asked Melvin.

"Don't think we've much of a choice. I'll ask what everyone else wants to do, but I believe they'll all want to come. If you'll have us."

It was a bigger task than Elora had first expected. She had sent Jaygen back to Rams Keep to fetch the trap and cart which was driven by Norgie. They brought with them four other horses tied in-file behind the cart.

Cathy along with eight of the elderly that couldn't walk were bundled into the trap while a further twelve were seated upon blankets in the cart. Those that could, held some of the babies swaddled and wrapped for the short journey. The youngest of the toddlers was sat upon the horses, three to a saddle with one of Melvin's crew to each horse, most with a baby strapped to their backs in carriers. The few boys which didn't watch a horse were following on behind, pushing prams or buggies; babies lolled to sleep with the motion.

Walking in a second rank next to the horses and pushchairs were the rest of the children, all of them holding hands, with the boy with the broken arm at the front and Melvin to the rear, shotgun in hand. The two dogs were patrolling along the lines, eagerly sniffing the air for any danger. Elora rode up and down the column, constantly counting the children and encouraging the less sure while she scanned the roads and buildings for any threat.

They made a slow but steady progress, weaving through the town, stopping occasionally for the little ones to rest before carrying on. By nightfall the large group arrived safely at the inn. They were all hungry and tired, the babies ready for feeding and the elderly sore and uncomfortable from the journey.

Norgie set about making supper for everyone while Melvin and his crew sorted out the babies. Elora took all the toddlers into the bar room and under her guidance they helped to push the tables to the walls to clear enough space for them all to sit. There was a lot of frightened faces and tears but once the general rush of everything calmed down, they began to relax and soon began to eat the bread and soup that Norgie had somehow created in the short time given. Gurple appeared shortly afterwards, his arrival a shock to the children but they soon learned to trust the little wood troll, a couple of the younger ones falling asleep against him snuggling up to his warm fur. The dogs also settling down near the doorway as if keeping watch. Elora knew that at some point in the past, Staffordshire bull terriers were known as Nanny dogs and these two lived up to the name.

Cathy came into the bar room as Elora was handing out blankets and pillows, the children would have to spend the night in here, they were too tired for anything else.

"The oldies are in bed, I think the journey had taken its toll on them, but we made it. All of us," said the pregnant woman, smiling.

"Yep," agreed Elora. "Have you got yourself a bed?"

"They're all taken, but I'm fine. I'll just cosy down with these little ones."

Elora shook her head. "No, you won't, you can have my bed. It's clean and comfortable and private."

"But..."

"No buts, it's yours. I won't be sleeping much anyway and I've got other jobs that need doing." Cathy was ready to argue back until Elora held up a hand. "Please. I would feel better knowing that you were settled. Come on I'll show you where it is."

Midnight had long passed when Elora sat down on the edge of the well, leaning back against the wooden roof support. Norgie was by her side, the rich smell of tobacco drifting from his roll up.

"You did it," remarked the old man, flicking ash onto the ground. "You've saved over fifty lives."

Elora glanced at the inn which was dark and quiet. A couple of oil lamps were glowing through the open door, enough to see by yet not enough to disturb the sleeping children. The elderly were tucked up in bed, some having to share but none complaining. Cathy was asleep in her bed and the boys had found places either with the little ones or in the corridor. It wasn't perfect but it would suffice for now.

"They're what's left of a single town, a small one at that," Elora said fighting back the morose mood that was settling over her. "I've a lot more work to do. A country worth of towns and cities to save."

"Well, it's a good start," said Norgie giving her a wink.

Elora knew it was a good start and she did feel some spark of hope at actually beginning to take control. To take something back from the Dark Army.

"We need to find this Grimwolf character as well. I think he may have slipped across from the Shadowlands when the barrier lifted. Maybe we can recruit him to our cause, he seems to have something against the bulworgs at least."

"Aye. That's if you find him," said Norgie, dropping the end of his roll-up on the ground and crushing it beneath his shoe.

"If he's out there I'll find him and any other allies I can find on the way."

Chapter 3

Weakest

The cockerel's dawn chorus was interrupted by the wailing of babies hungry for milk, demanding a nappy change or just wanting attention. Why anybody wanted them in the first place escaped Elora.

She bent down to touch her toes, stretching her back which clicked in complaint. She had been awake through the night pacing the corridors with at least one baby in her arms, feeding or rocking them to sleep. With nearly twenty of them it was constant work, Melvin's crew helped in shifts and were as tired as she was.

"Coffee?" Norgie offered, a small boy clutching his leg as he wandered about the kitchen preparing breakfast.

"Please. Shoot me up with some caffeine," she said, rubbing the stiffness from her shoulder.

Norgie picked the boy up and sat him on the table as he busied himself with the boiling water. "Poor little lad," he remarked. "He feels lost without his parents, as do the rest of the children."

Elora smiled at the boy whose stare followed the old man around the kitchen. At least he was safe.

Melvin poked his head around the door. "Can I have a word?" he asked.

Elora followed him out into the bar room, the floor littered with the sleeping bodies of children.

"What's the matter?" she asked when she recognised the concern etched upon Melvin's dark face.

"We've got enough baby milk to last us maybe two days. And we're running short on nappies and wipes.

Probably going to need some other stuff soon. Some of them are coming off milk and going onto solids."

"It's fine, I'll go into Averton and collect supplies, just give me a list."

Melvin shook his head. "We've already bled Averton dry. Me and the boys were planning on heading out to Brecon. That's the closest town, but it's still twelve miles away."

"Then it will be a big trip, but if it needs taking then so be it. Make me a list of what you need, the essentials - I'll leave when I can."

"Thanks Elora." he said before leaving by way of the kitchen and almost knocked into Norgie as he came through the door, the old man's arm protectively covering a steaming mug in his hand.

"He's in a rush," Norgie remarked, offering her the coffee.

"Yeah, think we're going to need to make some house rules," replied Elora, sipping the strong drink. "Too many children, too many babies and not enough space. Things will soon go awry without some kind of routine."

"I dare say you're right. How the boys coped by themselves is beyond me?"

After breakfast Norgie set the children to task. He broke them down into teams of ten with one of Melvin's crew to each team. They each had their own tasks to do. A team to fetch water from the well forming a chain with buckets to the kitchen. Another team to help Jaygen in the stables, a third to collect eggs from the hen house and feed the chickens, goats, pigs and cows. And the fourth had tasks around the inn: cleaning, washing, fetching or anything else Norgie could find to keep them busy, even if that meant Gurple creating a mess so they had something to do. Each following day, the teams would be swapped around so that everyone had time with the animals. He promised them all a playtime or a walk around the lake in the afternoon once the chores had been completed.

The baby-care came to Melvin along with two of his friends. Cathy's responsibility was for the elderly; overseeing their care and delegating any jobs to the two boys left from Melvin's crew.

After everyone was settled into doing the jobs and tasks at hand, Elora approached Melvin for the list of things they needed for the babies.

She scanned down it raising a sceptical eyebrow at the amount of stuff required.

"I think I'm going to need the cart," she said. "And somebody to help load it all up."

"Take Windy and Doug," Melvin said. "They're the boys I usually send out foraging."

Elora nodded and set off to saddle her horse and find Jaygen to harness two more to the cart.

They left before dinner, Jaygen driving the cart with Windy and Doug sat in the back with Melvin's shotgun. Elora rode out in front not wanting to be eating dust kicked up by the rickety old cart.

Once through Averton they followed an arterial road that would take them to Brecon. Elora didn't like them being out in a place that was so open and easily spotted from the hills and fields they passed, but there was little chance of taking a scenic route with the cart and the road was the most direct course to take. With any luck they would be home before nightfall.

They passed many abandoned vehicles, but none that blocked their way, the lanes being wide enough to allow the cart to slip down the middle if the need arose. Elora kept her attention to the way ahead searching for bulworgs or soldiers and expecting an ambush around every bend. But she began to relax with the signposts they passed, bringing the town they headed for a little closer.

"Windy?" Elora probed when she dropped back level with the cart. "Not a common name is it?"

"No, it's a nickname," Windy replied.

"Yep," Doug said, elbowing him in the side. "He gets these windy bellies in the morning and lets out a ripping good tune from his arse."

"Do not," Windy argued, elbowing Doug harshly in his ribs. "My surname's Miller. They call me Windy on account of that. You know, like Windy Miller?"

Elora chuckled. "Shame, I like a good tune. Especially when it's blown differently."

Windy laughed. "Look, sorry about before. You know, back at the chemist when we first met. We shouldn't have tried to do what we did. Seems crazy now."

Elora remembered it well. Windy had been one of the thugs that attacked Bray while she was busy destroying a thug's arm; she discovered this morning that the boy with his arm in a sling was called Dev.

"You've more than made up for it, all of you have."

They made good time arriving at Brecon by mid-afternoon. The town was quiet and still. Crows stared at them from car roofs and lampposts as they rode through the centre - witnessing humans on the high street must be a rare sight these days.

It didn't take long to find the supermarket. Brecon was small, loosely built around an old wall that partially surrounded the Welsh town. Elora steered Daisy around the cars to the shop front, then nudged her through the remains of the door frame ducking to avoid being knocked off.

Glass crushed under her horse's hooves as she rode down the aisles, weaving between fallen shelves and discarded rubbish. The place had already been looted of anything useful and edible. Ceiling tiles had come down in places, racks that once held bread were slung against the empty milk cages; a split bottle lay crushed on a low shelf, milk forming a yellow white puddle that gave of a sour smell.

"It's empty," Elora told the boys when she rode back out of the shop.

"Try the warehouse around back," offered Doug. "That's where we found most of our supplies back in Averton."

Elora dismounted and tied her horse to the cart then led the group to the back door.

There was a steel fence and a tall barred gate wide enough to accept a wagon, with razor wire running around the top. Elora pushed against the gate, it rattled but didn't open. A thick chain and padlock held it closed. Through the bars she could see the service yard and ramp that led into the back of the supermarket. The metal roller-doors were down and appeared undisturbed.

"Stay here," Windy said. He put his back to the bars and placed his hands together. Doug put his foot in his hands and grasping the bars was boosted up to the top of the gate.

From a pocket he produced a pair of pliers and began to cut the razor wire. A section of it fell to the ground and rolled away leaving a wide enough gap for him to climb over and slide down the other side.

"I'll be back in a minute," Doug said as he ran over to a small frosted window beside the roller-door and using the pliers, smashed the glass through. He cleared the jagged pieces away from the frame then climbed in. A few moments later he came out of the fire exit swinging a set of keys around his finger.

"You boys have obviously done this before," Elora remarked as Doug unlocked the padlock and let it fall to the floor.

"Maybe three or four times," Windy admitted. "And that was before everything went crazy."

The gate swung readily open and they followed Doug back through the fire door.

Inside, the warehouse was dark, the only light spilling through the door but it illuminated the large space enough for them to see tall shelves filled with products, stacked on pallets or in roller cages on the ground.

"What did I tell you bruv?" Windy said, high-fiving Doug. "The stores haven't been touched."

"Ok, now we just need to get the supplies we came for," Elora said, taking the list from her pocket.

"I'll bring the cart around," Jaygen offered, stepping back out into daylight.

The two boys climbed the racking searching for nappies, wipes and baby food while she searched the roller cages for anything else they needed. By the time Jaygen had brought the cart around they had made a large pile by the door and he began to load it. It didn't take long to find what they had come for and they even managed to include spare clothes for the children and a few boxes of sweets.

They jammed the fire exit closed and relocked the gate once they were through. The supermarket was a good find, it still held a lot of supplies and was worth a return visit.

They put Brecon behind them and were just making the turning onto the main road that led home when the sound of gunfire echoed from the town.

The rapid crack and thump of a heavy machine gun startled the horses and caused Elora's heart to leap into her mouth.

She spun Daisy around, her blade already finding itself in her grasp as she faced the attack, yet saw nothing but the empty street.

Cracks filled the air once again followed by the thumps of rounds hitting brick and ending with the ping of a stray bullet as it ricocheted. It seemed to come from the other side of town.

"We're not the targets," Elora said to Jaygen and the two boys who had buried themselves amongst the supplies. Doug's frightened face visible beneath bags, the barrel of his shotgun poking through the slats of the cart.

"We better be getting home then before they make us the next targets," Jaygen said, resting an axe that had appeared from nowhere on the bench beside him.

"Yeah," Elora replied sliding her sword away. "You guys start heading back. Stop for nothing. You'll be home before dark."

"You're not coming?" Jaygen asked, a frown creasing his young face.

Elora shook her head as she kicked her horse back towards Brecon. "I'll catch you up," she shouted over her shoulder, not giving them chance to argue over her decision, which she saw readied on Jaygen's lips.

Elora skirted the town, careful to keep herself hidden behind walls or buildings as she neared the source of the gunfire. It wasn't hard to track. The noise breaking the silence every few minutes and when she was close enough to believe it was just in the next street it grew louder. The blasts came in quick succession, rising to an ear-splitting crescendo of eruptions, shattering brick and glass and ended with an equally ear-splitting explosion.

Daisy suddenly reared almost spilling her from the saddle as Elora fought to keep her horse under control. The echoes of the blast still ringing in her ears as she watched a black plume of smoke rise into the sky on the other side of the building, the acrid smell of gunpowder thick in the air - whoever these people were, she thought, they had some serious weapons.

When Daisy finally calmed she dismounted and walked her into an abandoned tyre-fitter shop. Quiet, dark and hidden from view her horse should be safe from prying eyes. She tied her reins to a car lift and softly stroked her neck to reassure her that she would be back soon. Elora gave a final glance to the tyre shop before vaulting silently over an adjoining wall to the street where the explosion happened.

She crouched low into a darkened corner of a side road that led out of a shopping centre, and observed the scene before her. Two men in army uniforms were kneeling beside the broken rubble and masonry of a bank, their rifles trained ahead of them into the hole they had made in a wall. On the corner of the building was a third soldier, chubbier than the others, facing away from the street, his finger resting against the trigger of a huge machine gun.

Elora absorbed the details, recognising the men as being British soldiers and the rifles they held were SA eighties, the heavy gun being a belt-fed GPMG. The information was delivered instantly to her mind - memories from Diagus; the last Shadojak to imbue his soul into her blade. What he knew, she now knew. The feeling was strange, becoming aware of facts as they happened, borrowing the knowledge of others yet not knowing she knew until it was called for.

A child's scream broke the air as a small toddler ran out of the hole, stumbling on a loose brick. One of the kneeling soldiers caught the girl before she fell. Her legs thrashed as she struggled to free herself, raining panicked slaps at the man, terror making her sob with every breath.

Elora slipped from her hiding place startling the man holding the girl.

"Let her go," she growled.

The soldier recovered his composure and levelled his rifle on her, the girl still kicking in his arms.

"Halt," he ordered, his comrades also swinging their weapons about.

Elora stopped in front him. "Put the girl down," she repeated, wondering if her actions at snatching his rifle away were quicker than his reflexes at pulling the trigger. She thought not.

The girl finally landed a kick to the man's crotch. He let her drop as his free hand held his injury, his face turning red as it screwed up with pain.

Taking the chance given, Elora stepped into the man and in a single movement snatched the rifle upwards, twisting it in such a way that the weapon's sling wrapped around the soldier's neck. She aimed the barrel at his partner's head and used the choking man's own body as a shield against chubby who she knew couldn't fire without hitting him.

It was a smooth move, snake-like as if her body reacted from muscle memory, yet she knew it was reactions born from the thousands of experiences held in her blade and now in her mind.

Trying to locate the girl, Elora tightened her grip on the rifle sling, the material biting into the soldier's neck as she pulled him around. She stopped when a solid object pressed against the back of her skull; the metallic click of a safety catch being released.

She hadn't realised there was a fourth soldier - how was she going to get out of this one?

"Let him go," came a deep commanding voice beside her ear. "Easy now."

Elora slowed her breathing and closed her eyes, reciting all the men's positions to her mind: the angle of the weapons, the likely trajectory of the bullets, the quickness of their actions to hers. Chubby still couldn't take a clear shot and she had the soldier to her front in line with the rifle she was controlling.

"If you shoot me in the back of my head, the bullet mixed with my bone fragments will more than likely kill this one." She increased the pressure on the strap, pulling his head in line with her own. "And my hand will most probably pull the trigger through a massive nerve reaction after my brain explodes killing your man there."

"Maybe," replied the unseen man behind her as he increased pressure upon the gun against her skull. "But I won't back down."

"Stalemate then," Elora said, going through her options and coming short of anything that wouldn't end her life.

"Stalemate," the man repeated, calmly.

Elora was about to lower the rifle when a cloud passed in front of the sun and a shadow touched her face. She smiled at darkness's tender kiss.

"Captain?" said the soldier directly to her front. "Her eyes are turning red. Bright red and they were a funny bloody colour to begin with."

A wicked grin spread across Elora's face as she called upon the darkness, soaking up its energies, its whispers, its power.

She suddenly burst into a million pieces.

Her body becoming so light it floated. A feeling of vertigo washed through her as she witnessed the scene around her from every possible angle. She was above them, below them, passing backwards - she was smoke.

The effect was dizzying yet felt natural as she passed over the soldier that held the gun against her head. The tiny dark particles that were once her body stroked his skin, his smooth face and teased through his short hair. She felt the stiffness in his broad shoulders and the creases in his uniform as her smoke flowed over the contours.

So this was what it was like to be smoke, it was what Chaos was, what her father was and now what she was.

Elora materialised behind the Captain. Her hand forming over his as she pulled it back and pressed the barrel of the pistol under his chin and tipped his head against her shoulder. When her other hand became solid it was already grasping her sword; the crimson blade pressing against the neck of the second soldier. His eyes widened and his jaw dropped open.

"Give the girl to me and I'll let you live," Elora said, controlling her voice and not showing how shocked she felt. Had she really just turned to smoke?

"I can't do that," the Captain said, flinching as Elora pushed the barrel deeper into his neck. "She is in my care and I'll give my life before you freaky bastards have her. And that goes for my men too."

Elora eased the gun back, yet kept her aim. "Care?"

"She was taken from our camp this morning. One of the other children saw it happen - said it was an old man with huge dog-beasts that snatched her. My men and I tracked them across town and pinned them in there." The Captain nodded towards the hole in the bank wall. "I've a sniper around the back if they try to escape."

Elora glanced at the other soldiers as their leader explained, watching for any signs of deceit but saw none.

She lowered her sword and took a step back. The Captain visibly relaxed and slowly turned to face her, raising a hand to his men and ordering them to lower their weapons.

"My name's Elora. I'm the Shadojak, not one of those bastards," she said, handing him his gun back.

Movement from the periphery of her vision caused her to bring her blade about. It was the little girl, she shot out from behind a car and ran into the Captain's arms knocking him back a step. He picked her up and hugged her close.

"It's alright, we've got you now. You're safe," he said, soothing the child, then bringing his attention back to her, he introduced himself. "I'm Captain Brindle, a member of her Majesty's SAS. These men are under my command until we find someone with a higher rank. If there is anyone." He eyed her curiously. "So you're with Grimwolf?"

"No, I've yet to meet him, but I think he's treading along the same path as myself. What do you know of him?"

"Not much, he brings us children, babies and survivors. Or tells us where to find them. He doesn't say much; we don't even know what he looks like as he hides his face beneath a wolf shaped mask. Strange bloke, but one I'd have on my side any day. He hacked a couple of the dog-beasts apart with his huge sword a few days back."

Elora noticed his gaze falling on her own sword so she slipped it away into the smuggler's pouch. He raised an eyebrow as the blade seemed to disappear before his eyes.

"There's been some crazy stuff happening lately, girls turning into smoke being amongst the strangest. The entire country has gone to hell. I don't suppose you can shed any light?"

"Not just the country, Earth," she answered, her gaze falling on the dark opening in the bank's wall. "But I think I better sort these beasties out before we talk."

"You're going in alone?" Captain Brindle asked.

Elora nodded. "That would be safer for all involved."

Dust fell from the ruined ceiling. The explosion reducing the plaster to shattered fragments and making the air thick with a gloomy haze. The bank's lobby was dark and quiet, the dwindling daylight barely penetrating through the gap in the wall and giving her surroundings a haunting look; the empty desks and cashiers, roller-doors partly down only adding to the effect.

Elora stepped carefully along the once polished floor, her cloak held to the side ready to draw her sword as the sour musky scent of damp dog reached her nostrils. There was at least one bulworg in the building with her, maybe two.

The tiled floor gave way to carpet as she ascended a narrow flight of stairs to the offices above. She paused on the landing, the corridor splitting to either side and ending with a door at each end. They were much the same, the only difference being the large gash taken out of the skirting board towards the left-hand door and the bloody paw print smeared along the magnolia wall.

Her heart slammed harder inside her chest as she closed the gap between herself and the door in three strides. She put her ear to the veneered oak and listened - nothing. Yet the whisper of darkness called and she felt it breathe within her, drawing her through and inviting Chaos.

There was three of them on the other side of the door. She felt it in her mind, in the fire that burned within her blood. Two bulworgs under the command of a grumpkin.

The sensation was strange. She could feel them, seek out their black hearts as easily as a water diviner. She could touch their minds, sense the desperate cruelty in the grumpkin and knew that he sensed her back. Elora guessed the bulworgs would have picked up her scent before she even entered the bank so the element of surprise was out of the question.

The veneered oak blistered turning black under her hand as she shoved it open, the darkness washing through her. Heat, pain and destruction ebbed away as Chaos used her as a conduit.

51

The office was dark, dwindling light casting through grey blinds that covered the two windows offering up the mess within. Desks upturned and shoved to the wall, chairs thrown into corners, papers, computes monitors, printers and other office furniture scattered about the room. At its centre lay a single desk, rope lay to each corner ,severed at the points which would have been tied to ankles and wrists. This was where the child had been, where she was to have been killed, skinned and eaten by the grumpkin. The creature was at the desk now, bony hands splayed apart upon the smooth surface, black beetle eyes staring into hers and a playful grin curling his saggy face. Tight suit trousers held the flesh to his bones whilst a stained shirt did little to hide the cracked belly that pushed through the button holes.

Elora stepped purposefully forwards showing no fear and feeling the darkness reach out, stroking its black tendrils around the room, touching the grumpkin, the bulworg at his feet and the one to her back which slammed the door shut, closing her off from any escape.

She felt its hot breath on her neck, heard the guttural rumble from its chest and recognised its evil intent.

"This grumpkin is pleased to see you," said the grotesque little man before her. His jowls bouncing as he spoke, his skin sallow and appearing several sizes too large. "My last little guest has run away. She didn't want to play with this grumpkin."

Elora knew that the grumpkin would have replaced his own skin with that of the girls, as if it was nothing more than changing clothes. She felt revulsion for the creature; a thing cursed to hunt the young for their flesh, but a curse they enjoyed all the same.

"Not to this grumpkin's taste, I likes them younger, but my baggies do need a swapsy." He held an arm up and jostled it about, the sagging flesh beneath flopped back and forth. "So's I can't be too choosy in the upsie, not just yet."

He nodded to the beast behind her and she felt huge claws grip her arms to either side pinning her where she was as the grumpkin eyed her hungrily.

Elora smirked, the expression causing the creature before her to pause. He cocked his bald head to the side like a dog confused by a command.

"What's so funny pretty girl? Don't you know this grumpkin's going to cut your skins off and be wearing them? My bulworgs will be eating your inners, the ones I leave anyway."

Elora's smirk spread into a grin. She could if she chose, reduce this entire room to ash in a moment. The darkness within her willed it, urged her towards destruction and she was on the precipice ready to consume the energy and release Chaos.

"Your eyes have turned red," remarked the grumpkin, scowling now that it was clear she didn't fear him. "You're not from the upsies this grumpkin is thinking. Not Earth-born, you are seeming wrong."

"I'm so very wrong," Elora said. "Yield in the name of the Shadojak. Yield now and I'll make it quick."

Rubbery yellow flesh wiggled viciously as the grumpkin laughed. His eyes momentarily disappearing amongst the roles of sagging skin.

"Shadojak she says. Little girl is a Shadojak."

Unflinching she held his gaze until he finished laughing, then bowed her head. "Shadojak."

"Only one Shadojak in the upsies, and only one this grumpkin would fear. The Pearly White and you're not him."

He kicked the bulworg at his feet and the beast stirred. It clambered to its hind legs, one paw pressing against an injury on its ribs; blood running through its claws. When it reached its full height its wolf-like head reached the ceiling and its shoulders blocked out an entire window. It was the biggest bulworg she had ever seen.

Elora raised an eyebrow. "I killed the Pearly White along with my father Solarius, the God of Chaos."

The grin fell from the grumpkin's face as he saw the truth in her eyes. "You're the daughter of Solarius?" Lumps of baggie skin shook as he stepped back and raised his bony hands. "Please my Queen, this grumpkin didn't know." He bowed his head. "This grumpkin is your servant."

"I'm the Shadojak and no queen of yours. Now yield."

The grumpkin's head raised high enough for her to see the subtle signal he gave to the bulworg that held her. A slight shift of his beetle eyes but enough for a well-trained beast to respond to.

Pain screamed from her arms where the bulworg's claws dug deep into her flesh as he opened his jaw and exposed the long white teeth ready to bite down into her neck.

Elora let the darkness in, the whispers of a thousand night-terrors rushing through her veins to entwine with the fire in her blood.

She yanked downwards in a crouch, then sprang up driving her head beneath the bulworg's jaw. The impact was hard, shattering his teeth as the jaw snapped shut, severing the end of its tongue.

Her arms were suddenly released and she fell, whipping her sword from the smuggler's pouch before her feet touched the floor. She spun on her heel and brought her blade about, taking the beast's head from its shoulders in one fluid motion.

The head thumped against a desk a moment before the body followed. She turned back to face the grumpkin as the head rolled off the edge.

"Please. Please. This grumpkin is sorry my Queen, I didn't know, I didn't know."

Elora approached him and placed her blade against his neck. She had come across one before and knew they couldn't be killed by stabbing them through the heart. Only by crushing the brain inside the skull or removing the head would he die.

"Please," the grumpkin continued. "I will give you this bulworg," he said, slapping a bony hand on the beast beside him which hadn't made a move to attack her. "He is yours to command. Very precious a bulworg this size. He's fast and very strong."

Elora ignored the bulworg and stared down at the grumpkin. "Kneel."

"No, no no," he pleaded. "I will tell you where to find others if you let me live. Lots of grumpkins around, lots of bulworgs and takwich. I know, I can tell."

If the grumpkin was any other creature she could have stabbed him through the heart and harvested his soul. Any knowledge he held would have come to her from the blade.

"Tell me what you know and I won't kill you," she said, deciding that information on her enemy was too precious to let go even if she didn't trust it, it may still glean some clues.

A sly grin returned to the grumpkin's hideous face. "Thank you my Queen, my lovely dark Queen."

She withdrew the blade from his neck but still held it between her and the bulworg, its yellow eyes seeming more intelligent than its brethren as it followed the conversation.

"Tell me what Silk is doing, where he is sending his army, what numbers remain in the country. I already know the mass of his host is crossing into mainland Europe."

The grumpkin nodded. "This is true. The takwich known as Silk is advancing on the bigger lands. He is growing his ranks with every town and every city. Taking each country, using every man woman and child to strengthen his rule."

"And what of you? Why do you remain and why do bulworgs still patrol randomly around these parts?"

"This land still needs occupying, the army needs feeding. Lots of juicy little ones left," he said, clapping his hands together. "We search dwellings, sniff out survivors. Take them to the cities to either join the ranks of the army or feed it."

Elora fought the urge to ram her sword through the grumpkin's face. Instead she swallowed her anger to gain more information. "How many of you are there?"

"Too many, my Queen. Grumpkins in every city, every town and bulworgs to serve them all. Not so many in the countryside, but enough to bring anyone we find to the big cities. Or anyone we don't eat." He elbowed the bulworg beside him. It winced as the bony joint dug into his wound.

"This bulworg not so interested in the eating though. He's big, powerful, but too clever in the thinking. He doesn't eat what we find. He is weak. Is the weakest. That is what we call him, Weakest."

Elora looked again at the bulworg, he did seem different to the others she had encountered before.

"This dog let my juicy child go. Cut the ropes and let her run," the grumpkin said accusingly. "My child, my new skin to replace my baggies."

He slapped the bulworg across its snout. The beast glared down at him but made no move to attack. "I starved him for days, he should have eaten what was given but instead chooses to die slowly. He hasn't killed or eaten since we came into the upsies, stupid dog." He struck him again, then glanced at her. "He is yours now. A deal is a deal. You have the bulworg and my precious information and this grumpkin can go."

Elora stared once again at the bulworg. "Shadojaks don't own any property."

"Then kill it then. I don't wants it if it can't follow orders. Won't kill, won't eat, not good things in a bulworg."

"Kneel," Elora ordered. The beast lowered itself onto all fours, even stretching its neck out to allow a clean cut.

"This is the only order it followed. Stupid dog," the grumpkin snapped angrily. He tried to kick the bulworg until Elora stopped him with her blade.

"Touch him again and I'll kill you," she said.

"No, deal's a deal. You can't be killing this grumpkin," the ugly little man said, saggy skin wobbling with each word. "Shadojaks must keep their word."

"You're right," she replied, her attention once again returning to the bulworg. "Weakest?"

The bulworg raised his head to look at her and she recognised surrender in his sad eyes, he wanted to die.

"Can you understand me?" she asked. The beast nodded. "Do you wish to die?" Another nod.

The grumpkin was watching the judgment, his hands rubbing together in glee.

"I've made my judgement," Elora said, sliding her sword into its invisible sheath.

Deep crevices above the bulworg's flat head creased together as he cocked his head in confusion. Elora knew that Diagus, the Pearly White, wouldn't have thought twice about killing both the bulworg and the grumpkin, yet she wouldn't kill the beast who'd helped the girl to escape, who'd refused to fight or kill for the grumpkin and tried to end its own life. Death by starvation, not a pleasant way to go but the only way it could.

"You've been judged," she said, turning her gaze on the grumpkin. "Your punishment is death."

"No! We had a deal. You cannot kill this grumpkin, no," said the hideous creature as he backed into the wall.

Elora felt a grin spread across her face at seeing the fear he permeated from that stolen skin. "I won't kill you. That would be too swift." She turned her back on him and laid a hand upon the bulworg's head, the darkness stroking over his lupine form. "Hungry?"

Saliva dripped from the beast's long teeth, a deep growl building in his chest - Elora felt it vibrate through her hand.

"Come to me once you've finished."

She gave a final glance at the grumpkin who had cowered away into the corner, the bulworg slowly stalking towards him. "And leave nothing."

Elora left the room as the grumpkin began to scream in earnest, the sounds of bones crunching beneath powerful jaws followed her down the corridor.

Chapter 4

Taste of the Enemy

Elora waited inside the bank for Weakest to finish his meal. It wasn't long before the bulworg padded down the steps; grumpkin blood staining the corners of his mouth. He sat before her and bowed his head, gaze fixed on the ground.

"Has he sated your hunger?" she asked. Weakest nodded. "Good. You will no longer eat unless it is something I have granted you. Neither will you kill unless I order it. You will only attack under my command or to protect somebody under my care. Do you understand?" Again he nodded. "And understand this, I'm not your master, you are servant to nobody. However, I cannot trust you to go free, the enemy may capture you or you may decide to change loyalties again."

Weakest raised his head at that. "Nev...er," the bulworg growled, his word almost inaudible amongst the deep rumble.

"Good, you will remain by my side for now under the protection of the Shadojak. If you run away you will be considered part of the Dark Army, the enemy and will be treated as such."

Weakest nodded that he understood.

Captain Brindle and his men lowered their weapons as Elora stepped out of the hole in the wall, but they retrained them on the bulworg as it followed her out.

"No," she said, placing a hand on top of the Captain's gun and pushing it away. "Weakest is one of us. It was his actions that saved the girl."

Brindle scowled at Weakest, his gaze wandering over the huge bulworg and then looked at the girl still held in his arms. "Is this true?" he asked her softly. The girl, her thumb lodged in her mouth gave Weakest the briefest of glances and then nodded.

"He need not fear my men, but I can't speak for the others back at camp - some will shoot him on sight."

"Weakest is the only exception to his breed," Elora said. "It is only right that they shoot any bulworg they see. But let me see this camp of yours. There's a lot that I need to explain and bulworgs are only a small part of the problem."

"Captain, we can't take her back," said the soldier that she had choked with the sling. "For all we know she wants to find out where it is so she can kill us all. We shouldn't trust her. She changed to smoke for Christ's sake."

"Calm yourself, Dent. I've got the feeling that if she wanted us dead we would be - and she could get this," he pointed to Weakest. "Bulworg to lead her to the camp."

"Sir. I'm just saying we shouldn't trust her," replied Dent.

"I don't trust her but she's still coming back. Now let's head home whilst we've enough light to see by."

The Captain whistled and a man suddenly appeared above the bank leaning out over the roof. "Slater, take point." The man nodded and nimbly slid down a drain pipe, sniper rifle slung over his back. Tattoos covered both forearms and dark camouflage cream was smudged in tiger-lines across his face. He flicked his eyes over them as he passed but said nothing.

"Pudding, take the rear and keep it covered, I don't want anyone following," continued the Captain.

"Sir," replied the chubby soldier with the GPMG.

"Dent, Mac - keep alternate arcs, we're moving in file."

"Sir," they replied in unison.

"Wait," Elora said. "I'll be back in a moment."

She deftly vaulted the wall next to her and entered the tyre-fitters shop, finding Daisy where she had left her. The horse snickered as she approached and nudged her with her nose. Elora stroked the mare's neck before leading her out of the building, mounted and rode back to the soldiers.

The evening had pressed on, the sun having sunk below the roofs bathing the street in shadow as the group set off. They moved quickly yet silently, the only sound coming from Daisy's hooves. Elora thought she should wrap them in cloth for the next venture from the keep.

Slater led them out of town over a cobbled humpback bridge and along a quiet lane, tall conifers growing to either side blotting out what little light they had to begin with. As they travelled Captain Bridle explained to her how they escaped the Dark Army's attack.

He was leading a platoon of SAS soldiers on a night exercise on the Brecon beacons. Something he and his men had done countless times before. They were to patrol to a location high upon the Penyfan Mountain where they were to do a dawn attack upon a platoon of infantry who were playing the enemy; dug into fox-holes and trenches getting cold and wet.

The electricity had already gone by then, but nothing stopped the special forces from training - even more so when the security risk had gone up, which it had considerably when the lights went permanently out.

The exercise went as planned, the dawn attack successful and Captain Brindle was happy with the way his men operated. It wasn't until they and the infantry were tabbing back to Sennybridge - the battalion's temporary headquarters - that they realised something was wrong. The entire place was deserted. Every soldier gone yet their kit remained. All the beds, personal possessions and even the food in the kitchens left untouched.

Brindle being the highest rank, split the groups into two. The infantry to remain in the camp while he and his platoon marched to the nearest town which was Brecon. They found children on the way. Lost and scared they gathered them up listening to them tell of their parents being attacked by vicious spiders, then becoming possessed and simply walking away to join the rest of the grown-ups. The entire town's population of fit adults had marched leaving all the small children behind. Some of them had tried to follow but were chased down by huge dogs and ugly old men.

They spent the night at Brecon, searching houses and collecting children, babies and the elderly. By the time they returned to Sennybridge they had close to fifty.

"We soon realised that help wasn't coming and so set the camp up to accommodate the vulnerable. We sent search parties out every day to patrol the area, villages and farms for other people, food or other supplies while myself and these men here set off for Hereford to try and get some answers."

"Why Hereford?" Elora asked while coaxing the girl from the captain's arms to ride on the horse with her.

"Hereford is where we were stationed; home to the special forces and where, if possible, we would find out what was happening. It took two days of a forced march to reach, but the barracks were empty." Brindle shook his head. "We had some of the most sophisticated weaponry in the country. Armouries full of rifles, rocket launchers, grenades - the world's best and enough ammo to keep an army well replenished. Yet there was no sign of a struggle, not a single round fired." He nodded towards Pudding who was pacing behind them swinging his heavy machine gun to face the rear every few steps. "We found Barker inside a 432 armoured personnel carrier. He'd been hiding in there for days and it took us some encouragement to get him to come out. After he realised we weren't going to hurt him he explained what had happened.

A few days previously, the Colonel had ordered the entire camp to assemble on the parade square, even the camp guards which was something out of the ordinary. Barker, or Pudding as we all call him, was a driver and had fallen asleep inside the 432 and only woke up after the parade had been formed up. Not wanting to draw attention to himself he'd remained hidden inside his vehicle and watched through the small rear window."

"That's right," chipped in Pudding who had been listening. "Watched it all happen. Bins, the Colonel that is, he orders all the men to stand to attention and keep still - as strange an order as it is, they all did as they were told, he was the Colonel after all. Well, no sooner did they do what he asked then the parade square was swarmed by insects. Huge black spider-things that crawled out of nowhere, all emerging at once and flooding around the soldiers as fluid as oil." Pudding's hand mimicked the crawling insects as he spoke, chubby fingers moving like spider legs. "Within seconds the insects were all over the men; jumping, scurrying, biting and the men were dropping like flies. Then, moments later they were clambering back to their feet, all of them having these sickening grins on their faces as if they were all in on a practical joke. The Colonel made these funny clicking sounds with his mouth, not quite human, more an insect like tak…tak…tak noise and the men, the entire battalion responded with the same sounds. Freaked me out some I can tell you." Pudding wiped sweat from his forehead as he relived the experience in his mind. "I watched from my hiding place as they all formed up into squads and simply marched from the camp."

"Later when I plucked up the courage to leave the 432 I discovered the entire base was deserted apart from the odd insect or two I saw scurrying about. I decided I was safer in the vehicle so I made my way back and locked myself in. The day after, I witnessed a dog-beast roaming around," he nodded towards Weakest. "Like him. It came over to my hiding place, sniffed about for a bit and left. The day after was when the Captain arrived."

"Yeah," continued Brindle. "We took as many weapons and ammo as we could carry and made our way back to Sennybridge. We've done the same trip another three times with more men to collect the rest of the weapons so now our new camp is more than capable of looking after itself."

"So you're planning on staying?" Elora asked, realising that the girl had drifted to sleep with the rocking motion of the horse and now leaned back against her. She put her arm around her to stop the child from toppling off.

"Possibly, we've got nowhere else to go and with every search party that goes out we find more survivors. Might be that we'll run out of space before long."

They passed over a small hillock and followed a tree line to a natural break in the woods revealing a deer track that wound down to a stream. Weakest paused at the water's edge to drink as they crossed and Elora noticed that the men trained their guns on him as they passed. She doubted they would ever trust the bulworg, she was still unsure of her decision to let him live but didn't feel any evil in the beast.

Above the stream was a bridleway that weaved through the woods for some distance before ending at an old gate. Slater held it open for them, chatting to another soldier who had been standing sentry. He saluted Captain Brindle as they passed through and gave Elora and Weakest a puzzled look.

"This is the back way into the camp," Brindle explained. "I thought it best to barricade the main gate and lay explosives and claymore mines around the perimeter."

"It didn't stop the grumpkin from taking this one though," Elora said, brushing the blonde curls of the sleeping child.

"No, it didn't. We're going to need to double the guards I think, and keep a better watch over the kids."

He carefully lifted the sleeping girl from the saddle and passed her to another soldier.

"If she wakes up give her something to eat and put her to bed."

"And if she doesn't wake?" asked the soldier taking the child and gently settling her head against him.

"Then put her to bed. Sleep is what she needs after going through what she did, poor little mite."

They dropped down onto a concrete road with old army billets with wriggly tin roofs to either side. The faces of children were poking out of doors and windows to see what was going on. Green canvas tents were erected in between the billets with men dressed in army uniforms laying on camp beds or sat up cleaning weapons, glowing red embers of cigarettes in a few mouths. The parade square at the centre of camp was covered with more tents, either the green army kind or some that were taken from camping shops. They were erected in neat rows with buckets of water outside each with towels and clothes strung on lines between posts. Children played together in small groups, a few of the older ones reading to themselves or out loud to the younger kids. Elora felt them watching her as she rode towards a larger two-story building with a flat roof.

"This is where we store the weapons. The entire ground floor is an armoury with a small store at the back for equipment, maps and rations," Brindle pointed to the upper floor. "We keep the babies and the small children up there."

"Above all the weapons and explosives?" Elora asked, incredulously.

"Safest place for them. Besides, if the camp is attacked we would retreat to this building. If the babies are already there then it saves having to run around collecting them under fire."

"I suppose," Elora said, admitting that the Captain was probably right. She climbed down from the horse and followed the Captain inside, putting a hand on the bulworg's back before she passed under the threshold. "You'd better stay out here. And Weakest - try not to look so mean and aggressive." She grinned as the huge beast sat on its haunches and cocked its head in the puzzled way of a dog not understanding a command.

Yellow candlelight bathed the large assembly room revealing boxes and crates, some stacked taller than a man and one almost touching the high ceiling. Various rifles were placed in neat rows upon tables that surrounded the walls, all seeming cocked and ready. Elora recognised most of them from the standard SA 80 to Kalashnikov's, Amourlights to MP 5's. An open crate revealed high powered shotguns nestled tightly in foam along with boxes of 12 bore cartridges. Sniper rifles, pistols and even a 50 calibre anti-aircraft gun that lay in a corner. Her gaze roamed over the weaponry, surprised at the firepower that was in the room, surprised that the men had hauled it single-handed from Hereford.

"What are you planning to do with this lot?" she asked, wondering if somehow she could use it to attack the Dark Army. Although she knew that even with the highly trained special forces on her side - if they were on her side - they could do no more than make a small dent in the enemy. Little more than make a nuisance.

Brindle shrugged as he laid his own rifle on the table. "We haven't made any plans as such. We're still trying to work out what's happening. Who the enemy is."

Another soldier slipped into the room from a side door, its contents hidden in shadow. "We all signed on the dotted line pledging our allegiance to Queen and country. Nothing's changed, unless she's dead of course," the newcomer said.

"This is Corporal Scott. A medic," Brindle said, introducing the slim soldier who leaned against a crate of grenades pushing his glasses further up his nose. "Scott, this is Elora...actually I don't know what you are."

"I'm the Shadojak," she said, feeling more eyes on her as the rest of the unit joined them. Slater, Pudding, Dent and Mac sat themselves on boxes or tables, folding their arms or in Pudding's case, biting into a chocolate bar.

"I don't know what that is," Brindle admitted, his solid stare taking her in. "But we all saw what you can do: move like lightening, produce swords from thin air, turn to smoke and reappear somewhere else."

"And other things too, I'm new to the job. Being Shadojak means that I'm a balancer, judge and if needs be, executioner."

"You're not human," Slater remarked, a tattoo of a carp bunching up on his forearm as he flexed his muscle.

"Partly human. But not Earth-born," she explained, withholding the full truth that she was a demigod, the daughter of Chaos and the Queen of Darkness.

Brindle nodded. "So you're from the same place as those dog-beasts and those insects that possessed everybody."

"No, they were created in the Shadowlands, part of the Dark Army who had swept through this world to spread Chaos. I was born on Thea but lived most of my life here. I only found out I wasn't Earth-born a few weeks ago. A lot has changed since then."

"You're not kidding," continued Brindle. "So this thing has effected the entire planet?"

"Even America?" put in Dent, rubbing the back of his neck and making his dog tags clink together. "Thought at least the Yanks would have a contingency plan."

"I doubt anybody would have a contingency plan against what's happened," Scott said, joining in the conversation. "Nuclear holocaust, alien invasion, probably even a zombie apocalypse - they'd have people making plans for the lot, yet this thing that has happened goes beyond anyone's imagination."

The Captain nodded his agreement then returned his attention back to her. "So what the hell are we fighting and how the hell do we fight it?"

"Men, bulworgs, takwich, grumpkins..." Elora said, reeling them off on her fingers. "Grimbles, demons, trolls and other monsters - even a dragon called Grycul if she's escaped. They've been waiting thousands of years for this very moment, waiting in strategic places covering the planet; hungry to take the world, which they've done. I've pledged my life to taking it back."

"How?" Brindle asked, taking a step closer.

"I haven't worked that bit out yet," she admitted, her gaze wandering over the arsenal in the room. "But maybe you've got a few toys I could borrow should the need arise."

"Once the children are safe then you may have some men to play with those toys too. If the men agree."

Elora smiled. "There's a place twelve miles east of here that's safe, self-contained, although we may need to arrange how to shelter you all."

"How safe?" Brindle asked.

Elora chuckled. "It's protected by a fairy charm." She watched the soldiers' mouths drop open. "It's true. The Dark Army doesn't know where it is and couldn't penetrate the charm even if they knew where to search."

"I'd need to see this place for myself before I commit the children to your trust."

"Of course," Elora replied.

Brindle nodded and paced across the room to a small ammo box. He picked it up and brought it back, placing it down on the crate in front of her.

"Slater caught this a few days ago," he said. "One of those insect takwich things that possess people. Tried biting Pudding until Slater butt-stroked it and shoved it in here while it lay stunned."

"Thought we might learn something from it, you know, do some experiments or some other crap on the ugly git," Slater said.

Elora approached the ammo box and flipped open the steel clasps. "You might want to step back," she warned Brindle and the sniper as she gripped the lid.

The darkness that still lingered within her sensed the takwich inside the metal box. It passed through the steel container as if it was lighter than air. Stroking the creature's body, feeling its dark intentions, legs coiled ready to spring, pincers raised ready to strike.

The darkness wrapped around the takwich and soothed its violent mind while luring it into a false sense of security. Elora didn't understand how she was doing it, but felt that the creature was under her control.

It lowered its pincers, its head dropping as if under her spell. She flipped open the lid and wrapped her fingers tightly around its body. She gripped it in such a way that it couldn't move its head to strike her.

"Careful," Brindle warned, slipping a pistol from a shoulder holster and cocking it. "Don't let it bite, I wouldn't want to shoot you."

Elora ignored him, her attention given fully over to the insect in her grasp. She hadn't seen one up close before, let alone touched one.

71

It was an ugly little thing. Smooth shiny shell, black like its intentions, hard like its demeanour. Its mandibles worked viciously as the triangular head thrashed around attempting to sink its fangs into her. Large bulbous eyes sat atop its head, red like blood, red like her own when she let the darkness sink in.

Elora stared into those red orbs, caressing the takwich with the darkness, easing its frustration as it sought to bite her. She cocked her head to the side, the creature cocked its head to the side. She turned her head to the opposite side, the takwich mimicked her move. Elora released her grip and opened her palm out flat.

Gasps escaped the soldiers around her, yet the creature remained motionless, its gaze locked on hers, hypnotised.

"What are you doing?" Brindle demanded.

Elora didn't know what was she doing? The momentary lapse in concentration as her mind sought an answer was all the takwich needed to refocus its attention.

Pain shot up her arm as her father's creation sunk its teeth into her bare wrist, fangs piercing the skin and veins as it locked on.

Elora felt the presence of the takwich in sharp clarity as its soul sought to take charge of her body. She felt its consciousness seek out her nervous-system, sensed its desire to rule her, to take her.

The darkness smiled and she grinned with it. The takwich faltered, attempting to rush back into its insect body as it recognised the devastating mistake, yet it had died the second its fangs touched her.

A hissing sound escaped between cracks in the creature's shell, along with grey smoke as its inners cooked. Flames erupted from the puncture wounds in

Elora's wrist catching the takwich, devouring its head as the red orbs shrank; steaming green puss oozing out in disgusting tears.

A heartbeat later the legs gave way and the creature curled up into a tight smouldering ball upon her hand. Elora clenched her fingers, crushing through the hot armour as the insect crumbled to dust.

She turned her hand upside down and watched the remains of the takwich drift to the floor - ashes to ashes, dust to dust; if God doesn't want you then the devil must - Elora felt the grin still upon her face, formed from the pleasure felt by the destruction.

The grey dust fell to her feet, two thin black legs amongst the pile still twitching. She let the grin fall, it wasn't her, it was the darkness.

"Interesting," Scott remarked as he nudged the pile of dust with his boot.

"That's nothing, you should see her when she turns to smoke," Pudding said as he opened a packet of crisps.

Brindle slipped his gun away. "So where's this place of yours?"

"I'll meet you at Averton town square in the morning," she said, brushing the remnants of dust from her hand. "And bring Corporal Scott," she smiled at the medic. "How are you at midwifery?"

"Why?"

"We have a lady that's due any day now and you're the closest thing we have to a doctor."

Scott paled.

"Fine," Brindle said, slapping him on the back. "I'll bring him and an engineer. Are you going to be safe traveling back alone? You know yourself there's some real mean creatures out there."

The grin on Elora's face was her own this time. "I'm the meanest creature out there. Besides, I'll have Weakest with me."

"The bulldog?"

"Bulworg," Elora corrected.

Stars twinkled blue white as the moon cast pale light on the dark road, reflecting off the abandoned cars. Weakest stalked alongside her, weaving between the vehicles, silent an almost unseen, his dark fur soaking up the moonlight. An owl hovering above a field mouse, ready to make a kill was startled as they passed. It disappeared from view, Weakest staring after the bird and following its path into the night.

"Does it hurt?" Elora asked the bulworg, nodding down to the wound on his ribs.

Weakest shook his head no, the motion causing Daisy to jolt away from him. Elora guided the nervous horse back, stroking her behind the ears and reassuring her.

She tried reaching out to the bulworg with the darkness, attempting to touch him the way she had done the takwich earlier, yet couldn't detect him in the slightest. This was why he seemed different to her when she was in the presence of the grumpkin. She had felt the evil intent in both him and the other bulworg but not Weakest. Perhaps the darkness could only sense others of the same nature. Elora was sure she had the truth of it and felt relieved at knowing that Weakest wasn't part of the Dark Army.

She cast her gaze to the way ahead and guessed that they were roughly halfway home when Weakest paused.

The bulworg raised its wolf-like head and sniffed the air, a deep growl issuing from his chest.

"Dangerrr," he groaned.

Elora stood up in her stirrups and scanned the surrounding area, yet saw nothing. The road was quiet and the surrounding fields and trees empty. Closing her eyes, she concentrated on throwing out the darkness as far as she could, reaching maybe a hundred metres and still felt no danger. None relating to the Dark Army at least.

When she turned to Weakest, about to suggest that they continue a flash of movement startled her horse causing her to rear. Elora was thrown from the saddle and landed hard in a ditch that drove the wind from her lungs.

The sounds of Weakest snarling intermingled with his yells of pain brought her back to her knees. She struggled to take in a deep breath as she shook the dizziness from her head.

As her blurred vision refocused, Elora climbed from the ditch slipping her sword from its invisible sheath as she rose. In front of her was Weakest, crouching low, ready to pounce at a huge silver coloured wolf that stood on hind legs towering over him.

The silver wolf wore a long red cloak that billowed in the breeze and held the biggest sword she had ever seen, ready to chop down into the bulworg.

Elora's body reacted before she thought how to attack.

Dissolving into smoke her body drifted across the space in less than a heartbeat, materialising back into her human form in time to catch the huge sword with her own.

Sparks flew as the blades met, the force of her attacker was animal strong yet she deflected his blow, tipping the beast off balance whilst thrusting her fist into his stomach.

Elora expected to drive a winding blow to the wolf, but her knuckles struck metal and only drove the attacker back a few staggering paces. Undaunted, she pressed the attack following the creature before it got its footing and smashed the hilt of her sword against his chest.

The impact jarred her arm after striking metal once again. The wolf was a machine, but again the force knocked him back, pushing him up against a car; his arm flying wide and smashing a window. She stepped into him ducking low and swept her sword about to cut him across the knee joint; she could have taken his snarling head but she wanted answers before his life ended.

The wolf blocked her swipe with his huge sword and shoved her in the chest with a gauntleted hand, knocking her back a few paces – he was strong. She made to lunge at him but he held a hand up.

"Enough," he said, his voice sounding like the whisper of drawn steel. "My dispute is with the worg, not the Shadojak."

Elora held her blade out ready to strike but paused, taking the strange beast in as she caught her breath.

The wolf wasn't a machine but a man wearing thick armour. The breast-plate was intricately carved like a torso of a wolf, the detail so fine that each hair of the fur appeared real. His lobster gauntlets were shaped like claws, his shoulder guards also delicately carved and the helmet and visor were shaped like a snarling wolf's head. She felt his stare through the black slits where the wolf's eyes should have been.

"Grimwolf?" Elora asked.

Chapter 5

Grimwolf

His name hung in the air like a question - an accusation, spoken from delicate lips by a voice made to sing and made to touch his heart.

"Grimwolf?" The girl repeated, her sword held between them, its edge so sharp it made his teeth itch.

"I've come for the worg, not the Shadojak," he said. The roughly spoken words sounding the exact opposite of Elora's softly spoken question.

The girl raised her blade, the point inches from his face; violet eyes staring into his.

"The bulworg is under my protection, he won't harm you," she said, gesturing for the worg to step back and lower down. Surprisingly the beast did so. "How did you know I was the Shadojak?"

"Black cloak, god-created blade," he replied.

"Is it that obvious?"

He nodded wanting to say more but not trusting his voice. The worg lowered into a sitting position, its gaze still locked on him yet seemed less inclined to attack than his ever-violent brethren - strange.

"I've no quarrel with you Grimwolf, put your sword away," Elora ordered, her sweet voice teasing his lips into a smile that was hidden behind his helm.

His blade made a rasping sound, steel scraping against leather as he slipped it into his scabbard. He didn't doubt that the Shadojak could end him and that strike to his chest still hurt, there would be bruises tomorrow.

The girl lowered her own sword and spirited it away into a smuggler's pouch, her gaze never leaving his. "Will you remove your helmet or at least lift your visor? I'd like to see who it is I'm speaking to," she said.

Grimwolf didn't move. No good would come of revealing his face. When it became clear he wouldn't do as she asked she continued.

"We are not enemies. In fact I owe you a thanks for helping save the children and killing bulworgs in the area. Perhaps we could be friends?" She absently stroked the worg's head and the beast leaned into her hand, eager for the touch. "There is a war coming or at least a rebellion and I would prefer to have you on my side."

Pale moonlight reflected from her face, only adding to her beauty and revealing her vulnerability, her insecurities. This all powerful Shadojak was still just a girl. A girl that had stolen his heart from the very first time he saw her many moons ago.

"You don't say much, do you?" she asked, stepping closer and attempting to peer inside his visor.

He lifted his head preventing her from seeing who he was, she could never know; the knowledge would ruin everything.

"I don't even know if you're human. Did you come from the Shadowlands with the Dark Army or were you here already?"

Again he didn't answer. Words could trip you up, trap you or reveal answers that you wished to remain hidden.

"When the war starts I doubt there will be room for rogue fighters. You will either be with me or with them and you've already proven you're not with them."

The silence was awkward but necessary, for now at least. Grimwolf averted his gaze from those violet eyes that seemed to batter at his soul to root out the truth.

"My name's Elora, I don't live far away. Why not come back with me? We could talk this over. I'm not sure if I'm comfortable with an armoured wolf or whatever you are stalking around on your own."

He shook his head again, keeping quiet like a bashful child.

"Is there a way of finding you if the need arises?"

He heard the disappointment in her voice and fought not to remove his helmet, not to show her the truth and have done with it. Instead he shook his head. "If there's a need, I will find you."

It wasn't what she wanted to hear, he could see that from the hopeful expression dropping from her face.

"Then I'll be patiently waiting, Grimwolf. But don't take too long in your solitude, the war comes closer with each new day."

He remained still as she climbed up on her horse and began to ride away, giving him a final glance before she vanished around a bend in the road.

"Elora," he whispered into the empty night as he wandered in the opposite direction. He took a path through an unkempt field, hay almost shoulder height and well passed time to be cropped. It was perfect to hide his horse.

The stallion snickered as he mounted the saddle, throwing his head back and flicking his glistening mane. Grimwolf patted the horse's neck, dull metal gauntlets delicately touching the black silky skin.

He felt more alone than ever as he rode east in the same direction as the girl, but took a more scenic route preferring to cross fields and woods than take the road. Visions of Elora ruled his mind, every minute detail of the girl which had stolen his heart. Love, a mystery that had belonged to others had somehow been discovered by himself.

Lost in his own dreams his horse steered itself along a stream that weaved through a deep gorge that lay on the edge of a forest. The steep rock to either side blocked what light came from the starry sky, yet Grimwolf knew this place well, had ridden its path a thousand times before as did his horse. Hooves splashed the shallow waters displacing shingle as they ascended into a cave system that fed the stream. Tall and narrow the opening swallowed them, its dark inner sanctum blocking out the world.

A network of tunnels lay inside, carved from running water over millions of years. A labyrinth he knew well. The horse moved more silently now, the floor of the cave being sand, yet nobody would hear any noise they made.

"Elora," Grimwolf said into the darkness.

"Elora," The dark rock echoed back.

Captain Brindle greeted them with a smile. He waited with three others as Elora and Jaygen rode into Averton on the stagecoach. She recognised Slater, Pudding and Scott, yet had never seen the fourth man before.

"You came then?" Brindle said as he slung a rifle over his shoulder. "I was beginning to doubt the events of last night ever happened. That's what broad daylight does to you; evaporates any nightmares you've had, although some sights these days are best left for the dark hours."

"I know the feeling," Elora agreed, shaking hands with the Captain. "Climb aboard."

Once the soldiers had seated themselves into the back of the stagecoach Jaygen gave a flick of the reins that set the four-horse team back the way they had come.

"This is Jaygen," Elora offered, placing a hand on the teenager's shoulder. "A friend."

She felt him tense under her touch and withdraw. She guessed he was shy, meeting so many new people at once was something he wasn't used to, not after spending most of his life with only his parents for company.

"Nice to meet you Jaygen," Brindle said. Jaygen nodded but kept his head forwards concentrating on the road. If the captain found him rude Elora thought, he hid it well.

"You met these boys last night," continued the Captain, gesturing to the three men in his team. "And this is Smudge - or Sergeant Smith, he's our engineer."

"Smudge is fine," said the amiable Sergeant as he leaned over the seat to shake hands with her.

"Elora," she said, seeing a subtle resemblance to her uncle in the soldier who appeared a good twenty years older than the other men. He smiled warmly and sat back.

"How far away is this place of yours?" he asked. "The Captain tells me it has some kind of fiery protection."

"I said fairy protection, Smudge," chuckled Brindle.

"You know, I thought that's what you said but didn't for a second believe that's what you meant to say. Fairy protection. So how's that work?"

"I don't know how," Elora said. "But it's kept the place secret for hundreds of years."

"Sorry, I've a hard time believing in magic," admitted the engineer.

"Don't know about magic myself," said Slater, setting his rifle down on his lap. "Some of the things I've seen lately are all kinds of crazy. See."

He pointed ahead of them to where Weakest sat atop an abandoned car.

"I get your point," Smudge said.

Elora had ordered Weakest to scout ahead of them as she and Jaygen rode into town, not wanting to leave the bulworg at Rams Keep while they were gone.

She had a hard time explaining him last night. To Norgie and Melvin in particular who argued about the safety of the children. In the end Weakest spent the night locked in the dungeon, Elora stayed on a bench outside desperate to catch what sleep she could before sunrise.

Things hadn't altered much in the waking hours. Suffice to say that nobody wanted Weakest around, especially Jaygen who had been in a morose mood since their return.

As they rolled passed the bulworg Elora ordered him to follow on, taking care that they were not being followed.

The rest of the journey was pleasant, Smudge filling any silence with conversation, talking about nothing in particular which was fine with Elora. In truth she was tired. She had been since leaving Aslania and if left to roam around for itself her mind would drift to Bray, who could be absolutely anywhere as he sought a way to return to her.

Weakest darted amongst the trees as they rode into the forest, scouting around the stagecoach as they neared the ruins of Rams Keep.

"I know this area well," Brindle said, "studied maps and tabbed over nearly every hill and wood this side of

Wales, yet have never heard of this place. It's huge, how could I have missed it?"

"Because it's not on any map. It's hidden from above by the tree canopy and you can't merely stumble upon it," Elora answered. "I suppose the MOD think it's privately owned and local farmers believe it's owned by the MOD."

Elora didn't know the answer herself until the question was asked. What else was imbedded within her mind, what knowledge did she have ready to reveal itself with the right questions? The thought of it alone would make her dizzy if she let it.

"Impressive," Smudge remarked as the carriage rolled to a stop before the remains of a large stone tower. One side of the round structure rose two stories high, the spiral staircase intact and open to the elements; thick vines growing through the countless steps that were missing or crumbled to misshapen rock on the ground below. The other side of the tower rose higher still, but with no roof or floors the entire structure was a broken shell outlining the original shape.

"It's all in the same condition?" the Captain asked, not seeming as impressed as the Sergeant.

Elora nodded. "I don't think there is a roof intact in any of the buildings, but the foundations are strong and some of the thicker walls have stood the test of time."

She climbed from the stagecoach and gestured for them to follow.

Weakest padded by her side as she ambled over piles of rocks and masonry, weaving between partial walls and remains of doorways and arches. Some of the paths and corridors were still intact, solid cobbles and stone tiles coated in dirt and fallen leaves, yet was firm.

Every now and again, the engineer would pause and tap at a wall or in one case, kick it. Jotting down notes in a pad with a pencil as he gazed about the ruins. When they arrived at a well at the keep's centre, Pudding attempted to bring the bucket up, but when the pulley jammed and he used force, it gave way. The pulley rope and bucket disappeared into the well, clattering around the brickwork before splashing into the underground stream.

Smudge shook his head as he scribbled on his pad.

Nobody spoke as they carried on, only Slater tssking at Private Barker who shrugged at the general mishap as if it wasn't his fault.

Elora led them around the entire site, only stopping once more at the tower that led into the dungeons and the many rooms and chambers beneath the keep. The place where she had spent the night and where, many weeks ago, she - that other her had been awakened.

"This is the only place out of bounds," Elora gestured to the wide structure no less intact than the other towers but held so many secrets below the stone and grass surface. Secrets that even her predecessors were unaware of.

"Why?" Brindle asked.

"It's dangerous," she lied, not wanting the men exploring within the underground labyrinth of tunnels and corridors. "Some of the foundations here have crumbled and this part is liable to collapse. The rest of the keep is yours to use, just stay out of here - especially the children."

"She means you, Pudding," Slater said with a scowl.

Brindle gave a final glance about the ruins before turning to his Sergeant. "So what do you think?"

The engineer glanced down at his notepad. "I think it's going to be a lot of work. But doable. Very doable." He tapped his pencil against his bottom lip as he spoke. "We're going to need to visit a hardware store and a timber yard. Could do with a couple of cement mixers too and plenty of men. A lot of the stone can be used to rebuild the walls and where it can't we can use bricks. We're probably going to need a lot of scaffolding to fix the roofs or in most cases, actually put a roof up. Elora's right about the foundations being solid though."

"So what do you think?" Elora asked. "Will Rams Keep be suitable for your men?"

"If this fairy circle of yours actually works then the place is perfect. Or will be after Smudge has put a few things right."

"Great, let me show you the inn and introduce you to your new neighbours."

"If it's all the same to you Sir," Smudge said, addressing the Captain. "I'd rather stay here and get a good feel for the place and make a few more notes."

Brindle glanced to Elora for approval and she nodded with a smile. "Very well Smudge. I'll leave Pudding with you. We'll pick you both up before we head back to Sennybridge."

The engineer gave a half-hearted salute and began to wander back through the ruins, a reluctant Pudding by his side.

Norgie and Melvin came to greet them as the carriage rolled in front of the inn with at least a dozen children at their heels.

Elora introduced the Captain and his men. Melvin seemed less than pleased; most probably taking a natural dislike to authoritative figures, unlike Norgie who appeared thrilled to meet the Captain - which Elora guessed was due to him being ex-military himself. He chatted enthusiastically as he led the group into the inn, talking about his time in the Marines.

"I don't know if I like this," Melvin admitted, holding her back as the men disappeared into the building. "I mean, you only met them last night. Can you trust them?"

"I only met you once before I brought you here and that was when you levelled a shotgun at me and attacked my boyfriend with your thugs."

"Aye," he said, sheepishly, "You've got a point. But still..."

"Melvin. There is a war coming, in fact it's already begun and I'd rather have these soldiers on our side than not." She turned to Jaygen who had taken to staring sulkily at the bulworg. "That goes for you too. Weakest may have been part of the Dark Army once, but he's fighting for us now and we need every single fighter we can get our hands on."

Jaygen shook his head. "Do you really think we have a chance against them? They've taken the entire world."

"Don't you think I know that?" she snapped. "It's my responsibility to take the world back. And I will, by any means possible or die trying."

Elora took a deep breath and calmed her rising anger. No good would come of shouting at Jaygen, he was only venting his worries.

"Look, we've found survivors. British soldiers with enough weapons to supply a small army and that's just around here. Perhaps there's other survivors in other

86

towns and villages. In the cities, in London maybe, Silk couldn't have taken them all."

"And you'll gather them all up and march us to certain death. Is that your plan?" growled Jaygen, his knuckles turning white as he gripped the side of the carriage. Weakest picked up on his threatening tone and began a low growl himself. Elora steadied him with a stare.

"No, I just need you to survive. The only one going to battle is myself."

Weakest sat straighter, lifting his jaw and baring his teeth. "And Weakest, of course."

"Two against the biggest army this world has ever seen?" Jaygen said, shaking his head, but the anger had mellowed from his voice.

"If needs be. And Grimwolf; he's got some kind of grudge against the Dark Army too." At the mention of the stranger's name, Elora noticed Jaygen stiffen.

"He is real. I met him last night."

"I told you," Melvin said excitedly. "That dude is hardcore bad."

Elora smiled feeling the tension lift, yet recognised the sullen mood return to Jaygen.

"I wouldn't go putting my trust into Grimwolf. He may not turn out to be what you expect."

Elora felt that he knew more than he was letting on. She was about to ask him what it was, but before the question came to her lips he gave the reins a flick and set the cart rolling once again.

"What's gotten into him?" Melvin asked as they headed into the inn.

"He's only recently lost his father. I think he partly blames me for his death."

She asked Weakest to stay outside which he only seemed glad about, before entering the inn.

Cathy had joined the group by the time Elora stepped into the bar room. She was introducing herself and some of the children while Norgie set about making a cup of tea.

"Is it your first one?" asked Scott, nodding towards her bump.

"Yeah," Cathy replied, absently laying an arm across her belly. "I still can't get over it - me being a mother any day now."

"Oh, I was hoping you'd have given birth before," Scott said. "So you could talk me through the procedure."

"Why?" Cathy asked, suspiciously.

"Because," Elora intervened, since the medic had gone a bright shade of red. "He's your midwife."

"Midwife? How many births has an army doctor experienced?" Cathy asked as she placed her hands on her hips.

Scott cleared his throat. "None. And I'm not a doctor, just a medic."

"But the closest we have to a doctor," Elora said before Cathy could protest.

A heavy silence filled the room as the pregnant woman stared at Scott, only broken as Norgie re-entered carrying a tray of steaming mugs.

"What did I miss?"

They spent the next hour discussing how to coordinate transferring the camp at Sennybridge to Rams Keep. They came to the conclusion that they would do it in several trips, detouring through the countryside and using woods and forests for cover. Marching the entire camp in one go along the main road would present too much of a target and they could be easily followed.

The cart and carriage would be used to transport the weapons, but not before gathering what Smudge needed from the timber yard.

As the afternoon drew on, Elora showed the group around the rest of the grounds, allowing the children to splash around in the lake when they came to it.

Gurple had chosen that time to make an appearance, holding hands with two small toddlers who were timid around the adults. The soldiers were unsure of the wood troll at first but soon relaxed around him as they watched how he was with the little ones.

"This place is really something," Brindle said, a rare smile forming dimples in his cheeks as he was splashed by an excited boy chasing a duck.

"Yeah," Elora agreed, smiling herself. The fun the children were having was contagious. They both laughed as Norgie, attempting to stay dry was pulled into the water by the playful children and was soaked up to the waist.

After the children became tired and hungry they decided to head back to the inn. After Elora counted the children and turned to leave she noticed a figure standing alone on the other side of the lake. A cloak billowing out to his side as the wolf-shaped helmet faced her.

"Wonder what he wants?" Brindle said as he stared at Grimwolf.

"I wonder how he found this place?" she replied, setting off towards the armoured man.

"Do you want me to come with you?" the Captain asked.

Elora shook her head. "No, I'll be fine. Go back with the others, I'll catch you up."

She skirted around the lake with Weakest at her side, her gaze locked on the solitary being and Jaygen's last words playing on her mind - I wouldn't go putting my trust in Grimwolf, he might not be what you expect.

He stood a good foot taller than herself, as big and wide as Ragna had been; dark slits in his snarling helmet staring down at her.

"How did you find us? Rams Keep is protected from those that are not shown the way," Elora asked, skipping any greeting.

"I was shown a long time ago," he replied, his whisper sounding as harsh as it did the night before.

"Shown by who?"

Grimwolf didn't answer. He could have been mistaken for a carved statue rather than a man wearing armour. When it was clear he wasn't going to speak Elora asked. "Why have you come?"

"To warn you of a scraw-harpy in the next valley," he whispered. "It's been circling the area for days now, it knows you are close."

Scraw-harpy. The name was new to her ears but manipulated a memory and unlocked the knowledge she didn't know she had. A creature of the skies, similar in size and appearance to a vulture with an extended hooked beak and vicious talons. The scraw-harpy flew high above the ground, its keen vision helping to locate and track an enemy while communicating its thoughts to its owner, either man or beast. They had an incredible sense of smell too, able to follow scents left by a prey and seek them out from above. Elora knew it had to die and soon.

"It's linked to the Dark forces in the area. When you killed the grumpkin last night it came a step closer. If it stumbles upon Rams Keep it will bring an army against you."

Elora heard the truth in his words. "Thank you for the warning."

Grimwolf declined his head in a subtle nod, then surprisingly presented her with a bunch of flowers. She wondered how his claw shaped gauntlets held the bundle without crushing them.

Elora took the exotic plants wrapped in bracken leaves. The flowers were similar in appearance to the bird of paradise. A delicate decorative flower with large tear-shaped petals. It was deep purple at its centre, becoming azure blue as it spread out. Yellow barbs sprouted from the middle of each flower with separate strands of feathery plumes, bright yellow in colour and each ending with a tiny gold spear.

"They're beautiful," Elora said, failing to remember the last time somebody brought her flowers. She inhaled the rich aroma, a pungent mix of sweetpeas, lavender and wild lilies. "Thank you."

Grimwolf remained silent. Did he feel awkward or shy beneath all that armour? Elora couldn't imagine someone so fierce being bashful.

"I love them but you should know my heart belongs to another," she said, hoping that she didn't offend him.

"The flowers are to mask your scent; you won't get close to the scraw-harpy without it."

Elora felt a warmth flood her cheeks - how stupid could she be? How vain she must appear believing that Grimwolf had taken an interest in her. She cleared her throat thinking of something clever to say, yet it was

Grimwolf that spoke first. Either ignoring or not noticing her embarrassment.

"Crush the heads to powder and soak them in oil overnight. The perfume it makes will mask your human scent."

"How will I make the scraw-harpy land?" she asked.

"That's your problem, you're the Shadojak. But If I were you I'd use your new pet." His wolf's head shifted to face Weakest whose large paws flexed against the earth. "He may still be able to link with it."

Elora thought she caught a glimpse of skin, a slither of light bouncing off a pale cheekbone inside the helmet, yet the moment she caught it the light shifted so she couldn't be sure what she saw.

Grimwolf gave her one last glance before he paced away towards the forest, his cloak billowing out behind him as he entered the tree line.

"Bye then," Elora said as the armoured man disappeared. She inhaled the flowers once again, their scent was as beautiful as they were pretty. It would be a shame to crush them.

"Bray won't be happy with you," Norgie chuckled as she caught them up at the well. "Accepting flowers from a stranger."

The group had remained by the lake, watching her exchange with the mysterious Grimwolf.

"It's not like that," Elora said, as she swatted his arm playfully. "Have you any spare cooking oil in the kitchen?"

"I'm sure I can find some, why?"

"I'll tell you later." Then turning to Slater she asked. "Are you any good with that rifle of yours?"

The frown Slater gave her reduced his blue eyes to slits. "Never miss," he said, without a hint of boastfulness as if merely stating a fact.

"Can I borrow you tomorrow?"

Slater raised an eyebrow. "You better ask the Captain."

"If it's important, yes." Brindle said as he playfully bounced a small boy on his shoulders. "Slater could put a round through a crow in the sky and hit it again before the body fell to the ground."

"Good. He's the man for the job then," Elora said.

Chapter 6

Descent of the Scraw-harpy

Slater was already prepared for stalking. Green, black and brown camouflage cream masked his face in tiger stripes, his sniper rifle matching the pattern of his uniform; the standard multi-camouflage of the British army.

"What is it?" he asked her as Elora passed him the bottle of perfume. Unscrewing the cap, he gave the contents a sniff and screwed up his face.

Elora shrugged. "Just think of it as another layer of camouflage. Trust me, we won't get near the target without it."

"Fine," he said, grudgingly. He tipped some of the pale blue liquid onto his hand and rubbed it into his bare neck, then splashed a few drops on his clothes. "But if the lads back at camp smell me I will never live it down."

They were crouched beneath a tall oak on the outskirts of Rams Keep with a good view of the valley before them. There were few clouds in the morning sky so they should spot the scraw-harpy quite easily if it turned up.

Weakest lay on the ground beside her, wrinkling his nose as the scent of the perfume passed his nose. Elora smiled, it took her an entire hour to crush the flower heads to powder the previous night. Scraping them around a mortar and pestle dish while she made Norgie filter the oil through muslin. It felt a shame that she couldn't spare one of the flowers, it would have looked beautiful in a vase. Maybe she would ask Grimwolf where he found them so she could pick her own. They were not native to Earth she was sure of that.

"So this bird is something special, right?" Slater asked as he lay down on the forest floor and rested the rifle stock against an exposed tree root. He stared down the barrel and turned the dials on the telescopic sight - three clicks left for the wind and two clicks up for the distance.

"Special is maybe too good a word for a creature of the Dark Army. But yeah, the scraw-harpy is a prized asset."

Slater scowled, shifting his body to manoeuvre his shoulder against the stock and peered through the sight. He made another adjustment, a final click.

"Reckon we could take it alive, you know use it against them. Try at least to get some information."

He kept his gaze steady as he spoke, index finger pressing lightly over the trigger.

"If you can make the shot that will drop it without ending it then do that. It's paramount that it falls though, so if the shot's too hard just go for the kill."

"Check."

Elora had similar thoughts, if she could reach the bird before it died then she could harvest its soul with her sword.

It was almost midday before Slater tapped his grey beret and pointed into the valley. Elora followed the direction he was pointing and saw only empty sky. A moment later her eyes picked out a dot, black against the silver clouds in the far distance. How the sniper had spotted it she didn't know - then again, he was a sniper.

They watched as the dot came closer, growing in size until she could just make out the blurred shape of a large bird, its wings spread wide as it soured high up. Elora guessed that it would have most of Wales in its vision.

"I don't think he's coming any closer," whispered the sniper.

He was right, the scraw-harpy was making slow circles where it was but not appearing to be coming towards them.

"Leave it to me," Elora said.

She indicated for Weakest to follow her and headed down into the valley using the trees as cover. They moved swiftly and silently, avoiding twigs and dried leaves, sweeping through the foliage like a breeze. When they were as close as Elora dared go, she ducked low below the canvas of an elm and ordered Weakest to wander out into the open.

Elora lay still and was touched by the shadows about her. Hearing the urgent whispers speaking her name again and again. The darkness crept inside her as she watched the scraw-harpy, wondering if she could throw out her sense to the bird and coax it down. No, it may sense her and take flight before Slater took his shot.

From her hiding place she watched Weakest pace lazily out into the open, acting as though he was sniffing around and picking up a trail. The scraw-harpy took the bait and descended towards him but had no intention of landing.

"Don't miss," Elora prayed under her breath. They couldn't mess this up. One chance was all they had, one shot, one attempt. If the bird suspected anything or sensed one of them or even if the sniper missed - it would leave in a heartbeat and return with the strength of the Dark forces knowing where they were.

It circled the bulworg a couple of hundred feet above, still too high to make out any distinguishing marks as it sought a connection with Weakest.

Elora held her breath as the bird circled wider, gliding on the natural thermals rushing through the valley. Closer she willed it, come closer.

Weakest acted as though he hadn't noticed the flying creature. He continued to paw at the ground, yet Elora could feel the effect of the scraw-harpy trying to connect with him. She sensed an invitation to link with its mind, to share visions and thoughts, felt the birds hunger for information that this random bulworg may have. Yet the beast on the ground ignored it still.

The bird suddenly shrieked in anger. A high-pitched caw that echoed around the hills. It shrieked a second time startling wood pigeons from a nest; the smaller birds flapped widely, panicking to leave the area where this strange monster ruled the skies.

The scraw-harpy descended again, bringing it within a hundred feet, close enough to make out its dark brown feathers, close enough to see those sharp talons and hooked beak, close enough to see the evil in its eyes and close enough to kill.

The bird jerked in mid-air, its entire body spun sideways as the crack of the shot ruptured through the valley.

Elora watched the bird fall; loose feathers floating down following the spinning tangle of the scraw-harpy. Bent in half with its legs raised above its talons, reaching for the sky, its beak open as it shrieked protests to an unseen god above.

Bones shattered like fine glass rods as it thudded into the hard earth. The head whipped back on its rangy neck and bounced off the ground, snapping its beak shut with a loud clap.

Elora approached the fallen creature, waving a hand for Weakness to step out of harm's way. Broken and pathetic it may appear but it still had control over the vicious talons and a desperate will to use them.

She stood above its head, large yellow eyes watching her as she slipped her blade from the smuggler's pouch. The scraw-harpy's breath came in ragged bursts, blood beginning to coat its beak from a ruptured lung. Elora noticed a large hole in the flesh that bridged one wing with the body. This is where the bullet hit, shattering the bone beneath. A good shot, a sniper's shot.

Elora placed her boot down on its twisted neck to hold the body still and stared into those evil eyes as she drove her blade into the scraw-harpy's heart.

Blood spurted onto the god-made metal, a final pump from the now motionless organ and with it came a green flame. No bigger than a thumbnail, it drifted up the length of the sword, absorbing into the weapon before it reached the hilt

The soul was felt by Elora. A tiny flicker of life that flashed across her mind to join the thousands of other souls and memories that were held in the blade, mingling with her own thoughts to be recalled when she wanted.

"You killed it?" Slater asked as he joined them before the scraw-harpy's carcass.

"I got what I wanted. Great shot by the way. Perfect," she said.

Slater nodded as if she was merely stating the obvious. He nudged the bird with his foot, inspecting the shot that brought it down.

Her attention went to Weakest who hunkered down beside them, panting with his mouth open, wet tongue hanging out. Elora realised that the bulworg hadn't eaten for a couple of days. He kept his promise not to eat unless she gave permission.

"Hungry?" she asked.

Weakest's belly answered for him, growling from being empty. Elora nodded and began to walk away leaving behind the grizzly sounds of flesh being torn from bone as Weakest ate.

"So what did you learn?" Slater asked, pacing beside her.

Elora wiped the blood from her sword before sliding it away. "That we're safe enough, for now, anyway."

She worked through the memories the scraw-harpy gave her with its soul. "It's nested in a tower near the city of Cardiff. There's an entire division of Dark soldiers stationed there. Several battalions of men, thousands of takwich who have taken the bodies of civilians, and platoons of bulworgs commanded by grumpkins."

"How the hell do we fight that?"

"We don't. They are a reserve force left to hold the ground. I think there is another division like that in the north and an even greater force in London. But they don't know we're here."

"Yet."

"Exactly. In the meantime it would be advantageous to make Rams Keep as impregnable as possible." There were a few more flashes of memory coming to her but she would need more time to dwell on them before they came clear. "I'll speak with Captain Brindle later," Elora continued. "Scraw-harpies will be another beast best avoided."

The next few days passed in a blur. Elora spent the time helping to clear rubble from the base of a tower which Smudge had sighted to be the best place to start construction. Over half the soldiers from Sennybridge had arrived to help, the other half coming at a slower pace with the children. Captain Brindle, along with the rest of his team brought the weapons, aided by Jaygen and the cart.

By the time the sun had fallen below the tree tops on the final day of the second week, a crude, yet solid roof had been erected above the tower. Made mainly from canvas and tarpaulin it kept the elements out while giving the men cover, ready to rebuild the walls and floors.

Tents for the soldiers had been erected amongst the ruins while tents for the children had been set up in the field next to the inn. Elora thought they would feel more comfortable staying closer to the other children. The babies had been placed along with the others so now Melvin and his crew had their work cut out for them.

Elora's back, shoulders and arms ached from lifting stone and carrying timber, yet she felt satisfied that things were working out well. She thought it was close to midnight by the time she'd made her way back to the inn for something to eat and a soak in a bath, although by the time she climbed in the water was tepid. Once clean she made a final check on the babies and the children asleep in the common room. Satisfied that all was well she settled herself into a chair in the kitchen. She stifled a yawn, her eyes lids growing heavy with the warm air coming from the dying coals in the fire. Folding her arms upon the table she rested her head thinking that a quick nap might freshen her up.

"Elora," came Cathy's voice, reaching her in her sleep and dragging her into wakefulness.

"Yeah?" Elora answered, the word coming out slurred as she hadn't properly woken up. Couldn't she just get a few minute's rest?

Fighting the growing irritation Elora sat up and rubbed her eyes. It was then that she realised it was daylight. Morning had crept on without her knowing.

"Sorry Elora," Cathy continued. "I left you as long as I could, but the Captain's been asking for you down at the keep. Nice flowers by the way."

"What?" She still sounded groggy as she rubbed the stiffness from her neck. It was then that she saw a bunch of flowers in a porcelain vase sitting on the table she had slept against. The same kind that Grimwolf had given her. The colours radiated the sunshine that came through the window, reflecting blues and golds onto the wall.

"Where did they come from?" Elora asked touching the delicate tear-shaped petals and inhaling the fragrance.

"I've no idea. I came down a couple of hours ago to heat some milk for the babies. You were sleeping like a baby yourself, but the flowers weren't there then. Somebody has obviously got a thing for you. I wish somebody brought me flowers like that, they're beautiful."

"You can put them in your room if you like," Elora said, thinking that they may get damaged being left on the table.

"Are you sure? I mean, somebody went to an awful lot of effort to give you them in the middle of the night. How they got passed the guards I've no idea."

"Me neither," and that went doubly for Weakest who she saw sitting by the kitchen door. Had it been

101

Grimwolf? He was the only person who knew where they grew and he must have realised she had loved them from her initial reaction at seeing them at the lake.

"So, Captain Brindle wanted to see me?"

"Yeah, I don't know why. I don't think it's urgent though - have something to eat first."

"I'll have a coffee if there's any hot water left."

The coffee had been bitter, swallowing it down with a thick slice of bread as she headed out of the inn. She paused briefly at the well to wash her face with the cold water then set off to find Brindle.

The cement mixers were turning as she approached the tower, somehow the engineer had removed the motors from the machines and rigged up a chain that fed from bicycle wheels. Soldiers were peddling away and turning the drums, wet cement slipping around inside as other men shovelled in sand and water.

"You're making great progress," Elora said by way of greeting. Smudge smiled as he surveyed the tower.

"The men have been working hard. They've been at it since sun-up."

Scaffolding had been erected to the highest point of the structure. Men were busy laying stones and bricks around the top, rebuilding it a layer at a time.

Ropes were fed through pulleys, one end tied to buckets of masonry on the ground whilst the other was tethered to a horse. Jaygen controlled the heavy set mare, hoisting the loads up the scaffolding. Elora waved out to him, but he either didn't see her or chose not to notice.

"Have you seen the Captain?" she asked.

"Down by the well. Tell him I'll be needing another ten men when I hoist up the beams."

"I will."

102

She found Brindle where Smudge had said, overseeing a pair of soldiers that were abseiling down the deep well.

"How's it going?" Elora asked, Weakest sat beside her watching the men at work.

"So far so good. The water down there," Brindle said, gesturing down the hole, thick arms resting against the stone brick work. "Is fresh and clean. The men are just retrieving the broken bucket and the ancient rope-and-pulley system. Smudge will build a new one this afternoon."

"Yeah, he's really doing well, the keep's coming along fine. By the way he needs ten more men for hoisting beams."

"Ok. But while you're here, I wanted to tell you something."

They strolled through the ruins as he spoke, Elora taking in all the men about her, each to a job and everybody busy. Several men were collecting stones in wheelbarrows, others hacking down the vines and trees that had grown into the fallen building and adding to the decay. Another team were pulling up the grasses and weeds that were poking through the cracks in the cobbled pathways and corridors. The soldiers saluted the Captain as he passed and he saluted them back.

"My men keep sighting Grimwolf," Brindle said, a crease deepening his brow.

"He's not an enemy."

"No, and he has helped us in the past, yet I don't know if I fully trust him. He hasn't revealed himself to us. It could be anyone under that armour."

"Yeah, I know what you mean. But he has helped. He's the one that warned me about the scraw-harpy and gave me the means to approach it."

Crows burst from a nest in a tall archway above them, startling a soldier that was clearing the stonework and he almost fell from a ladder. Weakest snapped at a passing bird, teeth clashing together as he missed.

"I've posted sentries around the keep and pairs of scouts are patrolling the grounds. They've all seen him coming and going. Spotted him walking through the forest, at the inn and here, in the ruins. Some of the scouts try to follow him, but he's like a ghost. He'll be there one moment, then simply gone the next."

They stopped besides the tower which hid the dungeons beneath.

"He's been spotted here a few times also, more frequent than anywhere else. Except from around you."

"What do you mean?" she asked.

"He was seen yesterday, watching you while you helped Smudge. He followed you back to the inn and was seen entering the building last night. He's watching you and Weakest very closely. It's like he's stalking you."

Elora didn't know what the armoured man was doing, stalking her - it just didn't feel right. Why would Grimwolf take such an interest?

"Thanks for the warning Captain. I'll keep an eye out for him."

She left him there and headed back to the inn. The creeping sensation of being watched making her cautious. Was Grimwolf stalking her now? Was he spying on them, hidden within the shadows of the trees or was it just the Captain's words that put her on edge? At least she now knew who brought her the flowers.

104

Grimwolf watched Elora as she spoke to the Captain, a pang of jealousy causing his fingers to flex above the hilt of his sword. He fought against the emotion, allowing it in could only bring more pain. Elora would never be his.

He had been a fool to take her flowers in the dark hours. An idiot trying to please a girl that had feelings for another. The infatuation needed to be brought under control before it became an obsession.

Elora delicately picked her way through the ruins as she returned to the inn. Grimwolf followed her, careful to keep downwind of the worg by her side, a trick easily done amongst the working soldiers but a skill as he entered the forest, although none knew the place as well as he did.

Now and again the Shadojak paused, feigning to tie a boot lace whilst checking the path behind her or the tree line he hid in. She was getting suspicious and her eyes almost fell on him twice. Only the depth of foliage and the shade the canopy provided keeping him out of sight.

If she did see him what would he do? Run? - Weakest would bring him down. Pretend that he simply stumbled upon her by accident? - she would see through his lies and trust him even less. Neither was an option so best not let her see him at all. Best to just let her go. Best to just fall on his own sword and have steel puncture his heart where love never will.

His cloak suddenly snagged against a prickly bramble bush. His already dower mood sank lower as he snatched it away causing a tear in its thick cotton side. The sound made Elora pause once again and glance in his direction.

Grimwolf only released his breath once she continued the journey, watching her until she fell from sight, then cursed himself for being a fool. One part a fool for almost being seen and two parts a fool for almost wanting it.

Thin branches of a rowan snapped at him as he plunged deeper into the forest, his steel-plated boots catching the lower plants that festooned the floor, mocking him, attempting to trip him up. They tore as he drove onwards, scrambling over the undulating ground as it rose and dipped. He almost toppled when his foot found a tree root which sent him tumbling into a solid oak. Teeth jarred as his helmet struck the wood and he could taste blood where he bit the inside of his cheek.

Anger propelled his clawed gauntlet into the trunk, dislodging the bark and leaving an animal like gash. The blow was the start of a flourish of punches, each biting deeper into the oak in rapid succession.

Unsatisfied he screamed into the woods and withdrew his sword about to hack through the tree which still swayed with the impacts. Only pausing the swing at the last moment and taking a deep breath.

It would do the blade an injustice to use it like an axe. It would do the god-created suit of armour and the name that came with it a dishonour to act like he did. Grimwolf wasn't a petulant teenager with no control of his temper. He was a Knight.

Composing himself, Grimwolf surveyed the damaged tree, one side of the trunk reduced to pulp. He wanted to fight, but realised the enemy he sought was Grimwolf. How can you battle against yourself?

The sword whispered back into the sheath as he carried on with more care than before, allowing his legs to take him south on a wide trek back to the ruins. It was then that he stumbled upon a group of men as they marched along a deer track heading towards the inn.

Dropping swiftly into a ditch he crouched below the roots of an elm, hidden from the track by bracken and bramble. This time his blade slipped out silently as he leaned on his belly against the ground and watched the group through the foliage.

Ten men and a woman, none of them Earth-born. Grimwolf recognised the black cloak of a Shadojak worn by a lean man with dark skin. A few strands of grey hair curled from beneath a white turban matching the grey in his neatly cut square beard. By his side strode a younger man wearing similar garb who must be his Shaigun. A large scimitar sword swung from his hip, the sheath and hilt plain and undecorated - tools for use and not for show. This wasn't a good sign.

Behind them were six men dressed in dark uniforms with black boiled leather armour. Each carrying a spear and each wearing a sword. Grimwolf thought these were Shades, soldiers from the Shade Army that served the Shadojaks.

At the front of the group was a Shaigun he'd met before, Bray. Large green eyes scanning the way ahead as he led the group through the forest. To one side of him was a thin man of the same age. He wore the cloak of a Shadojak yet had a thick silver thread trimming the garment which seemed to be of a higher quality than the others.

Grimwolf's teeth clenched as he watched the figure to Bray's other side. She carried a melancholy expression, blue eyes cast ahead with dogged determination, yet held a sadness. His heart almost jumped as he recognised her too. Only the last time he saw her she was in better spirits and the Norsewoman's hair had been long and golden, tied in a braid that hung well passed her shoulders. Now it was cropped short, appearing as if it had been hacked harshly from her head leaving only blonde spikes.

Grimwolf fought the urge to rush into her arms, to embrace her, to keep her safe, but couldn't. He couldn't show himself to her like this. Not yet.

Chapter 7

Bittersweet Reunion

Norgie was waiting for Elora when she returned to the inn. Anxiety written in his deepening wrinkles as he came out onto the doorstep.

"What's happened?" Elora asked, dreading the answer.

"It's Cathy. I think she's gone into labour," he said. "Scott's with her but the lad's flapping like a turkey at Christmas."

"Well, it was going to happen sooner or later," she said, wishing that they had prepared for it better. "Have you plenty of boiling water and clean towels?"

"Yeah and Gurple's boiling some more."

"Good, the best thing is to keep calm. It's a natural thing giving birth. Let's not worry Cathy any..." Elora paused mid-sentence as she watched Norgie's face tighten with shock, his gaze locked on something behind her.

She turned to see what had the old man so worried and froze. Her mind doing a double-take as she absorbed the approaching figures. Her heart suddenly squeezing tight as recognition sunk in, was this truly happening?

Bray strode purposefully out in front of a group of men. Green eyes alive with what, excitement, fury? His face was locked in a stern expression. Trepidation halted the smile forming on her lips. Something was wrong.

"Keep Scott calm," she ordered Norgie. "I'll be with you as soon as I can."

She ushered him inside the inn and shut the door, willing her own heart to keep calm as she stepped out to meet Bray, Weakest padding beside her, his hackles raised and teeth partially on display.

Ejan dashed out in front of the group as they entered the courtyard. A forced grin setting her face, yet her eyes spoke otherwise. She bowed her head as she knelt before her.

"Well met, Shadojak," the Norsewoman said, speaking formally as if addressing royalty instead of a friend. She glanced at the bulworg momentarily before continuing. "I humbly thank you for providing me with your Shaigun to aid my return home."

Elora saw the intensity in her stare and realised that she was trying to tell her something but couldn't make out what. It was clear that Ejan didn't want her to act like herself. This was only confirmed by Bray's words.

"It has been a long journey Master," he said as he knelt before her, bowing his head low. "And I am glad to be in your service once again."

His words and the way they were said rooted Elora to the spot. Bray kept bowed, hiding the gorgeous face she'd been dreaming of kissing for the past few weeks.

She suddenly became aware of the other men spreading out around her. Six of them were soldiers, unlike the Imperial Guards these were dressed in black, hands resting on hilts and ready to draw in an instant. They were Shades: soldier, assassin and tools of the Shadojak Supreme, which led to the dark-skinned man. A Shadojak from the hot plains of the south. His blade was a scimitar, god-created and belonged to one of the Dark Knights that were ruled by her father. He kept it sheathed for the time being although his copper eyes watched her with the intensity of a predator, as did his Shaigun; a figure that her new memories couldn't place. The last man, with long blonde hair set in a centre parting, dressed in the blacks of a Shadojak was also somebody that evoked no new memories, although she recognised the silver trim that laced his cloak. They all seemed eager for her response.

"Rise Bray, you're not a dog," she commanded, trying her best to imitate something that Diagus would say.

Bray rose and nodded briefly before standing by her side. Close enough to touch, to smell, to wrap her arms around and close enough to kiss. She clenched her teeth as she watched the other men, their stares becoming no less intense, yet none had drawn a weapon.

"Master. Let me introduce you to Flek, the Voice of the Supreme Shadojak," Bray said, holding his arm out towards the man with the long blonde hair. "It is his wish that you return with us to Thea. To Rona and the council of the Shadojak so you can be properly sworn in."

Flek nodded, a playful smile curling his thin lips. "Or not," he said, using the common tongue of Thea which Elora, through her soul infused memories, could now understand.

"Elora, isn't it?" he asked, not bothering to wait for a reply. "I'm afraid I cannot call you Shadojak until you officially hold the title."

"If she holds the title," cut in the dark-skinned Shadojak, sharply. His copper eyes glaring with malice. "I doubt the Supreme would grant her it. She will forfeit the blade; it would be blasphemy to do anything less. She even owns a bulworg."

Weakest stiffened, long claws digging into the earth as if preparing for the command to attack.

"The bulworg is free from any master. He is free to go should he wish it. But while he stays here he is under my protection as is everyone at Rams Keep."

Elora knew that to forfeit the blade would be the end of her life. She would lose it as the Soul Reaver was plunged into her own heart to harvest all those memories of her predecessors.

"Forgive the Shadojak his cruel words, Elora. But you have been the topic of every heated conversation back in Rona. Most however, tread along the same path as..."

"Sibiet," Elora finished, the name of the Shadojak swimming to the front of her mind, much to the shock of the man who owned the name.

"It is true then. You killed Diagus. You murdered the Pearly White and have gained all his abilities, all those memories," Sibiet said.

"Blasphemy," declared his Shaigun, drawing his scimitar.

Elora instantly took stock of her surroundings, opening herself up to the threat that was before her. The six Shades spread wide, forming a semi-circle, each drawing their own swords and adopting the attack stance of the scorpion; blades held over head, open hand out to the front. Sibiet snatched his scimitar from a smuggler's pouch and stood beside his Shaigun.

Elora weighed up her options, her brain working through all the minute detail, seeking the best course of action that would keep her alive. It took only a heartbeat to realise her chances were not good.

The six Shades would be hard work by themselves before adding the Shaigun's attack. Elora guessed that she may survive long enough to make a single strike against him but the ShadojakSibiet, would be her

112

undoing. He was her equal and more experienced. He could probably kill her alone.

She felt Bray tense beside her, his arm positioning itself ready to draw his blade. Ejan too slipped a dagger into her palm and Weakest crouched low, his fangs glistening bright. Elora couldn't let them die.

Sibiet's huge curved sword swung before her, the god sharpened tip pointing at her face. She stared down its length, marvelling at the way the dull green metal shimmered along its fine edge. She was staring at death.

"Do you yield?" the Shadojak growled.

Before she could answer his Shaigun stepped between them and raised his own sword. "No, Master. Allow me to take her, I demand the duel rights," he said.

Elora's mind swiftly processed what the duel rights were.

It was a privilege given to any Shaigun to offer a duel to a new Shadojak. If they killed the master they would instantly become the next Shadojak, proving that they were worthy enough to gain the title and the blade.

"Fool," cursed Sibiet. "She killed Diagus. She's as evil and devious as her father was."

Elora saw a flicker of doubt in the Shaigun before her, a subtle tremble to his hand before he regained his composure. He meant to attack.

She was about to pull her sword free to defend herself and begin the sequence of her own demise when a loud crack thundered through the air.

A flash impacted upon the Shaigun's scimitar, wrenching the sword from his grasp. It spun over the group before imbedded into the soft earth beside the well. The weapon wobbled side to side, a wisp of smoke spiralling from a perfect circle that had been punched through the blade.

Elora heard the sniper rifle being re-cocked, the bolt feeding another bullet into the chamber. She couldn't see him but knew Slater was hidden within the tree line. A smile played on her lips, their chances of surviving had vastly improved.

Shock was written plain across the Shaigun's face, an expression mirrored by Sibiet and the Shades. Elora felt the tension rise as their minds tried to process what just happened. Silence followed the rifle shot that still resonated over the forest as Captain Brindle emerged from beside the inn followed by a red faced Pudding who was out of breath, a huge machine gun slung over his shoulder.

The group stared at the Captain as he approached, drawing a pistol and pointing it into the face of Sibiet.

"Any problems Elora?" Brindle asked, calmly. Dimples forming from his grin as he stared at the large scimitar held before him. "Seems somebody brought cutlery to a gun fight."

"Who's this?" Bray whispered beside her as he scowled at the Captain.

"A friend," she whispered back. Then grinned at the Shadojak. "I suggest you put your blade away."

An eerie quietness settled around them as Sibiet glared at Brindle, broken only by Pudding pulling the huge bolt of the GPMG back and releasing the heavy spring forward.

It was Flek that moved first, laying a gloved hand on the Shadojak's arm.

"It may be prudent to seek the path of peace this time," he said, then flashed a smile at Elora, showing neat small teeth. "Perhaps you could ask your men to withdraw their cannons. They're not from Thea so don't know the consequences of threatening a Shadojak. I will only let that happen this once."

"I think they've got the message, Captain," Elora said.

Brindle lowered his pistol and stepped away from Sibiet, his grimace not softening as he re-sheathed his sword.

Flek raised a gloved hand and signalled for the Shades to put their weapons away. "Elora, we have no quarrel with you, but the Supreme has conveyed his wishes. You will return with us to Rona to face judgement. If that means that I must return with a battalion of Shades and the other six Shadojaks, then so be it."

"I will go to Rona and face whatever. Even death if that's what's judged. But I won't leave Earth until I've purged it of the Dark Army." She rested a hand on Bray's shoulder wanting so much to pull him into an embrace, wanting it so much that her fingers pressed tightly into him. "And my Shaigun stays too."

"You won't succeed," Flek argued, pushing his blonde hair from his face. "And you will lose your sword in the process. Or worse, it will fall into the hands of the enemy. I cannot allow it," he cocked his head to the side as if coming to a decision. "However, return with us and you may persuade the Supreme to aid in your purging. Better yet, if you can win the ear of the Emperor, perhaps he may help."

Elora played his words over in her mind. There was wisdom in them, a way to have numbers sufficient enough to make a difference. But there was also a risk. If she left with them to be judged at Rona, what would become of Earth if she came on the wrong side of the

115

balance? Would anybody take up the cause to save the world? Would anybody care?

She was about to tell Flek to go to hell when a scream pierced the air. A painful wail, wrought with agony rupturing from inside the inn.

Cathy.

"This matter can wait," Elora spat at the Supreme's Voice. She then turned and grasped Ejan by the arm. "Come, I need your help."

They arrived at the front door as it was flung open. Scott was out of breath, his face white and panic-stricken as another scream echoed through the inn.

Elora pushed passed him and rushed to her old chambers, vaulting up the staircase taking four steps at a time. She wrenched the door open to find Cathy lying on the bed, legs spread wide, dressed hitched up to her swelling belly and Norgie at her shoulders holding her hand.

Cathy turned to face her, cheeks bright red and clammy, hair stuck to her forehead with sweat.

"Get it out of me," she growled, before her lungs opened up once again to scream.

Norgie held tight to her hand but it was clear from his worried expression he didn't know what to do.

The room was in disarray, towels had been spread on the floor, two buckets of boiling water laid at the end of the bed, a medical journal lay in a puddle; the open pages soaking up water.

"What in Odin's name..." demanded Ejan as she entered the room. She took one look at the mess, then at Cathy before bursting into action.

"You," she ordered, pointing at Norgie. "Roll that dress above her belly, it's trapping the little mite."

She removed her traveling cloak and pushed her sleeves up to her elbows before dipping her arms in the boiling water.

Another scream filled the chamber as Norgie struggled to lift the dress. Elora moved quickly, taking her dagger and sliced the dress open. Cathy's belly instantly dropped lower as the mother to be let out a long deep moan.

The door burst open once again as Bray came in with Captain Brindle and the Shadojak.

"Get out, all of you," Elora snapped as she advanced on the men. She gave Bray an apologetic look as she ushered him from the room.

The men left hastily since this was no place for them. Elora caught hold of Scott's arm before he also disappeared. "Not you," she said, propelling him back into the room.

Ejan shook her head. "I leave Rams Keep in your care for a few days and look what you've done with the place," she said teasingly as Cathy gave another cry of pain. The Norsewoman's face became stern as she placed her hands against the exposed belly.

"Are you a doctor?" Cathy asked between sharp intakes of breath.

Ejan exchanged a look with Elora before answering. "I'm a Viking."

"But the only person around who has actually given birth," Elora added seeing the concerned expression on both women.

"I helped ease births in my home village when I was younger," Ejan offered.

"Is it supposed to hurt this much?" Cathy asked, her face screwing up in pain.

117

Ejan nodded apologetically. "Hurts like a bitch. But the baby is in the right place, shifting lower and wanting out."

"I. Want. It. Out!" Cathy cried, clenching her teeth so hard that Elora feared they might crack.

Scott busied himself putting a morphine injection into Cathy's arm. "It'll take the edge off the pain," he said, placing the spent needle away.

"Take the edge off?" Cathy spat. "How much more have you got? Bloody give me everything."

"It will kick in soon. Just try to breathe," Scott said, blowing air through his own mouth and looking like a goldfish.

"Push girl," Ejan encouraged, now sitting on the floor. "I can see the head. Push."

Elora squeezed Cathy's other hand as she closed her eyes and pushed.

"That's it, the head's out," Ejan said, her arms disappearing from sight as she helped the baby. "A little more. It's nearly over. A few more pushes."

Cathy gave a final push, screaming with the effort and a baby's own cries joined that of the mother.

Ejan wrapped the tiny pink baby in a dry towel as Scott cut the umbilical cord. She brought the bundle around the bed to Cathy and gently placed it in her arms.

"Congratulations," she said, "you have a daughter."

Elora's eyes welled up as she watched Cathy place a kiss on the baby, her tiny little fingers opening and closing, a tuft of blonde hair poking through the towel.

"Thank you," Cathy said, smiling through the tears. "All of you."

"She's a real cutie," Norgie said as he pretended to rub something from his eyes. Scott could only nod, colour beginning to return to his ashen face.

Elora leaned down to place a kiss on the new arrival, then another on Cathy's cheek. "Have you a name for her?" she asked.

"Genella?" Ejan suddenly said, as she paced across the room.

Elora watched her delicately pick a single flower from a vase that was sitting on the windowsill soaking up the midday sun. She put it to her nose and inhaled, a sad smile forming from her mouth. "Ragna used to bring me genellas. They are my favourite, but they only grow in one part of the forest and only he knew where. How did you come by these?"

"A friend," Elora said, "Grimwolf."

At Elora's answer, Ejan's head snapped up as if from shock. "Grimwolf? He doesn't exist. He's a myth."

"He's real and he brought me those."

"Describe him," Ejan ordered, setting the flower carefully back in the vase.

"I haven't seen his face, but he's tall,"

"As tall as Ragna was?"

Elora nodded. "And as wide. He wears a suit of armour, god-created and shaped like a wolf."

Ejan was quiet for a moment, a single tear rolled down her cheek. "Grimwolf was a folk legend, a story to tell children. Ragna would tell the story to Jaygen when he was small. You should have seen the big five-bellied lout acting out the scenes and knocking things over." She wiped away the tear. "I think it's time I found my son."

As her hand fell on the door, Cathy called out to her.

"What was the name of that flower again, it was beautiful, just like the flowers themselves."

"They're genellas."

Cathy looked down into the bundle in her arms, face beaming with pride. "Genella. A beautiful name for my beautiful daughter."

Elora helped clean Cathy up and arranged for Melvin to bring baby clothes, nappies and anything else the newborn needed. By the time she left her in the capable hands of Scott, the evening was drawing on and she had still to find time to seek out Bray. He had been a constant presence amid thoughts all afternoon, she had a thousand questions but would put them all aside for just one kiss and for him to wrap her in his arms.

She found Flek, the Shadojak and his Shaigun breaking bread in the common room. They sat at a table while Norgie poured them wine. When he noticed her, Flek motioned at the chair beside him with his gloved hand. Reluctantly Elora approached but held Norgie by the arm before she sat.

"Have you seen Bray?" she asked, observing the tense expressions of the men at the table. "I need to make sure my Shaigun has kept up his training."

"He's chopping wood. We're getting a bit low," he replied. Elora nodded, seeing through the ruse. There was plenty of wood in the store shed. Bray would be waiting for her in the forest.

"We are not your enemy, Elora," said the Supreme's Voice as he poured her a glass of wine. The Shadojak and Shaigun glared as if it was a sin just to speak with her.

Elora stared at the glass but made no move to drink. "That wasn't what it looked like earlier."

"Yes, that was an unfortunate clash of ideas. But you must see it from our point of view. You have a Soul Reaver blade, you're untrained in the ways of the Shadojak and..." Flek took a deep breath as he brushed his blond curls aside. "The daughter of Chaos."

"You're a blasted demigod for mother's sake," Sibiet spat as he leaned over the table, a vein pulsing in his temple.

Elora raised an eyebrow, staring right back into his copper eyes that seemed so full of hate. She wanted to push her thumbs through them, crush the whites until they ran red - burn his skull...She took a deep breath, letting go of the darkness that had crept inside.

"Calm yourself Shadojak," Flek continued, pushing Sibiet back. "The judgement will be made when we return. Until then she is under my protection. That is, under the Supreme's."

Sibiet sat back, the vein in his head throbbing all the more. Had he seen the change in her? His young Shaigun appeared ready to take action until his master pushed his rising body back into his seat.

"As I was saying, we are not enemies. However, you will be returning with us and soon. Is that clear, Elora?"

"But I've vowed to take Earth back from the Dark Army."

"Your father's army," the Shaigun pointed out, his words thick with malice.

"His seed made me, nothing more,"

Elora could feel the darkness rising once again. The whispers of Chaos touching her ears.

"Seed or no, you won't conquer them," Flek said. "But maybe you could persuade the Emperor to help." He drank deeply from his glass leaving a small bead of the red wine at the corner of his lip. "Or not. Refuse to come with us and you will die along with your impossible cause."

Elora fought the desire to smash the top of the glass and grind it into his face and watch the pretty patterns of his blood mixing with the wine. "I'll do what you ask," Elora said, eager to leave before she did any damage. "But give me a few days to allow things to settle here."

"I'll give you two," Flek replied, finishing his drink.

Elora rose and downed her glass of wine in one go. "Fine," she said coldly, stepping out of the common room and into the night.

A cool wind picked up dust spinning it around in a waltz as she dashed across the courtyard. Elora pulled her cloak tightly around her shoulders, feeling the first signs of an early winter. It wouldn't be long before there was frost on the ground.

Leaves crunched as she entered the forest, the first of many that would blanket the floor as the season stripped the trees bare. With any luck Captain Brindle would have Rams Keep habitable before too long. Winter would be harsh amongst the stone ruins, yet she wouldn't be here to witness it, not if she was returning to Thea to be judged.

A twig suddenly snapped behind her. Elora spun, ready to draw out her sword, but stayed her hand as she recognised her pursuer.

"I never did catch your name, Shaigun," she said, feeling annoyed at being followed.

The Shaigun remained still, calm, although she saw the defensive stance beneath his cloak, ready to strike in a moment.

"Drifid," he snarled.

"Drifid," Elora repeated. "Why are you following me?"

The trees swayed in the wind, a glimmer of light passing through the branches casting pale light over the Shaigun's pinched face, his expression was one of loathing; dark eyes sparkling with hatred.

"You can't be trusted. My master wants you watched at all times. You cannot be left alone."

"I'm not alone, Weakest is behind you."

The bulworg stalked from the shadows, a deep growl rumbling as he padded passed the Shaigun to stand beside her. Drifid glared at him but made no attempt to attack.

"And I'm meeting my Shaigun. So you can run back to your master and leave me alone."

"Bray is also watched. The Shaigun that bends his knee to a demigod is as blasphemous as the creature he serves."

Elora took a step towards him feeling her anger rising once again, the darkness propelling her to destruction. She felt Weakest move with her, knew his claws were drawn, his teeth displayed.

Drifid stood his ground, raising his chin up and stared down his nose at her and she saw his hand shift above the hilt of his sword, ready to draw the scimitar.

"The duel right still stands," the Shaigun said. "Draw your blade."

"Why so eager to die?" Elora asked, the whispers of darkness goading her on, seeking blood and wanting destruction.

Drifid snatched his sword from its sheath and levelled it at her face. "I'll take your Soul Reaver and plunge it into your black heart before I take your dog's head. Bray's too, no doubt he'll attempt to avenge his whore."

At the mention of Bray, Elora's control over the darkness collapsed as she launched herself at the Shaigun.

Drifid's jaw clenched, preparing to arc his sword across her body, yet as she reduced herself to smoke the blade passed harmlessly through her.

She sensed the Shaigun from a thousand different angles, from every view possible as she flowed along the scimitar, caressing the dull steel, passing through the bullet hole in the metal and streaming up his arm. Parts of her weaved between strands of his loose hair, others curling beneath his hood to re-join behind him.

As Elora solidified her forming hand wrapped around Drifid's wrist, applying pressure to the soft flesh below his hand until he let go of his sword. It struck the forest floor as she twisted his arm around his back, jamming his elbow at a painful angle. Her other hand applied pressure to his throat, thumb biting under the Adam's apple, eager to hook it out and let him choke.

The Shaigun's vertebrae clicked as Elora stretched his spine back. She grinned feeling him struggle, the muffled gasps of pain terminating beneath her hand. Should she break his neck or crush his spine and leave his paralysed body to the foxes and rats of the forest?

It was Weakest that brought her out of that frame of mind. His lupine body rubbing softly against her leg, concern in his face as he gave a subtle shake of his head. She swallowed back the pleasure she was experiencing, replacing joy with control and fought the cruel darkness.

When the voices in her head calmed to a whisper she trusted herself to lean closer to the Shaigun's neck, feeling the pulse beneath his tanned skin as her lips brushed his ear.

"When the time comes I'll be judged by all of you," Elora said, her voice sounding as harsh and menacing as if it was Diagus himself speaking through her. "If I'm still alive afterwards then you're welcome to die at the end of my blade."

She let him go, his body crashing to the ground in a painful heap.

"Go back to your master, Drifid. While my conscience restrains me from taking your soul."

She placed a hand upon Weakest's head, scratching him behind the ears. If it wasn't for the bulworg being here she would have torn the Shaigun apart.

Drifid struggled to his feet, a tentative hand searching his throat where she had left a swollen red welt in the shape of her thumb. His bloodshot eyes stared with anger as he limped over to retrieve his sword. He opened his mouth to speak but pain forced it shut.

Elora watched him hobble away, swatting branches out of his path like a spurned teenager. He was probably concocting a story to tell his master, Sibiet.

When he disappeared she turned to Weakest.

"Thank you. You saved me as well as the Shaigun." Weakest nodded, licking her hand before starring in the direction Drifid had gone. "Follow him. Make sure he returns to the inn; I don't trust him or the others."

Weakest gave a final nod before stalking after the Shaigun as swift and silent as the wind.

With a heavy heart she stepped deeper into the forest, walking purposefully to the place where she had first passionately kissed Bray and where she had made him swear that he would kill her if she ever turned into that other, darker girl.

An owl hooted from a tall oak as she entered the small clearing. An axe lay embedded in a tree stump, the moonlight in the steel head reflecting against a barrow full of split logs. Elora glanced about and realised she was alone. If Bray had been here he was now gone.

She pulled the axe from the stump and sat down, feeling tears prickling her eyes as she thumped the back of it against her palm. She wanted to hold him so much the disappointment of not finding him here was almost too much to bear. Where was he?

Tension had been building inside her all day. Seeing him stroll into the courtyard earlier, acting strange when all she wanted to do was hold him, kiss him. The stand-off against the Shadojak and Flek. Genella's birth, a near fight with Drifid - all done with the thought of Bray on her mind, all leading up to this one moment. This one place which was theirs.

Frustration fuelled her movement as she drove the axe deep into the tree bedside her. The impact splintering a crack deep in the trunk whilst leaves rained from above. The noise would have been heard at Rams Keep but she didn't care as she wrenched the axe free ready to strike a second blow.

"These are not the actions of a Shadojak."

The words startled her, halting her mid-swing as somebody stepped out of the shadows.

Nobody could sneak up this close without her knowing. No human. She let the axe fall.

"Elf boy?" she said as her heart suddenly soared.

Bray grinned, his smile the most beautiful sight she'd seen since they were last together in another place, another world.

"Master," he replied cockily.

"Shut up and kiss me," Elora growled, her frustration finding another target to vent itself upon.

His lips were soft yet hungry; moss-green eyes penetrating hers as strong hands pulled her close. Elora melted into the hard body, the solid chest and wide shoulders - hands reaching behind his neck to draw him closer still, wanting more. This was it. This was the moment her entire day had been leading up to.

Fire, raw and hot was building inside her stomach. A primitive energy that wanted release, demanded it and she felt the same burning from within Bray. She slammed him against the broken tree and felt a giddy rush - could the heat transfer into the wood? Will the forest burn? She felt like a tinder box, like an inferno building to a crescendo. All she need do was apply the spark.

Breathe.

Tears ran down her cheeks; the tension finally released as they pulled their lips apart, yet her fingers remained curled around his dark hair.

Sweat clung to Bray's shirt, to his heaving chest and rippled abdomen, his grin returning once again.

"What is my master's bidding?" he asked, huskily.

Elora grinned with him as she licked her lips, tasting him upon them.

"She demands another kiss."

Chapter 8

Bad Dreams

Bray could still taste Elora on his lips as he watched her leave, returning to the inn before him so as not to aid suspicions of their love to Sibiet and his Shaigun. He still felt the tears she left against his cheek made cold by a light breeze stirring the night. Tears born out of frustration that they both shared at being so close to one another yet forced to be apart.

It had been hard for him to explain what they must do, how they must be. It had been harder for her to accept; her eyes glowing demon-red and flaring with anger before cooling to their beautiful violet once again. After a quiet moment she reasoned that it would be better living the lie and being close than admitting their love and being dead, which is what would happen if they were found out. Death may be what greets them in the end anyway, but death was a companion he had danced with for the better part of his life. A silent friend he learned to live with but now began to fear, for Elora's sake.

Picking up the fallen axe he began to split logs once again. Placing the wood upon the stump and imagining it being Sibiet's head. He tired of their questioning and accusations on the entire journey from Aslania. Always in his face, accusing fingers needling at him, pushing him, goading him to anger and revealing the true feelings between them. If Flek wasn't there to come between them, Drifid may well have had an accident before they arrived.

The logs split with a satisfying crack. He picked up the two halves and threw them in the wheelbarrow imagining copper eyes spinning in the air.

Replacing another log, he raised the axe and split Drifid's head in two. The pieces fell to either side of the stump in unison. The Shaigun's menacing smirk falling apart from his pinched sour face. He picked up the halves and dropped them in with the broken head of the Shadojak - if it was only that simple.

But killing the pair would be just the beginning. Their thoughts were echoed back in Rona. It seemed they would find few friends amongst the other Shadojaks and Shaiguns, but plenty of enemies. The judgment was already heavily against Elora; being a demigod and the daughter of Solarius was bad enough without throwing love into the mix. With no support she would face death at the end of her own Soul Reaver.

Leaving the axe in the stump he steered the wheelbarrow back towards the inn, fresh worries about Elora rising with each step he took: could she mask her emotions under the scrutiny of the others, could she control her anger and keep that other her in check?

Witnessing the confrontation earlier, between Elora and Drifid, he worried she may have less control than he thought. Her turning to smoke had been a shock, the sight had rooted his feet. Elora was more her father than he guessed and he was sure she would have ripped the Shaigun's throat out. Drifid was only saved by the bulworg's timely intervention. And that was another worry, Weakest, an enemy within Rams Keep. Which led to the other new arrival within the fairy protection, Grimwolf. A mythical creature who he'd never heard of until today. Something that was other worldly yet showed allegiance to Elora. As it also seemed, Captain Brindle was. A man who stirred another emotion in Bray. When he saw the soldier standing beside her earlier, offering help and protection the first thing he felt was jealousy; an emotion he had never experienced before. But that's what came with being in love. A chemical reaction which was far less pleasurable, but one which could be as painful and doubly dangerous.

Leaving the logs beside the woodshed he entered the inn, slipping the cold emotionless mask upon his face and calming the fire burning within his heart - becoming the Shaigun he once was, although this time his master came with a world of complications.

The bar room was quieter than he expected this time of night. The room covered in sleeping children all mixed up together in blankets and sheets. One of Melvin's boys sat vigil over them, a baby in his arms drinking milk from a bottle.

Bray nodded him a greeting as he weaved between the sleeping children, making his way to the kitchen.

Drifid's voice punctuated the quietness, drifting through the closed door. Bray paused outside the kitchen to listen.

"...I saw her with my own eyes. Smoke. She flew through the air and attacked me like a ghost, like a demon possessed. The bitch would have torn my throat out if I didn't escape."

Bray shoved the door open more forcefully than intended, entering the kitchen and cutting the conversation short.

"Come on in lad," Norgie welcomed him as he stirred soup in a pan above the fire. "Hungry?"

"I can eat," he said, staring at the three men sat at the table.

Flek gave him a courteous nod although the ShadojakSibiet and his Shaigun regarded him with the same coldness they had shown the last couple of weeks.

"What was that about smoke?" Bray asked as he sat beside Flek, facing the others.

"It seems your chosen master has a secret...power," the Supreme's Voice said. "The ability to change to smoke." His thin lips curled back in a grin challenging him to deny the fact.

Bray said nothing.

"Your silence, Shaigun, is confirmation," Sibiet spat, slamming a fist against the table. "You see Flek. The spawn of Chaos cannot be trusted. Kill her now and spare Rona the threat of her return."

"That is not how we do things Sibiet. You know the code. She has taken the blade and so must return for judgment."

"But she tried to kill me," Drifid squealed.

"She defended herself," Bray shouted, rising from the table. His own hand slamming against the rough oak as he leaned across, his face inches from the Shaigun's. "You drew your blade first, you demanded duel rights."

Drifid's hand dropped to his hilt, fingers turning white as he slipped the sword partially from its sheath but paused, his face seeming uncertain as if he'd started something he didn't want to finish.

Bray grinned, his fingers and thumb spreading and opening up the smuggler's pouch. "Draw your steel Drifid. Let me open up your lying worm-ridden guts for all to see."

Please, he thought, just pull out your scimitar so I can finish you; so there's one less enemy, one less blade to battle against. I'll cut down Elora's antagonists one at a time if needs be; the entire Shade Army so she can live.

"Enough," Flek said as he rose, taking the higher position of the Voice as he glared at Bray before his gaze fell on Drifid. "Is this true? Were you the first to draw your sword against Elora?"

Bray relaxed back, folding his arms as he watched the Shaigun squirm beneath the Voice's question.

Drifid's head dropped as he pushed his sword back into the scabbard. He grunted something unintelligible as he sat back down.

"You know the rules Shaigun. You will have your opportunity for duel rights once we're back in Rona. Until then, if you draw your sword against Elora I'll let her finish you off without retribution. Do I make myself clear?"

Again Drifid grunted, not bringing his eyes up to meet Flek's. Unsatisfied with his Shaigun's response, Sibiet cuffed him hard around the back of his head.

"Answer the Voice, boy. Or I swear by the Mother I'll leave you with the Shades and take on another Shaigun."

"I understand," sputtered Drifid.

Bray let his grin drop although he was enjoying watching the Shaigun redden in shame. But it appeared that Flek wasn't finished speaking. He turned on him and prodded him in the chest with his gloved hand.

"You, I will speak with outside. Come."

Flek paced from the room, exiting through the rear door.

Bray followed him out, pausing briefly to pat Norgie on the arm. "I'll take the soup for breakfast in the

132

morning," he said before pushing through the door and back out into the night.

He found the Voice waiting outside the forge. His blonde hair appearing grey in the darkness and his face taking on an uncharacteristic pained expression.

"It appears to me Bray, that Elora's chances are shrinking with each day."

Bray couldn't argue with the point; her chances were practically non-existent but why would the Voice care?

"It may be prudent to start thinking about your own path. What would you become once she was judged?"

Bray knew Flek from long ago, they were in the same platoon together in the shades and even began the Shaigun training at the same time. That was before Flek severed his thumb in sword mastery practice and got instantly disqualified from the Shaigun path. Bray glanced at the man's gloved hands, wondering which one lacked the opposing digit.

"She will be judged worthy of being a Shadojak and I would follow no other," he said, flatly.

"Bray, I wish I had your confidence in Elora. I really do. From what I've seen of Rams Keep and of how she handles herself around innocents and even delivering babies, there is no doubt in my mind that she is worthy of the title. But I am just a Voice." He held up his right hand. "Even if it was whole, my hand doesn't count in the vote. Only the seven remaining Shadojaks and the Supreme may vote."

Bray leaned against the stone wall of the forge and studied Flek. "And what are the thoughts of the Supreme?"

The Voice was the personal assistant of the Supreme Shadojak. A secretary that travelled with the Supreme's

133

authority to convey wishes and watch over tasks, to voice opinions with the Emperor or to settle judgements in his name. In truth, the Voice was an extension of the Supreme, being privy to his thoughts and council and the only person to be with him in the inner sanctum and chambers at Rona.

"It makes little difference what the Supreme believes when all seven hands will be going against."

"So he doesn't think as the rest do? But he holds the deciding vote," Bray felt a brief flicker of hope.

"He doesn't think much at all these days. Not for himself anyway. And in truth, it would only be the deciding vote if the judgement fell evenly split."

"What do you mean, he doesn't think for himself?"

Flek stared at the ground, kicking a stone across the cobbled ground and watched it skitter into the stables before answering.

"Old age. It catches up with all of us in the end. Some days he is the same Supreme he's been for years: wise, devious yet a good balancer. Others, he's like a child, remembering little and sinking into quiet wonderment. Twice now I've caught him talking to himself. Speaking as if there was someone else in the room that I couldn't see."

"Saying what?"

Flek shook his head. "Gibberish really, nothing that makes sense."

"But shouldn't you tell the others? Surely if the Supreme has become ill or weak in the mind he needs replacing."

"And so you see my dilemma. Who do you think will step up to the job?"

Memories of the other Shadojaks tumbled through Bray's mind: Gunwahl, with the mighty broad sword, Yaul-tis-munjib, with the huge hammer. Both as deadly as any Shadojak but equally as barbaric as their weapons. Quantico with the Soul Reaver rapier and his brother Quantala with the samurai-like sword. Both good judges and balancers yet neither the true qualities of a Supreme leader. The long limbed Indian, Hashim with the flat tipped spear may be a good contender but was little liked amongst the Shadojaks, and little Dwenal the dwarf with a double-headed axe, had an incredibly bad temperament and had an instant disregard to anyone taller than himself, which was almost everybody.

That left Sibiet. Bray let out a deep breath. If Sibiet became Supreme then Elora's fate was as good as sealed.

"Why tell me?" Bray asked.

"Because I trust you."

Bray didn't know what he was expecting but it wasn't that. Flek took a deep breath, his face suddenly appearing older than its years.

"There's more." The Voice took a brief glance at the kitchen door, then led Bray towards the stables his voice dropping to a whisper. "I've found...things amongst the Supreme's files, hidden in his desk or stuffed behind old tomes on shelves."

"What things?"

"Scraps of paper, torn scrolls full of scribbles, diagrams. Some scrawled in the Supreme's handwriting with ink, some in child-like squiggles with blood. Some are recent, whilst one large parchment belongs to a time before the great rift. Even the older scrolls, written in a language that isn't spoken any more. I needed to find references to work out what they meant."

"And what was that?"

"They all say the same thing. 'Chaos will unite the worlds - Chaos will set us free,' or something along those lines."

He pulled a small scroll from inside his sleeve and unrolled it. "Have you ever seen this symbol before?"

Bray stared at the dark circle overlapping the white circle. It was similar to the emblem Silk uses. Above the circles was an old swirling text he couldn't read, but guessed that it said, 'Chaos will unite the worlds - Chaos will set us free'.

Flek pulled a scrap of parchment from inside his cloak and handed it to Bray. "This is the latest one I found. I think it was written by the Supreme, although when I asked what it means he denies ever seeing it before, but it's in his handwriting."

He took a step towards the inn. "I better be getting back inside before Sibiet and that idiot Shaigun of his start accusing us of being lovers."

Bray waited until the Voice had entered through the kitchen door before unfolding the scrap of paper.

On the inside were two roughly drawn circles, one dark overlapping the white. It was similar to Silk's symbol, although the ink was fresher and the parchment less brittle. The text above was written with an unsteady hand, jagged spider-like but he was able to read the words.

'Elora will unite the Worlds, Elora will set us free.'

Elora stared at her reflection in the black mirror. She was disoriented and out of breath from running, her blood thumped inside her ears, rushing to keep up with her hammering heart. Where the hell was she?

The Elora staring back grinned, her eyes alive and sparkling crimson red. In the mirror image she had a dark figure looming behind her. Elora snapped her head about, blade already in her hand but nobody was there, just the empty blackness of her surroundings.

She returned to stare into the mirror once again and choked. In the image her blade was in her hand, dripping with blood and she held a decapitated head in her other, moss-green eyes wide open in shock; mouth pulled tight in a soundless scream.

Elora's own scream filled the void.

"Bray!"

"Bray. Bray. Bray." Her boyfriend's name echoed about her in a thousand whispers. Her reflection grinning cruelly as the dark looming figure stepped closer, armoured hands clutching her other self's shoulders. Flaming wings spreading out either side and a menacing smile splitting his raven black beard.

"Elora," her father said. "Your army awaits you, Chaos is coming and it will set you free."

'No!"

The Soul Reaver darted out to strike her father, the blade's tip passing though the black glass a heartbeat before it exploded in a silvery shower of fractured pictures.

When the glass cleared she found that her sword had impaled Diagus, blood spreading out from his heart in an intricate snowflake pattern to devour his white robes.

As Elora tried to pull the blade free, the Pearly White snapped his eyes open and glared at her, the whiteness vanishing from the pearl in his socket to become onyx black.

"Do the right thing," the former Shadojak said before bursting into flames before her.

Elora opened her mouth to scream again, but it instantly filled with acrid smoke from Diagus's charred corpse as it crumbled to dust.

"Elora. Elora wake up!"

She felt herself being shaken, her struggles against the unseen being useless, the blackness closing in, the whispers echoing her name. Elora, Elora...

"Wake up."

Daylight pierced her vision as she forced her lids open. She blinked heavily, still struggling against the grip that held her.

Curling her fist into a tight ball she threw a punch, but held it at the last moment.

"Jaygen?"

Elora glanced around and saw that she was in the stables, curled up in the hay where Daisy usually slept.

"You were having a bad dream," Jaygen said, helping her to her feet. "I heard the horses kicking at the door to get out so I came to see what had spooked them. Seems you were having a nightmare."

Elora dropped her clenched fist and rubbed some feeling back into her face. That nightmare was more real and more horrific than any other she'd had. The terror was still with her as she gathered her thoughts.

She remembered walking around the inn after leaving Bray chopping wood. Checking in on Cathy and the new baby Genella. Calling in on Melvin and making sure the children were tucked up in blankets before coming to check on her horse.

Elora remembered the hay still warm from Daisy's body and seeming so inviting. She only meant to take a light doze, but because the sun was high in the sky realised that it was mid-morning.

"Are you alright?" Jaygen asked, his hazel eyes filled with concern.

"Yeah, I'm fine. Like you said - just a bad dream."

She grasped his offered hand and rose to her feet, stretching the stiffness from her back. It was then that she saw that some of the hay was singed and white ash lay on the ground beneath where she'd been sleeping. She kicked it loose with her boot before Jaygen noticed.

"Think I'll go freshen up at the lake. The walk might clear my head," she said, but in truth wanted to be alone so she could mull over her nightmare and maybe catch some time with Bray.

She paused at the stable door and turned to Jaygen once again. "If you see my Shaigun, can you tell him his master requires his presence at the lake."

Jaygen nodded, face taking on the sullen look once again. Elora felt that he was still coming to terms with his father's death. It must be so hard for him.

The water was icy, causing goosebumps to appear along her bare arms as she washed in the lake. Elora dipped her face under hoping that the shock of cold would chase away the bad dream. When she pulled her face out Bray was standing beside her, reinforcing the nightmare once again.

"Are you alright? You look terrible," Bray said, quickly scanning the area to check they were alone before pulling her into an embrace.

"Just a little tired," she lied, folding her arms around his waist and leaned into his chest.

It felt good having him close. He made her feel safe, loved and if she closed her eyes she could almost forget the world of troubles that plagued her mind. His lips touched the top of her head leaving a gentle kiss before he let go.

"You smell of horse," he laughed.

"What?"

She knelt at the water's edge and slapping her hand against the surface, splashed him.

"Hey, that's not fair. You're the smelly one," he joked, placing his arms over her and prevented her from splashing him again.

She struggled against his strong arms, unable to brake his hold. Laughing, she changed tactics and closed her eyes, concentrating on the element of water itself.

Ducks suddenly broke into flight, their webbed feet slapping the lake's surface as they took to the air. Startled birds flew from the great willow beside them as a huge wave struck the bank, smashing into the tree before showering herself and Bray.

"Argh, not fair," laughed Bray, as he let go of her arms and threw her over his shoulder.

Elora giggled like an excited schoolgirl as she struggled to free herself, kicking her legs in a futile effort.

"Put me down," she demanded as Bray stepped into the lake, wading waist-deep then she was pleading between breaths, her stomach aching from laughing. "No, no, don't you dare."

He let go of her and they both splashed into the water.

They were both laughing hysterically now as she playfully punched his arm and splashed water into his face. He splashed her back before pulling her once again into an embrace. They sank lower into the water until only their heads remained above the surface.

"I love you," Bray said, mischief sparkling in his eyes; his hands pressing against her lower back and drawing her closer until their noses touched.

"Love you too, Elf boy. Now shut up and kiss me."

After what seemed only a few seconds Bray pulled away, his face taking on a frown as he stared out across the lake.

"We need to talk about Rona."

"Don't scowl so much you're ruining that gorgeous face of yours," she said, wanting nothing more than to taste him once again, to be held by him.

"I'm serious, Elora. The judgment will be soon and if we don't turn at least three of the seven Shadojaks to your cause you'll be..."

"Judged, I know," she kissed his lips and spun in the water so her back was resting against his chest, pulling his arms over her shoulders. "Must we talk about it now?"

She felt his lips brush the nape of her neck sending a pleasurable wave of heat down her spine.

"I think we can trust Flek. He's got a kind of plan of sorts. Still a long-shot though."

Elora felt a glimmer of hope. Could the Voice be on her side? She wouldn't have thought so but if Bray said it was true then who was she to say otherwise.

"There is something else too. Something Flek discovered in the Supreme's vaults. Flek thinks it is linked to you and has a connection with Chaos."

Elora suddenly felt cold and not because of the water.

"He's found symbols and texts saying that Chaos will unite us - Chaos will set us free."

Elora spun, seizing Bray by the shoulder. "I had a nightmare last night. I dreamt about my father, he told me that the Dark Army awaits me and that Chaos will set me free."

She watched Bray's face change as he absorbed her words. He was about to say something to her when the noise of footsteps, fast approaching from the direction of the inn caused them both to pull apart.

Jaygen ran to the water's edge, red faced and out of breath.

"Prince Dylap has returned. He's got news about Silk," he shouted, waving for them to come out of the water.

Elora glanced beyond Jaygen and saw the reason he had approached at such haste. Following him was Sibiet and Drifid, both wearing matching scowls as they came towards them.

Elora felt Bray briefly squeeze her hand before they pulled apart and began to wade back to the bank. Thoughts of what he told her mingled with the memories of her dream. She felt that they were impossibly linked somehow, but now wasn't the time to dwell on it. She wanted answers from the fairy. Finding Silk was her priority.

Chapter 9

Return of the Farrosian

Elora's boots squelched as the small group hiked towards the keep, replacing the silence that Sibiet and Drifid brought. She knew that they were waiting to catch her and Bray out, wanting to prove that there was love between them and hammer another nail into her coffin.

Of course the Shadojak had demanded a reason for them both being in the lake together. Bray had explained that they were practicing sword play in the water, building strength with resistance training. Jaygen told the Shadojak that was what he witnessed when he arrived at the lake and without any other proof, Sibiet had to accept what he'd been told. Elora resolved to be extra careful in the future.

Weakest joined them as they wound around the cobbled bridleway, quietly padding from behind thick bracken to stalk alongside her. Elora heard Sibiet snort and was sure Drifid muttered 'dog beast' under his breath before the silence returned, seeming somewhat thicker than before.

"Has it been raining?" Smudge asked, looking her up and down as he walked out to meet them by the tower he was working on.

"Something like that," Elora laughed. "Where's Captain Brindle?"

"He's away with the fairies," the engineer replied, then chuckled after realising what he had said. The humour died when he glanced at Sibiet; the Shadojak's face a mask of impatience.

"They're on the southern edge of the keep, near a ring of moon daisies. When you see the Captain, you can tell him we've completed the second floor here and beginning to work on the third staircase."

"Already?" Elora asked, surveying the tower before her.

The tarpaulin sheeting tied to the scaffolding above swayed in the wind revealing some of the turret wall set with fresh cement. Soldiers were busy picking through stone rubble and finding pieces that fitted into the structure and bringing it back to its original state.

"Yeah, the boys have been busy. The well's up and running, temporary barracks have been built with a separate shower block fed from the stream. We built a kitchen too - well a brick oven anyway and a huge stone larder full of supplies. This tower has two floors complete, the spiral staircase was fiddly but it's as good as new. I've set men to clearing the passageways into the building and the ones beyond that." Smudge pointed towards the low walls and partially fallen archways that lay further into the keep where soldiers were busy filling wheelbarrows with rubble. "The Captain wants this area rebuilt before winter, for the children or any more survivors that we come across. That inn of yours is getting full."

"Great work. I'll pass on the information to Captain Brindle," Elora said as she led the group to the fairy circle, eager to receive news about Silk, but also fearing it.

They found Brindle, Slater and Pudding by the fairy circle, the Captain attempting to communicate with Prince Dylap, was using hand-signals and gestures yet it was clear they were having problems.

"I still can't believe I'm talking to a fairy. A real life fairy," Brindle said as he noticed them.

"He's not a fairy, he's a Farrosian," Elora explained.

Prince Dylap took to the air, steering his black falcon towards them. He dropped from the bird and glided down to Bray's shoulder, folding his lightning blue wings before he landed.

The tiny Farrosian whispered into Bray's ear as everyone else became silent and attempted to listen, even though Bray was the only person present who could understand the Prince. Elora cursed herself for leaving her tinker's tongue charm at the inn.

Prince Dylap seemed irritated by the new arrivals at the keep, especially the bulworg who hunkered down beside her, his nose resting on large front paws.

Bray spoke back to Prince Dylap, she heard him say Weakest while gesturing to the bulworg. He then pointed to the rest of the group, introducing Captain Brindle and his men, then Sibiet and his Shaigun.

Satisfied, Prince Dylap spoke again, less animated this time. Now Bray turned his attention to her.

"The capital city has been taken, almost every human has been possessed by the takwich and marched south through the Channel Tunnel into Europe. Small pockets of survivors remain, mainly the children and the elderly or those with bodies deemed useless to fight."

"Why south?" Captain Brindle asked.

"We don't know," Bray continued, translating for Prince Dylap. "They're pushing into France and joining the main host. An army so large, that when it marches it's like watching a black ocean rise and fall over the countryside and growing in strength and numbers with each village, town and city they pass as they travel east towards Russia."

"And what of Silk?" Elora asked.

"The takwich calling himself Silk still remains in London. He has command over the occupying force there. Some fifty or sixty-thousand. Armed with rifle, blade or tooth. He's surrounded himself with bodyguards and another creature spat out from the Shadowlands - Charwigg."

"I don't care what he surrounds himself with. I'm still going to kill him," Elora said, finding that she had curled her fingers into a fist. "This Charwigg too if its part of it."

"Charwigg's part of it, girl," Sibiet said. "She's your father's creation. God-created, like that beast there," the Shadojak pointed at Weakest. "Created for dark purposes like his daughter."

Weakest growled as he slowly rose, grey fur rising on his hackles until Elora rested a hand on his head to calm him.

"When I deliver Silk's head will that satisfy you?" Elora asked, anger lacing her words.

"It matters not. London is a five-day hard ride away and we leave for Rona in the morning," Flek said as he joined the group; the six Shades at his heel.

Bray quickly introduced the Supreme's Voice to Prince Dylap.

"Not to mention the army of dark fighters you're going to have to get through to reach him. Smoke or no they'll cut you down within minutes of the first blade being drawn," the Voice continued. "And that's if you're lucky enough not to meet Charwigg. That beast is as destructive as the dragon, Grycul."

146

"I don't care," Elora snapped. "I'll find a way."

"I admire your courage Elora. But the answer's no, Rona awaits your judgment."

Elora caught Drifid smirking and wanted to cut it from his face. Instead, she focused her attention on Flek.

"Please. Silk is destroying Earth and everyone in it. I don't have time to travel to Rona, wait to be judged and then travel back. If I'm going to kill Silk it has to be today, it has to be now."

"Impossible," Sibiet snorted. "You wouldn't survive the judgement anyway. Let her go Flek and she will take her father's place and have the Dark Army at her disposal."

"No, she wouldn't," Bray said, stepping between her and the Shadojak. Prince Dylap also seemed to be quickly grasping the situation and stood as tall as he could on Bray's shoulder, lightening intensifying along his wings.

Sibiet raised an eyebrow whilst regarding him with his copper stare. "You know nothing Shaigun. Step away from your false Shadojak or do I need to balance you also."

"Nobody will be balancing here," cut in Captain Brindle. "Judging or any of that crazy stuff you lot are spouting about. There's no law here and as far as Elora's concerned she can do whatever she wants."

"Stay out of this Earth-born," Drifid said, clicking his fingers for the Shades to surround the Captain.

Elora realised the situation was quickly getting out of hand.

"Stop. We're all on the same side. Bray, back off."
She turned to Brindle and smiled apologetically. "You're right, there isn't a law here, but as a ShadojakI have a

147

code to abide by." She turned to Flek. "I will return to Rona with you. I've given my word already. But tell me, how will we pass into Thea - charm key?"

Flek confirmed her suspicions with a nod, an amused puzzlement crossing his features as he wondered where this was going.

"So even if we crossed into Thea in the morning, we would still need to ride through several kingdoms to reach Rona." She fumbled through her soul memories and knew there was four or five, depending on which route they took.

Again, the Voice nodded.

"So with best speed and unhindered we would reach Rona in about two months."

"Yes, Elora, but I fail to see your point."

"My point, is this. If you grant me a few days to attempt to assassinate Silk, I will deliver us all to Rona within a day or two of my return."

Silence consumed the group as minds worked through her words. It was Sibiet that broke it first.

"Impossible," he blurted out, pointing a tanned finger at her. "She tries to deceive you. The moment you release her the Dark Army will gain their figurehead and ruler."

"And if say, you did kill Silk and return, however unlikely that is. How will you deliver us to Rona with such haste?"

Elora smiled. "The Necrolosis."

The last syllable of her words still hung in the air as Sibiet burst into action, his body moving in a rapid blur.

Pain hit her behind her ankle as she was spun around and forced to the ground, knees driving into the stone path as her neck was exposed. She barely had time to register what had happened before the Shadojak's

148

scimitar was resting against the top of her spine, its sharp edge grazing the top layer of skin.

She realised she was at his disposal, like a hostage to a desperate gunman.

Before she could stop him Weakest launched at Sibiet. She watched the progress of his shadow travel towards its target, his ferocious growl suddenly ended in a yelp before the bulworg's body landed in a crumpled heap beyond the Shadojak's feet.

She sensed Bray moving for his sword, Captain Brindle also cocking his pistol, but neither attempted to attack. It would only take the subtlest of movements for the Soul Reaver to slice through her neck and they knew it. The entire group of men watched on silently, unmoving.

"See what she is?" Sibiet snapped. "Owning bulworgs, loving her Shaigun, daughter of Chaos and now has command of the Necrolosis."

"Shadojak, remove your sword," Flek ordered. He took a step closer and paused, unsure of how to proceed.

"No, she needs judging now. If we wait any longer she'll bring the Dark Army down on us. I will not allow that risk to continue."

"I am not one of them," Elora argued, trying her best to keep her neck from moving as she spoke.

"You're in league with General Zionbuss. No wonder you're so keen to meet Charwigg. Who's next, are you planning on releasing the dragon Grycul and taking up where your father failed?"

"No."

"I judge otherwise."

"It's not your place to judge," Bray said. Elora could sense the tension in him, desperate to act but fearing to bring any harm to her.

"He's right," Flek agreed, raising his gloved hands toward the Shadojak and attempting to calm him. "This must be done in Rona."

"It must be done now."

Elora closed her eyes, expecting the cold blade of the sword to cut though her. Would she have time to change to smoke or would the shift kill her being too close to the Soul Reaver?

Sibiet had caught them all off guard, giving nobody the chance to react. She was at his mercy, which was something he was lacking in. If she died now, who would save Earth?

"Sibiet, please. The Supreme has to be the one to judge her. Him and the rest of the Shadojaks," Flek pleaded.

It was the first time Elora had heard the Voice act with anything short of authority. "There are other things at stake here, things that you are not privy to."

"What things?" Sibiet demanded.

"It's not for me to say, but for the Supreme. Some things are just beyond our understanding."

Elora couldn't see the Shadojak's face from her position on the ground, yet she could almost hear the cogs spinning in his head.

"We could bind her wrists and put her in the dungeon under lock and key. At least until we leave for Thea," Flek offered, reasoning with him.

The silence dragged out, Elora's fingers digging into the stone as she prayed to whatever god who'd listen that she wouldn't die just yet. At least let her live long enough to save the world.

"Very well," Sibiet said, withdrawing his blade. "But I want her watched and guarded at all times."

The dungeon was cold but the steel manacles about her wrist were colder. Elora thought that locking her in here was a little over the top, yet Sibiet refused to budge on the matter. Three of the Shades posted outside the heavy oak door only added to his insecurities.

She sat on the stone floor resting her back against the wall. The last time she was in this cell, Zionbuss had awakened her to that other girl: the daughter of Chaos, the Queen of Darkness. The same place where she had struck Diagus, thrown Bray against the wall and almost killed her uncle.

It seemed so long ago now, she had been to a different world and back since then. Met her mother, killed her father and become a Shadojak and now a prisoner.

Candles were set on the floor in each corner, the yellow light revealing that someone had made a rudimentary attempt at sweeping the dust that clung to the dirt and cobwebs, yet had done no more than brush it into the cracks and fissures.

She wondered how many lives had perished within these walls. How many poor souls had let out their final breaths, their bodies passing from life after the final death rattle. Their remnants still remained within the dust. If she stayed here she would join them and if Sibiet had his way, this is where she would rot.

Escape was her only option, the world's only chance of survival was her ability to live and for that she needed to find a way out.

She looked around for inspiration while slowly sinking into desperation. Then heard shuffling from the other side of the new door. Ragna had put the Fist of the North through the last one, the great war hammer reducing the oak to kindling. She heard the bolt on the other side being slid back before it was pushed open.

Flek stepped into the cell with Bray at his side.

"What have you done with Weakest?" Elora asked, drawing her legs up; her cuffed hands resting upon her knees.

The bulworg had been the first to react to Sibiet's attack and had lunged at him, teeth bared. But the Shadojak had been prepared and drove his other fist into Weakest's throat. The punch strong enough to choke the windpipe and render the beast unconscious.

"He's chained to the wall in the tower above us," Flek answered. "Howling like a crazed wolf at the moon."

"You've come to set me free?" she asked, hopefully.

Bray remained silent as Flek stepped forward, pulling a piece of parchment from his cloak and dropping it on her lap.

When Elora looked at it she recognised the twin world symbol, a dark circle overlapping the other, like the one on Silk's business card.

"I thought Chaos is supposed to set you free," he said.

Elora frowned, did Bray tell him what her bad dream was about. She glanced up at him and saw the truth.

"It's too much of a coincidence isn't it?" the Voice continued. "These notes, these symbols and writings stemming back through the ages. Your Shaigun has told you what the Supreme's been scribbling?"

"Elora will set us free," she answered.

"Elora will unite us. Strange isn't it? Do you know what they refer too? I can't see there being another Elora that's linked to the God of Chaos."

She picked up the parchment and passed it back. When Flek reached down for it she grasped his wrist and pulled him close so their noses were almost touching.

"You need to let me go so I can kill Silk. I don't know what these symbols mean or what hand Chaos has in it. But Silk seems to know. At least if I kill him it's one less threat. I'll return once the deed is done."

"Not that easy I'm afraid," Flek replied as he peeled her fingers from his arm. "Sibiet's got the only key to your manacles and he's..."

The steel cuffs struck the floor. The clattering of metal on stone echoed throughout the chamber as the Voice glanced down. Elora held up her bare wrists just as they materialised from smoke.

Bray grinned. "I told you she could do that."

"I will be leaving for London," Elora informed him while rising from the floor. "I'd prefer it if you gave me your permission. Otherwise I'll be going through those Shades guarding me and whoever else is set to stop me."

"Bray said you might do that. Your Shaigun knows you well, Elora. Thankfully I've already come to the decision to let you go, that's why we're here. The Supreme's on to something with these drawings and scribbles."

"What about Sibiet?"

"The Shadojak doesn't know," Flek replied, brushing dust from his shoulder. "And neither will he until you've gone. I dare say he won't be best pleased, but what can he do once you've left?"

"I don't know what to say. Thank you Flek."

"Just make sure you return; I'm taking a great gamble letting you go. If your Soul Reaver falls into the Dark Army's hands then I'll be the one being judged on returning to Rona."

"That means, Master," Bray said while folding his arms. "That if you can't find a way to reach him, you don't go on a suicide mission. The same goes if you see the demon Charwigg. She was one of Solarius's nastier creations. If she's there you will return immediately."

"Funny, I thought I was the master and you the Shaigun," she said, reminding him to act as such.

"Forgive me Master."

Flek chuckled. "Come, if you're to go it must be soon before Sibiet or Drifid realise what we're about."

The brightness of the daylight reduced Elora's eyes to slits as she marched over to the chained bulworg and in a single stroke slipped her blade out and cut the steel chain about his neck.

"He's coming with me," she told Flek before he questioned her. She rubbed the raw skin on Weakest's neck where he had fought against his restraints and added. "If he wishes."

Without hesitation the bulworg bowed his head and rubbed up against her leg.

As they made their way back to the fairy circle Bray slipped something into her hand. She glanced down at the tinker's tongue charm, the small magical device fitting snuggly into her palm.

She made an act of attempting to place it in her ear without fixing it on properly.

"I always have problems fitting this in," she said pausing. "Bray, attach the damn thing on before I break it."

"Yes Master," he replied taking the device and placing it in her ear.

She watched as Flek and Weakest walked on before placing a hand against his. Checking that the Voice wasn't about to turn around she swiftly planted a kiss on his lips.

"Don't worry about me, I'll be back soon enough."

She stared ahead again as Flek waited for them to catch up. Bray moved her hair out of the way as he clipped the tongue charm on, then delicately kissed the nape of her neck.

"I know. Doesn't stop me worrying though."

He broke the contact as Flek turned around. "There Master. You should be able to understand Prince Dylap now."

They hastily joined the others and continued the small walk to the fairy circle.

As they neared Elora was surprised to find Grimwolf looming above the wall, regarding them through the slits in his snarling wolf helm.

Below him was Captain Brindle, Slater and Pudding; armed with rifles and shotguns, they appeared ready for action.

"Need any help?" Brindle asked.

Elora offered him an apologetic smile. "I wish I could take you with me, but you wouldn't survive the journey. Only fairies, gods and those they create can travel in a fairy circle."

She glanced up at the armoured man, his red cloak gently swaying in a light breeze. "I don't know about you. Your suit's god-created, but will it protect you?"

"Maybe," he whispered, his voice deep and grating.

The armour, as thick and hard as it appeared moved with a lightness as he dropped from the wall and strode into the fairy circle, stepping delicately between the tall moon daisies.

Prince Dylap landed on the stone cobbles, his black falcon giving Grimwolf's steel-capped boots a curious tap with a sharp beak.

Weakest vaulted over the ring, the flowers gently rocking in the wind he created. He padded around the perimeter before settling down.

Elora was about to join them when she noticed Ejan walking from the direction of the inn. She paused when she saw Grimwolf, shock written in her expression. Without taking her eyes from him she approached with an unsure step before halting at the edge of the fairy circle.

Her fingers played with a bracelet she was wearing, one that Elora recognised as being made from Ragna's beard. Ejan had cut the plaited strands from his chin before the huge Viking sacrificed himself so that they may live. A last token to remember him by.

Ejan stared up at the huge armoured man, cocking her head this way and that, seeming to absorb as much detail as her hungry eyes could take.

"So, Grimwolf," she began, a touch of anger to her voice. "You know where to find genellas?" she asked accusingly.

"Yeah," Grimwolf replied after a moment's hesitation.

"Funny that, only my husband knew where they grow."

After another awkward silence had passed, Grimwolf replied, "That so?"

"My husband used to tell stories about you to my son. Great tales about a mystical man in a snarling wolf suit of god-created armour. Ragna spoke so vividly in his tales, his descriptions seemed so real it even had me believing in you."

"That so?" his words carried like the sound of stone grounding against stone.

Elora watched the exchange, wondering where it was going, why Ejan seemed so worked up by Grimwolf's presence.

"That's so," the Norsewoman said, "he also described your huge sword with the wolf's head set in the hilt. Big heavy thing that needs a big heavy man to handle it."

The silence grew longer this time, Grimwolf's gauntleted claw resting against the wolf's head of his sword.

"I watched Ragna die. Watched my Raggie fall, screaming out his last salute to Odin. I grieved the sorrow more powerful than any widow's and I waited the painful days and weeks until they rebuilt the bridge at the pass so I could collect my husband's body. Just so it could have the proper respects it was due. I'd already built the funeral pier."

"That so?" Grimwolf said, his voice sounding less sure now.

"That's so. I was one of the first across and saw the mess he'd left. The bodies of the Imperial Guards; arms missing, arrow strewn, guts laid open for the air, skin turned a marble white from the snow and ice and packing them as fresh as the day it happened, like meat for the winter. But Ragna's body was gone."

"That so."

"Yes, that's bloody so!" Ejan snapped, cheeks glowing red. "I knew the spot he died in, the very place his soul left the mountain. I'd spent days watching it from across the pass. No movement, no trail, no nothing. There was no sign of snow jubbs having been there and mountain cats would have left tracks. It was like his body had just risen and walked off."

In the silence that followed Elora watched Ejan, her fingers now clenched in fists, then at Grimwolf who stood as motionless as a steel statue and just for a split second wondered if the man inside the armour was Ragna.

Tears streaked down Ejan's face as she sunk her teeth into the knot that tied her bracelet before she yanked it from her wrist.

The rest of the group stared at her, looking uncomfortable at watching the Viking display her emotions and probably feeling that they were intruding on her privacy.

The stare she gave Grimwolf was full of hate, yet Elora also saw a haunted wanting in them.

"When you return, I want words," she said, then hurled the bracelet at him.

It struck Grimwolf's breast plate and slid down his armoured torso. He caught it before it fell to the ground.

Elora wished she could see through the snarling wolf helm. See the man wearing it. She understood Ejan's anger, yet wondered if she was merely venting her frustrations and found a target in Grimwolf. If it was Ragna then Ejan would make his life hell. But how could it be? She watched the great Viking die.

With all eyes on the Norsewoman wondering what she would say or do next, Ejan turned and strode away, leaving an eerily still quietness behind. Elora watched as she disappeared behind the trees, the desire of going after her to give her some comfort was strong, but she knew that time was against her. And to confirm her last thought, Sibiet stormed from the opposite direction, his Shaigun, Drifid struggling to keep up.

"Time to go," Elora said.

The moment her feet entered the circle the moon daisies began to crackle with static. The air above them shimmered like the translucent waves of a mirage.

Elora watched the Shadojak advance on the fairy circle, copper eyes alive with violence, teeth bared ready to begin a tirade of shouting. Sibiet seemed impossibly angrier than he had in the morning, his dark completion turning scarlet.

Elora had just enough time to smile at the Shadojak and childishly blow him a kiss before a sudden sense of vertigo opened up a void in her mind and she was flung backwards.

Chapter 10

The Hedge Witch

Weakest yelped as Elora slammed into him. His large body absorbing the force she would have felt if she'd crashed into the ground.

As her vision slowly returned she pushed herself off his body, her fingers sinking into his warm fur. They were in the grassy glade full of flowers that was in the cellar of Norgie's London home. The glade was how she remembered it. The large tree with magnolia coloured fruit, beside the turquoise stream was almost bare now, the lilies that floated upon the water were now no more than green pads but it was the same place. All within a huge snow-globe shape that ended where the cellar walls and ceiling began.

"Sorry, Weakest. Are you alright?" she asked, worried that she'd broken his ribs.

The bulworg grunted as he slowly shuffled to the stream and delicately drank, his huge tongue dipping into the turquoise water. He didn't look well.

Stretching her neck and back she shook the dizziness from her head. It was then that she noticed Grimwolf lying on the grass, motionless.

Kneeling beside him she placed a hand against his steel chest and tapped the metal.

"Grimwolf?"

The lack of response had her worried. In the armour she couldn't tell if he was even breathing.

"Grimwolf, can you hear me?" she asked, more urgently, banging her knuckles against his chest once again.

Shifting towards his head she leaned over the snarling wolf helm and peered inside the eye slits but it was too dark to penetrate the shadows within.

Her hands searched over the suit as she sought out a way of removing it, yet there were no buckles or clasps, not even a gap where she could wedge her fingers in between to get a grip - how did he put it on?

Working her way around the helmet her thumb brushed over the steel canine teeth and felt something give. It was a thin hinge, fine and intricately worked into the side of the carved mouth. She found another below and pushed her fingers around to the other side of the mouth where she spotted a clasp in the shape of a tooth.

"Grimwolf?" she tried one last time then worked the clasp loose.

The metal tooth twisted smoothly and the steel face sprung open a fraction. She placed her fingers into the formed crack and lifted the visor open. Time to reveal who Grimwolf was.

Her heart leapt as a steel claw suddenly wrapped around her wrist, pulling her arm away from the helmet.

"Sorry," Elora said, as his other claw moved swiftly to refasten the clasp. "I thought you might be injured or dead."

She rose and went to stand by the strange tree, feeling that she may have encroached too far in attempting to reveal who he is. Prince Dylap was sat upon his bird, perched on a branch beside her and watching the scene unfold.

"When I'm dead you may open my visor. Until then, don't touch."

"Understood," Elora replied, watching as he struggled to his feet and shaking that wolf's head of his to chase away the grogginess. She still felt a little nauseous herself, traveling in the fairy circle would be something she didn't want to do regularly.

Prince Dylap left his bird and glided down to land softly on her shoulder. He was so small and light she wouldn't have known he was there if she hadn't have seen his electric blue wings spread out. He closed them as he neared her ear.

"Silk is half a day's walk, even with your long strides. We should begin the journey before nightfall," he said in a soft high-pitched voice.

Elora felt the small disk in the tinker's tongue charm vibrate, moulding the Farrosian's words into her own.

"We're not going to Silk right away," she said, striding out of the daisy circle and heading for the door. "We're going to see the hedge witch. Grendal has something we need."

When she pushed down on the handle the door gave way, forcing her back into the cellar as bricks and burnt wood crashed through the opening.

When the dust cleared she saw that the entire doorway was filled with masonry and charred timber.

"I forgot that Bray and Norgie were attacked here before they left for Rams Keep. Silk destroyed the house rather than leave it," she said to the others who stared at the blocked doorway.

She studied the mess that lay in their path, if they pulled it out of the way it would only be replaced by more rubble from above. "We're trapped." She turned to

162

Prince Dylap, "Is there another way? Another fairy circle?" she pointed at the flowered glade and made a circle in the air with her finger. The tongue charm only worked one way, she could understand them, but her spoken words were in her own language. Luckily he took her meaning.

"No," he replied pointing down at the moon daisies. "This is the only one near the capital."

"Great," she returned her gaze back to the blocked doorway. "Better get digging then."

Weakest sniffed hungrily at the air behind her. Padding over to the wall his nose led him to a wooden board nailed into a frame. With an easy flick of his paw he reduced the board to splinters revealing a fractured window that looked out onto the front garden.

"Nice work," Elora said as she stood on tip toes to peer out.

The garden was pretty much how she remembered it. The lawn was tall and unkempt, the grass gone to hay with the large willow reaching over the crumbling path. There was no sign of people, neither survivors or the Dark Army itself. The entire street seemed deserted, quiet and empty.

Unlocking the window, she pushed it open. The rusted hinges screaming in protest as it swung outwards, flattening the grass that had grown against it.

The already fractured glass fell harmlessly out of the frame as Elora tapped it through using a wooden chair leg that she found on the floor.

Prince Dylap flew out of the gap, his falcon cawing in the air as he joined him. Elora was next, scrambling up the wall and squeezing through the window.

163

She gazed at the devastation around her that she hadn't been able to see from below.

Norgie's terrace, as well as both neighbouring houses lay in a blackened ruin. The homes reduced to an ugly pile of rubble, only the charred remains of a roof frame, secured at one end to the end terrace house, appeared to float above. Bereft of tiles it gave the appearance of skeletal fingers, erect and rigid reaching from the grave in a final stretch.

Glancing back at the cellar window she watched Grimwolf, his head and shoulders taking up the entire gap she'd climbed through. There was no way he would fit through it.

She was about to suggest that they wait while she cleared some of the rubble away so he and Weakest could exit through the door, when his huge gauntlet gripped the cross beam and pulled the entire window frame from the wall, including several bricks.

Grimwolf wriggled through the opening, his shoulders taking another brick as he forced himself out. Weakest scrambled out easily, bending his lupine form, he was sitting beside her before Grimwolf had risen to his feet.

"We need to move swiftly yet quietly," Elora said as she opened the garden gate. "How are you at running in that armour?"

"I'll keep up."

Elora wondered if that was possible, the wolf suit must weigh as much as a grown man without the grown man inside it - if that was what he was. She didn't question him as she broke into a steady jog.

They ran out of the road and along the adjacent street, keeping to pavements where possible to avoid the mess of abandoned vehicles strewn along both lanes.

Grimwolf kept pace with her, the only sound created by his cloak which whipped from side to side with his motion.

The tall blocks of flats that towered above gave them some cover from scraw-harpies that may be circling in the sky, as they darted between the buildings aiming to reduce the length of time they spent in the open; if they were spotted she would have no chance of reaching Silk.

As they vaulted over iron railings having dashed over a roundabout, Weakest growled at the way ahead and nudged Elora towards a truck that straddled across the verge having broken down mid-manoeuvre. She got his understanding and crawled under the trailer, hiding behind the huge wheels. Grimwolf dropped to the ground and rolled sideways until he lay next to her. Weakest hunkered down to her other side.

She watched the direction where the bulworg growled. It was a shopping precinct with all the windows smashed. A crushed bin jamming the broken door open. Her eyes picked over the second and third floor above which had a large billboard that originally advertised a sports drink and now had two circles drawn over the top; the shaded one over laying the other. Above the shapes, written with a dark brown paint were the words 'Chaos will unite us.' Then beneath, scribbled with the same substance which she guessed was dried blood was something that raised the hairs on her neck. 'Elora will set us free.'

Sharp movement brought her eyes away from the billboard.

Three men suddenly burst from the precinct and sprinted across the roundabout. The youngest at the front stumbled in his haste, hitting the concrete and spilling his rucksack full of tins and crisps. As he attempted to pick them up his friend yanked him upright and pulled him on away from the shop fronts.

They fled passed the truck, feet slamming hard against the floor, all three of them panting and stealing glances behind, eyes full of panic. Elora remained out of view watching the teenagers make it to the other side of the junction where they leapt the iron railings and disappeared down an alley.

The sound of glass smashing brought her attention back to the precinct as a bulworg landed on the pavement outside the shop front. The window he'd crashed through raining down in sparkling shards as he took off in the direction of the young men.

She tensed as it bounded passed their hiding place, its teeth set in grim determination on chasing down its targets. Elora knew it would be on them in moments.

Several other men exited through the shop window. Armed with assault rifles they took off after the bulworg, yet at a slower more controlled run and allowing the beast to catch the fleeing teenagers while they caught up to arrest them.

As they passed, Elora realised that they were takwiches. She sensed the darkness within each, feeling the touch of her father's soldiers and recognised the possessors inside the stolen bodies.

Elora watched Grimwolf shift his hand over the hilt of his sword, ready to burst into action. She placed a hand atop his and shook her head no. If they followed it would lead to a fight. A fight they would win, but the noise would attract others and they couldn't risk that over the mission. They only had one attempt at reaching Silk.

She waited for the takwiches to disappear before slipping from under the trailer, remorse hanging heavy in her mind at leaving the teenagers to their own devices.

"Come, we need to press on," she said to Grimwolf and Weakest, who stared towards the ally.

With reluctance they followed her as she set off running in the opposite direction. Prince Dylap flying above, his shadow trailing along the road ahead.

Before becoming a Shadojak and acquiring Diagus's soul memories she wouldn't have been able to navigate London. Even when it was still functioning properly she had never visited the country's capital. Yet the route she was plotting came so naturally it was like she'd been here all her life; knowing the boroughs, the streets and side roads, recognising the skylines and little quirky cobbled lanes from a long ago era. So much so that they arrived at the back passage to Grendal's house just as Elora realised where they were. Where she'd first met the late Shadojak. The Pearly White had saved her from Rueben and two takwiches.

Gunfire and the crashing of hammers erupted from the other side of the wall. She crept to the gate that opened into Grendal's garden and peered through.

Four men were firing rifles into the back of the building, although their bullets were crushed flat against an invisible force before dropping harmlessly to the ground. Beside the men, there was a clay golem. The eight-foot tall creature was swinging a large hammer against the door but met the same impenetrable shield. The hammer sending a shock wave through his clay arms and shoulders, yet the golem remained relentless as he continued to bombard the door with swing after swing.

Then she heard insect like clicks and clacks. Glancing down she watched two takwiches scurry under the gate, their pincers snapping at the air; black oily shells reflecting in the sunshine.

She backed away and slipping her Soul Reaver from the smuggler's pouch, traced their movements as they scuttled towards them.

Then they attacked.

The one closest sprung towards her face, its legs spread wide; hooks at the end of its feet ready to gain purchase, mandibles open, fangs pulled back anticipating to sink into her flesh.

Reflexively she brought her sword across, the blade passing through the takwich and severing it in half. Its shell spinning away whilst its legs and head tumbled to the ground.

Taking another step back she adopted a defensive stance just as the second launched towards her.

Grimwolf caught the creature in the air, its pincers and fangs working against the steel gauntlets. He brought the insect towards his helm for a closer look, turning it over as if examining it. Then with a shrug he closed his hand into a fist, the takwich exploding in a tangle of broken legs, shell and black ichor.

"Nice," Elora remarked sarcastically, then stepping back to the gate gave her companions a sly grin. "Shall we?"

The gate swung open crashing against the brick wall as she strolled purposefully into the garden.

The men stopped firing and turned puzzled faces towards her whilst the clay golem halted his hammer inches from connecting with the wall.

She took another step closer feeling the growing excitement in her, sensing the rising tension and almost tasting the blood about to be spilt. But rules were rules, she needed to offer them surrender, it was the code.

"In the name of the Shadojak, Yield!"

The bigger of the men appeared to be the leader. He re-cocked his rifle, feeding another bullet into the chamber. This was the sign for the remaining four to do the same.

Elora's grin spread. "Thought so."

Spinning the sword in her hand to reverse the grip she dove into a forward-roll, springing up before the closet target and arcing her blade in an upwards thrust. She sliced through his wrist severing his arm from his trigger finger.

She carried the motion forwards, sidestepping and ducking under the second target's barrel - high-powered rifles were a lethal force but the wrong weapon for close combat. Her sword bit into his lower back cutting his spinal cord before a single shot was fired.

Weakest was a blur of grey fur on the outskirts of her vision. His shape lunging into a rifle man, his teeth finding an exposed throat as his weight brought them both to the ground.

Continuing her circle, the momentum brought her before the golem. She arched backwards feeling the wind from the hammer as it skimmed her face. As it passed she launched herself at the wall behind the clay giant, her feet pressing hard into the brickwork before she propelled herself over him, curling into a somersault.

The golem glared up as she passed above him, his smooth clay features blank of expression as the creature was no more than an animated statue brought to life by a mage.

Elora thrust down with the Soul Reaver, the blade entering his open mouth and as she came down to the ground she yanked hard, tearing the golems jaw clean off.

It smashed on impact, the fragments striking her shins as she landed before jumping out of the of his swinging hammer, the clay man being oblivious that he'd lost the lower part of his face.

One of the remaining men finally fired a burst of rounds, she heard the bullets impact against metal and guessed that Grimwolf had been hit but couldn't bring her eyes away from the golem to check if he was alright. He'd need to fend for himself for the moment.

Her original target was pairing-up with the clay man, his useless arm forgotten as he came at her with a sword of his own, blood pumping from the stump and spraying the wall they'd tried to break through.

She caught his blade with her own, the crash echoing strangely as she dissolved to smoke, feeling her entire being wash over him, flaming embers grazing his face and singeing the hairs above his wrinkled brow.

When she solidified on the other side she had barely enough time to duck before his head jerked back, blood and teeth following the hammer as it passed over. The dead body struck the wall before sliding into a heap. The head crushed grossly out of shape, white splinters of skull rupturing through the skin; grey matter clinging to lank hair.

Elora rose behind the hammer as it came at her from the back swing. She cut up and broke through the golem's elbow, the arm shattering as the heavy weapon thudded into the body of the fallen.

She spared a glance at Grimwolf in time to see his broadsword decapitate a soldier. The unfortunate's head tumbled over in the air, face still grimacing as blood sprayed from the neck; the dark droplets spinning and making a swirling pattern above the teetering body.

Grimwolf kicked it over as he came to stand beside her. They watched Weakest tear the throat of the remaining man, swallowing it in one gulp as the soldier choked, his body shuddering as he fought to suck air into his lungs. He went still as the bulworg came to join them. The three of them spreading out to surround the golem. It surveyed them with unseeing clay orbs, the remaining portion of its head looking like something from a horror film.

"We need to break it open and destroy the mage's mark," Elora said, dodging a punch from the clay being's remaining arm.

It kicked out at Weakest, connecting with his legs and knocked the bulworg over. Snarling, he rose back to his feet ready to lunge but Grimwolf held a hand out to stop him.

The armoured man re-sheathed his sword, stepped closer to the golem and punched his fist through its head.

It shattered like an expensive vase, yet the golem still kicked, its feet cracking against Grimwolf's steel boots as Elora stepped in from behind to cut through both knees.

The torso fell to the ground as Elora stomped down, smashing the chest and waist to pieces. Amongst the clay rubble she found a small scroll and picked it up as the larger fragments of clay still twitched and moved of their own accord.

A strange letter, like a rune but one she didn't recognise was written over and over again. Repeated in a spiralling pattern that ended at the scrolls centre.

The arm of the golem still moved, fingers clenching and unclenching as they sought an object to grip. Elora narrowed her eyes at the scroll in her hands and it burst into flames.

As the paper curled back the runes glowed bright red, the flexing limb at her feet gave a final stretch before the scroll was reduced to ash.

Elora looked around at the devastation she'd done. The mutilated bodies of the dead, the blood still oozing from gaping wounds, trickling in black streams to mix with the fragments of shattered clay. It was Chaos.

Before the bodies were taken by the takwiches they were ordinary people, going about their lives and harming nobody. They probably had wives, children and the last thing they deserved was to be butchered, their bodies left to rot in a stranger's back yard.

The excitement she felt before the fight belonged to that other her, the girl of darkness. The tears that now ran down her face belonged to her, to Elora. Using her sleeve, she wiped them away. She was a Shadojak now and better start acting like one.

"Grendal?" she shouted. Her voice echoing back from the quiet house. She thought it was empty until the door slowly creaked open and the hedge witch poked her head out.

"Come in," she said waving her hand anxiously. "They'll send more. Come in while you can."

Elora entered the home first and held the door for the others. Grimwolf stepped in having to duck to avoid hitting his head, followed quickly by weakest, blood still dripping from his mouth as they filled up the small kitchen.

"It's ok Grendal, he's with me." Elora offered seeing the frightened look the hedge witch gave him.

Finally, Prince Dylap flew in, his falcon landing on the table and she shut the door.

"I don't for a moment understand why you have come, but I am glad you have," Grendal said, embracing Elora with her unusually long arms. "Is the Shadojak with you?"

Elora pulled away. "I'm the Shadojak now. For the time being anyway." Then she introduced the others. "This is Grimwolf, Weakest and Prince Dylap,"

Grendal nodded to them all. "Thank you for coming. But I still don't understand why you did."

"We will find a way of bringing you back to Rams Keep with us. You and your son Darrion, but our intentions are not as kind as you're led to believe. We're here to kill Silk and you've got something we need."

Grendal chuckled. "Don't I always? That's the reason Silk wanted to break into my shop in the first place. That golem has been hammering at the door day and night, non-stop for the past couple of weeks. He'd have kept it up until the barrier failed, which wouldn't have been much longer. Truth is, we ran out of fresh water a couple of days ago and I was in a mind to surrender."

"What do you have that he wanted?" Elora asked.

"I don't know how he knew I had it, but he was after the box containing the djinn. Or the remains of the djinn."

"He knew because a spliceck told him," Elora answered.

"Reuban?"

"Exactly, I'm afraid I'd been tricked all along. That spliceck had taken over my uncle and led me along a path to free Solarius."

Grendal sat down at the kitchen table, rubbing the despair from her face with long fingers. "So that's what's happened. The Dark Army has truly ascended onto Earth."

"I'm afraid so," Elora said taking the chair opposite. She took hold of Grendal's hands in hers. "But I'm here to send them back, somehow."

"What is it you've come for? What do I have that you need?"

"The same thing Silk wants, the djinn."

Grendal remained quiet for a moment, soft eyes regarding her beneath a heavy brow.

"This djinn is priceless. It maybe my only bargaining chip to offer for my Darrion's life, I care not for my own over his. What would you do if I refused? You are the Shadojak now, are you to be as ruthless?"

"I'll do what I must, Grendal. But I will still take you back to Rams Keep regardless, whether you gave me the djinn or if I simply took it."

The hedge witch leaned back in her chair letting out a heavy sigh. "If you think it can be any use against Silk, then please take it. But I must warn you I don't know how powerful it is. It's just the remains of a djinn, I've never seen proof of its actual worth."

The box was how Elora remembered it when she first saw it in the Aladdin's cave of treasure which Grendal had in an upstairs room. The box had been the centrepiece, sitting on a velvet cloth. It still appeared charming yet maybe a little less magical as it was placed before her on the kitchen table.

It was plain, the size of a shoe box with a barrel-shaped lid and made from polished rosewood with brass edging and lock.

Elora put her finger to the clasp and unlocked the box.

"Be warned," Grendal said before she lifted the lid. "The djinn are known to be deceitful and untrustworthy. If you let it trick you, you'll be paying with your soul and an eternity trapped in the box."

Elora felt the others around the table shift uncomfortably as she breathed deeply and opened it.

Fine tendrils of black smoke drifted out, wisps of ghostly fingers curling and coiling but never reaching further than a hand's width from the box. Elora watched the spectral phenomenon, wondering how you communicated with the djinn inside. When she had last seen it, Grendal had explained that a djinn was a kind of wish granting demon, similar to a genie. Should she then be rubbing the side of the box or was that just lamps?

Prince Dylap stalked across the table top, poking at the smoke with his javelin. He stared up at her, shrugging his shoulders and shaking his head.

"I don't sense any powers from within," he said spreading the spines of his wings. Electrical blue forks of lighting sparking along them as he flew above the box to peer inside.

He hovered there for a few seconds before letting go a tiny bolt of lightning that ran down his javelin and fired into the dark depths of the smoke.

Nothing happened at first, then all of a sudden a black wisp snapped out like a whip and flicked the Farrosian across the table.

Grimwolf caught him before he slid off the surface, his little body seeming impossibly fragile in the huge gauntlet.

"So there is something in there," Elora said.

Before Grendal could stop her, Elora reached inside the box; her fingers suddenly becoming cold when it touched the smoke.

She reached further inside expecting to meet the bottom where her eyes were telling her it should be, but her elbow passed out of sight before she felt something solid or something solid found her.

Icy fingers wrapped around her own and yanked her towards the box. The lid pushed fully back and the opening stretched like a mouth ready to receive her.

Weakest locked his jaw onto her cloak and Grimwolf wrapped an arm around her waist, preventing her from disappearing inside the box.

A sharp stabbing pain pierced her wrist, like a scorpion sting. She felt a drop of blood run down her palm, the icy fingers gripping tighter as something slug-like and wet licked the wound, tasting her.

A heartbeat later the box jumped and began to shake violently, the smoke sucking back inside, the fingers instantly releasing her but before they let go completely, Elora dipped her hand in further and grasped the icy fingers herself.

"No you don't! Taste my fire djinn, feel my worth - realise who it is that has you." She pulled fiercely at the hand she grasped. The bodiless fingers pulled back but it showed signs of weakening as if the fire in her blood was beginning to devour its strength.

"No!" came a voice from inside. "I have not the powers you seek. Leave me be, leave me to rest."

Elora stopped pulling but kept a tight grip on the hand. "You've tasted me, djinn. You know who I am, what I am - and I demand a wish."

"Rest is all. I'm no longer a djinn. I'm but the dust of a memory, ashes of a dead demon. Let me rest in peace."

"I'll let you rest once you've granted me a wish."

"I am but a memory. Even the threats from the daughter of Chaos could not draw power from where there is none."

"So you do know who I am?"

"I hear the darkness whisper your name. Now there's a power you should be harnessing. What is it you seek, what is the favour you wish?" The Voice became more steady as Elora softened her grip, yet did not let go.

"I wish the Dark Army to retreat. All of it, and for the takwiches to abandon all the bodies they've taken."

"The wish would have been too great for my former self to perform. There is only one being alive who could command such a power should they wish it."

"Who?" she asked, feeling hope once again.

"I'll only tell you if you lay me to rest. True rest, the eternal sleep."

"Death, but how?"

"It's simple, you just need to empty my ashes from this box, from this vessel which has been my prison for over three millennia."

"I will. On my word as a Shadojak."

"The word of a Shadojak, the honour of a demigod. Very well, Queen of Darkness. Although you may feel cheated by my answer, yet it is the truth and only solution to your riddle."

Elora wanted the answer. If there was a person so powerful who could grant her this wish she would do anything to reach them.

"Tell me who can purge Earth of the Dark Army," she demanded, feeling anxious should the djinn be tricking her.

Everyone around the table leaned closer to the box, including Prince Dylap who scowled at the opening, javelin in hand and ready to throw.

"Elora, daughter of Chaos, Queen of darkness, you are the only being who can unite the worlds and set them free."

This was a trick, yet she sensed no treachery in the demon's words.

"But how?" she asked, knowing that she alone couldn't defeat the Dark Army.

"Chaos. It's what you are. It's what you command."

"But..."

"I've kept up my end of the bargain. Now you must keep yours. Chaos is fickle, random, patternless; neither good nor evil. It flows on a whim; it trickles along its own path as should you. I can say no more."

Elora felt cheated, she had learned nothing from the djinn. And before she had chance to ask anymore the cold fingers she held reduced to ash.

She removed her arm from the box, her hand cupping the charcoal coloured dust. She wanted to hurl it back inside but she had given her word.

With a sense of loss, she crossed the room carrying the box. Grendal opened the door and she flung the ashes out, then upended the wooden vessel spilling the last remains of the demon.

A breeze suddenly picked up and carried the black dust away. Elora watched as it spun in a tiny whirlwind, flowing over the wall and disappearing along with the only plan she had. The reason she came to find Grendal was because of that djinn and what it could have done. Now she was back to square one.

She dropped the box back on the table and sat down. How was she going to kill Silk now? How was she going to break through the vast army that surrounded him?

"How am I supposed to set the worlds free when I can't even reach one man in one city."

"Chaos? Maybe there is something in that," offered the hedge witch as she sat beside her and grasped her hand.

"Or just the ramblings of a memory, the ghost of a demon wanting an escape," Elora grumbled.

"At least Silk didn't get his hands on the djinn. The Blessed Mother only knows what he could have done with that power, probably nothing but he will still feel cheated. He will still break down my barriers to get what he wanted but now there'll be no djinn for him to find."

Elora stared at the empty box; the lid left open and now empty of the djinn. It was nothing more than a plain wooden vessel, yet an idea was formulating in her mind.

"Who's to say, Silk can't have his djinn," Elora said, smiling at the others around the table.

Chapter 11

Unwanted Gifts

Grimwolf flinched as the door slammed like a coffin lid, shutting him out with the enemy. He stood on the steps outside the front of Grendal's house, now committed to seeing this crazy plan through. There was no going back.

He swallowed down the rising bile as he stepped towards the horde of takwiches. The thirty or so possessed men appearing as surprised to see him as he was to being in their company.

Rifles were cocked and trained on them, fingers itching to pull triggers as they watched him approach. Glancing down he saw that Weakest was as unsure about this as he was. Well, a problem shared was a problem halved - little comfort when half the problem still meant a few thousand of the Dark Army's meanest.

"Halt," shouted a man on horseback.

Grimwolf took him to be the leader of this platoon. He appeared older than the rest, wearing boiled leather armour and an old breastplate bearing the twin world symbol. Unlike his men who were merely wearing whatever clothes the people happened to be in before they were taken: jeans, t-shirts, tracksuit and even a three-piece suit, shirt and tie. Takwiches numbered so many that they couldn't be spared armour.

Be brave, he willed himself. This would only work if he appeared as mean or meaner than the soldiers themselves.

Grimwolf stopped and waited for the horseman to trot forwards, two other horseman flanking him either side.

Hawking up phlegm the leader spat on the ground, missing Weakest's paw by an inch.

"Who are you and what business have you with the hedge witch?" he asked, nodding towards the front door which had already vanished. His matted beard twitched as he spoke, a tic that made his already fierce demeanour have a mad quality.

"My business," Grimwolf replied, making his voice sound meaner than that of the horseman.

"And what business is that?"

"None of yours."

After several twitches of the tic the leader leaned down, his face inches from Grimwolf's. "Nice armour," he pulled a dirk from his belt and slid the tip of it down Grimwolf's shoulder plate. "Think it might fit me just fine."

"Think my blade would suit you better," Grimwolf growled. "But it seems my hands are full."

Glancing down at what Grimwolf held in his hands the leader grinned. "Is that the box we've been after?" He turned to the man beside him. "We've got Silk's djinn."

"I'll take that," said the rider holding his hands out for the box.

"I wouldn't trust you incompetent fools with this. Do you know what a djinn would do in the hands of a mortal? I'm taking it to Silk myself."

"Listen to me, whomever you are. Silk's on the other side of town. You won't get far on foot."

Weakest began to growl as he sensed the same hostilities approaching. The men would act soon, only seeing the pair of them as an easy challenge. Violence was a certainty, the only language the Dark Army understood.

"Then give me a horse," Grimwolf said, putting as much authority into his voice as he could muster.

The leader grinned again, the tic working his beard. "I don't have a spare."

Arms extended from the rider beside him, hands reaching closer for the box. Grimwolf saw his opportunity and slammed his head into the soldier's face, feeling his skull crunch beneath his wolf's helm.

The rider flopped out of the saddle and fell unconscious to the floor.

"It appears that you do have a spare," Grimwolf said, placing his foot in the stirrup and mounting the horse before the leader had time to think.

It was a pivotal moment. Grimwolf watched the leader for his next actions. Dark eyes darting about as his dark mind worked. If he didn't do something his men would think him craven. If he drew a sword against him, it may be his own death.

Grimwolf made the decision before the leader forced a bloodbath.

"Captain, you will escort me to Silk and ensure the safe delivery of a precious gift to our illustrious Commander." He subtly shifted a hand from the box to rest upon the hilt of his sword, the gesture meant for the leader's eyes only. "That is if your men are worthy to be an honour guard."

Clearing his throat, his tic working double-time, he looked to his cohorts. "We have honour enough for that and for aiding you in retrieving the djinn."

"Of course," Grimwolf said. "I'll inform Silk of your heroic deeds in defeating the hedge witch."

The Captain puffed his chest out at that. It seemed to Grimwolf that you could find vanity anywhere, even in the ugliest and cruellest of men.

Weakest padded next to him as they rode through the city, his nose constantly sniffing for more trouble and his teeth regularly on display, but it wasn't the bulworg that was constantly watched by the growing amount of soldiers they passed. Every man, beast or demon glared his way, puzzling at the stranger in the armour, at the god-created wolf that was being escorted.

Grimwolf tried to act as casual as he could, staring ahead and ignoring all the sharp steel that was on display, all the rifles cocked and menacing stares; death at the end of each. He felt cold to the bone beneath the suit.

The population of soldiers grew thicker as they neared the city centre, they were on every street, standing or sitting around the abandoned vehicles, cooking on open fires, sharpening swords and axes, sparring with each other or patrolling in great numbers. Like ants taking over a termite hill they were everywhere. Their silhouettes rimmed every building, flat or office block; every concrete monolith and filled every window.

Grimwolf realised that they could never have fought so many.

The Dark Army swallowed the small group as they rode through, heading for the tall glass building ahead. Red flames illuminating its roof and giving it a sinister appearance in the dimming daylight. Red like the devil, red like blood.

Grimwolf's heart was in his mouth, Elora had planned only to get in and reach Silk, she hadn't mentioned how they were to escape afterwards.

He swallowed his fear and put trust in the girl he loved. That was the reason he came after all. Even though she loved another.

The Captain led them into the car park beneath the glass tower. The compound full of armed men, takwiches and bulworgs amongst other unsavoury creatures. They dismounted before a huge rock troll at the building's entrance.

"What you want, human?" said the rock troll, spitting the name of the species as if it left a bitter taste on his tongue.

Thick granite muscles flexed along wide shoulders, biceps bulged as huge flat fingers gripped his halberd. His naked body blocked the entire double door giving Grimwolf a nasty suspicion that they were not getting passed him so easily.

"Got me something for Silk, something he's been after for a while," said the Captain, spitting on the ground at the troll's mammoth feet.

Grimwolf cringed as the rock monster's beady grey eyes narrowed on the man that led them here, huge square teeth grating against each other as his square head leaned closer, dwarfing the man.

"Got 'pointment?"

"I've got a bloody open invitation you stupid brick! Let us in or I'll make you fodder for the catapult."

Grimwolf gripped the box tighter feeling the approach of an ugly fight and sensed Weakest crouching low, readying himself for the same onslaught. This would be the end. Death in a car park, hundreds of miles from home in a cold concrete city amongst the enemy.

"Dat's where my brother ended up. Flung over wall at da siege in Cragghuff. Smashed he was, putting a hole in one o those sloping towers them craggys likes building."

"Plenty of walls around here that could do with holing," added the Captain, his hands caressing the stock of his rifle.

After a moment of mulling over the words the troll stood aside and let them pass. His gaze cast down in a sorrowful stare, probably remembering his sibling and feeling the loss, if rock trolls were capable of such feelings.

Grimwolf followed the Captain into the huge glass building, an overwhelming sense of dread hanging around his neck as the impending doom glared back from the floor that was filled with soldiers and more rock trolls.

Untroubled by the sharp weapons and hostile stares, they were led to a steel room. Small and cramped the tiny chamber had barely enough room for himself, Weakest and the Captain - let alone the dwarf with the huge wooden mallet.

"Silk's floor," ordered the Captain.

"Aye," replied the dwarf, pulling a lever set into a machine attached to the steel wall.

A loud metallic clunk started a cog spinning around that fed a chain onto a bigger cog. Grimwolf got the impression that larger chains and cogs were working outside the room as the whirring of machinery appeared to echo from above.

"Clear the door," shouted the dwarf, then picked up the mallet and struck a thick pin. It released the rope it was holding and the whole steel room juddered before

Grimwolf felt his chest being forced through his stomach.

Almost dropping the box, he watched in disbelief as the tight chamber swiftly rose, the floor they were on disappearing below them. Weakest darted away from the open doorway in fear of losing his tail between the huge blocks of concrete and black cables that whooshed passed.

"This human elevating machine was a wonder in itself working from Earth magic," explained the dwarf. "Me and the boys spent weeks working out the chains, gears and pulleys." He scratched at his beard with a child-sized chubby hand while working a lever with his other. "It takes a god's age to reset the counterweights too. Trolls are the only things that are strong enough to wind em back down."

Floor after floor zipped by, flames from sconces illuminated the presence of men or takwiches everywhere in the huge building. Each level another barrier to be breached in their attempt to escape. Grimwolf glanced at the wooden box he carried and gritted his teeth.

"Hope you know what you're doing, Elora," he whispered.

With a jolt that caused Weakest to leap a foot in the air, the chamber halted.

"You'd best get out before the counterweights are unhooked," advised the dwarf, sniggering as the bulworg landed and leapt through the doorway. Grimwolf swiftly exited, not wanting to travel in the cramped box room again.

Striding purposefully down the expensively adorned corridor, the Captain puffed his chest out, licked his fingers and brushed them through his beard - hacked up phlegm, was about to spit it on the plush carpet but thought better of it. Swallowing it down he paused outside a guarded door.

"Tell Silk, I've got what he wants. I've brought the djinn," he said to the takwich that stood to attention outside a door.

The takwich nodded as he instructed them to wait there. He disappeared into the room for a few moments before reappearing, a huge man in a black suit at his side. He spoke in the clicking language of the takwiches before seeming to remember he was addressing a human.

Ignoring the Captain, he stared Grimwolf up and down as if sizing him up. "Who are you?" asked the takwich, who was almost as big as the rock troll and twice as nasty. Grimwolf guessed he was a personal bodyguard or manservant to Silk.

"Grimwolf," he replied, attempting to pronounce his name with a mean edge, but feeling like a chicken that had wandered blindly into a fox's den.

"Never seen you before."

"Why would you have? Don't suppose you get to the front lines when you're wiping Silk's arse." Inside his armour Grimwolf flinched. It was a hair's breadth of a line between being tough enough to gain the respect needed or being seen as an arrogant bigmouth that needed knocking down a peg or two.

The bodyguard's black suit tightened as he folded his huge arms, his shirt collar stretching to accommodate a neck thicker than his head. "Inside," he growled.

Grimwolf straightened up as he stepped passed him, Weakest was close to his heel.

"Not you," snapped the bodyguard.

187

Grimwolf turned to see the Captain being pushed back into the corridor, hurt contorting his features as the door slammed in his face.

"This way," growled the huge man, ushering them into a large room that must have taken up the greater portion of the tower's floor. A crystal chandelier hung from the centre of the high ceiling, flames flickering from hundreds of candles and reflecting from the glass walls that stretched down two sides. Beyond the walls Grimwolf could make out the tombstone skyline of London's buildings with its flat, steeple or domed roofs stretching away into the night. The walls which were not glass were a rich mahogany, gilded with gold to match the frames of expensive oil paintings that were hung up, depicting various countryside scenes or the heads of lavishly dressed people from a long ago era. Grimwolf didn't care, his eyes only grazing the furniture of the room before falling on the large oak table at its centre; frost coated runes carved around the edge, the white standing strikingly out against the dark wood. In the middle of the table lay the remains of what was originally a man. Or something that was roughly the shape of a man.

The skin had been removed and left in clumps, blood drying in congealed pools. Swollen red muscle clung to bones and along one arm it had been carved away leaving a skeletal hand. A mask lay across the dead face, made from thick green scales that followed the contours of a jaw line and down the neck with no apparent join. Then he realised it wasn't a mask. The dead creature had actual scales instead of skin.

"Charwigg's work," offered the bodyguard as they passed the table. "She's been torturing that Dragon

Guard for days. Extracting information on how to reach Grycul through the mountain they occupy."

Grimwolf had heard stories about the dragon guard. Originally men that were left to guard the mighty Grycul who was chained to a mountain for her own protection. But as the thousands of years passed, living in close proximity to the large dragon, the men slowly changed into scaled beings as ferocious as Grycul herself. Even the armour and shields were carved with thick fireproof scales that the dragon had shed over the years. A few hundred of them still remained, guarding the mountain and setting traps so nothing could get near Grycul until Solarius himself rises to free her. Which, now thanks to Elora, will never happen.

Pulling his eyes away, he fought the rising nausea. What that poor soldier must have gone through at the hands of this Charwigg, was a whole new level of hell. It took a special kind of evil to carry out what she had done. He just hoped he would never have the misfortune to meet her.

The large takwich knocked on a door, paused a moment and then entered, gesturing for them to follow.

This room was half the size of the previous one, with a smaller table littered with maps and scrolls instead of a tortured carcass. Lamps burned along the walls, fighting back the night that blackened the outer glass wall. An aged man slowly turned from staring through the window to regard them with dead eyes. His thin mouth curling into a grin as he glanced at the box.

"It is a rare treat that somebody brings me a gift without an order. Initiative is a scarce commodity amongst the Dark Army," said the old man.

He addressed his bodyguard and made several clicking sounds before returning his attention to them. "Do you know who I am?"

The bodyguard slammed the door before crossing the room to stand beside his master.

"Silk," Grimwolf said, looking the old man up and down yet saw nothing special about his appearance, although he sensed a sinister energy radiating from the Lord of the biggest land army this world had ever seen. What was he expecting to see, a giant of a warrior all buffed up in armour and bristling with weapons? No, this was the first takwich to break through the barrier from the Shadowlands. He would have possessed the first body available, even if it was old and frail.

"That I am, but I know nothing of you gift bringer," Silk said, slipping silently closer and placing his aged hands on the table, eager eyes fixed on the box. "Yet here you are, appearing from nowhere and commanding the biggest bulworg I've ever seen. Do you have a name?"

"Grimwolf," he answered, leaving Weakest's name out of the conversation. He may not recognise the beast but may have heard of the bulworg.

Taking a step to the table he placed the box before Silk.

"Grimwolf? Not a name I'm familiar with, what about you, Charwigg?"

"Norse legend," came a voice from behind him, startling his heart into a double beat.

Grimwolf slowly turned to see a dark-skinned woman leaning lazily against the wall; bare arms folded as she stared him over with wide black eyes - the lanterns seeming to burn brighter within their inky reflection.

Where the hell had she come from?

She wore what seemed to be black leather bandages wrapped tight to her body, although from the grain of the material, Grimwolf guessed it hadn't come from cow hide; the leather being too fine and smooth. Human? He let out an involuntary shudder beneath his armour.

"You're a long way from home, Viking," Charwigg said, her voice sounding deep and throaty as she stalked towards Silk, hips swaying in a feminine swagger although not seeming quite right.

As she passed Grimwolf, she trailed a sharp-nailed finger down his breast plate, a crooked smirk twisting her face and forcing her flesh to pull overly tight around her cheek bones. Tiny lumps beneath her skin, like flowing beads of bone, shifted to allow her face to reform to its original shape.

From up close, Grimwolf saw that her skin was actually white and only appeared dark due to runes and symbols finely painted onto her body. The scroll work covered every inch of her, the runes seeming to move on their own, swirling and turning. It made him feel giddy when he tried to focus on any one spot.

Charwigg made a popping sound as she moved, like she was made of knuckles and joints that cracked with each step until she stood beside the box, her hand caressing the wooden lid.

"Did you get what you wanted from the dragon guard?" Silk asked.

"Not everything," Charwigg replied. "His body was tough, it took days of cutting and slicing to tease a song from him. In the end he'd given just enough to allow me into the foothills. I could work the rest out from there. Unless..." Her fingers tapped a beat against the box.

"Unless you had a wish to remove Grycul's chain?" chuckled Silk. "Perhaps, if there's no other way, but I don't want to waste a wish from the djinn just yet."

"If the djinn still holds power. I sense something beneath the wood, but I can't tell what," Charwigg said.

"We'll soon see." Silk then turned his attention back to Grimwolf. "And what do I owe you, Norseman? Why the gift?"

"A token of my loyalty. This world has fallen and it's time to choose sides," Grimwolf said, unable to come up with a better answer, he just hoped that Charwigg didn't see the lie in his words.

"There are no sides to this world, only Chaos. Yet you've proven yourself worthy, I can find you a place amongst my forces. Never let it be said that the Dark Army doesn't accommodate for those a little...different."

Silk placed his hands either side of the box, his aged face alive with excitement. "Now let us see this djinn."

The moment the lid creaked open black tendrils of smoke began to lick out. They stretched, twisted and reached towards Silk and Charwigg, weaving a random pattern as the dark vapour cast tiny red embers that burned the air.

Grimwolf took a cautious step back, silently slipping his sword from its sheath as all eyes were on the djinn. He cast a glance at Weakest who had crept behind the bodyguard.

Things were about to get ugly.

Chapter 12

Jack-in-a-Box

Blinded inside the cramped confines of the box, Elora could only listen as the journey unfolded. The sound coming to her, not through her ears but arriving within her mind in perfect clarity. The same way in which she felt Grimwolf's actions as he delivered her, sensing his fear and trepidation in his thumping heart. She had felt Silk's presence the moment they had entered the building and every other dark being in the tall hive; a tower of evil waiting for the command to kill, to spread Chaos.

Tension built inside her as she readied herself to strike, waiting patiently for the trap to be sprung - like a Jack-in-a-box waiting to make the innocent child jump.

The lid lifted and she spread herself out into the air, pushing searching fingers towards Silk. He hadn't changed since she last saw him on the canal bank by the Molly, her uncle lying unconscious at his feet.

Elora's hands were the first part of her to materialise, one grasping his neck as her body reformed behind him, her other placing the Soul Reaver against his back; blade biting into a kidney and ready to be pushed upwards into his black heart.

Weakest reacted before any of the others, rising on his hind legs and swiping a heavy paw across the bodyguard's head, sending the huge takwich crashing into the table and scattering splintered wood, maps and scrolls across the room.

A map slowly fluttered to the floor, Grimwolf's boots pinning it down as his sword cut up towards Charwigg's face, the point halting inches from her unnatural nose. She raised her hands slowly in surrender.

"Elora?" Silk asked, chuckling despite the sword digging into his flesh. "A dramatic entrance if ever I saw one, but quite unnecessary. If you'd wanted to visit you could have simply strolled in."

"Shut up," she growled, feeling her temper rising. Months of pent-up anguish finally coming to the fore, ready to quell itself against the man that brought so much pain into her life.

Increasing her grip around his throat she felt the cartilage in his throat sink beneath her fingers.

"What do you want?" Silk asked, the words no more than a painful rasp squeezed through his restricted windpipe.

Elora leaned closer to his ear, fighting the impulse to bite it off. "I want the Dark Army to halt its move east and to disappear back into the Shadowlands. I want every person that has been possessed by a takwich to be returned and every single life that has been lost to be given back."

"You want the impossible."

"I want you dead."

"That's the only wish likely to happen," Charwigg remarked.

Elora peered around Silk to stare at her. Her skin was like that of the demon Zionbuss, god-created, the writings that covered her body swam out of focus when she concentrated on them. The demon's face also seemed wrong. It moved and shifted beneath the skin as if a nest of beetles lived in there. Never resting, always on the move, making popping sounds with each crawling step.

"And what's your part in this, Charwigg?" she asked.

"What do you think daughter of Solarius? I was created by your father. Crafted by the God of Chaos, yet only as an after-thought, using the scraps and left-overs after finishing his Dark Army." She smirked, the skin shifting and popping to accommodate the movement. "A chaos of parts, a toy built on a whim, made for destruction and carnage. I am Chaos itself. The part I play is this, dear Elora – I am your sister."

"You're a demon."

"How delightful," Silk said. "You even bicker like sisters."

Elora applied more pressure to her hand and prevented the takwich from speaking.

"You're no more my sister than Zionbuss is my brother," Elora spat, willing herself to stay in control.

Charwigg laughed. "Zionbuss, the traitor who would have commanded the Dark Army before switching his allegiance. It is true that we were made differently to you, crafted instead of spawned. Yet we're all his children."

"Just say the word," Grimwolf whispered, edging the tip of his sword closer to Charwigg's face; ready to thrust his blade through her head. Yet the threat hadn't the power to rub the smirk from the demon's lips.

"Please forgive me, I've an errand to run, a dragon to free," Charwigg said, then in a single motion slapped Grimwolf's sword away with one hand whilst punching him in the chest with the other.

Elora watched in disbelief as Grimwolf propelled backwards into the outer wall, the impact of his body fracturing the thick glass before slumping to the floor.

Weakest suddenly launched himself upon Charwigg, his weight knocking her back a step while his vicious teeth clamped down onto her bare forearm.

The bulworg thrashed his head to either side but could not gain a hold, the skin seeming impervious to his attack. It was like trying to sink his teeth into steel.

Laughing, Charwigg aimed a brutal kick that sent Weakest tumbling onto his back, a yelp escaping his lungs as he slammed down. She raised her hand out, flexing her fingers and working the muscles in her arm.

"Only a god-created weapon can harm me," she boasted, eyes flicking down to Elora's blade. "Maybe."

Silk's body dropped like a sack of rocks as Elora slammed the hilt of her sword against the back of his head. Then turned the blade on the demon.

"Only one way to find out," Elora said, then as an after-thought added. "Yield?"

Charwigg shook her head. "Not likely."

Elora leapt towards her, swiping her blade through the air and aiming to slice the demon's head from her shoulders. But shifting as if made from water, Charwigg ducked and spun away, planting a foot atop Weakest's body and flipped over. Her passing foot caught Elora across the jaw.

White stars fizzled in the corners of her vision, the flashing images of the blow making her dizzy as she dropped and rolled away from a fist that skimmed passed her nose.

The Soul Reaver cut through the air before her, guiding her attack as she rose, yet met nothing.

Charwigg had already bent impossibly backwards, her spine folding over to avoid the sword. A loud pop, echoed around the room as the demon's body righted itself. Snapping erect like a cobra and elbowing Elora in the chest.

The force knocked her off her feet, the pain only registering as she landed on top of Silk's unconscious body.

"Had enough, sis?"

Charwigg approached casually, her skin shifting awkwardly to show a hideous smile.

"Not until you're dead."

Elora raised herself off Silk, kicking her legs around and feigning to swipe Charwigg off her feet, but changed to smoke in the last moment.

The demon was already leaping from her initial attack as Elora vaporised. She swarmed around Charwigg, flowing over her human skin bandages, smoke condensing into knuckles as she landed a punch against a mouth.

It felt like punching a bag of marbles.

Beneath her fist, solid beads of bone shifted, wrapping around her hand and began to crush it. Charwigg's facial features twisted until her mouth reformed over Elora's fingers.

She vapourised her hand before teeth bit into her flesh then reformed it to slap the demon across the other cheek.

Hoping that was enough to disorientate Charwigg and gain a few precious seconds, Elora reformed fully and thrust her sword down into the demon's chest aiming for the heart.

The blade glanced off a chest bone, barely grazing skin as Charwigg snapped her body rigid and drove the flat of her hand forwards.

Elora doubled over, the wind crushed from her lungs. She struggled to breathe as she clambered back to her feet, hands gripping tight to her sword but unable to stand straight.

"Don't feel disheartened," Charwigg said, playfully. "You're the first to ever draw blood from me."

Elora lifted her head to see a gash running up the demon's chest and over her collar bone. Dark blood already congealing in the open wound. Charwigg touched her fingers to the opening and held her hand out.

"See, I do bleed."

She wiped the hand down the wall, smearing a sickly black line with her blood.

"But I don't have time to play today." She dipped her fingers once again into her wound and painted another line below the first. "I have an appointment with Grycul." She drew a third line and formed a triangle on the wall.

Elora clenched her teeth and forced herself upright just as the triangle filled with an inky blackness to match the demon's eyes. It shimmered as Charwigg placed a foot, then a leg inside the gate.

"I'm sure are paths will cross again, Elora. Until then sweet sister, goodbye."

The demon dipped her head into the black triangle, followed by the rest of her body her sharp-nailed hand giving a final wave before disappearing.

"No!" Elora screamed as she pushed her body onwards, her slow steps gathering speed as she dived towards the gate.

White stars flashed cross her vision for the second time that evening as her head struck the solid wall.

"Ouch," Silk said sarcastically.

Elora pushed herself up from the floor to see the old man grinning maniacally at her, having already risen himself.

"She is special that one. Probably half way to Grycul as we speak,"

Elora spat blood from her mouth as she clambered over to Weakest, the bulworg only just coming around and shaking the dizziness from his head. Grimwolf was already on his feet, clawed gauntlets testing the chin of his wolf helm as if it didn't fit right.

Seeing that the pair were still alive, Elora stepped closer to Silk.

"Let's get this over with," she said.

Silk was still grinning as she placed the tip of her sword beneath his chin and forced his head up. One thrust, one flick of the wrist and they could go home.

She leaned in closer forgetting the pain that came with every breath, her broken rib scratching the inside of her flesh as it flexed.

Sucking the blood from her teeth she spat into Silk's face, fire erupting as it touched the air and then burning his skin as it struck. His grin dropped as pain fed from the affliction.

Elora felt no satisfaction from making him suffer, but the other her - the darker her revelled in it. She allowed enough of the princess in to balance what she must do. Maybe that other her was closer to Charwigg than she liked but only evil would enjoy others to suffer.

"Tell me how to stop the Dark Army. How do I purge my father's forces from this world?"

Her blood had finally stopped burning leaving his aged face red and blistered.

"That power is already with you," Silk answered, "I have no real command over your father's army. Chaos rules. Only Chaos can set them free."

"You're not making any sense," she said, applying more pressure to her sword; the tip breaking the surface of his chin, a tear-shaped drop of blood running down the blade.

He could cry every bloody tear from his worthless body and it still wouldn't put right what the takwich had done.

"Why are they heading east? What's there?" Elora asked, beginning to slowly twist her wrist; the tears becoming a steady red stream.

His eyes met hers, the whites had gone a yoke yellow, veins bulging as he winked. "Chaos. They know where it is, where to begin digging. Your father's last orders being carried out by the unstoppable for the unstoppable. You can't bring them back, not yet, not until it's found. Only then can you command your father's legacy, your birthright."

"What are they digging for?"

Silk's fingers curled around her blade, gripping the edge tight enough to cut deep, fresh blood mixing with the dark fluid that was already running down the Soul Reaver.

"Chaos. It will unite the worlds. It will set us free."

Then gripping her sword tighter he raised his head, eyes locked on hers. "You Elora, will set us free."

Silk buckled his own legs and suddenly dropped. The weight of his body driving his head onto the sword and as his last words finally met her ears her blade had already passed through his chin, the point exiting through the back of his skull.

Elora yanked the Soul Reaver out and watched Silk's lifeless body fall to the ground, a feeling of loss niggling at the back of her mind. They came here to kill the takwich, to rid the army of its leader. But now she felt more lost than before. More confusion as a myriad of fresh questions plagued her. And now as he passed into death Silk could no longer provide the answers.

A gentle tapping noise came from the door, bringing Elora out of her morbid trance. She turned to see a takwich poke his head around the door.

"Is everything alright...?" began the takwich in the butler's uniform, his expression becoming that of sheer panic as he took in the sight before him.

Grimwolf took a step towards the horror-struck man as he ran but he'd already slammed the door.

"Not good!" Elora hissed, joining Weakest as they chased after him.

They reached the corridor in time to see the takwich crash through the fire exit doors that led to the floor below, his shouts bouncing back up to them through the stairwell, followed by the clatter of a lot steel being drawn and rifles being cocked.

"Not good," Grimwolf repeated, echoing Elora's prior words as the footsteps of heavily armed men rushed up towards them.

Elora pulled the double doors shut as the head of a bulworg appeared, ascending into view above the steps.

"I'll hold them," Grimwolf said as he slammed the doors shut. He gripped the handles in his steel gauntlets as the beast collided with the door from the other side.

"I don't doubt it, but there's a rock troll down there, I can feel him," Elora said as she dashed back into the room they'd just come from. After a momentary search she returned with a table leg and jammed it through both door handles making it secure; that was until the rock troll punched through the wall.

"The elevator chamber," Grimwolf said, pointing down the corridor. "If we can make it to the ground floor we could fight our way out."

Elora glanced where he was pointing.

"Down the lift? No, there's got to be a hundred thousand men, bulworgs and trolls down there - not to mention the scraw-harpies that would pick us off in the open."

Thumping and crashing ensued from the fire escape, the doors pushing in and back with every strike and beginning to fracture the table leg.

"So you don't have an escape plan?" Grimwolf asked.

"I had, but it died with Silk."

She was going to use him as a hostage, believing that the army wouldn't move to hurt their leader.

"You?"

Grimwolf shook his head as the cables on the lift brought the top of the carriage into view.

"Maybe."

Elora watched as the armoured man lunged towards the rising lift, moving with a swiftness that belied his size in the cramped corridor.

He slid to a halt at the lift's opening just as the carriage revealed men tightly packed together, rifles pointing towards Grimwolf through the widening gap.

Two of them managed to get a shot off, the bullets harmlessly ricocheting off his armour as he sliced through the cable above.

The carriage juddered, the faces of the men taking on a worried expression before the lift dropped from view.

The cable that supported the counterweights beginning to smoke as it rushed through the pulley.

A sickening explosion erupted from floors below as Elora felt the sudden loss of dark energy; the life blinking out of the men in the lift. It was a strange experience yet one she couldn't ponder on at the moment.

Snapping her attention back to the here-and-now, she ran to help Grimwolf pull in the slack of the cable. She didn't know what he was up to but by the time they had coiled it all up there must have been over a hundred metres of it.

"You planning on climbing out of the window?" she asked as they rushed back into the room where Silk's body lay atop that of his bodyguard.

"Kind of," he replied, punching out the rest of the window that his body had already shattered when Charwigg threw him against it. Satisfied it was clear of glass he secured one end of the cable to the chandelier above and gave it a testing yank.

"Hate to ruin your plan, but we can't simply climb down," Elora said, taking in the sea of armed soldiers at the base of the building.

"Not down, across," Grimwolf explained, pointing at the multi-story car park across the street. "I just need you to take this over there and secure it tightly."

Elora took the free end of the cable, dropped the slack on the floor and taking three long strides dived out of the window.

She vapourised in mid-air, drifted across the street and on to a lower floor of the car park and landed with more force than intended - she was still getting used to her new ghostly powers.

Checking first that she was alone amongst the few cars, she threw the cable around a concrete pillar, tied a slipknot and pulled it tight.

Signalling to Grimwolf that she'd done what he'd asked she realised that he was no longer there, the window was empty. The sound of clashing steel broke through the muffled grunts and shouting of men as she watched shadows thrown by the chandelier, dance in the room she'd come from.

Elora leapt back out into the air, her body reducing to smoke as she flowed up the taut cable.

As she reached the window she saw that soldiers had infiltrated the room, a tangle of bodies already on the floor at Grimwolf's feet while he wrestled with the rock troll.

Materialising with her blade in hand she joined the melee, catching a sword as it was about to hit Weakest in the back. With her free hand she jabbed at the soldier's throat and collapsed his windpipe. Before his hands reached to his neck Elora had already spun onto the next target, thrusting her sword into the heart of a takwich as he brought a rifle about; his mouth opened in surprise, reflexes working his trigger finger and spraying the bulworg before him with bullets, both falling to the ground in unison - comrades in life and now also in death.

Becoming smoke to avoid a lethal blow from an axe, Elora flowed between the two remaining soldiers in the room, dancing out of harm's way as Weakest swiped a paw across the axe wielder's chest while she grasped his weapon and drove it into the other's shoulder.

The curved steel bit deep enough to almost sever the head, spraying blood against the wall as his body toppled over.

"We need to get out now," she shouted to Grimwolf whose arms were locked against the rock trolls, both struggling against each in a violent embrace while exchanging head-butts.

"Weakest, go," she ordered, nodding towards the cable.

The bulworg glanced at the cable then back at her, shaking his head to either side.

Elora realised that he couldn't use the cable as he had no opposing digits on his paws.

"Will you hurry up," she snapped at Grimwolf as she shoved Silk's body off that of his bodyguard. She undid his belt buckle and slipped the belt from his trousers just as the unconscious takwich was waking up.

She punched him in the face, putting him back into a sleeping state.

Flicking the belt over the cable, she waved Weakest forwards.

"Bite down on this," she ordered.

The bulworg complied, his sharp canines piercing the leather.

"Don't let go."

Elora shoved hard against the beast and watched as he slid down the cable, using it like a zip-line, his body dangling above the long drop at the mercy of the belt.

She let out a held breath as he landed safely, two floors down in the opposite building.

Turning her attention back to Grimwolf she watched him dig the claws of his gauntlet under the rock trolls chin and drive it in. Grunting with the effort, he followed it up with a final head-butt, the snarling wolf's helm crushing the troll's nose flat before it fell heavily against the doorway, partially blocking it up.

"Now go," she ordered, pointing at the window.

Grimwolf bounded across the room in three easy strides, leapt and grasped the cable.

Blue sparks flew from his gauntlets as he slid down to join Weakest.

"Stop her!"

The command came from behind the fallen troll as takwiches poured over the rock beast to reach her.

Lunging for the window, Elora vapourised once more, slicing her sword through the cable as she drifted down to the car park. The steel wire whipped against the building making a metallic crack as she landed between Weakest and Grimwolf.

"Run!" she shouted, her order echoing around the floor, bouncing off the vehicles and concrete pillars.

Leaning hastily over the wall she glanced down at the mass of soldiers sprinting for the car park's entrance; swords drawn, axes brandished, rifles cocked and evil intent drawing them on.

"We don't have long," she said.

Elora sprinted down the ramp onto the next level, the floor as dark and quiet as the one above, the rubber smell of old tires, oil and petrol hitting her nose as she turned the corner.

The three of them pelted along the floor, herself and Grimwolf pumping their arms for all they were worth, gripping tightly to swords while Weakest pounded easily ahead. His four legs making short work of the run as he changed direction to descend to the next level.

The excited shouts of the crowd drifted up, dulled by the concrete floors between them but sounding no less menacing. It grew louder with each level they dropped down and with each floor the Dark Army rushed up until she saw the tight mass of bodies raging ahead, the sounds of clattering steel, the eager screams of wanton violence urging them closer.

Ahead of her Weakest slid to a stop and raised onto his hind legs, head brushing the ceiling as he readied himself for the wave of oncoming slaughter.

Elora sprinted passed him but instead of turning down the final ramp and meeting death she ran on.

"Jump," she shouted as she dived over the chest-high wall, trusting that they had already come down enough floors so that the fall wouldn't kill them.

Arms wind-milling to keep herself from spinning head first, she watched the ground race up to meet them. A swifter death than if they had stayed, but most probably just as messy.

Vaporising at the last second she saved herself from splatting against the paved walkway. She became solid in time to see Grimwolf slam into a large white van beside her. He crashed through the roof with enough impact to blow out all four tyres.

Weakest landed in a large elm tree along the quiet road, its thick foliage and limbs snapping as they broke his fall. He leapt down, shaken but barring no major injuries as Grimwolf's sword pierced through the vans side and cut a hole in the thin metal, large enough for him to climb out.

All three of them stared up at the drop and at the soldiers staring back, some of them debating whether to jump themselves yet most disappearing as they raced back the way they came.

"We have to keep moving," Elora said.

She led them down a narrow pathway between the buildings away from the crowded streets of soldiers, their feet pounding the ground as they tore after them. The pathway opened out into office blocks and business holdings. Tall grey skyscrapers made from brick and glass, steel and thick plastics, separated by roads and intersections which lay shrouded in shadow; the traffic lights and street lamps were nothing more than shapes now, useless and as dead as everything else electrical.

Tearing towards them, erupting from hidden doorways and around corners were the Dark Army. The darkness seeming to regurgitate them from all directions at once, including from above.

Elora ducked and rolled as a scraw-harpy cut through the air where she had just been; so close her hair snagged the bird's talons, yanking her head back.

Its scream of triumph was cut short by Grimwolf's sword cutting the winged creature in two. Both halves crumpled against a wall leaving a trail of blood as they fell to the ground.

Scanning ahead Elora witnessed a swarm of darkness running at them; teeth, claw and steel glinting with what light the moon provided as Elora sought desperately for an escape route.

"Down there," she shouted, pointing down a narrow alley.

They barely made it in as the Dark Army pressed in behind them, bodies squashing together and jamming the opening so tight that the leading men were crushed beneath the weight of the crowd behind them.

Elora's hope that they might break free of their pursuers was short lived. Cutting around the corner were several soldiers running at them while screaming unintelligible battle cries, but their raised swords made it easy to understand.

Leaping in the air Elora turned to smoke through the front soldier, her own sword slicing his head from his body. She reformed long enough to kick herself from the alley wall where she cleared the thrust of the second, her blade meeting the top of his shoulder and gouging him on the back swing.

Carrying her momentum on she felt more than heard Grimwolf smash the bodies out of the way as he came through, following in her wake of death.

The third and fourth soldiers fell simultaneously after Elora rolled between them, ducking their cuts while severing hamstrings. She was already rising for the fifth when Weakest finished one screaming man while Grimwolf decapitated the other.

The next target she smashed in the face, launching herself before him. She parried his strike with her blade and drove her knee into his nose before landing, rolling and throwing the Soul Reaver at the sixth and final soldier.

The sword entered tip first, piercing armour and embedding half a foot into his stomach. Elora jumped on the falling body grasping her sword and yanked it free while flipping over and landing once again into a roll.

She skidded to a halt as she emerged from the alley, exhausted and panting for breath.

Weakest leapt in front of her ready to take down the next man, but back-peddled against her legs as Grimwolf paused beside her.

The alley had opened out into a high street. Shops with dark or smashed windows running along both sides, tall buildings standing behind them. Cars, vans and a truck lay abandoned along the road. At the top of the street was a cinema complex, its wide glass front, housing posters for the latest Pixar film due out soon which nobody would ever watch.

The sadness Elora felt for that fact was dwarfed by the immense fear of seeing what lay between them and the cinema.

The crowds of soldiers that had chased them down the alley slowed; their haste to reach their foe subdued in the realisation that they had them trapped.

As the first of them emerged, Elora slowly stepped away and following her unlucky companions put her back against the wall of the shop next to them. They faced the black sea of the enemy which stretched out in all directions.

They had unwittingly run into the entire division of the Dark Army. A mass of at least ten thousand stood before them, armed and ready.

Bulworgs covered the vehicles in the road, archers and riflemen stood beside them while sky-harpies turned the moonlit sky a darker shade of night. Movement from the roof tops above brought Elora's attention to the snipers and machine gunners getting in position to reduce them to lumps of meat.

"Don't fancy the odds much," Grimwolf remarked, his wolf's helm wandering over the vast army before them.

"I'm sorry I dragged you into this," Elora said, placing her hand atop Weakest's head to include him. "I think we've gone as far as we're going."

She watched the closest men advance, rifles levelled at them as row upon row of the soldiers formed a semi-circle, pinning them against the shop.

Grimwolf stretched his neck from side to side and gave a practiced swing of his sword before levelling it towards the crowd.

"To die amongst friends is a glory in itself, companions in life and into death."

"I would never have guessed you were a poet," Elora said, feeling a bitterness wash over her, wishing she felt Grimwolf's words in herself instead of a growing hatred.

"Yeah," continued the wolf-armoured man. "But I'm still going to take as many as I can of the bastards into hell with me!"

He screamed the last words, goading the enemy on.

Elora felt a shift in the air, a rumble that began at the centre of the crowd. A rumble like the entire army had begun to stamp their feet although they approached no quicker. The noise flowed over the sea of soldiers, deep growls and thunderous clashing; working its way from the shadows and drifting down from the night as wailing.

The noise was deafening, although Elora realised she was the only one hearing it.

Elora...Elora...Elora...The darkness spoke to her. Whispers from a thousand voices spiralling inside her mind, speaking not to her but to that other.

Elora...her name echoed out from the rifles being cocked, Elora...scraping from approaching boots, Elora...whispered as steel slid against steel.

"Elora?" Grimwolf asked, taking his gaze from the enemy for a moment to glance at her. "Your eyes are changing."

Ignoring him she glared across at the Dark Army, her father's army...her army. She felt the corner of her lip pull back in a snarl, her teeth bared like a wild animal.

"Kneel!" she screamed, the word wrenching painfully hot from her chest.

The order ripped from her throat leaving a burning sensation. The single word bouncing about the street reducing the entire city to silence as the advancing soldiers halted, bulworgs paused and nothing stirred for several long breaths.

A scraw-harpy suddenly broke the silence, cawing as it dropped from the sky; talons raised before it and aiming for her face.

The entire front row of soldiers fired their rifles, the cracks and thumps from thirty SA 80's filled the night as the large bird of prey was pulverised by the bullets.

It fell to the road before them, hitting the concrete with a wet thud.

Elora glowered at the scraw-harpy killed by its own side to protect her. Her gaze then cast up to the Dark Army as she watched them lower their guns, their swords and axes. She felt astonishment as they dropped to one knee and thousands of heads bowed to her.

Feeling a wall of heat behind her, Elora spun to see that the interior of the shop had burst into flames. White and red fire licking the air, scorching the glass with her at its centre.

No, it was only a reflection. She still felt the heat at her back, the fire in the mirror image was either side of her, flaming wings sprouting from each shoulder.

Mesmerised she watched as each wing unfurled and spread out, stretching further than two arms lengths. Her reflection grinned wickedly, crimson eyes sparkling with menace as she brought her wings together and buffeted the shop front and shattered the glass into sparkling splinters that showered to the ground in a random pattern of chaos.

Chaos. She spun back to face her army, the fear she felt evaporating along with her reflection in the glass, along with her fiery wings for they didn't exist outside the reflection, yet the sword she held was burning bright and fierce as the Soul Reaver lit the night.

The souls of every man, takwich, bulworg and scraw-harpy - every rock troll demon and grumpkin swam before her as she embraced their adoration for the God they followed, for her.

She wanted an army to rid the world of her father's legacy, a way to scourge the darkness from Earth. And now she had one, her own army and the world was hers. There was no going back to Rams Keep, back to Sibiet and that fool Drifid. No going to Rona to be judged. Who in Chaos's name were they to judge her? Fools, the lot and she would burn them, burn them all.

This was her world now, her arms of darkness that were spread across the lands to do her bidding.

For the first time Elora felt free, felt alive and felt the grin cracking her face - she was Chaos.

"Elora?" Grimwolf said softly. "Shadojak, we need to go."

Shadojak? And her life became her own again, the word hitting her like a slap across the face waking her from a delirium.

"Elora?"

"I'm fine," she answered, slipping her sword away into the smuggler's pouch as a vision of Bray flickered across her. She wouldn't betray him, wouldn't turn her back on the world.

"They won't harm us, put your sword away," she instructed.

"But…"

"I can't explain it now. We need to leave before they realise I'm not the person they believe me to be."

The dark soldiers parted allowing them to leave; heads still bowed, weapons lowered, claws retracted and teeth hidden - the army remained still.

When they had put a few streets between them Elora settled into a steady run, Grimwolf and Weakest easily keeping pace, although remaining as silent as the army they had left.

It suited her. She had many things to think over. The biggest riddle being Silk's words: Chaos will unite us, Elora will set us free.

Whilst she was that other her, she thought she knew the answers, understood what they meant and what part she played but her knowledge drifted away when she awoke back into herself and it now hovered just out of reach. Teasing; along with the truth of what her armies sought in the east. Something which was big, a weapon of some kind. A machine long ago buried and forgotten.

Struggling to see more into her mind the memory slipped away until it was gone, leaving just the ghost of a thought. Maybe if she became the daughter of Chaos once again she would remember. Yet she knew the idea was flawed. If she became that other her, would she have the strength to come back? - She didn't think so. If the Queen of Darkness regained control, then that was who she would remain and Earth would fall under her own hands.

No, she came to kill Silk. That had been done and although his death left more questions than answers the mission had been a success. She just hoped it would be enough for Sibiet and the rest of the Shadojaks.

Chapter 13

Beneath the Armour

Moon daisies slowly became solid as Elora focused on the blurred image in front of her. She was lying facedown on the ground, mouth open and dry, her cheek pressing hard against the gauntleted hand of Grimwolf. He too had succumbed to the harsh experience of traveling in the fairy circle and was on his back, wolf helm staring up at the sky as the dawn sun crept above the forest to turn the few clouds pink.

"Elora?"

The familiar voice of Bray, tinged with panic and full of concern refocused her as he gently pulled her from the cold ground and into an embrace.

"Are you hurt?"

The broken rib she received from fighting with Charwigg was now nothing more than an irritating itch.

"I'm fine, just tired. Have you been waiting here since I left?" she asked.

"Pretty much," he chuckled. "What else could I do?"

Grimwolf clambered awkwardly to his feet, as did Weakest who immediately sat back down again.

"Grendal?" Bray asked, astonished as the hedge witch and her son unwrapped themselves from the blanket that allowed them to travel within the fairy circle.

"Hello Shaigun," Grendal replied as she and her son Darrion stepped outside the moon daisies without any sign that they had suffered a discomfort.

As she passed Elora, she held up the blue and green blanket.

"Weaved by the God Alubis. I was reluctant to try it as I wasn't sure it was genuine, but..." she looked herself up and down. "It worked as good as anything god-created."

"I might need to borrow that sometime, then I don't have to watch Elora travel without me," Bray said.

"Come on," Elora said, taking Grendal by the elbow." Let me take you to the inn, Norgie will have breakfast ready and I need to sleep."

As they set off Grimwolf pulled her to one side and taking her hand dropped Ejan's bracelet on her palm, the hairs from Ejan's late husband's beard woven in an intricate pattern.

"I need to show you something. Meet me at the dungeon tower this evening - And bring Ejan, she's as much right to know the truth, if not more."

"I will. What's this about?" she asked, but Grimwolf had already begun to stalk away in the opposite direction, his red cloak billowing with each stride. She didn't even get the chance to thank him for his help.

The walk back to the inn had been slow and arduous. Elora was more tired than she'd ever felt before and was reluctant to let go of Bray's hand as he'd been supporting her, yet a red faced Sibiet met them by the well.

The Shadojak stood with arms folded, his Shaigun, Drifid, standing beside him, mimicking his master's stance. Their cold eyes regarding them as she approached.

Several children who'd been collecting water must have sensed a hostility in the air and made a hasty retreat to the inn, two of them struggling with the heavy bucket.

"Well?" Sibiet asked.

"Silk's dead," she answered, stopping in front of him.

If she wasn't so exhausted she would have felt satisfaction at the Shadojak's surprise. He'd expected her to fail or to not return at all.

"If you say so," Drifid said, sneering at her; his pointy face appearing even more pinched. "And Charwigg? I suppose you killed her too?"

"No, we exchanged a few blows but she escaped. She's planning to release the dragon, Grycul."

Sibiet's brows knitted together. "We'll see about that. If she succeeds then Earth will suffer greatly."

"We need to stop her." Elora slumped against the wall of the well, leaning back against the thatched roof.

"No. This is not our concern right now. You've done what you set out to do, the takwich, Silk is dead. Now we travel to Rona, your judgment is pending."

Elora wanted to scream in his face that he could shove the judgment where the sun doesn't shine, but instead pushed passed him. After all, she'd given her word that once Silk was dead she'd go to Rona. Yet the journey to London had given her even more incentive to stay and fight or at least to get answers.

"We go to Rona tomorrow," she said, walking away and not giving the Shadojak the chance to argue. She needed today to think and to sleep.

"Master?" Bray's voice sounded distant as if calling her from some far-away place. "Master, it's dusk."

Elora stifled a yawn as she struggled into a sitting position and when she opened her eyes she found that they were stuck together with sleep. It took several moments of rubbing them before Bray swam into focus.

"You've been asleep all day - thought it best that I wake you so you can have some food."

He closed the door to her old chamber; Cathy and her baby, Genella, had vacated for the day. He sat on the bed beside her, taking her hand.

"Have you been watching me the whole time?" Elora asked, feeling her face go red as she realised what a state she must have appeared.

Bray nodded, a playful smile forming on his lips. "I didn't realise you snored so loud."

Elora slapped his chest. "I don't snore. Do I?"

"Yep, thought we had a snorklepuss in here. You drool as well, by the way."

"Do not," she laughed, as she wiped her chin with the back of her hand.

"Thick long strands that ran from the corner of your mouth down the pillow to the floor." He chuckled, then pulled her into his arms. "But I still find you gorgeous."

She could stay like this all day, but knew she had errands to run, jobs to do and Drifid would be hovering around the inn ready to catch them in each other's arms.

"I took the liberty of running you a bath, Master."

"What, you think I smell now as well as snore and drool?" She mocked a shocked expression.

His lips touched the nape of her neck and softly laid a kiss. "Pretty much."

"Then maybe you should join me in the bath and help scrub me to your standard," she said, and laughed when his eyes widened in surprise.

Elora's smile faded as the events of the previous night entered her mind. Guilt at feeling pleasure in Bray's company as millions of lives suffered.

"Last night, before Silk died, he said that I had the power to control the Dark Army, to command them."

Bray shifted around on the bed until he was facing her. "How is that possible, Elora? The Dark Army is hell bent on evil."

"No, Chaos. And the takwich repeated the words you spoke to me, the same words spoken by my father in my dreams. Chaos will unite us and I will set us free."

Bray took her hands in his. "I can't say they're just ramblings, a coincidence. They're linked somehow, but since we don't know what they mean I wouldn't worry about it too much for now. We've your judgment to think about."

"And there was something else, something happened to me when we escaped."

She pulled him back on to the bed, wrapping his arm over her and interlaced his fingers with her own.

"We were trapped, thousands of the Dark Army pressing the three of us tight - we had no escape, but the darkness spoke to me, whispered my name and I became that other me."

"If she helped you escape it wasn't a bad thing," Bray reassured her, planting another kiss on her cheek.

"No, it was more than that. She commanded the army, they knelt at my feet, thousands of them responding to my order."

"There was no other way to escape, her actions - your actions let you live."

"A part of me wanted to stay. I wanted to spread Chaos throughout the world. I wanted to be Chaos."

"Yet you didn't, you came back."

Elora pulled his arm tighter around her. "I don't think I could do it the next time. If I ever became her again I wouldn't be coming back."

A loud knock on the door startled them and Bray jumped from the bed as Norgie poked his head into the room.

"Dinner's ready," he said cheerfully. "Oh, and Jaygen wants a word with you Elora, he'll be waiting in the stables."

"No rest for the wicked," Elora said as Norgie disappeared.

"Shame," Bray said, planting a kiss on her lips and attempting to lighten the mood. "I was looking forward to scrubbing you down."

"Another time."

"I'll hold you to that," Bray replied as he slipped from the room.

Elora bathed and changed into fresh clothes before dinner. Norgie had excelled himself by laying on a banquet-like feast and Elora caught his gaze more than once falling on Grendal. Could the meal be for her benefit?

Afterwards she excused herself and visited the stables as the sun disappeared behind the tree line.

She found Jaygen in a candle lit stall, brushing his black mare's coat to a glossy shine.

"You wanted to speak with me?" Elora asked as she stroked the horse down its slender neck.

"Funny, he wanted to speak with me too," Ejan said as she stepped into the stables and gently took the brush from her son's hands. "You'll not get her to shine any brighter than she already is."

Elora recognised a sadness in Jaygen's eyes, a firmness set in his lips which she hadn't noticed before.

"I ought to leave you two to talk," Elora offered, feeling that she was prying on their emotions. They must have a great deal to talk about.

"No, he wants you both there. Wants to show you who he really is," Jaygen said.

"Who?" Elora asked.

Jaygen met her gaze. "Grimwolf."

Ejan stiffened at hearing the name, narrowing her eyes on her son. "And what do you know of Grimwolf?"

Jaygen shrugged his shoulders as he stepped out of the stables, taking a lamp down from its hook. "I know he loves you. Both of you."

It was Elora's turn to stiffen. "What do you mean, he loves me?"

Jaygen didn't answer the question, instead pacing away towards the Keep. "Come, he's going to meet us at the dungeon tower."

They followed him down the dark lane, the lamp swinging in the gloom, the only light in the motionless night.

"Here," Elora said, placing Ragna's beard bracelet in Ejan's Palm. "Grimwolf told me to give you this."

Ejan remained quiet rubbing the bracelet through her fingers. "Do you think it's him?" she said after a while. "Do you think it is Raggie?"

"How could it be, we both watched him die," Elora answered. "And besides, he says he loves me too," but she didn't say that out loud.

"But Ragna's body wasn't there when I searched. And his was easily the biggest, the heaviest amongst all the other dead, his was the less likely to be dragged off."

"Well, we're about to find out. Just don't let hope run away with you. If he is Ragna, he would have revealed himself before now."

"Perhaps," Ejan said, tying the bracelet around her wrist. "But if it is him, I'm going to kill him."

Jaygen led them through the ruins of the keep stepping through the maze of broken stone and passageways with the confidence of someone who knew the place like the back of his hand. They finally arrived at the dungeon tower, the huge buckled door laying on the ground; years of neglect and rot having destroyed what battering rams never could.

"So where is he?" Ejan asked, impatience thick in her voice.

"Below," Jaygen said, descending down the stone steps and into the chamber beneath the tower. Shoving an old table aside he opened the trap door that lay hidden and disappeared down the spiral staircase that fed into the dungeons and the labyrinth of tunnels that spread out beneath Rams Keep.

They continued below the dungeon level and passed another darker tunnel, Elora and Ejan stayed close to Jaygen, his lamp the only source of light casting an amber glow onto the damp stonework.

When they reached the bottom the staircase carried on spiralling down into dark water. Elora was glad they didn't need to drop into it, she was cold enough as it was.

"This way," Jaygen said, leading them down a musty smelling tunnel.

Splashing through puddles that lay stagnant on the tunnel floor they followed the light, Elora noticing that the walls were more dirt than stone with sharp stalactites dripping a milky liquid from the arched ceiling above.

"I thought these tunnels had caved in years ago," Ejan said, her words appearing loud in the confined space.

"Some have, but several more exist with intersections that lead back into chambers that have survived."

"And you know your way around them all, because...?" Ejan asked, her motherly annoyance coming through at her son for putting himself in danger.

"Da, showed me a few - I found the rest myself."

They passed through a doorway that was missing a door and led into a square-shaped room. Dirt and dust piled high in each corner, broken boxes; wood long ago rotted lay in heaps against one filthy wall.

Jaygen crossed the space to a hole in the opposite side, the brick work smashed through leaving a gap large enough for them to pass through.

"Mind your step there's a bit of a drop," he warned as he climbed inside. He held the lamp out to guide his mother through and she in turn grasped Elora's hand, not that she needed help, her eyes were growing accustomed to the dark.

The tunnel rose in a slight gradient, turning this way and that before opening into a larger space, this filled with ancient chests and crates, the wood faring better than the that in the previous chamber.

"What's in those?" Elora asked, curious.

"Empty mostly, a few pieces of rusted metalwork, cutlery, tin goblets, old coins. Nothing of any value."

The mouth of a cave gaped wide from a corner and the sound of running water met Elora's ears.

"That way leads down to the gorge that runs outside Rams Keep. Da told me he thought there was a secret passage that fed into the stream. I only found it a few months ago, the path passes through water-logged catacombs."

"Catacombs? I can't believe you've been digging around down here, what if you'd have been injured?" Ejan seemed less cross and more hurt at the fact he'd done it. "What were you searching for?"

"Da told me that Grimwolf was buried down here somewhere. Rams Keep was the last stronghold in a battle fought years ago, before the worlds had split. The legend went that the king at the time hired Grimwolf in desperation; a final attempt at keeping his kingdom - I just wanted to see if the stories were true."

"So why did he think he was still here? I mean, that war must have been fought thousands of years ago," Ejan said, her scepticism was shared by Elora.

"Da said this is where his stories ended. The legend went that after the great war Grimwolf remained at Rams Keep after falling in love with a princess."

"And they lived happily ever after?" Elora chuckled. "Just like a fairy story."

"Well, this story was true," Jaygen replied as he pushed open a solid oak door, the hinges appearing to be oiled and well maintained. "I found him."

They entered a large circular chamber, burning torches slotted into the wall revealed the dry stone work. Tall posts jutted up from the ground, the wood chipped and gashed away as if some animal had taken its anger out on them and at the centre of the chamber stood Grimwolf. The flaming torch light reflected from his armour, the slits in his snarling wolf helm regarding them coolly.

"Raggie?" The name tumbled from Ejan's lips, barely a whisper but it was loud enough to fill the room.

Grimwolf remained silent and motionless as Jaygen placed his lamp upon a stone box and approached him.

"He's not Da," he said.

Jaygen reached up, his finger releasing the catch on the helm which was in the shape of one of the teeth. The visor sprung open to reveal it was empty.

Elora released the breath she didn't know she had been holding. Was Grimwolf a ghost, a spirit that only occupied the armour in times of need? It would explain why he was thousands of years old.

Jaygen twisted the wolf's head and it came away from the body so the suit appeared decapitated.

"I don't understand," Elora asked. "Where is he, where's Grimwolf himself?"

Placing the helm down beside the lamp, Jaygen tapped the stone box. "In here."

Now Elora had a better look at the box she realised that it was a coffin; a faded wolf carved into the stonework and script written in an old language that may have been Latin.

"I found this chamber, this tomb by accident. The door had been bricked over with only a steel emblem of a wolf's head no bigger than a coin, inserted in the wall. When I pried it out with a knife some of the brick work fell away to reveal the door coated in wax."

"So that's why the door hadn't aged," Elora said, staring at the coffin containing Grimwolf.

Jaygen nodded. "I think the king had it sealed that way to preserve the suit."

Elora watched as he unclasped the red cloak from a shoulder plate and stepped behind the armour to fiddle with other clasps.

"Am I missing something?" Ejan asked. "If he's been dead for so long who's been walking around in that...."

Ejan's words ended as she watched her son step into the armour and refasten the cloak. He flexed the claw like gauntlets and grasped the wolf's helm before slipping it over his head and closed the visor.

"I'm Grimwolf," Jaygen said, his voice now a full octave lower and sounding gravelly.

Memories suddenly clicked into place in Elora's mind. The nights he'd spent by himself, hidden even from Norgie, the injuries she'd seen on his back and neck that first night she returned from Thea. His knowledge of Rams Keep and how he managed to sneak inside the inn to place flowers beside her without raising suspicion.

"That explains the genellas then," Ejan said, placing a hand atop the deadly gauntlets. "I really believed you were Ragna." A tear ran down her cheek and Jaygen caught it on his claw with a delicateness that belied the suit. "Your Da would have been proud."

"When I finally pulled the bricks away and opened the door, I knew I had found him. This armour was propped up against a post, un-aged and without a blemish; not even dust lay on it. It took me days to find the catch on the helm to open it." Jaygen opened and closed his claws, bringing them up to his visor. "But once I did the rest was easy and before I knew it I was in the armour - I was Grimwolf."

"And these marks in the wood?" Elora asked, running her fingers over the damaged posts that stuck up from the ground.

"I brought them in afterwards for practice. I spent hour after hour, night following night in here, swinging the sword, building muscle memory, teaching myself and

227

practicing what you and Da had already taught me about swordplay."

"Why now? Why didn't you tell me before?" Elora asked.

"Because to you I was just Jaygen, the stable boy. In this suit I was something more, a man, a warrior. I thought you'd look at me differently; the way you look at Bray."

Then it clicked. His words only a couple of hours before, 'he loves both of you'. Jaygen had strong feelings for her.

"You're leaving for Rona tomorrow and I wanted you to know the truth before you left."

Elora was unable to see his face but heard the sadness in his voice. He loved her or at the least he thought he did. Yet he was only fifteen, barely a man grown; surely it was more like a first crush. After all, he didn't get chance to see many girls while growing up at Rams Keep.

She was desperate to say something, to explain she didn't feel the same way about him, but he beat her to it.

"You love Bray, I know. I could never be him." He took a deep breath and picked up the lamp. "Come, I'll show you the way out."

Chapter 14

Passage through the Shadowlands

The dark grey cloud that had been looming above the inn all morning had finally burst, saturating the forest and the small group of people who gathered around the great oak.

"Is this some kind of trick? I don't see a gate?" Sibiet said, his mood matching the weather. "Take note, Flek - she wishes to deceive you further by saying she has lost the portal to the Shadowlands."

Elora offered him a smile as beads of rain water gathered on his turban before running down his nose.

"Do you think I would leave the gate open; visible so anyone could just walk in or anything to crawl out?" she answered She pulled down the large limb of the tree until it touched the dirt where Bray had hammered a stake through its forked branch to hold it in place. It formed a triangle with the trunk, branch and ground.

Elora produced salt from a pouch she held and sprinkled it along the branch and soft earth before shaking some onto the damp bark of the trunk. When the mineral overlapped and made a complete circuit it began to crackle, like static from an old radio.

Elora took a step back as the triangle instantly filled with an inky blackness, shimmering like polished onyx.

"Impressive," Flek said, touching the substance with his finger, the digit partially disappearing until he pulled it out.

"Déjà vu," Norgie remarked as Elora felt his arms crush her in a hug. "Same place as I said goodbye to you the last time."

Ejan joined the hug. "Same place, different Shadojak."

"Different girl, that's for sure," Elora agreed, hugging them both back. "You ok running things here? Captain Brindle and Smudge should have more rooms at the keep soon, so the inn will be less crowded."

"We'll be fine, it's you I'm worrying about," Ejan said, concern creasing her brow.

Elora shrugged. "It's out of my hands now, but I'm confident the judgment will be fair. I'll be back before you know it."

"What you deem fair may not be what I perceive it as," Sibiet said, copper eyes boring into hers.

"There will be nine votes, Sibiet," Flek cut in, as he took some of the sting away from the conversation. "And the Supreme counts twice."

The Shadojak snorted his disdain, glancing away as if he'd found something of interest in the forest's shadows.

Flek smiled at the group before turning to the oak. "Well, let's not make a song and dance of it, Rona beckons." The Voice of the Supreme gingerly placed a foot through the gate and when he felt solid ground confidently stepped through.

The six Shades followed carrying packs of food, clothes and water skins. They strode into the black triangle without showing any signs of fear; an emotion that was easily put aside by their harsh training. Drifid was next while his master, Sibiet waited for Elora to pass before him, his hand hovering over his smuggler's pouch.

She flicked her hood up, gave a final hug to Norgie and Ejan then waved out to Captain Brindle, Melvin and Cathy who pulled her baby in close against the rain. In the distance Elora could just make out the form of Grimwolf standing against the willow beside the lake, Weakest by his side. Elora thought it was for the best to leave the bulworg behind under his care. The pair seemed to get on with each other and she trusted them both to protect the keep and all those she was leaving. Jaygen hadn't wanted to wave her off or even say goodbye. Maybe he felt stronger in the armour, she gave them a nod, then stepped through the gate and into the Shadowlands.

The bright vista full of black mountains and cracked bedrock, reduced Elora's vision to slits. Red dust instantly clung to her damp clothes and made Sibiet and the Shades appear like the terracotta soldiers she'd once seen in pictures.

"So where's the Necrolosis?" Sibiet asked, steam rising from his turban which had gone a shade of pink.

"Zionbuss wasn't expecting us, we may need to find him and his ship," she answered as she strode off, skirting the edge of a deep gorge that swept down to cracked plains - the same route they had made the last time she entered this barren wasteland.

Gravel and dust ground under foot as the group followed after her, Bray now at her side.

"Will it really be that easy?" he asked, checking behind him and making sure his words were not heard by the others.

"Zionbuss will know I'm here," she said, removing her hood and baring her face to the baking air. "I just hope he's the only demon in the area."

She scanned the ridge ahead and could just make out the chimney stacks protruding from the ground; dark red rocks silhouetted against a lighter red sky. She had forgotten how everything was in shades of reds and oranges. At least there were no dots of black on the flat cracked lands below, which would indicate soldiers of the Dark Army. The last time she was here there had been a sea of them.

"Keep clear of the chimneys," she warned the others as they passed between the tall structures.

Drifid scowled at her as he strode closer to a smoking stack, showing that he wouldn't be taking any warnings from the likes of her.

The chimney chose that point of time to cough and splutter before spitting a head sized lump of lava from its smoking top. Drifid yelped as he jumped back, the liquid rock striking the ground where he had just been and splattering against the charred stack.

Elora faced ahead to hide the grin spreading on her face and heard Bray chuckle. He gave her a wink and shared a rare smile as Sibiet cuffed his Shaigun on the side of his head.

"Wake up boy. This cursed land is hers. If she says to stay clear, you damn well will." Sibiet snapped.

"Yes Master," Drifid replied.

Elora could almost feel the Shaigun's scowl deepening as his eyes glowered into her back.

As the chimneys began to thin out she saw mounds of red dirt on the ground and dust that had been swept up in knee-high drifts against man sized shapes. Elora slowed her pace, these were not here before.

The wind teased away the top layer of dust as she passed the closest mound, revealing rusty coloured fur.

Her blade was in her hands before her next heartbeat. The scraping of steel behind her indicated that her companions had also brought their arms to bear.

"What is it?" Flek asked. The only person in the group without a sword in hand.

"I don't know," Elora answered, taking a step closer and prodding the furry lump with the tip of her blade.

The Soul Reaver pushed easily through the skin and struck bone, yet the creature or whatever it was didn't move. It was dead.

She withdrew her sword and nudged the mound with her boot. Dust fell from the beast in large clumps to reveal the remains of a bulworg. Dry and wasted it was nothing more than a furry sack of bones, its teeth long ago fallen from its skull where a yellow cheekbone poked through the paper-thin flesh; an old arrow imbedded in an eye socket.

Bray kicked another mound, the dust falling around his feet to reveal another bulworg, its head removed from its shoulders and sitting skinless by its ribs.

"These are the bulworgs we killed when we were last here," Bray said, returning his sword to his smuggler's pouch. "See, that's Ejan's arrow."

Flek nudged another shapeless lump, dirt shifted to reveal a skeletal muzzle. "But these were killed a long time ago, years even."

With no immediate threat Elora slipped her own sword away. "Time works differently here. Months have passed since we killed these, but months on Earth and Thea could mean decades in the Shadowlands."

"So that's how you can deliver us to Rona so swift," Flek said. "It's relative to where you are. We could spend half a year wandering through this baking desert and only days would have passed in the worlds. Remarkable."

"It may have escaped your notice Voice, but we only have provisions for a few days and I see no rivers, lakes or even clouds in this hell. Which means no water," Sibiet said, scanning the area before them. "Just dust and rocks."

"That's the beauty of this place, we don't need provisions," Bray offered. "Do any of you feel hungry, thirsty?" He glanced around at the men, only a couple of the Shades shaking their heads no. "That's because your body stays in the same condition as it was before we passed over."

Elora nudged the bulworg with her boot and its skull flopped to the side.

"Unless of course, you get killed. Then the Shadowlands claim your body."

Flek shook his head in wonder. "So that's why the Dark Army has remained in prime condition, fresh to fight after so many thousands of years."

"Your father knew what he was doing when he created this place," Sibiet said.

Elora caught the disdain in his voice but didn't rise to the bait. Instead she kicked dust back over the body and continued walking along the ridge, following the dirt mounds of the fallen and trusted Zionbuss to arrive soon or at least hoped he would.

What seemed like hours passed by as they waited on the cliff's edge; Elora was sat on a black rock, hands resting on her knees as she stared out over the vast plains before her, searching for a white ship floating on a green sea but saw no sign of the Necrolosis. Doubt began to seep into her mind and pick at the edges of her hope. What if he didn't come? What if he was so far away he didn't know she was here or if Zionbuss did know and he didn't care?

The clashing of steel upon steel brought her attention to Sibiet and Drifid. The Shadojak and his Shaigun circling each other as they sparred; their huge scimitars spinning this way and that in a duelling dance.

The curved flat blades were constantly moving, cutting the baking air, balanced by heavily balled pummels. Elora marvelled at the precise and accurate cadence, the beat and rhythm to the pair. Even the Shades watched, nodding approval with each cut, block, counter block and parry.

Fighting with a scimitar was a different discipline to her own sword, which was more like a samurai. The footwork was also different, the position of the body which flowed around the heavier swords always moving, continually turning and spinning, whereas she would use her blade as an extension of her arms.

Sparks flew as their blades met, Drifid's sword making a whistling sound through the bullet hole that Slater had made, but being no less deadly for the effect.

Elora watched Sibiet change his step, lean forward and make a cut across, slicing the air between himself and Drifid. She recognised it as a ploy to knock the other out of sequence and the Shaigun fell for it.

Drifid's almost peaceful face changed as he too realised his mistake, but the weapon being as heavy as it was he was unable to stop its momentum. His blade found empty air as Sibiet slammed the pummel of his sword down on his Shaigun's arm, knocking his scimitar from his grasp.

"Stay focused, boy," the Shadojak growled. "Or I swear to the Mother I'll replace you."

"Yes Master," Drifid replied as he picked up his fallen weapon.

Elora thought that Drifid had fought well until then, but she knew from watching Diagus spar with Bray that there was always room for improvement and the lessons were always harsh.

Sibiet's gaze turned to a glower as they fell on her, his blade held in both hands, point almost touching the floor.

"Perhaps the girl wishes to take a lesson," he snarled, knuckles turning white as he took a step towards her.

Bray moved before she did, his blade already out as she rose from the rock, her hand reaching for the smuggler's pouch.

"Stop," Flek demanded, the Shades pulling their own swords free and stepping between them. "Any fighting between Shadojaks will be done during the judgement. Not here and not now."

Sibiet's copper stare still bore into hers brimming with vehemence and burning with fury. Elora could taste his passion rising, the hate spreading from him and she readied herself for an attack, her finger and thumb spreading to open the smuggler's pouch - she also felt that other her wanting this to happen, goading the incensed Shadojak on and felt the beginnings of a smile forming on her lips.

Elora spun to face the other way and forcefully folded her arms. If she allowed the daughter of Chaos to take over here in the Shadowlands, in her father's creation; she would never gain control again.

"Very well," Sibiet snarled. "But the lesson will come, the punishment too."

She heard the dust being kicked up as he paced away from them, his Shaigun trailing after.

"It was most probably the hot blood of battle that brought that on," Flek offered apologetically. "This place, the heat and the death that it permeates only adds to it."

Elora took deep steady breaths as she listened to his words. The Shadowlands put everyone on edge. It picked at nerves, irritated the mind and brought the worst out of people. So why didn't it affect her in the same way? She even sensed an uneasiness from Bray, like she had on her previous visit yet she felt at home.

"What's that?" Flek asked, coming to stand beside her and stretching a gloved hand towards the black mountains on the horizon. "It's Grycul," he said, his voice rising an entire octave. "The dragon's been freed. May the Blessed Mother have mercy on us all."

Elora focused on where he was pointing. "Not a dragon. It's a ship. It's the Necrolosis," she said, watching it grow bigger as it neared.

Within moments the shape of the large sails came into view as it rode on thermals, the green sea of souls glowing brightly in the red sky.

Elora turned to the Shades, their swords still out as they watched the ship approach.

"Put your weapons away, he won't harm us," she said.

When Flek saw that they didn't react he gave them a curt nod and they instantly slipped their blades into sheaths.

"This Zionbuss, he's a friend of yours?" Flek asked.

Now the Necrolosis was almost upon them, the Voice had a concerned look upon his face.

"Friend? Perhaps. He's sworn to serve me - a way to escape the servitude under Solarius. Either way, Zionbuss is not to be harmed," she stared at Sibiet. The Shadojak grunted as he folded his arms, unimpressed by her words.

"As you say, Elora," Flek said. "We have no quarrel with the demon unless he harms us."

"He won't."

They watched the huge galleon descend, the patchwork of skins that made the sails being furled as the bone hull gently touched the cliff. The dark face of Zionbuss leaned out over the gunnel, black eyes twinkling as he looked down.

"My Queen," he said, deep voice rumbling. "I longed for the day you would return."

Beside him stood several of his sailors. The animated corpses were armed with bow and arrow, nocked and aimed at them. Zionbuss raised his arm and they lowered their weapons. He gave another order and a plank made from bones and rope was lowered to the ground by two of his dead crew. "And who are these strange fellows that accompany you?" he asked as he swaggered onto the ground.

"Hello Zionbuss," she said, staring up at the demon who towered above them all.

He was as big as she remembered. A huge slab of a man that dwarfed even Ragna, sharp horns either side of his head making him appear even taller. His naked torso and arms were thick with muscle and sinew - his skin, much like Charwigg's, was covered in ancient writing and diagrams that seemed to blur before her eyes if she tried to focus on them.

"Friends. They're escorting me to Rona," she answered, unsure if Flek or the Shadojak wanted their identity revealed.

"And what awaits you at Rona?" Zionbuss asked.

"Judgment," Sibiet said, sharply.

Zionbuss approached the Shadojak, a huge hand with sharp nails scratching his thick chin. "What kind of judgment?"

Elora saw no fear in Sibiet as he stared up at the demon, although the closer Shades took a cautious step back.

"The kind that has death well balanced on its scales," he answered, hand brushing his smuggler's pouch.

Zionbuss sniffed the air before him. "You remind me of Diagus and you've the scent of a Shadojak," he said. "I hate Shadojaks." His grin revealed large white teeth filed to points.

"Then you'll hate me too," Elora said, attempting to channel some of the rising tension. "I'm also a Shadojak."

Zionbuss turned, large black eyes growing wider. "How is that, my Queen?"

"I killed Diagus."

The rigging and bone planking of the Necrolosis creaked as nobody moved or spoke. Zionbuss frowned, Elora could almost see her words being played over in his mind - what if he abandoned them here? Could she find her own way back?

"Seems to me there's a story that needs telling," Zionbuss said as he dropped to one knee before her and lowered his head. "As always my Queen, I am your servant - the Necrolosis is at your service." He rose again to his feet, so tall that Elora's face came level with his stomach.

"My price is that you only tell me the story. Shadojak or no, you're still my Queen."

She followed him onto the ship. The plank bouncing with the weight of them, hundreds of feet up between the cliff and the Necrolosis. The smell of death and decay reached her nose as she stepped passed the sailors which were in various states of decay themselves.

Bray came to stand by her side as the rest of the group anxiously boarded, Sibiet scowling as he glanced over the floating vessel as if he would like to do nothing more than set fire to it.

Once they were aboard, Zionbuss had his men bring in the plank and the ship rose higher into the sky. The sails unfurled and snapped tight as the wind picked them up and began to propel the vessel.

Stumbling with the sudden motion, Flek gripped the side of the ship and paled. Elora smiled encouragingly at him as her hair flicked out in a breeze. It felt good to be on the Necrolosis once again.

"How long will take us to reach Rona?" Flek asked once he regained his balance.

Zionbuss shrugged his huge shoulders. "Perhaps an evening will pass in the worlds, but...a long, long time here. Might I suggest you make yourselves comfortable, we'll be in the air some time."

Elora still found it difficult getting to grips with how time worked in the Shadowlands, as she guessed the others did too.

"So if we took a slight detour, would that add much time...in the worlds of course," the Voice asked.

"Depends where the detour takes us," said Zionbuss. "Shouldn't make much difference outside the Shadowlands, but to us it will. Where's this detour?"

"If it's not going to take us too far out of our way, I would like to gather some intelligence on Grycul."

Zionbuss let out a loud laugh. "The dragon is secure - always has been and always will be."

"Even if Charwigg is planning on freeing her?" Elora added.

The demons laugh dissolved into a frown. "What do you know of Charwigg?"

"I've met her. Even exchanged a few blows before she escaped. She is planning on freeing the dragon."

"She won't find that easy," Zionbuss said, his hands resting on the gunnel as he stared out over the vast red lands, concern creasing the scroll-work on his brow.

"She had a Dragon Guard held captive and tortured him for information," Elora argued.

"And he gave away the secrets of the mountain?"

Elora shrugged, "She seemed confident that she would release her."

Zionbuss turned to face her, the grin returning but lacking the confidence it held before. "She will still find it hard. Maybe it would be wise to pass over the mountain. As it happens, it's not too far out of our way, but I'm not landing. Not if Charwigg is there." He put an arm, thick with muscle over her shoulder and led her towards the Captain's chamber. "Now about this story. How is it you are now a Shadojak?"

Sometime later, Elora couldn't tell how long, she found herself on the foredeck next to Bray, leaning out over the rail, hands close to each other's but not touching. With Sibiet and Drifid so close by it wasn't worth the risk.

She had spent a long time with Zionbuss, telling him all that had happened since she was last aboard the Necrolosis. He listened intently, never interrupting and only nodded, his face a mixture of anger, hurt and anguish as she told him how she was used to release her father and how he unleashed the Dark Army onto Earth before she killed him and before she killed Diagus.

"Zionbuss wants us to stay with him in the Shadowlands," she admitted to Bray. "He built himself a palace a long time ago. On top of a mountain that's only accessible by the Necrolosis. He tried to grow trees there once, with seeds he scavenged from both the worlds. It even has a spring with fresh water which he tricked a mage into creating."

Bray didn't say anything, he just continued to stare out, his face blank.

"Zionbuss never uses it – he says it's ours if we want it. We could live there until the end of time, literally."

"And Sibiet, Flek and the others?" Bray whispered.

"Zionbuss has his means to kill them - this is his ship and these are his lands."

"He's got it all worked out, hasn't he?"

Elora nodded. "It would be a ticket to a new life, a safe life together - forever."

Bray sighed as he turned to her. "You said no, didn't you?"

"Of course I did," she risked a glance behind them before placing her hand atop his and stared into those dark green eyes. "I made a promise, several of them."

"Not resting until you've saved the world, that kind of thing."

"Exactly. And I'm still a Shadojak," she let out a sigh of her own. "Maybe one day, we'll get our happy-ever-after. It's just not yet."

She let go of his hand as she heard footsteps behind her.

"We're getting closer to Grycul," Zionbuss informed them as he joined them at the foredeck.

Elora focused on where he was pointing and saw a lone mountain that was jagged and tall, black and grey - like a sharp tooth cast down from the heavens or a crooked tombstone that had withered with age. At its foot was a long shadow, a stain on the red ground that spread out in an odd pattern. Then she realised it wasn't a shadow at all.

"Are those soldiers part of the Dark Army?" she asked.

Zionbuss nodded. "They think they'll take the mountain by force. Using sheer numbers, but even if Solarius's entire army descended on that stronghold, the dragon guard would still not break."

"And Charwigg?" Bray asked, eyes glowering as the huge mountain grew bigger.

"If she's tortured secrets from a guard then she may get close to the dragon herself, yet she will still face Grycul's wrath and have no means to release her."

"So the dragon doesn't want to be released?" This from Flek who had joined them to stare at the approaching jagged tooth.

"A tethered bull will still attack the person who tries to free it. When beasts are full of rage they just see red."

The soldiers at the foot of the mountain slowly took shape. They crowded around several tunnels, spears and halberds thrusting at an unseen enemy in the darkness.

Other groups of men and bulworgs had attempted to scale the black rock itself. They failed miserably as the vertical face was unclimbable and any that managed to scale up even part way we're knocked from the ladders or ropes by rocks hurled down by the dragon guard.

"Higher," Zionbuss snapped as he commanded his crew.

The skeletal sailors jumped about the rigging, hoisting ropes and cranking wheels as the Necrolosis began to gain height.

"Higher," he repeated, then turning to Elora, explained. "Last time I was here the Dragon Guard attacked me in the air using a large scorpion and catapult."

And on cue, as if the Dragon Guard had heard Zionbuss speak, a loud clunk echoed from the mountain and a car-sized rock hurtled towards them. It passed harmlessly below the ship, wind whooshing behind it as the Necrolosis wobbled in its wake. The demon displayed his sharply filed teeth, grinning as if to say I told you so.

"Perhaps it would be more prudent to skirt around the mountain," Flek suggested. Elora heard the tinge of panic in the Voice's softly spoken words.

"No." Replied Zionbuss, grin growing wider. "We fly directly over. They won't fire above them, because what goes up."

" Must come down," Elora finished.

"Indeed, my Queen. And besides, it wouldn't be a clever move showing them the ship's broad side. That scorpion of theirs is pretty accurate."

The sounds of battle drifted up to them. Steel clashing against steel; men's shouts, animal screams and the wailing of the dying - arriving in snatches brought by the wind. Elora squinted into the violence, somewhere down there was Charwigg or had she already gained entrance into the mountain's secret passages?

"How sure are you the chain will hold?" Flek asked.

"It was forged in Valeria. If it had any weak links Grycul would have torn free long ago."

Elora scowled. "Charwigg doesn't need to break the chain, she just needs to dig the anchor from the rock. It's what I'd do."

She watched Zionbuss's grin falter as her words sunk in, then vanish completely.

"You may have the right of it, but she still needs to get through the dragon guard."

The ship's shadow passed over the peaks of the mountain, deforming and reforming with the cracks and fissures before becoming solid as it stroked along a charred plateau. At its centre was a huge creature. Its scales were such a dark green it appeared as black as the ground it crunched beneath large sharp talons. An oval body and slender neck jerked about, tethered by a thick chain, its wings buffeting the rock and sending clouds of dust billowing about as it struggled.

It paused, watching the shadow pass in front of it. The creature's huge head slowly turned up to face them, yellow eyes narrowing to slits as it opened a long vicious mouth; rows of sharp teeth visible even though they were at least a hundred feet up.

It craned its neck before rocketing it forwards, coughing out white fire in a roaring plume. The heat hit Elora just before she ducked beneath the gunnel as the ship rocked.

Flek wasn't as quick as the rest of them as he frantically flapped his hands against the flames on his cloak.

"If Grycul gets free then we are all doomed," he said, giving up on putting the flames out and just removing his cloak and throwing it overboard.

Elora risked another peek over the hull. The dragon stared up at them, tilting its head and baring teeth, yellow eyes gleaming with hatred. She sees me - she knows who I am, what I am. The beast's mind forcefully probed her own, Elora could feel a reptilian presence skittering through her memories.

The air suddenly grew tight around her chest and pushed in on her, everything and everyone becoming a dark blur as the world shrank to just the two of them.

With an immense effort she pushed the creature's mind back, anger helping her to drive the beast out of her head.

A scream ripped from her mouth as she slammed her mind shut. Grycul screamed simultaneously, fire once again burning the air as she roared.

Elora felt herself being pulled back from the side of the ship as flames engulfed the hull. "Elora, are you hurt?" Bray asked, worriedly.

"I'm fine," she croaked, although her head told her otherwise. It throbbed with a sharp pain, white heat pulsing with each heartbeat.

"No, you're not," he argued, then turning to Zionbuss. "We need to leave this place, now."

The demon nodded, a large hand covered in writing, fingernails long and sharp meant for ripping, for killing, gently rested against her arm. "Grycul can sense him on you, smell your father's blood in your veins."

246

The sounds of chain links snapping tight as the dragon thrashed against her restraints echoed up to her. An ear-splitting shriek closely followed by the thunderous boom of its feet slamming against rock.

"We shouldn't have come," Elora said, rubbing her thumbs against her temples.

"You're right," Zionbuss agreed. He yelled in his language and some of the sailors brought bows to arms and began to rain arrows down on the dragon.

The pressure in Elora's head suddenly lifted making her feel lightheaded. She struggled to her feet and watched the beast snap viciously at the wooden shafts as they came down around her to bounce harmlessly from her thick scales, but it was enough of a distraction to stop the creature attacking her mind.

A bugle was blown, the noise coming from somewhere inside the mountain and armed men began to run onto the plateau from several different cave entrances and tunnels, kicking up black dust as they rushed to surround Grycul. Elora thought they meant to attack her, thinking that some of Charwigg's soldiers had found a way through but she was mistaken.

They formed circles around the dragon, each man holding a large tear-shaped shield which was the same dark green as Grycul. They faced away from the beast to protect her from the arrows. Others knelt between the shields, while notching arrows of their own and began to send them arcing up at the Necrolosis.

"The dragon guard," Zionbuss explained as he signalled for his crew to steer the ship out of harm's way. "Tenacious little bastards. Their armour is made from Grycul's own scales as she sheds them. Not that they need it - they've been in the dragon's company for so long that even their skin has grown scales." He grinned. "So you see, Charwigg will find it none too easy, freeing her."

The sails cracked tight in a fresh wind, pulling the ship higher as they drifted out of reach of the arrows and began to put the mountain behind them.

"Why doesn't the Dragon Guard free her if they worship the dragon so much?" Bray asked, a question Elora was about to ask herself.

Zionbuss stared at the scaled soldiers, growing smaller by the minute. "Grycul is a wild creature, extremely dangerous and unpredictable. Without Solarius to control her she would burn everything. At least here they have some control over her."

Elora watched the dragon as they put more and more sky between them, sure that the beast was also watching her.

"Grycul needs to die," she said.

Chapter 15

Rona

Bray stood beside the portal, the wind curling the red dust from the runes that were carved out of the circular rock and forcing him to narrow his eyes. He watched Elora step through and was about to follow her when Sibiet lay a hand on his shoulder, pulling him aside from the black swirling gate.

"Tell me Bray, what are your plans after the judgment?" he asked, copper eyes staring after Elora as the tail of her cloak vanished.

"I will serve my master," Bray answered, deadpan.

Sibiet blasted air through his nostrils as he regarded him.

"Elora will not live beyond her judgment, boy. Don't be a fool," the Shadojak said, shaking his head.

"She will," he argued, wanting to scream it into the southerner's face, but restrained his emotions.

The Shadojak shrugged.

"Perhaps...maybe the spawn of Chaos can tip the balance in her favour, but I doubt it. And when her life has ended what will you do?"

Before Bray could argue further the hand on his shoulder applied more pressure.

"Don't scowl boy. All I'm saying is, keep your options open." Sibiet's hard face softened. "You've a real talent. One of the best Shaiguns alive and many would see you take the Soul Reaver. The Pearly White trained you well and it is only fit that you take his sword and become a Shadojak."

"I am not ready."

"Nobody is ever ready. Yet you've done the training, learned to control your emotions and you've walked the path of the Shaigun. None of these things the girl has done and that will reflect against her at the judgment. That and the fact of who she is."

The Shadojak raised his chin and glared down his nose.

"When the time comes, after the balance has being passed, the Shadojaks must move as one to take her blade - do not stand against us."

Breathing deeply, Bray glared into those mocking copper eyes.

"My master will survive her judgment."

He pulled his shoulder free from Sibiet's grasp and stomped into the portal, but not before Sibiet's final words reached his ears.

"We will see."

Elora pulled her hood down against the drizzle that clung to her dust coated cloak. The wind rushed up the bare hillock and howled around the bleak countryside teasing out her golden lock of hair and whipping it against her face. She tucked the loose strands back into her hood as she glanced at the portal, the grey rock barely showing against the darker grey of the sky - she couldn't tell if it was dawn or dusk.

Bray materialised through the swirling gate, closely followed by Sibiet. The Shadojak producing his sword and slashed it against the ring of glowing runes, the god-created metal causing sparks against the slate.

Instantly the portal vanished leaving scarred rock. The runes blending with the natural veins and grains, leaving it camouflaged from the untrained eye.

As Bray paced passed Elora she noticed him glaring at the Shadojak and sensed anger in him as if they'd just been quarrelling - what had happened on the other side?

She caught his attention and raised an eyebrow, but with a subtle shake of the head he indicated that it was nothing.

"Any ideas where we are?" Flek shouted above the driving weather.

"We're south of Rona, sir. Perhaps a day's ride," offered one of the Shades, pointing into the gloom.

Elora only saw sparse rolling hills and the occasional dark patch of woodlands in large fields crisscrossed with dry stone walls. As her eyes lingered she noticed a thick cobbled road stretching from one horizon to the other, cutting through the countryside as if a giant had sliced a mighty scythe through the land.

"There's a farm over the next rise," continued the Shade. "If my memory serves me well, there will be horses."

"Very good. Lead the way," ordered Flek.

The farm was small, a simple stone cottage with a thatched roof; smoke dancing out of the crooked chimney at the mercy of the wind. The door was already open as they approached, a squat figure silhouetted against the warm glow of a fire from within as a dog yapped at his feet. He stepped out of the cottage and levelled a large crossbow at them.

"If it's shelter yer after, there's a sheep barn over the next rise - ain't much but it'll be dry. If it's food, there's a little stew in a pot but not enough to feed all of us. And

251

if it's trouble you're about," he raised the crossbow into the crook of his shoulder, the steel point of the arrow catching a glow along its deadly edge. "The first one of you will get stuck in the face and I've three more sons with crossbows trained on yer."

"By order of the Shadojak you will lower your arms," Sibiet ordered, slipping his sword free as he approached the farmer.

"Shadojak?"

The farmer's eyes widened as he glanced first at Sibiet and then at his sword. "I beg your pardon sir, I didn't know."

He lowered his weapon to the ground as he knelt before them, bowing so low his grey beard touched the mud.

"Don't worry yourself," Flek said as he lay a hand on Sibiet's arm. "You were not to know."

The farmer's bushy eyebrows raised and Elora saw hope in his wrinkled weathered face.

"Now, I hear that you have horses," he said, a sly smile curling his lips.

"Aye," replied the farmer rising to his feet and not appearing so hopeful anymore. "Got two mares in the stable."

"Just two?" Sibiet asked, slamming his sword into his scabbard. "We have a pressing engagement in Rona."

"Sorry my Lord, there's just the two cobs and a couple of oxen for pulling the cart."

Flek patted the man jovially on his shoulder. "Then we'll make do."

"I need the...," began the farmer, but stopped his protest when the Shadojak clenched his jaw. "I mean; they are at your disposal sirs."

"Good. Now if you would be so kind, have your sons saddle the horses and ready the oxen and cart."

"I have no sons my Lord. Twas just a lie to put off trouble. You can't be too careful these days. Not with people robbing honest folk and the likes."

"Indeed. Well, point us in the direction and we'll saddle our own mounts."

The old man's gnarled hand pointed to the stables, his face twitching in a scowl as the Shades splashed through the mud.

"Is there no honour amongst people any more that they must result to stealing from the innocent and hard-working folk?" Flek asked rhetorically, bending to stroke the yapping dog which snapped at his hand.

"Appears not," the Farmer replied, watching his horses and oxen being taken away.

A short time later Elora was sat in the back of the cart with the Shades, being jostled about as the wheels found every dip and rut in the road while watching the farmer glower from his porch, gripping tightly to his crossbow.

"What will happen to his horses once we reach Rona?" she asked.

Bray flicked the reins in his hand but the oxen only kept to the same slow but determined plod.

"They'll be handed over to the Emperor's treasurer. He'll decide their worth and whatever cost the farmer will incur from their loss."

"So he gets paid?"

Bray nodded, yet is was Flek who sat beside him that answered.

"The farmer will most probably get them back with the next trader that comes this way. Along with a few coins for his trouble. In truth he'll be better off."

"He didn't look too happy about it."

"They'll always be resentment against the Empire, especially from the common folk. People don't like being forced to do anything, but a Shadojak can demand what they like with the power of the Emperor himself. Those that refuse will pay by death."

"That's awful."

"That's the Empire, but he'll be better off. The Emperor always pays his dues and with interest."

The sun rose as a pale disk above the rolling countryside, thinning the clouds that had drenched them to a scattering of white smears. A mist began to rise from the damp cart, the hedgerows and puddles in the cobbled road and from their saturated clothes. Even the oxen added their own vapour, sweat exhuming from their hides as they plodded on.

Sibiet steered his mount closer to Flek; Drifid flanking the other side and gloated down at them in the cart.

"I'm pressing on to Rona," the Shadojak said, a hint of a smirk on his face. "Your beasts are far too slow. With any luck we can have the judgement this evening."

"No, it would be better if we arrive together," Flek replied, adjusting his gloves. "I insist upon it."

"You forget yourself Flek. We're in Thea now and so your appointment as the Voice is over."

"My appointment as the Voice still stands until Elora is delivered to Rona."

It was the first time Elora noticed the Voice appear perplexed, his fingers curling into fists before he relaxed them and brushed his blonde parting aside.

Sibiet grinned. "We shall see boy, yet once through the Imperial gates you'll be no more than a manservant with less authority than a common valet."

The cob snorted as he kicked her into a trot, hooves flicking up water as they departed. Drifid left after him, but not before treating them to a mocking bow.

"I don't like this," Bray said, staring at the pair as they disappeared behind trees on the approaching bend. "They'll sour the judgment before we even arrive."

"You need to trust the system better Bray," Flek offered. "Although I surmise that Sibiet won't waste time giving his views to the others. Yet he is still a Shadojak, so won't lie."

"Just bend the truth to fit," Elora said, realising that today could well be her last.

"Perhaps, but don't underestimate the other Shadojaks and the Supreme himself." Flek said, turning in the seat to stare down at her. "They'll come to their own judgment after meeting you and hear what you have to say."

"And if they don't like what they see or hear? After all I am the daughter of the most destructive God the worlds have ever known."

"You're still a Shadojak." Bray said, offering her a sad smile, his green eyes alive with hope.

"That's right and with a great Shaigun to back you."

Flek gave the reins to Bray and pulled himself up before clumsily climbing into the back of the cart.

"Come Elora, you should be sat up front with Bray. Sibiet was right, I'm no longer the Voice so you, as Shadojak out-rank me; besides, you'll get to see this countryside and Rona itself is the most beautiful city in all of the Empire."

They travelled for a time without speaking. Elora watched the rolling hills and woodlands as they passed by; listening to birds, the creaking planks and springs of

255

the cart and the snorts from the oxen and attempting to let her mind wander from the judgment ahead. Somewhere along the journey Bray's hand had found hers. She squeezed it, offering him a reassuring smile while she swallowed back the fear and dread that filled her stomach. The impending doom was on the horizon.

"Rona," Bray said, nodding ahead.

Elora stared at the spires that towered above the next rise. Large gold and blue monoliths that scraped the sky, the sun glinting from hundreds of polished points and reflecting off thousands of windows. As they approached more of the city revealed itself. Tall arches, domed buildings and slanting roofs sat well below the monoliths but were no less beautiful. Elora squinted against the bright alabaster wall which surrounded the city and seemed to radiate with an inner light while the swimming reflections of a circular lake danced along its parapet.

The oxen pulled them across a bridge, its golden gilt carved in a flowing design of intricate flowers and ivy inlaid with precious stones. A structure which put the Tower Bridge to shame. Imperial Guards stood to attention as they rolled by. Tall pikes and halberds resting against the ground as they thumped fists against shining breast-plates.

"They're saluting the Shadojak," Bray whispered as he leaned closer.

Elora was about to ask which Shadojak when she realised that she was the only balancer here. Feeling like a charlatan she fixed a stern expression on her face and nodded to them.

Bray halted beyond a gatehouse and ordered one of the Shades to take the oxen and cart to the treasury to be processed, while she soaked up the sights within the city walls.

The opulence that was on show outside the city was shared within. Buildings carved from smooth soapstone curved along the street making up the shops and traders; from cobblers to silk merchants, beauty parlours to restaurants. Each structure varying in size and colour, displaying their wares and trades outside stained glass windows. The people that walked the marble streets and the traders themselves were dressed in equal splendour. Elora was amazed with the wealth on display.

"Come, Master," Bray said, guiding her by the arm. "The city is large and our destination lies to the land beyond the east wall, across the city."

Elora followed Bray along the street, the people around them pausing in their daily routine to bow or curtsy, making her blush with the attention. She was glad when they entered beneath an archway into a tall building with a large domed ceiling. Steam billowed out of long vents that ran around the roof in spirals.

People were queuing along a platform, much like that found in a train station. Angry glares soon dissolving as they neared, parting to allow them to the front. Once clear, Elora noticed that there were indeed train tracks running along the ground. They disappeared around sweeping bends in both directions. She was about to ask Bray what the building was when an explosion of thunder blasted towards them. She stared in the direction of the sound, hand reaching for the smuggler's pouch when a steam train clattered into view surrounded by a cloud of steam.

Brakes squealed as the wheels locked up, the huge steel beast screeching to a halt several feet passed her.

Elora closed her open mouth and stared at the train. It was similar to the old machines they had on Earth, yet this had a large cone-shaped nose and thick pipes that fed from what must be the engine, behind which sat a large silver cylinder. A thicker pipe protruded out of the top, curling over the drivers roof to funnel plumes of steam up towards the dome ceiling.

"What, you didn't think we would have trains on Thea?" Bray asked, raising his voice above the noise of the thumping engine. "Just because we don't have electricity doesn't mean we're not advanced."

He opened a carriage door and held it while she climbed in.

Crushed blue velvet padded out the comfortable seats, matching the plush curtains and trim. The golden sun of the Empire was stitched boldly upon every surface, reflecting the warm light cast by brass lanterns fixed to the mahogany walls.

Elora stared through the carriage window, watching the driver and an engineer as they attached a hose to the engine and locking it in place with a wrench.

"They're filling her up," Bray offered as he closed the door and came to join her.

Nobody else came into their compartment - it appeared that Shadojaks liked to be left alone or rather the people wanted to be left alone away from the Shadojaks.

"Where do they put the coal?" she asked, not remembering seeing the store of coal that usually sat behind the engine ready to be heaped into the furnace.

"It doesn't burn coal," Bray replied with a grin.

Now they were alone he slipped an arm around her waist. "They're pumping water into the boiler - ramming it in with huge amounts of pressure."

She watched as the engineer removed the hose and opened another smaller pipe next to the first. He then pulled thick goggles over his head and donned gauntlet-sized leather gloves as he placed a silver hose to the pipe. The man let out a sigh of relief as they two connected.

"Liquid fire," Bray explained. "Created by the spell casters and binders - pretty potent stuff. It reacts violently when mixed with pressured water and the steam produced powers the engine."

The carriage door suddenly swung open and Flek entered with the five remaining Shades. Bray let his arm drop from her waist before it was seen and offered Elora the seat by the window. She sat and returned her attention to the scene outside.

The driver and engineer unattached the hoses and climbed aboard the train. A moment later there was a loud clunk followed by a sudden cloud of steam that hissed out from beneath the wheels. Then they were in motion.

Bray sat beside her as the train picked up speed, the people on the platform becoming a colourful blur as they left them behind. She felt his body press against hers as the track took them into a bend. Her hand crept towards his but she pulled it back when Flek spoke from the seat behind her.

"The Emperor's at his city residence then," the Voice said, pointing out of the window.

The train was now out in the open and rising above the ground, the tracks taking them upon the city wall itself as they skirted around the perimeter at high speed.

259

The roofs rushed passed and only the huge monoliths at the city centre appeared still like giant pillars of gold and azure reaching into the heavens. From this vantage point, Elora could see another inner wall surrounding the base of the monoliths and a circular ring of sparkling water surrounding that. Inside the wall was a beautiful palace of light blue soapstone, appearing like something straight out of a fairy tale with peaked roofs, golden balconies and flowing flags depicting the sun. Between the tallest of the towers were bridges, linking the palace to the monoliths and at the very top of the colossal structures, silhouetted against the sun itself was an airship.

"Yeah, which means the brothers will be with him," Bray added.

"Brothers?" Elora asked.

"Quantico and Quantala. They're the Shadojaks appointed to babysit the Emperor."

"You don't seem happy about the fact."

Bray breathed out. "Your judgment would only go ahead once all the Shadojaks have cast their vote. I was hoping they were away so you might have longer. But it appears that Sibiet will get his way."

"Maybe," Flek said. "Although I imagine delaying the judgment might work against you. Sibiet is respected but not well liked - he's more akin to Diagus in that regard, yet the longer he has to grow the seed of doubt in others the harder it would be for you."

"Besides," Elora said, "I'd rather get this over and done with. The sooner I'm judged the sooner I can return to Earth; either with the Emperor's help or without it."

They disembarked from the train at the other side of the city and climbed aboard a stagecoach. The winding road they travelled on weaved between hills and over

260

rivers and farmland. After maybe an hour they turned off the road and down a track which ended in a huge stone gate, two Shades standing guard saluted her as they rolled passed.

The gate gave way into a cobbled courtyard, bereft of any ornaments or even plants and seeming a world away from the city she had just left. To the other end of the courtyard was a tall building, stone pillars erect either side of huge oak doors. It loomed three stories high and appeared as cold as it was grey.

As the stagecoach stopped before the building a platoon of Shades rushed out and flanked the carriage doors and at the head of the soldiers was Sibiet.

The Shadojak had been back long enough to wash, shave and dress in clean clothes and a fresh turban. That would have given him enough time to spread whatever rumours he wished about her.

Elora climbed out off the coach with trepidation heavy in her stomach, but met the Shadojak's copper stare - this wasn't good. A fact only made stronger by Sibiet's smile.

"What is the meaning of this?" Flek asked as he joined her.

"Elora's under arrest. The Supreme thinks it only prudent to lock her in a guarded cell until her judgment at dawn."

Elora felt Bray move, his hand already upon his smuggler's pouch and ready to slip his sword free. She placed a hand atop his to still him.

"I will go willingly," she said, quelling her anger.

"Don't worry Elora. I'll see the Supreme directly and find out exactly what's happening," the Voice said.

Sibiet chuckled. "You do that Flek. Return to your master - I think he's been missing his favourite valet."

The Shadojak returned his attention to her. "Now surrender your blade."

"No."

The soul memories in her mind worked swiftly, assessing the situation and what was being asked. They had no right to demand that she surrender her sword. Not even the Supreme nor the Emperor himself could demand it. They could only ask, but the very nature of the Soul Reaver made it impossible to take without being challenged and she wasn't going to give it up so easily.

The Shadojak's smile dropped.

"Very well, but know this Elora," he said as he edged closer, his voice dropping to a whisper. "If you attempt to escape, you will be caught and killed. If you leave the garrison walls before the judgement, you will be hunted."

"Fine," she hissed between her teeth.

Reading her memories from their previous owners she knew that the garrison was one of the biggest in Thea. Some five thousand Shades were stationed at any one time and hundreds of new recruits, already soldiers in training. It was also the school of the Shaigun and blade masters. Some of the world's most lethal fighters were within these walls.

Flanked by Shades either side of her she was led away.

"Not you," she heard Sibiet say and turned to see he had prevented Bray from following. "The Supreme wishes to speak with you."

Elora offered him a smile; she would be fine - she hoped.

The Shades were silent as they marched her inside the grey building, the heavy door slamming behind them with the finality of a coffin lid. Wind whistled through the cathedral-sized hall and jostled flags and tapestries that hung from the stone walls. A myriad of bright colours and emblems that were trophies brought back from wars fought over the thousands of years since the forging of the Shadojaks. Elora felt only sadness at seeing so much material, some little more than blood-stained rags and the lives that had been pointlessly lost over the battles and skirmishes they represented - will they hang a flag for her after she is judged?

They passed through the hall and descended into another courtyard. The sounds of battle reaching her ears before they stepped back out into the fading light.

Shades were sparring in the cobbled grounds, exchanging blows with swords, spears, axes and nets. Some practiced with longbows; shooting arrows at straw targets set at the far end of the practice yard. Others fighting open-hand combat under the tutoring of drill sergeants; they all paused mid-blow to watch her escorted through. Even the instructors stared, proving that Sibiet's words had spread like wildfire. Elora wondered what the Shadojak had told them.

Men's grunts, the flashing of steel and the thrumming of bow strings resumed when they passed under an archway and down a dark passage. Torches burned along the narrow walls, the flames flickering in their wake and making the shadows dance along the stone floor. Elora felt the heat they gave off as well as the fire itself: an energy that stirred something deep inside her and excited her blood. It tingled like static, giving her a rush of adrenalin and quickened her heart. She glanced at the Shades surrounding her - just men, easily tricked, easily killed.

Elora breathed deeply and pushed the thoughts of violence away before her body responded. The fire, much like the whispers of darkness, spoke to the daughter of Chaos and that was the one person who she needed to escape from. Yet how do you escape from yourself?

The Shades paused outside a doorway which was guarded by a further two men, both briefly glancing at her before continuing to stare silently ahead. The leader of the Shades unlocked the cell and motioned her inside. The chamber was small and dark, the only furniture was a wooden cot and a bucket. She entered and glanced out of the barred window which looked onto the courtyard. Two more guards were stationed beneath it, their helmets catching the setting sun - it seemed the Supreme was taking no risks with her.

The cell door creaked shut and thick bolts were slid into place on the other side, followed by the heavy thunk of a key being turned in a lock.

Bray glanced about the Supreme's office, a once meticulously tidy room that was now in disarray. Flek began to rearrange scrolls and manuscripts on the bookshelf, while wiping dust from tombs with his sleeve; a disgruntled look on his face.

It had been a few years since Bray had been last standing at this very spot, staring at the Supreme as he was given his title as Shaigun to the Pearly White. A decision that he had thought a punishment at the time but had come to realise was the correct one. Diagus had been a great Shadojak to be apprenticed to.

"I've heard the truth from Sibiet," the Supreme said, touching his fingers together above his desk and forming a steeple as he stared over his spectacles. "Now I want to hear it from your own lips. Are you Shaigun to this imposter, this blasphemous creature that is spawn of Solarius?"

Bray met the icy glower of the most powerful man below the Emperor himself. A man who had been a Shadojak for over fifty years before becoming the Supreme. A giant in his day, as much feared as the Pearly White and who still held a Soul Reaver.

"I am, Master."

Wrinkles deepened upon the old man's face, crow's feet growing long and showing him older than Bray remembered him to be.

"Can you be persuaded from this path, Bray?" the Supreme asked, his aged voice softened. "I'm sure others would take you on as Shaigun."

"I cannot," Bray replied.

"No," the Supreme mumbled, sitting back in his chair and blowing air between his teeth.

He held Bray's gaze before it fell down to the disorganised paperwork on his desk, his thick bottom lip protruding almost childlike as he began to push the parchment around.

"Elora," he said, making it sound like a mystery there was no solving.

Bray watched the paperwork being shuffled around by shaking fingers. Some of the parchment was old, crumbling with stains that appeared equally as ancient while others seemed more recent and written with the same shaky hand that now jumbled them around. Yet the symbol on all of them was the same - the twin worlds.

"Chaos will unite us. Elora will set us free," the Supreme whispered, his hand now hovering above the mess on his desk; fingers making circles in the air.

"A scribe Flek, for the love of the Mother, give me a scribe," the old man screeched suddenly, acting like a totally different person.

Flek rushed to his side with a bottle of ink and a feather quill. The Supreme snatched the quill and with the aid of Flek guiding his shaking hand, dipped it into the ink. Then the quill touched the paperwork, scribbling in wide circles while he mumbled under his breath.

"Set us free, she will set us free."

Bray glanced to Flek whose sad eyes could only watch as his master spoiled the pen, snapping the quill and tipping the ink bottle over the desk. Black liquid ran over the scrolls, thicker than visceral blood.

"Master?" Flek said laying a hand on the Supreme's shoulder, yet the man appeared oblivious to them being there as he dipped his fingers into the spilt ink and continued drawing circles.

Flek met Bray's eyes and shook his head apologetically.

"He would sink into moods similar to this before I left, but not this bad. Not so rapidly."

"What is it?" Bray asked, seeing the Supreme in a new light. Seeing him for the aged old man that he was and feeling pity.

"It's a form of delirium, a state that effects the elderly. I'm afraid he won't recover."

Guiltily Bray could only think about how this would affect Elora's judgment. If the Supreme wasn't there to rule over it, either it would be postponed or somebody else would take his place.

"We need a physician, a healer," Bray said, striding to the door.

"No."

266

Bray paused with his hand on the doorknob.

"If word of his afflictions reaches the others he'll be forced to stand down, forced to relinquish his Soul Reaver," Flek said, panic touching his words.

"The blade's peace," Bray whispered as he let his hand fall.

Flek nodded.

"The worlds will unite us," the Supreme mumbled, his finger now trailing black circles along his bare arm. "Chaos is the worlds."

"I'll fix him a calming draft and clean him up."

Flek slowly took the old man's hand in his own and began to clean it with the gentleness a mother gave a child. "For Elora's sake, he needs to be well for the judgment tomorrow."

"And if he decides against her?"

"I'll talk to him. I've seen what she has done on Earth and the pains she goes to for others. I can't make the decision for him but will make him see a truer picture than Sibiet gave him."

"I hope so."

Bray watched the face of the Supreme brighten as his aged eyes finally focused on him, a thin trail of saliva dripping from his chin.

"The worlds will unite us…Elora is Chaos."

Chapter 16

Judgment

Elora opened her eyes to darkness, the remnants of a bad dream dissolving to nothing more than an empty feeling. It had been another nightmare. One she couldn't recall or wanted to, although the proof lay beneath her palms; handprints scorched black into the wooden cot. She wrapped her cloak around herself and clambered from the solid slab of wood, crossing the floor to stare out of the window into the empty practice yard. The garrison was a cold, harsh place devoid of any comforts. All hard edges and sharp angles shaped from stone and rock and open to the elements to be carved harsher by the wind and stinging rain. It was a hard place, producing hard men.

The guards either side of the window appeared to be carved from the same stone. Sentinel statues feeling less emotion than what was contained in the spears they grasped. Breath escaping their mouths in fine mists were the only indication that they lived at all - would these be the same men who escorted her to her judgment? Dawn was little more than an hour away.

About to return to the cot she glanced to the bars at the door and was startled to see dark eyes staring back.

"So you're the daughter of Solarius," came a softly spoken voice, the speakers face hidden in the shadows created by wall sconces in the corridor outside her cell. "You don't seem much."

"Just a girl with freaky eyes?" Elora finished for him. "Quite."

"But looks can be deceiving."

She caught the outline of a grin from the man outside her door, his teeth catching the lamp light.

"That they can, Elora. I'm Hashim."

"A Shadojak?"

Hashim gave a single nod.

There was a loud metallic clunk and the door swung open. The Shadojak stepped into her cell, having to duck beneath the doorframe and remaining stooped inside the room - his bald head shining in the gloom. He was tall and slim with the wiry frame of a Kenyan Masai Warrior. He carried a long spear with a leaf-shaped tip - she recognised the dull green metal to be god-created. The weapon was a Soul Reaver.

"I'm here to escort you to the pinnacle," Hashim said.

Elora sighed. "To be judged."

"To reset the balance of things."

He stood aside and raised his hand towards the door, "After you."

Cold air caressed her face as they made their way across the practice yard flanked by two pairs of Shades. Their boots cutting parallel tracks in the dewy grass as they headed for the knoll beyond. They took a path that twisted around the mound and rose up a steep hill, bare of trees and shrubs - the wind picking up as they ascended and pulling at their cloaks.

"Will my Shaigun be at the pinnacle?" Elora asked, not being able to see the summit beyond a grey cloud that hugged the hill.

"Bray is elsewhere in the grounds. There will be just the Shadojaks and the Supreme."

His spear was held loose, carried almost casually, yet Elora sensed that Hashim could bring it to arms swifter than she could draw her sword.

The path forked at the top of the hill. One branch ascending towards another - Elora could make out the orange glow of sconces set into a stone structure at its peak, while the other way led down to a cave, the wind whistling at the man-sized mouth.

Hashim paused at the fork and the group halted with him. The Shadojak glanced up at the pinnacle then down at the cave.

"It is said, you know nothing of the path to become Shaigun."

"This is from Sibiet?" she asked. Hashim acknowledged with a nod. "It is true; Bray hasn't spoken much of his training or his time before we met."

"And your soul memories?"

Elora stared at the cave entrance. It was familiar, like a place she might have visited as a child, yet now seen through adult eyes it had changed in a way that things did from a different perspective, although she knew she had never been here before.

"Diagus was never a Shaigun."

"No. And those memories of your blade's wielders before him?"

"Vague."

The Shadojak stared at the cave, then back at Elora, his dark skin shining in the torchlight. "Allow me to show you something," Hashim said and strode down to the cave.

Elora trailed after him, leaving the Shades at the fork with concerned expressions, yet they didn't follow.

"This is the final test the Shaiguns take before being apprenticed," Hashim explained. "The training is the hardest thing they'll ever do. They come as promising Shades, standing out amongst others either for being great thinkers of having creative prowess in combat. And the training to become a Shade is brutal enough."

They reached the cave entrance and stopped. The echoes of people speaking bounced out to them and Hashim smiled.

"It appears we've arrived at a fortunate time. A Shaigun is about to progress through his final test."

Putting a slender finger to his lips he indicated for her to follow.

Torchlight flickered deep within the cave, casting shadows against the worn walls as it guided them to a large chamber with two tunnels leading off in different directions. Elora counted six men dressed in simple grey tunics standing around wooden statues which were dressed in civilian clothes. A seventh man stood beside a large table filled with an array of herbs, strange coloured powders and bottles of ointments.

"You stumble across this distraught family in the dead of night," said the man behind the table, his arm sweeping towards the wooden statues dressed to represent three adults, one of which held a doll swaddled in rags, and two children standing beside them. "The babe has received scratches along its face from an unknown attacker while sleeping peacefully in its crib. The wound is superficial - three straight lines along the forehead that barely break the skin yet they appear infected, the flesh red and swollen and the babe is struggling to breathe."

271

Elora glanced at the doll and the red lines drawn upon the carved brow, then at the six Shaiguns assembled to assess the scenario.

"One of the children had been playing earlier in the day and seen a strange goblin lurking by the well. He only caught a glimpse but described the beast as small with pale skin and pointy red ears. It ran away when approached but not before poking a forked tongue out at the child.

You are alone, cut off from your Shadojak. Yet have the right antidote and elixir at your disposal." The aged man waved a hand above the table before him then glowered at the Shaiguns-to-be. "Act quickly - make the right choice and reset the balance."

The Shaiguns approached the table, each beginning to mix potions or grind powders with a pestle and mortar. They acted swift and confidently, three of which created the same mixture - a brown paste - while another two made a fowl smelling liquid which fizzled with bubbles. The remaining Shaigun took longer as he ground a black root to dust and placed it in a silk cloth before soaking it in water.

Finished, the men approached the babe. The first three applying the paste as a salve to the dolls brow. Once done they stood before the instructor, his stern face revealing nothing as he indicated for them to pass through one of the two tunnels. They disappeared down the dark passage without a word or glance back.

The next two Shaiguns poured the liquid into the dolls mouth before approaching the instructor - they too were indicated to take the same tunnel as the three previous.

The final Shaigun applied the soaked cloth to the dolls forehead and tied it in place with a bandage then stood before the instructor. After a moment's thought he pointed at the same tunnel the Shaigun's fellow trainees had gone down. When he had gone the instructor approached the wooden figure of the mother and baby and removed the cloth and wiped the doll clean, shaking his head in disappointment.

"Six more failures," Hashim said as he stepped fully into the chamber.

The instructor glanced up and saluted. "Yes, sir. Only one of these concoctions would have reacted with the wound. But only to prolong its life by another day."

The instructor's eyes found Elora and then widened.

"Yes, Delwyn. This is she," Hashim explained. He poked his spear towards the table of concoctions. "She has no Shaigun training and I am intrigued to see what she would choose."

Elora was about to protest but realised that Hashim maybe testing her as a means to prove her ability. To show she was worthy to be a Shadojak. If she wanted his vote at the judgement she needed to get this right. And to refuse the test would certainly put him against her.

She approached the table and stared at the multitude of ingredients in bowls, bottles and vials. Varying in shape texture and colour, she wracked her soul memories but still only recognised a few of them. If Grendal was here she would have fixed the correct draft already.

"Be swift, Elora," Hashim said. "The longer you take the worse the condition."

Elora picked up the same root the last Shaigun had ground down - if this was the mixture that would prolong the symptoms maybe she could enhance it for the cure. Hastily she ground down the root and added a tryella stone - this she knew would give the mixture a potent kick.

"Quickly now, the babe is dying," the Shadojak said.

Elora ignored the pressure Hashim was attempting to place her under. Feeling more confident, she sprinkled in a pinch of lemon frost which she knew would stave off the fever, then wrapped the compound in a silk cloth and dipped it in goat's milk.

"She's beginning to convulse," Hashim said urgently.

Carefully taking the cloth, Elora rushed to the doll in her mother's wooden arms and was about to apply the dressing when she paused. Something niggled at the back of her mind, telling her this was wrong. She re-traced the words of the instructor: scratches, swollen, fever, - what was she missing? - breathing, scratches...fever?

"Hurry."

Elora glanced at the tunnels. What had the others missed? What was the right thing to do?

...child, well...goblin...Goblin - pale, red pointy ears, forked tongue.

"The babes dying..."

The cloth hit the floor with a wet thud. Elora stepped back and in a single fluid motion slipped her sword free and sliced the baby in half, then followed the momentum through decapitating the children before lunging her blade into the wooden statues of the father and finally the mother.

Returning her sword to the smuggler's pouch she turned and caught Hashim smiling.

"Why?"

"It was a ragretch fiend, not a goblin," Elora explained, the soul memories providing her with the knowledge. "The babe was already dead and all in contact we're dying, even though they felt nothing at the time."

"And if it wasn't a ragretch?" Hashim asked.

"Without proof we can only assume the worse. The risk outweighs the lives involved, the balance has been found."

"Well judged. And as a Shadojak your next course of action would be?"

"Burn the bodies, seal the well and hunt the fiend."

Hashim's smile broadened. "Spoken like a Shadojak. Now come, dawn is upon us and we have an appointment at the summit."

Elora swallowed her nerves as she stepped beneath the stone frame of the pinnacle. Eight arches leaned together to form a dome. The seven Shadojaks and the Supreme stood in each, their Shaiguns beside them, facing inwards to the centre where she now halted. Feeling all eyes of the judgment upon her she forced to herself keep still, pushing the whispers that taunted from the shadows and the voices in the flames that danced in the torches set at each arch calling her name.

"Elora, you have been summoned in front of the entire league of Shadojaks for judgment," an elderly man said.

Elora took him to be the Supreme, tufts of his grey hair waving in the wind. She gave a single nod.

"You have been accused of heresy, not just by your own actions but by your bloodline. Do you deny your lineage?"

"I do not. Solarius, God of Chaos was my father."

Sibiet filled an arch to her left, face set hard and expressionless although Drifid to his side had the look of the cat that got the cream.

"Yet it was you who killed him," the Supreme continued. "With the help of the ShadojakDiagus, who was killed in the same vicious attack."

Elora nodded, attempting to show a calm exterior while inside she was fighting the impulse to reduce herself to smoke and leave.

The Supreme folded his arms. He appeared dazed for a moment; deep wrinkles rising in bewilderment as if he'd just woken and lacked the knowledge of where he was. Flek, who had been standing behind him, approached and placed a gloved hand on his shoulder and whispered in his ear. A smile finally broke on the old man as if he suddenly remembered where he was. He inclined his head to the men around the arches before speaking once again.

"Those are the facts, laid out to you in their simple form, although the layers that build behind them are many. If any of you have need to speak freely, ask questions - then do so now." He glanced at each of them, glowering beneath thick wiry eyebrows. "Each of you have a vote and each of you will cast it."

"Blasphemous," Sibiet blasted spontaneously. "Her father was the very being the Shadojaks were created to protect the worlds from. The Chaos that created that burned half of Thea and his blood runs think in her veins. The monster has already inherited her father's Soul Reaver and has taken the souls of many in the months since she stole it."

"I didn't steal it," Elora snapped before she could stop herself.

"Silence. You will have a chance to speak at the end," the Supreme said, angrily. Then indicated for Sibiet to continue.

"Not only did she take the blade, but she slew the previous owner - the Pearly White himself, Diagus." Sibiet paused for dramatic effect. "In the few days I have known the spawn of Solarius it has become clear that she is as evil as she is cunning. Twisting others to do her bidding, even Bray; who has become her Shaigun has been fooled by her devious nature. Taunting him with false emotions, dangling love in his face and teasing him into submission. Now the poor boy follows her like a lost puppy - that's the power she has."

Kill...kill him, the voices of darkness whispered at the edge of her perception. ...tear his heart out...take his soul...kill him...kill them all... Taking a deep breath she pushed the violent impulses away.

"And what's more she has taken a bulworg into service. A bulworg that is known to have served the Dark Army, her father's army and now it serves her."

The Shadojaks listened intently, scowls growing deeper and in the case of a huge beast of a man with a war hammer; teeth angrily clenched and knuckles turned white as he gripped his weapon. Elora couldn't see the Shadojaks that stood in the arches behind her but guessed they were feeling much the same. All except Hashim, the tall man smiling pleasantly as if this entire ordeal was a lighthearted discussion amongst friends.

"My Shaigun, Drifid, has borne witness to some of her powers. Experiencing first hand as she attacked him, although he fought bravely and would have subdued her by blade if she hadn't used demon powers and turned herself to smoke."

The big man with the hammer snorted angrily through huge nostrils, shaking his head in disbelief - this judgment wasn't going in Elora's favour. She bit her lip and wondered where Bray was, if he was close or if he'd been kept in another part of the garrison for his own protection. Would she ever see him again?

"I've seen firsthand what the bitch is capable of and how she manipulates others. I know her better than any here and so cast my vote with confidence. I judge her unworthy of the blade, unworthy of the title and the re-balance can only be achieved through her death."

His copper eyes locked on hers. "I vote against."

The others around the pinnacle nodded in agreement, Sibiet's words having struck a chord and twisted their judgment.

"Wait," Flek said as he took a step into the torchlight, his gloved hand wringing together as he glanced at the men around the stone structure.

"Masters, I know I speak out of turn and have no right to make judgment. But please hear me out."

"You are not a Shadojak, you have no right," Sibiet protested.

"I've known Elora for as long as you have Master and have seen the good the girl has done."

"Silence, valet. Know your place."

"I would like to hear what he has to say," came the soft words of Hashim.

"Very well. Flek held the title as the Voice and has been witness to Elora for the last few days. So he will speak freely." The Supreme said.

Sibiet folded his arms angrily, yet said nothing.

"Some of what ShadojakSibiet says is true, but taken out of context," Flek said as he paced inside the dome, speaking with ease as all watched on.

"Elora did kill her father, a being that had no hand in her childhood. In-fact she had only known him for the

278

few minutes before she ended his life. It is also true that she killed Diagus. Yet it was the Shadojak himself who wished it, sacrificing himself so Elora could slay the God of Chaos. There was no other way."

"And the bulworg?" Asked a Shadojak. He was a dwarf, stocky and well-muscled; his axe held in a tight fist, the bearded point grazing the ground.

"His name is Weakest. Although the name falls somewhat short of the beast himself. It is also true that he has served in the Dark Army but had deserted, refusing to kill in the name of Chaos. This bulworg is rare amongst his breed. Having a high intelligence and an intellect that gives him a level of understanding between right and wrong, a conscience over his actions. He doesn't serve Elora - he is free but chooses to remain alongside her people as a protector." The former voice paced the before the arches, addressing the Shadojaks as a whole.

"Within minutes of our first meeting she had helped a mother give birth during a difficult delivery. She had already filled Rams Keep with children left over as the Dark Army ravaged Earth. She'd committed herself to save the lives of the innocent and vulnerable and still found time to kill bulworgs and grumpkins, and even a scraw-harpy that came close to the keep." Flek brought his hands together as he glanced at them all once again, holding his audience captive. "Elora came with us willingly, knowing that death may be what she received from the judgment. Yet she still came, but not before risking her life in killing Silk - a takwich that ruled the Dark Army.

And as far as the accusations of love between herself and her Shaigun - I have seen no proof. They are close, but then are you not all close to your apprentices?"

Flek bowed before returning to his place beside the Supreme. He gave Elora an encouraging smile and a shrug. She didn't know what good his words had done, but felt a wealth of gratitude towards him. At least she had one person on her side.

Hashim cleared his throat. "I am concerned about her bloodline; these things shouldn't be taken lightly. And she hasn't the experience of the Shaigun training." He smiled warmly at her. "Yet she seems to have a wise head, the coldness to make the right decisions and the mettle to see them through." He stared confidently at the Supreme. "My vote is for."

The next Shadojak around the ring was the huge man with the hammer who filled his arch better than any other. Yaul-tis-munjib's muscles rippled beneath his tunic, pulling the grey material taught. The Shaigun that stood beside him was cut from the same cloth - thick arms and a neck that was as wide as his square head.

"I'm with Sibiet. I vote against this daughter of Chaos," the giant Shadojak boomed, slamming the butt of his hammer against the ground for emphasis.

Elora remained quiet, putting on the bravest face she could while feeling ice creep up her spine. That was two against her, another three and she was dead and any hope of saving Earth along with it.

"I don't recognise this killer of the Pearly White as a Shadojak," came the voice of Dwenal. "I vote we kill her and take the soul blade back."

Elora turned to face the dwarf. His axe was as tall as he was and standing next to his Shaigun, a man of average height, gave him the appearance of an angry child. Albeit with a beard, a head shaved into a mohican and a jaw clenched so tight she could hear his teeth grind. That was three against her.

From her soul memories Elora recognised the next Shadojak as Gunwahl. A man of little words but was infamous for his prowess in battle. He had led many skirmishes in the north against Vikings as a young man and earned the right to become a Shade early in his career. From there he became Shaigun and challenged his own master to a duel. He had won and taken the soul blade - a broadsword which had been pulled from its scabbard and now rested against Gunwahl's shoulder.

"Against," he said flatly and without emotion. Short, simple and another nail in her coffin. Elora forced herself to unclench her fingers as her fate became grimmer by each vote cast; four against, one more and it was over.

Quantico slouched easily against the upright of his arch, arms folded casually as if he was merely passing the time and not deciding on somebody's life.

"Love's overrated," he said in a thick northern accent. "I've had my fair share in my youth but thank the Blessed Mother the Shaigun training put me right. If the girl thinks she's in love, it can be easily fixed." He raised an eyebrow toward her. "Are you in love?"

"Love is just a chemical released by the brain," Elora said, glad that Bray wasn't in earshot. Chemical or not it still warmed her when she thought of him.

"So true. And as for your lineage - you can't help being kin of your parents. If my brother and I was an ounce of my father we'd have drunk Rona dry years ago."

"Aye," Quantala agreed. "And sowed our seed in every wench in every brothel from here to Roseland."

The brothers were so alike in appearance that Elora wondered if they were twins.

"It is true," his brother Quantico, agreed. "So I cannot vote against her purely on who her father was."

"She is the epitome of what we stand against." Sibiet snapped.

"No, she is a Shadojak. She is one of us. I vote for," Quantico said.

Quantala nodded in agreement. "I'm with my brother on that."

Elora could have kissed them both, although that still left her short of a balanced decision. Only the Supreme himself was left to cast his vote and his counted twice.

All heads turned to the aged man as he drew his sword free from its scabbard. Arthritic fingers curled painfully around the hilt, yet he glowered with the power of his position.

Elora's own fingers drifted down to her smuggler's pouch, ready to draw the soul blade. At the same time, she noticed Sibiet shift. Planting his feet and readying himself to dash towards her. As did the giant with the hammer and the dwarf. The grey dawn was alive with anticipation.

"Elora, you have been judged by your fellow Shadojaks. Three votes for and four against." The Supreme spoke firmly, his words ringing around the dome of arches and echoing around the cloud-filled hill.

Drifid exchanged a look with his master who in turn gave a subtle nod to Gunwahl; his own body adjusting into an attacking stance. It was obvious to her that the Shadojaks had already spoken and planned on this outcome. They'll hit her hard and fast. Cutting the daughter of Chaos down in a single brutal strike before she had chance to defend herself.

They could go to hell.

"And so the final vote goes to myself. The judgment and the rebalance of things," the Supreme said.

Elora breathed deeply, calming her thumping heart as she slowly placed a foot forward and shifted her weight onto the ball of the other. She glanced at the men surrounding her. Seven Shadojaks and five Shaiguns. They will attack as one, even Hashim and the brothers who voted for her - once the judgment was made it needed meting out.

Elora shut her eyes, locking the Shadojaks locations and probable movements to memory as she chose her path. One against one, she may have been equal to any of the men before her. Seven to one was a different matter.

Clearing his throat, the Supreme took a step towards her.

"My vote is for."

Elora slipped her blade free as the words sunk in.

"Elora, you are one of us. You are a Shadojak," the Supreme said, lowering his own weapon as did the dwarf and Gunwahl, although somewhat reluctantly.

"But she's…" Sibiet protested, scimitar still in his grasp and raised towards her.

"The first sister in the brotherhood of Shadojaks," Hashim said, a wide smile beaming. Then inclining his head he bowed to her. "Welcome sister."

"Welcome sister" was repeated by the brothers and Flek while the giant slammed his hammer into the earth and snorted. Dwenal shrugged his shoulder and slung his axe on his back.

Elora released the breath she'd been holding and nodded gratefully to the Supreme. Still not believing what had happened - she was alive.

"You can lower your sword now," Quantico chuckled.

In the revelations of her judgment, Elora had forgotten she was still holding her blade in a defensive stance. She was about to slip it away when Drifid pushed passed his master.

"I demand duel rights," he said, face turning red.

"Don't be an idiot, boy," Sibiet snapped as he grabbed his Shaigun by the arm. But Drifid shrugged him off.

"It is my right," he shouted, grim determination filling his face with fury.

Nobody made a move to stop him as he approached her, swinging the long curved blade of the scimitar about his body as he began his dance of steel. The heavy weapon sliced through the air, the bullet hole making a whistling noise as he spun left then right in a blur of movement.

The first rays of dawn struck the steel as it whirred overhead, reflecting a golden beam against the stone arches. Drifid bent low in a feint, stepping to the side before dipping back and swung his scimitar, striking for her face.

Elora tipped her head back, allowing the weight of his sword to carry him passed - it was a good strike, an attack made to decapitate. She sidestepped his spinning body, curling her foot behind his ankle and landed a swift punch to the nerves below his armpit.

Drifid yelped as he slammed into the ground, scimitar sent spinning out of the dome. His head bounced off the hard earth as his now useless arm became pinned beneath his own body.

Elora casually placed a foot on his stomach as he struggled to rise.

"Yield?"

The point of her blade touched his shirt above his heart. A part of her wanted him to resist, a part of her desired to push her sword into his life-pumping organ and claim his soul.

"I yield," Drifid panted, scowl softening in submission. "I yield."

Without removing her sword, Elora settled her eyes on the other Shadojaks and Shaiguns that surrounded her, filling up the arches of the dome.

"Is there anyone else? Anyone who demands duel rights?" She met the copper stare of Sibiet; his knuckles turning white on his scimitar. "No?"

After a moment he glanced away, his grip softening. As did the others who voted against her.

Drifid suddenly squirmed beneath her, a moan escaping his lips as she realised her blade had cut through his shirt and bit into his chest, turning the material red. Elora took a shuddering breath and eased her sword off.

"Well judged Elora, although some of us would have killed him," Hashim said. "If others believe you will mete out mercy it may persuade them to attempt duel rights themselves."

Elora slipped her blade away. "I stand corrected, Hashim. But then, that wasn't much of a duel: more of an irritation. The next attempt on my life will end with a death and it won't be mine."

Once released Drifid scurried back behind his master, shame forcing him to stare at the ground. Sibiet hissed through his teeth as he glowered at his foolish Shaigun. Elora hoped they had both learned a lesson from this.

The Supreme left his arch to stand beside her as he spoke to the rest of them.

"Elora is one of us now, this judgement is over." He then turned to her. "Is there anything you require, Elora?"

"My Shaigun?"

Chapter 17

The Emperor's Deal

Bray stared out of the library window, the pinnacle appearing like a black crown against the dawn rising above the hill. He caught himself fidgeting with the hem of his cloak and forced his fingers to drop the loose threads he had worked free. Old tombs lay at his feet, the parchment so brittle it flaked to the floor when he turned the pages. The scrolls didn't fare much better: vellum that would have been well aged before the great rift, was now little more than dust. He had come here expecting to find nothing and nothing was what he had found. An errand given by the Supreme to keep him out of the way, to stop him from interfering with Elora's judgment. He didn't have to try the door to know it was locked with Shades posted outside.

The first red rays from the sun crested the hill, briefly shining through arches before rising above and forcing the structure into shadow. The judgment would be over.

Bray's eyes glazed over as he strained to focus on the pinnacle, wondering if she was dead - surely he would have felt it, sensed the loss of her life, her passing. The thought was like a spark to dry kindling.

His foot kicked through the pile of books and sent them crashing into the shelves and exploding against the wall. The ruined pages and paper scattering about the floor in an unruly mess.

What if she was dead, what would he do - what could he do? The frustration was like nothing he had felt before and he only restrained himself from punching the window through when he caught movement through the glass. People, little more than black dots descending down the hill.

Bray counted them, then counted again. But the notion was as pointless as him being in the library - he didn't know how many went up there to start with. To the back of the column were four Shades bearing a stretcher - it was her. It was Elora's lifeless body.

No, it moved.

As the dots neared and slowly took shape he focused on each person until he settled on the stooped shape of the Supreme, alongside him was a shorter person with a female shape, loose strands of hair blowing in the wind - Elora.

She was alive. A Shadojak now and that would bring its own complications, but she was alive.

Flek had been right, the Supreme's secretary had told him not to worry, he was sure that his master would vote for her as would the twins who served the Emperor. He didn't know how he knew, but Bray owed Flek a great amount of gratitude.

The window shrieked open and the wind came in to stir the dust about the musty room. Bray knew that the guards wouldn't open the door so he climbed onto the window ledge and dropped the two floors to the ground.

The garrison was beginning to wake up. Troops were already exercising and the clash of steel was echoing from the practice grounds. The Shades he passed saluted him, slamming fists to breast-plates. He acknowledged them with a nod, eager to reach the Shadojaks and Elora.

They met at the base of the hill.

"It seems your Shaigun has found us," the Supreme said as he approached them.

Bray heard the words but in that moment his world was focused on Elora. So much so that he didn't notice Quantala as he slammed a playful punch into his ribs.

"Great to see you, Bray," the Northman said. "Your new master is a damn sight better looking than Diagus was, eh?"

Bray smiled. It was the first time he had seen the brothers since the Shaigun training some five years ago. They had gone through hell along with Flek; a bond which brought men closer together as they shared hardships of becoming a Shaigun.

"How is the babysitting duties?" Bray asked.

"Drab. Don't get me wrong, it has it perks but it's a boring business," Quantala said.

"Yeah," Quantico agreed, joining the conversation. "Who's going to attack the Emperor? Nobody can get within a hundred paces of him without an invitation and even then you'd be searched within an inch of your life."

"Which reminds me." Quantala turned to Elora. "The Emperor has formally invited you to meet him at your earliest convenience."

"Which is to say, at his earliest convenience," Quantico continued.

"Which would be this morning," his brother finished.

Bray grinned at the way the twins spoke together, taking a sentence each as if it was only the one person speaking. They had done that a lot in training and it seemed they still did. Yet his attention was firmly locked on Elora herself and he fought hard not to pull her into a crushing embrace.

Although appearing exhausted, Elora's face lit up at the brother's words.

"I also wanted to see the Emperor. I'll come immediately," she said. Then looked down at herself, lifting a corner of her cloak up. "Maybe I've time to wash and change before being in the company of the Emperor."

She let her cloak drop from her fingers and dust from the Shadowlands floated to the ground.

"That might be a good idea," the twins said together.

"And my Shaigun?" she asked, turning to the Supreme for permission.

The old man shrugged. "He's your Shaigun now, where you go, he goes."

Her smile grew wider and Bray thought he had never seen a more beautiful sight.

"We'll inform the Emperor that you've formally accepted his invitation and will meet with him shortly," Quantala said.

They said farewell to the Supreme and stalked off down the hill into the garrison proper. The trail of Shadojaks and their Shaiguns tailing behind. Sibiet gave a final glance back, his face filled with thunder as he followed the Shades bearing Drifid.

"So the judgment went well, Master," Bray asked, now that they were alone.

"I'm alive. And so Earth still has a chance," Elora replied.

Bray heard sorrow in her voice, but decided not to press the issue, instead he nodded after the group. "What happened to Drifid?"

"Duel rights," she scoffed. "Almost got himself killed. But I think it gave the others a warning."

"No doubt, but I don't think we've seen the last of Sibiet's wrath."

Elora's violet eyes scanned the ground below them, a lone tear making a slow track down her cheek. Bray wanted nothing more than to wrap his arms around her and hold her close. His arms even began to swing towards her but he checked himself before they touched.

"What's wrong?" he asked.

She blinked the tear away and wiped her cheek. A sad smile forming on her lips. "It's still sinking in. I'm officially a Shadojak."

"Yeah."

"And you're officially my Shaigun."

Bray chuckled. "So I'm yours for keeps - to boss around and..."

"Never to touch, to hold, to kiss. Shadojaks don't feel love remember."

Her words were like acid. A corrosive concoction that imbued his heart with pain.

"We can...work something out," Bray said, his words sounded pathetic, even to himself.

They began to walk down the hill, the sun now fully up and turning the few clouds pink. On another day, Bray might have recognised the splendour in the Rona countryside but today he saw it as an ill omen.

"At least you're alive," he finally said as he took his place beside his master.

"For now. Let's just hope this Emperor will help in saving Earth."

"And after Earth has been liberated?" he asked, fighting the temptation to place his arm around her waist.

"I haven't thought that far. I can't. Not even about us - it's adding too many complications."

That stung him. Another painful stab to add to the acid feeling.

291

"I love you," Bray said, but the wind chose that time to pick up and steal his words away. After a moments silence he guessed that she hadn't heard him until they reached the bottom of the hill where she turned away so he couldn't see her face.

"Love is just a chemical in the brain," Elora remarked, coldly.

Bray stared at her back as she stalked away; hood now up and concealing her face. He wanted to yell at her, to scream that love was more than that and that she knew it. Instead he trialled behind, feeling the creeping realisation that they would never be together. No more closer than a Shaigun and his master.

Rona was full of life. The city hadn't changed much since he was last here over three years ago. They left the train station and Bray escorted Elora around the busy streets to the bath houses and then onto the tailors for new clothes.

Elora acted the authoritative Shadojak. Her face set in mild irritation as the tailors busied themselves around her, measuring her body for a new shirt, tunic and trousers while he stood patiently by the door.

They both left with new cloaks and boots, the tailors having pushed their finest wares upon them and would no doubt bill the Emperor's treasury for triple their worth.

Neither of them spoke as a stagecoach carried them across the city to the inner walls of the palace. Bray found it hard to stop staring at Elora and he often found that his gaze wandered to her reflection in the window. He relaxed the muscles in his face and slipped on a mask of indifference. If she wanted things to be uncomplicated between them and take up the position of Shadojak seriously then who was he to pursue her differently? He wasn't going to make things any harder for her. Once things had calmed down she may open up her feelings to him.

The carriage gently rocked as it rolled over a bridge and into the grounds of the Emperor's city home. The huge airship blotted out the sun, momentarily throwing them into shadow. The huge flying vessel was the only one created. The Emperor wanted to be the only ruler of the sky, although the funds needed to keep the craft flying were extremely costly. Bray glared at the airship and the huge balloon that kept it afloat, wondering if all that money could be better spent on the Emperor's people instead of himself.

They were met by Imperial Guards at the foot of a marble staircase and was escorted through the grounds to an atrium.

"Good to see the people's taxes are not wasted," Elora said. Her dark curls falling over her face as she stared about the richly decorated room. She picked up a delicate crystal glass that was set beside a matching decanter on a side table. The reflection of her violet eyes refracted in the glass as she held it up to the light.

"I expect the wine to be worth many times more than the crystal," Bray said. Then added "Master."

Elora set the glass back on the table. "You don't need to keep calling me master."

"I know, I'm not a dog," Bray snapped, a little harsher than he intended. "But what else shall I call you?"

"You can call me by my name."

Bray heard the hurt in her voice and felt a pang of guilt. She didn't want this anymore than he did. Yet she had made it clear that she would put their love aside.

"No, I can't."

"Fine," she snapped back and turned her back to him.

"Fine, Master," Bray said, feeling his emotions beginning to slip out of control.

The door to the receiving room suddenly opened and Quantala stepped through, dressed in a fine uniform of gold and scarlet - the Empires' colours.

"The Emperor will see you now," the Shadojak said, mocking a bow while winking at Elora.

"Thank you," Elora said tersely and stepped out of the atrium.

"Feels a little chilly in here," Quantala remarked. "Have you already had a disagreement with Elora?" he asked, raising an eyebrow.

"I preferred arguing with the Pearly White. At least you knew where you stood with Diagus."

He followed Quantala into the huge receiving room. The Emperor was draped over his throne, a leg dressed in silk pantaloons dangling over the golden arm. He rocked it casually as he watched them enter, an amused smirk held along his thin lips. Imperial Guards stood beside the oval entrances on both sides of the room, gold-gilded armour shining in the crystal lamps. To Bray's surprise, Flek was already kneeling before the throne and rose as they entered.

"At last, at last," the Emperor said delightedly, clapping his manicured hands together. "The one they say is the daughter of Solarius - spawn of the God of Chaos. And now a Shadojak no less."

He clicked his fingers in the air and a servant hastily came forwards and placed a glass of wine in the Emperor's hand. He took a sip and dismissed the servant with an annoyed flap of the wrist.

"Why is it you didn't come to me when I first summoned you?" the Emperor asked Elora as she knelt to the polished marble and bowed her head.

"My apologies, Emperor. I had pressing matters on Earth," she answered.

"Pressing matters on Earth indeed. You are a Shadojak. Your pressing matters belong to the realm of this Empire and Thea." He took another sip, his eyes never leaving the top of Elora's head. "You may rise."

Quantala took his place with his brother behind the throne, his arms folding to match the stance of his twin.

The Emperor's gaze fell next on Bray who could see where fine makeup had been applied to his eyelids. Dark lines were painted into the corners and brushed against his delicate lashes.

"And this is your Shaigun?"

Bray knelt. "I am, your Excellency."

"You've an elvish look about you," the Emperor remarked before taking another sip from his glass. "A half-god Shadojak and a half-breed Shaigun. These are strange times we live in." He finished the wine and flicked his fingers. A servant hastily approached, armed with a fresh bottle of wine, but the ageing man instead gave him the empty glass and dismissed him with a wave of his hand.

"You may rise."

Bray rose. "Thank you, your Excellency."

"You've taken the Soul Blade from the Pearly White -
is that right?" the Emperor asked, addressing Elora once
again.

Elora nodded.

"Then should you not be protecting the province or
country that the Pearly White had been doing previously,
is that not how these things work?" He inclined his head
to glance at the twins behind him. "I don't pretend to
know how the Shadojaks select the areas or the rules; it
bores me so. Yet she will have a domain to protect.
Where in the Empire is it?"

"Your Excellency," Flek began. "The Pearly White
covered Earth. The Supreme hasn't instructed us
otherwise so I assume she will return."

"So she will return to Earth. I expect there's nobody
more suited to that realm than one who has lived there all
her life."

"I will return, your Excellency. As soon as I may. But
the Dark Army has conquered it and is laying waste the
population - those that have not been possessed by the
takwich anyway."

The Emperor rose from his throne and wandered to a
fruit bowl that lay upon a polished table. He selected a
ripe apple and bit into it; juice spitting to either side of
his mouth. He reminded Bray of a spoilt child who had
never experienced a hardship and always got what he
wanted.

"This is not my problem, Shadojak. It is yours."

Elora took a step towards the ruler of Thea, Bray saw
the agitation she held back as she breathed deeply.

"I accept all the responsibilities and will do whatever
is in my power to rid Earth of my father's legacy.

However, they are too big an army for me to crush alone."

"And so you will have me commit my own forces to your course? My Imperial Soldiers?"

"If it pleases your Excellency, yes."

The Emperor took another bite from his apple then discarded the remainder into the bowl he picked it from.

"It doesn't please me; no. I care not for the affairs of Earth. It matters not who rules there as long as the balance is kept in check."

Bray couldn't believe the arrogance of the man. He stepped beside Elora to address him.

"The Dark Army is marching east, across the plains of Europe. They've excavated a site in the northlands known as Siberia."

"To what purpose?"

"I don't know," carried on Elora. "But I believe it is some kind of weapon. Something my father created and left buried deep beneath the snow."

"Intriguing. But still...not my problem and one I won't risk my men for."

Flek cleared his throat. "And there is also Grycul, your Excellency. The demon Charwigg is planning on releasing her onto Earth."

"Grycul? But she is trapped in the Shadowlands, no?"

"Yes, for now. Yet this Charwigg won't rest until the dragon is set free and I believe she is capable of doing it."

The Emperor crossed the stately room to a balcony and stepped out into the daylight.

"Whoever rules the skies has the upper hand," he said, glancing up at his airship.

"Indeed your Excellency. And nothing can bring down Grycul," Flek pressed, as they joined the Emperor on the balcony.

"But if released, the dragon will be ruling the skies of Earth. Not Thea."

"Grycul has the power to shift between worlds. It is not in the nature of Chaos to remain in one domain but to spread and keep on spreading. Once Earth has fallen, Grycul will be the first to bring devastation to Thea."

Bray watched the Emperor chew on his painted lip, face upturned up to his airship. He wished he could read his mind.

"Who controls the dragon?" the Emperor asked, his manicured fingernails drumming on the golden rail of the balcony.

"Nobody, now," Elora answered. "Solarius had control over his creation but now he has been slain, Grycul will reap havoc. Charwigg may succeed in releasing her but will never rule the dragon."

"This is true," Flek added. "And the beast may decide to seek vengeance for her master's demise. I expect her to break on this side of the barrier before Earth." He shrugged his shoulders. "Who's to say what path it will choose; Chaos has a will of its own."

The Emperor's fingers ceased the annoying tattoo on the balustrade and Bray witnessed worry in his face as he paced back into the room. He resumed the throne yet sat with a more erect posture as he summoned a fresh glass of wine. He took several swallows before speaking.

"I will spare you five divisions of the imperial guard." The Emperor held the empty glass out to be refilled. "And six battalions of Shades. But it has a price."

"I will do whatever is needed your Excellency," Elora said.

The Emperor stared at her for a moment as if struggling with a decision. "Kill the dragon. Bring me Grycul's head and you shall have an army to march onto Earth."

Bray's heart filled with blood as he saw the determination in Elora's eyes.

"I will kill her. Charwigg as well," she said.

"Then we have a deal, Shadojak?"

Elora nodded and Bray wanted nothing more at that moment than to wrap his arms around her and steal her away to somewhere safe. Why was it she was always heading into danger? Racing from one disaster into another. Mere hours had passed since her life was held in the balance at her judgment. Now here she was, throwing it against another close to impossible situation. Well at least, he consoled himself, he would be with her.

"I will go with her to bear witness to Grycul's demise, your Excellency. The Supreme will demand it," Flek said as he knelt before the Emperor.

"Then we are settled," The Emperor sloshed his wine around in circles and watched the red liquid cling to the glass. "Although there is the small matter of those scrolls you're researching. Tell me, Voice. Have you come any closer to discovering the riddle - Chaos will unite the worlds and Chaos will set us free?"

Bray exchanged a look with Elora and it was plain to see she was as surprised as he was.

The Emperor chuckled. "You didn't think I had my own spies. I know what it is you're seeking, along with the mad ramblings of the Supreme. The twin world symbols are something my scholars have been researching for some time."

"Begging your pardon your Excellency, but what have they discovered?" Flek asked eagerly.

"Nothing more than riddles pieced together to form an incomplete picture. But the jigsaw does give hints to something buried, both on Earth and on Thea."

"This is what the Dark Army is excavating. I know it," Elora said.

The Emperor nodded. "And this so-called weapon has a piece somewhere on this world. And I dare say that there will be dark entities seeking it as we speak; if they don't already posses it."

"From what we can surmise from my own libraries is that the weapon, when whole, will be powerful enough to reduce both worlds to ruin."

He raised his glass for another refill and slouched back into a more relaxed posture, swinging a leg over the arm of the throne.

"Of course, these weapons are no more than myth. We have found no proof that they actually exist or even where they are."

"Surely we can't take that risk, your Excellency," Flek said. "We have searched our own libraries but have found little to indicate any weapons. Perhaps if I could search your archives or speak with your scholars..."

"I thought you were going to witness Grycul's demise? Besides, my scholars and historians have been working on these ancient scrolls and tombs for some time and have yet to bring up anything new."

"But maybe a fresh pair of eyes may help. With somebody who has had experience on both worlds," Elora offered.

"Who do you have in mind?"

Bray watched Elora's violet gaze as they settled on him, her face appeared strained as if fighting to mask her feelings.

"My Shadojak has lived on Earth for the last three years and has knowledge of this riddle. I could think of nobody better."

The words slammed into Bray in a sledge hammer blow. "But you will need me to kill Grycul...."

"Do I?" Cut in Elora, the hint of anger in her voice. "You will best serve me here, researching this weapon."

Bray looked to Flek for support but the Voice seemed to be thinking over the possibility as he slowly nodded.

"Master, I want to be by your side. There will be more at risk killing the dragon than a weapon that might not even exist."

"And if it does exist? I would rather you here. My mind is made up and you will obey."

"It is settled then," the Emperor said. "The next time we meet Shadojak, you will bring me the head of Grycul."

Elora knelt to the marbled floor, bowing her head. "I won't fail you your Excellency."

She rose, gave Bray a final glance then paced from the room. Flek knelt then hurried after her.

Bray watched them leave and fought not to run after them. How could she leave him like that? Shock - his entire world shrank to the doors as they slammed, cutting him off from her; from his love. Possibly the last time he would ever see her.

"Quantala will show you to the libraries," the Emperor said, bringing Bray's world back into the stark reality of where he was.

"Thank you, your Excellency," he heard himself say, although he didn't feel as if anything was real. He felt as though he was trapped in a cruel delirium or nightmare he couldn't wake from - he felt sick.

Elora also felt sick as she made her way from the palace grounds and only became aware of Flek's presence as he panted to keep up. Once he did, he pulled her to the side.

"Are you sure this is the right decision, Elora?" the Voice asked.

She glared at him, feeling her rising anger and frustration building and wanted something to vent it upon.

"You will call me by my proper title," she snapped.

Flek stepped back before bowing humbly.

"Sorry, Shadojak. I…"

Elora was suddenly hit by guilt and placed a hand against his arm, "No, it is I that am sorry. I shouldn't have flown at you like that. You've been a good friend these last couple of days."

Flek smiled, "I was only doing what's right. Are you still sure you won't take Bray with you? He is a capable warrior."

"I'm sure. And if I had been choosing with my head then he would have been my first."

Flek chuckled. "But instead you chose with your heart. It's alright Elora, your secret is safe with me. You would have to be blind to see that there wasn't any love between you and Bray."

Elora smiled herself and felt relieved that Flek understood her situation.

"Could you tell Bray that I'm sorry for forcing him to stay, I couldn't bear to see him getting hurt." She glanced about the empty street to make sure they were alone. "And tell him that I love him."

"But I'll be coming with you. I am to report Grycul's death to the Supreme," Flek said.

"No, you won't. I'll be taking Sibiet," she replied, the seed of a 'plan B' beginning to grow in her mind.

"Sibiet? But he'll attempt to get in your way. He wants nothing more than to prove you're not worthy of being a Shadojak."

Elora gave Flek a kiss on his cheek. "That is why I'm taking him."

"And me?"

"Help Bray find this weapon and decipher the riddle. I think he's in need of a friend."

Chapter 18

Balancing the Scales

The thick bone mast creaked as the sails snapped taught, catching a warm wind that propelled the Necrolosis into the air. Elora leaned out over the gunnel, letting her hair fall free as the ship of bones ascended into the red sky. She stared into the sea of souls below her and the trapped spirits within; each face locked in a silent scream as they floated the grizzly craft onwards to the dragon.

"What do they think about?" Elora asked, her question aimed at Zionbuss as he came to join her.

"Nothing," replied the demon, his long black nails digging into the bone rail of his vessel. "Or at least, nothing of any importance."

Zionbuss scratched absently at his chin, the symbols and runes painted on his body swimming and changing, making it hard for Elora to focus on any particular spot.

"How do you know? They look like they're in pain to me."

The demon shook his head, making a deep throaty chuckle. "My Queen, how can they feel any pain without a body?"

"Pain doesn't need to be physical," Elora said, sounding morose, even to herself.

The demon nodded, the huge horns that sprouted either side of his head dipping like a bull about to strike the attacking matador, although his filed teeth showed through a black grin.

"You're missing Bray. Tell me again why you didn't bring the Shaigun. I thought he'd be the better warrior to have with you for this task."

Elora knew that he would have been, Bray was her rock, her moral anchor that kept that other her in check; and that was the exact reason she didn't want him here. She shrugged and remained silent, not trusting herself to speak his name should the tears come – maybe not having a body to feel through wasn't all that bad.

"I'm sure you've got your reasons," Zionbuss said, when he realised she wasn't going to answer. He turned to nod towards his other passenger. "But why bring him? Isn't he the man that stands against you, hurling accusations and always attempting to bring you down?"

Elora shifted her gaze to Sibiet. The southern Shadojak was leaning against the mast, arms folded and glaring at the skeletal crew, at Zionbuss and herself and at the Shadowlands in general. "That is precisely why I brought him."

"I don't get it."

"You will," Then changing the subject, Elora asked, "any news of Charwigg?"

Zionbuss nodded, "She's reached the plateau and has begun to carve into the mountain the dragon is chained to. She has no god-created tools to break the links themselves, so she's going to dig the beast free."

"And the Dragon Guard are allowing this?"

"Charwigg has them under her spell, they're even helping. It won't be long before the beast is airborne and then things will start to burn."

Elora stared at the approaching mountain range. Tall black and jagged, they appeared like broken teeth scattered atop the red desert. A line of dust snaked up from the huge rocks showing where Charwigg and her men worked to free the beast. They would be there soon.

"How high can the Necrolosis go?" Elora asked as she glanced skyward.

"We can go high enough to dwarf those mountains to pebbles, but if we kept going we would sail straight through the top of this world and vanish into nothing - just cease to be. Why, have you a plan?" Zionbuss asked, a wicked grin splitting his mouth.

"I'm working on one, but we need to get above the range of Grycul's mind. I don't want her filling my head again." She involuntary shivered at the painful memory.

Elora followed the demon to the foredeck and leaned on the bow beside him as he took control of the wheel; huge hands grasping the bones and spinning it so fast that the skulls on the outer rim became a blur. He bellowed an order which sent the rotting crew scrambling up the rigging to unfurl new sails while others began to push barrels over the gunnel.

"What are in those?" Elora asked, as she watched the barrels roll out into the air before hurtling below.

"Ballast," replied the demon as he settled the wheel and began to make minor adjustments. "They're just full of rocks and dust."

The ship began to rise as Elora's confidence began to sink. How was she going to kill Grycul? That is, if she could even get passed Charwigg. Luckily it wasn't herself she was relying on, but that other her – and she was full of confidence. She just hoped she would have the strength to snap out of the daughter of Chaos before she hurt someone other than the intended.

The Necrolosis seemed to move slower, although she knew it was the influence of them being higher which caused the effect. Yet she could suddenly feel another presence; something other than her on the edges of her mind, attempting to press in.

"She senses me," Elora said, while concentrating on not letting the dragon into her head.

"As I feared, my Queen. She's linked with you once already; it wouldn't be hard for her to form that link again."

They were closer now, the ship's shadow beginning to work its way up the foothills of the black mountains.

Zionbuss made to spin the wheel until Elora rested her hand upon his thick forearm. "No, stay your course, you need to get me directly above Grycul - It's time for me to become that other." Elora closed her eyes and took a deep breath. "Wish me luck and don't let me harm Sibiet."

"Sibiet?"

"Yeah. I told you there was a reason why I brought him along."

Elora approached the southern Shadojak, stepping purposely before him as she leaned against the gunnel. She folded her arms and waited for him to speak – she didn't wait long.

"I still don't see why you insisted on bringing me back into this forsaken place," Sibiet said, his scowl creasing up into his turban. "I doubt you've any intention on killing the dragon."

Elora smiled under his copper glare. "I felt sorry for you, it must be lonely without Drifid," she noticed him stiffen and knew he took the bait. "I do feel a little guilty after putting your Shaigun on his back."

"You leave Drifid out of this," snapped Sibiet, his wide nostrils flaring. "That boy is worth twice your

Shaigun. At least he stands by his honour and doesn't go falling in love with any old whore."

That stung, but that was her aim. She felt her anger rise and the whispers begin to hiss at the edge of her hearing.

"Probably to do with his blood, I told the Supreme there's no room in the league for a half-breed."

Elora grinned as she listened to the voices. She opened herself up to the darkness, letting it fill her...kill...kill...kill. The sails cracked tight, the ropes and bone planking creaked her name. Elora...Elora. The voices were singing to that other being, the darker creature that she had swallowed and kept hidden and at bay. But now she eased the grip on her mind, letting loose the daughter of the darkness and 'she' was as greedy for destruction as the darkness which whispered to her.

Far below, she sensed the beast. Grycul was listening, probing and attempting to take her mind – I'm coming, dragon.

"You were lucky at your judgment girl, if it..."

"Girl?" Elora snarled as she approached the older Shadojak. She wanted to take his head in her hands and burn him. But she still needed to rein that other her in; she still had a job to do, a dragon to kill and to do that she must keep a little self-control. "If I'm a girl, old man; why fear me so much?" She pursed her lips and blew him a kiss. "Or do you wish to be in Bray's position? After all, you haven't had any female company in decades."

Spit flew from the corners of Sibiet's mouth as he screamed at her, "How dare you? You, impertinent demon-whore."

Elora felt her world shake as her head was knocked sideways by the Shadojak's slap. It stung; a flaming heat across her mouth and cheek and she could taste blood – thank you, old man.

Kill…Kill.

She smiled as she licked a bead of blood from her split lip before it caught fire, deciding if she should rake out Sibiet's eyes before she torched him.

She approached with the intent to kill the Shadojak, anticipating the enjoyment of watching him writhe in pain, but Zionbuss stepped between them. A hand pressing against her chest while his other rested against Sibiets's arm that was reaching for his sword.

"Enough my Queen. Grycul is the prey intended, not the Shadojak," said the demon.

It took a tremendous amount of willpower for Elora to halt her advance when she could easily knock Zionbuss aside and sink her fingers into the Shadojak's skull.

Taking a deep breath, she stepped away, her eyes never leaving Sibiet's.

"Now you are the Daughter of Darkness, shall I take us down?" asked the horned giant.

Elora peered over the rail and stared at the mountains thousands of feet below.

"No need," she cast her gaze about the Necrolosis. "This rag and bone skiff is far too cumbersome."

She leapt upon the gunnel and balanced on the balls of her feet as a harsh wind tore at her cloak. Turning, she put her back to the red void and blew the Shadojak a kiss. Then simply fell back into the sky.

Above the sudden rush of air and wind she caught the snatches of Zionbuss laughing, until the distance between the ship and herself became too great and the whistling wind drowned out everything else. She spun her body so she was now facing down, pinning her arms to her sides to gain more speed, although she doubted she could drop any faster.

The mountains grew bigger, spreading out before her and beginning to show more features than just the jagged peaks. She could now pick out the plateau and the green mass at its centre that began to take shape.

A ball of fire spat towards her. From this distance it was no bigger than her fist, if Elora put it in front of her; harmless as it was pointless. Elora's grin grew wider - I'm coming, bitch.

Grycul pulled her chain tight as she turned her huge head skyward and roared. The dragon screamed both into the Shadowlands and in her mind, but Elora wasn't the weak little girl that had cast her violet eyes at the beast, she was now the daughter of Chaos and her gaze was crimson.

The ground approached her at a frightening speed, the faces of the Dragon Guards that surrounded Grycul coming into focus; the spears and swords held towards her and forming a huge bed of sharpened steel - what fun I will have with these, Elora mused.

As the rock raced up and the points of the weapons reached out, the daughter of Chaos reduced herself to smoke; the force of her fall creating a plume of dust that raised from the plateau as she weaved between the scaled men.

She experienced the thrill of a coming battle, sensed the blood and heartbeats of those she touched and felt the hatred and fear permeate from the dragon. She watched it all from her mind's eye, seen from a million different angles and positions as she flowed like a hurricane through the army.

Elora solidified in the midst of the dragon's soldiers, her father's sword in hand and began to cut through the multitude; sweeping her blade like the reaper parting corn, although she was death and her reaver parted limbs, split torsos and severed heads. A blood harvest.

They fell like leaves, three, four or five at a time – screaming, shouting and dying in pain and surprise. She was a maelstrom, moving through and amongst them like the wind, becoming smoke to dodge a blade, to pass through a spear or halberd, to reform to slice and destroy; father would be proud. She felt an exhilaration, ecstasy; like she was invincible and the more she destroyed, the more blood she spilt – the stronger the sensation grew.

Grycul felt her approach and roared in fury, in fear; for she knew that her life's end was working its back way towards her. I'm coming, laughed Elora, as she reaped another's life, then she sensed the presence of a demon.

The ranks of Dragon Guards suddenly parted and formed a large circle on the plateau that Elora drifted into, the echoes of her laugh bouncing around the rocks as she reformed at its centre. She glanced about her, at the fallen and slain, at the limbless bodies, the bodiless heads and the blood. Her lips pouted as she absorbed the carnage, her chest rising and falling in euphoria. This was Chaos, this was her legacy and this was what she had to give to the world.

Grycul suddenly roared once again, scorching the air around them with fire. Yes, thought Elora, they'll be plenty of time to burn – after the fun.

She was about to turn to smoke once again and begin reaping afresh when Charwigg stepped into the circle, the soldiers parting their scaly shields to allow her through.

"What a sweet reunion," said the demon, her hips swaying as she snaked her way closer, delicately stepping around the bodies. Elora noticed that the black leather bandages, wrapped about her body, were coated in red dust.

"Been digging, demon?" asked Elora as she brought her Soul Reaver to the fore.

Charwigg, chuckled. "Only until you arrived, sis. But it's no fun clawing at this foul rock, the chain that binds Grycul is buried too deep. Still, we're making progress." Dark eyes glistened with mischief as she nodded towards Elora's drawn sword. "Unless I may borrow your god-created tool."

It was Elora's turn to laugh. "I doubt it," she shrugged her shoulders. "Maybe you could pry it from my dead fingers."

"Dead fingers?" said Charwigg, giggling like a child as she gestured to the many mutilated men scattered about them. "Have you not had your fill of death, Elora?"

The reaver whistled against the wind as Elora cut several slices from the air before levelling it out at the demon. "You can never have too much death. It is what everything is after all. Life is just that; death at different stages. Even a newborn, from when it takes its very first breath has begun a journey through the final door."

Charwigg began to step around the edge of the ring, black gaze never leaving hers as she circled like a shark.

"Time was against us when last we met," said the demon playfully as she skipped over the fallen wreck of a Dragon Guar. The shell of his armoured chest was sliced open and his gruesome inner-workings, slopping out of the crack. "Perhaps I should have stayed a little longer and taken the sword from you. Grycul would have been free by now."

The darkness laughed with Elora, a thousand whispers carried on the dusty breeze, goading her on.

"I'm not the same weak child I was then, demon. I'm so much more."

Charwigg nudged a head with her bare foot, while raising an eyebrow. "As I can see, but you won't defeat me in battle. Join me. Let us free the dragon together, let us rule the Dark Army and release Chaos into both worlds."

"Chaos is mine for releasing, as well as your blood," Elora said, feeling her grin spreading across her face. "You've almost reached the end of your journey, demon, you'll be passing through the final door in the next few moments, followed closely by Grycul."

Charwigg's face shifted awkwardly into a scowl, a million tiny beads shifting below her skin to reform into the angry expression.

"So be it, daughter of Solarius," she said, as she crouched low, ready to spring. "I gave you the chance of life, to rule alongside me."

"Rather his daughter, than a creature created from the leftovers."

Charwigg screamed in frustration as she sprang towards her, sharp nails raised and ready to strike.

Elora rolled left and slid her blade sideways into the demon's thigh, yet only grazed the skin; Charwigg's flesh already shifting and moulding around the reaver and becoming an extra hand, complete with long razor-like talons.

Twisting her blade free, Elora spun away to avoid a vicious kick to her midriff, but received a punch to the back of her head that sent her reeling into the surrounding Dragon Guards. Tears blurred her vision as she was roughly pushed back into the ring, shoved from the tear-shaped shields.

Kill…Kill…Kill – Elora vented a roar of her own, equal to that of the thrashing dragon, as she used the momentum of the shove and flowed it into a sprint. Anger now driving the thrust that she led with. Charwigg snapped her head to the side, narrowly avoiding the point of the sword, bending her body backwards in a chorus of knuckle pops as she changed shape once again; her legs becoming arms, dagger-shaped hands that flicked out lightning fast to jab at Elora's oncoming form.

Outside the ring, beyond the crowd of men, Grycul gnawed at her chains; metal screaming in protest but holding against the vicious onslaught. The dragon screamed in frustration and spat fire above the guard that protected her and filled the red sky with a white shade of heat.

"What makes you think you can control the dragon, if you freed her?" Elora asked as she blocked and parried every attack from the many-limbed, beast. "Once she's parted with those chains she'll tear through Earth. She's a beast of destruction."

"That's the intention. She can spread Chaos throughout the lands while I find that other weapon, the relic the Dark Army digs for."

As the last word fell from her sentence, Charwigg dropped to the ground and flicked her legs over her head; her feet connecting with Elora's chest and sending her onto her back.

Her breath was knocked out of her, Elora rolled away to avoid a kick to the head. She flipped back onto her feet and reflexively dodged Charwigg's teeth as they gnashed together by her neck, close enough for her to feel the snap.

"I'm intrigued - what's the weapon in the ground?" Elora asked, swiping an elbow into the demon's ribs and yanking it away when the god-created body began to absorb it.

"It was our father's final target, the mechanism in which Chaos will pulse through the worlds, uniting what had been parted in the time of the small gods."

"A mechanism? A machine?" The momentary lapse in concentration earned Elora a claw being raked down the side of her face, opening up a gash that oozed molten blood.

"Oops!" laughed Charwigg at seeing the pain on Elora's face. But the scowl swiftly returned as flames hissed along the injury and it healed up. "Yes, it's just a machine, one that when used, can never be undone. Life will change forever."

"Chaos," Elora whispered, narrowing her crimson eyes.

Charwigg nodded as she came on, four arms raised, hands shaped like spear heads.

"Then let's end this," Elora said.

She ducked the attack and reduced herself to smoke, passing over and between the demon to reform behind her - slipping her blade along Charwigg's neck and feeling her sword bite deep. When she spun around to face her opponent she watched the demon's partially severed head flop over at a right angle, slick black beads like beetle shells, spilling from the gaping wound.

The body fell to its knees as its many hands busied themselves at catching the falling black mass and pushing the head back straight. Wet popping sounds echoed around the ring as its flesh began to knit together, the swirling symbols tattooed on the body glowing red as a grin formed on the demon's mouth.

"The blade can't kill me. Not even yours," said Charwigg as her head was finally righted. "So I ask you one more time sister – will you join me?"

Elora answered with her sword, slicing through the neck once again, only this time completely.

The shiny black beads poured from the stump more readily, spilling to the ground as the head bounced from the dusty rock.

She might not be able to kill her with her blade, but she would make it difficult. Stooping low she picked up the head by the strands of lank hair. She held it before her and winked at the dark eyes that stared back, the demon's mouth working up and down; vacant of sound where only tiny beads fell out.

"I will come back to destroy you properly, but for now, I've got an appointment with the dragon."

Elora spun the head around and around before hurling it over the watching soldiers. It spun through the air, falling from view and hopefully from the plateau; Grycul screeching into the sky only adding to the drama.

With their champion bested and only themselves standing between her and the beast, the Dragon Guards moved as one.

They rushed to the centre of the circle, stomping over their falling comrades in a desperate frenzy to kill her. Steel blazed in the fire spat from the beast, an uncountable array of sharp weapons hacking their way towards her, ready to part her with her flesh.

Metal clashed as all sides converged onto smoke, stray blades and spears finding the men on the opposing end as the oncoming crushed those at the front. But Elora paid it no heed as she flowed through the throng; gliding over, under and between the masses in the maelstrom of anger she was before.

The dragon thrashed against her bonds as Elora materialised at her huge feet. It raised up on powerful hind legs, buffeting wind and dust as it fought to take flight. Long teeth snapped together as it realised its futile attempts of escape were useless. If it hadn't freed itself in the past thousand millenniums, it wouldn't do so now.

Elora stood tall, her blade dangling slack in her hand, the point resting against the ground. She stared up at Grycul, the monster looming no shorter than fifty feet above. Craning her neck, she gazed into the demented yellow eyes and saw anger, frustration, fear and Chaos – Elora saw herself.

The dragon opened its mouth wide, ready to spit fire; her sharp tongue curling back as the brimstone gas began to flame.

A large white-hot jet spewed forth, Elora reduced to smoke to avoid her flesh melting from her bones, then solidified once again and dropped upon the dragon's scaly back; sliding a leg either side of its neck. It felt cold to the touch, the opposite of the fire arcing towards her as the scaly flesh shifted beneath.

Elora, raised her sword high, gripping tight as she brought it crashing down, the blade slicing through air, through fire; before severing the thick links of the chains.

The sudden release of her bonds caught the dragon off balance as she struggled to keep to her feet. Elora took the opportunity to grasp the length of chain that was still attached to Grycul's neck and throw it over the beast's head to snap it tight into her gaping mouth.

The dragon thrashed anew, heavy feet slamming into the ground, its thick tail striking rock and men and sending parts of both crashing over the plateau.

Elora pulled the chain tighter, digging her heels into the muscled neck for purchase as the huge head gnawed at the steel in her mouth. The dragon's large wings battered the air, the downdraft strong enough to blow the soldiers over as Grycul began to rise above her army.

The beast jerked in the air, attempting to dislodge Elora from her perch, but she was comfortably sat in place, legs hugging the writhing monster beneath. Realising her efforts at shaking her burden were useless, the dragon snapped her head around, trying to bite Elora. But with every twist of her long neck, Elora pulled back, forcing the head straight, using the chain like a bit attached to horse's reins.

Increasing the pressure on Grycul, Elora kicked her flank, driving her upwards, above the plateau and away from the shouting men.

Amongst the scuffling guard, Elora's gaze fell on Charwigg, her many limbed body scrambling about the legs of the soldiers as it sought the head – there must be a way to finish the demon off.

The dragon climbed into the red sky fighting Elora as she rose; thrashing, biting and whipping her long tail yet failing to land a single blow. She spun in the air, forelegs kicking and narrowly missed the Necrolosis. Her huge wings wafting the ship's sails in a way that forced the craft to list to one side. Elora glanced at the wide-grinning Captain. Zionbuss was beaming with pride while Sibiet held fast to the gunnel, holding her with his copper stare.

They rose higher, the dragon neither letting up or slowing her ascent. Screaming out while spitting fire as Elora held on, the mountains below shrinking away from them.

Above them the ceiling of the world came into view, a blanket of red and orange fire that spread out into the distance. Elora felt the heat it permeated as it lit the Shadowlands. Zionbuss told her that if you passed through the ceiling, you simply ceased to be – well let us put that theory to the test, she thought.

"Higher!" screamed Elora, tugging the chain and steering the huge reptilian head upwards. "Higher, Grycul, you're not scared of dying, are you? Let us go together, let us see what's on the other side."

The darkness sang in excitement – willing her on, a thousand voices adding to the chorus...Kill...Elora...Kill.

The dragon roared in protest and spun upside-down at the final moment, the flames licking her belly before she began to descend.

Elora felt a pang of disappointment, as if the dragon had taken something away from her; the answer to oblivion, to cease to be. But her grin soon returned as they gathered speed, Grycul folding her wings in close, the wind howling passed her ears.

They fell at a rate more rapid than Elora's descent as she dropped from the Necrolosis. The mountains racing up to meet them at a furious speed as they headed directly for a jagged peak.

A heartbeat before impact Grycul flicked her wings out and spun, meaning to dislodge Elora with the rock. But seeing what the dragon was about to do, Elora reduced her body to smoke for the fraction of time that it took to pass.

In frustration the beast rolled several times and began to thrash once more, her entire green body dipping and bucking. Elora held tight, teeth now clenched as they passed between two tall pillars of rock before suddenly dropping once again and flying vertically down at the rushing ground.

Elora steered the dragon on, pulling her to the side and forcing Grycul to bank left in a long curving arc. She then pulled the other way, not giving the beast any room to make her own judgements. They flew in a large 'S' shape, sweeping through the sky before corkscrewing down.

Elora leapt from Grycul's back as the dragon crashed into the plateau. The beast's body gouged a deep channel in the ground, bowling over the guards before coming to a stop in a red cloud.

Landing deftly, Elora approached the beast as it snorted dust from huge nostrils. Grycul struggled to raise her head, shaking with the effort as she worked her mouth about. She roared at Elora, her mouth opening wide to reveal the rows of long teeth, some now trickling with blood from the impact.

Elora screamed in response and punched the dragon as hard as she could under its armoured chin.

"Kneel!" she shouted, contorting her face in rage as she pressed her nose against Grycul's and stared into those yellow eyes. "Kneel, before your master."

The daughter of Chaos stepped away as the huge beast clumsily raised its battered body from the rock, submission written plainly in its downcast gaze, slumping wings and shoulders. She gave Elora a final glance before bowing her head low and sinking to the ground.

Elora stared at the dragon, now heaving with exhaustion and now under her command. She felt the grin on her face as she turned to survey the Dragon Guards that had been advancing on her, weapons raised and ready to kill. They were now still, swords and spears lowering and as one they knelt; striking the rock with the base of their shields and bowing their heads low.

Surveying the throng before her, Elora began to laugh. She came to kill a dragon and had gained an army. Had come to slay the beast, yet gained the obedience of the most terrifying creature that Thea had ever known. Her father would be so very proud. But he had burnt to nothing in the Church of Minu by his own sword, wielded by his own daughter – funny how things work out. Chaos was unpredictable.

"Youuuu!" came a voice screeching with pain and fury. "You will rule beneath me, or I will kill you."

Elora turned and stared at Charwigg as she advanced, her crooked neck still popping in places as it righted itself. A thin trail of black beads glistened as the final remnants of the gash healed up. She held several swords, from several limbs. Six in all and pointing towards her.

"I told you I wouldn't be easy to kill; not even your god-created steel could end me. Nothing can," said the demon as she expertly sliced through the air, the many blades she held moving in a silver blur. "I'm going to keep coming back, no matter how many times you take my head. You will realise sister, that I am the superior power. I will rule the worlds."

Elora took a deep breath and blew through pursed lips, the wind-milling swords were so close now that she could feel the breeze they created. Yet she didn't give any ground, her eyes never leaving those of the demon's.

"Bend the knee to me, daughter of Solarius, and I will let you live."

Elora couldn't hide the smirk she felt forming on her mouth, the excitement at feeling death so near, so close she could simply take a step forwards and it would be upon her. But her time wasn't now and this wouldn't be the place.

"I bend the knee to no one," Elora said, then reflexively stepped away as a large shadow passed above and the powerful foot of the dragon came crashing down onto the demon.

Swords clattered away as Charwigg was crushed; her head and arms flailing out through the talons, thrashing against the weight that flattened her. Black beads spewed from her mouth, like blood it formed a puddle, but unlike before it couldn't reform with the overwhelming pressure pushing the body into the rock.

Dark eyes locked on Elora's, "You cannot kill me," gargled Charwigg, spitting the blackness out against large red scales.

"I won't kill you," Elora said, leaning down so her face was inches from the trapped demon. "Grycul will."

Turning away from Charwigg, Elora tenderly placed a hand against the dragon's nose then traced a finger over the huge mouth and along a long tooth.

"Burn the bitch," Elora ordered as she walked away from the beast.

Charwigg's screams echoed around the plateau as the foul smell of cooking flesh tickled her nose. There are many ways to die, thousands - but burning had to be right up there with one of the worst ways to go.

Another shadow passed above bringing Elora out of her morbid musings. She watched the Necrolosis as it hovered a few above the ground, the green sea of souls hugging the rock like a dense mist. A rope ladder was dropped over the gunnel and Zionbuss approached, flanked by the southern Shadojak and several of the skeletal crew.

"I knew you wouldn't kill the dragon," spat Sibiet, curling a lip in disgust as Grycul began to devour the charred remains of the demon. Biting down where the blacked stump of a head was and gulping the gruesome remains in three swallows. "When the Supreme hears about this, he'll have you…"

Elora hadn't realised she was going to punch the Shadojak until his body hit the ground; and by the stunned expression on Sibiet's face, a trail of blood leaking from a ruined nose, neither did he.

His shock lasted only a moment before his Shadojak reflexes kicked in and he sprang to his feet, brandishing his huge scimitar before him.

The curved blade cut across Elora, the sword aiming to decapitate, but she easily sidestepped the attack and grasped the scimitar over Sibiet's hand and wrenched it from him.

The Shadojak's own bodyweight tipped him off balance and he tripped over Elora's heel as he went down.

She was about to follow his falling body with a thrust to the heart from his own sword, when Zionbuss intervened.

"No, my Queen," said the horned giant.

"No?" Elora asked, feeling the exhilaration of a coming kill.

Zionbuss shrugged his huge bare shoulders. "You ordered me to not let any harm come to the Shadojak."

Elora laughed, the order had come from that weaker half she shared her body with. Shifting her gaze, she took in the pathetic man lying on the floor. Shaking, covered in dust and his turban had come loose to reveal loose grey strands beneath.

"Very well. Take him back to Thea - let him deliver this message to the Supreme, to the Emperor. Let them hunt me, let them bring more death and carnage." She tossed the scimitar at Zionbuss who deftly caught it. "And have a new sword. If you decide you want the soul memories on the voyage back," she nodded towards the fallen Shadojak, "then you know what to do."

Zionbuss, snapped an order to his crew and they began to carry Sibiet back to the Necrolosis.

"And what of you, my Queen. You will not return with us?" asked the demon as he tucked the scimitar into the belt around his skirt.

Elora grinned as Grycul stepped close enough for her to climb onto her back once again.

"No, I've got a world to conquer and a relic of a machine to dig up."

"Chaos to spread?"

Elora kicked her heels into the dragon's flanks and Grycul responded immediately. The huge beast crouched low before springing into the air, great wings spreading out either side to batter the rock with wind and dust.

"They'll be plenty of that," shouted Elora as she steered the beast into the red sky, feeling Grycul's mind linking with her own and just as eager to reach Earth.

Chapter 19

Betrayal

Bray put his shoulder to the door causing dust to fall from the frame. Lanterns picked up the ancient motes as they scattered about the dank tunnel and forced a cough from Flek.

"It moved," offered the Voice, pointing at the dark gap barely an inch wide. He set the lantern on the stone floor and joined Bray, adding his own weight to that of the Shaigun's.

Together they pushed against the old wood and with a high-pitched groan from the hinges, it finally gave.

Bray gripped Flek's cloak, preventing his overbalanced body from falling into the blackness of the room. Then pulled him out of the way as he picked up the lantern and strode purposefully in.

"Careful, Bray. Nobody's been in there for centuries; there's no telling what's inside."

Bray heard the words but didn't care. His mood matched the gloom and suited the darkness. And if he was being truthful, he wished the Voice would go back up to the vast libraries and leave him alone. There were thousands of scrolls, old tombs and charts to sieve through, which were better suited to Flek, while the catacomb-like maze deep under the palace was more suited to himself - especially in the black mood he was in.

The smell of damp mould and rotting wood permeated the room, Bray held the lantern aloft to reveal the secrets that were long ago locked away. The chamber was cluttered with simple chests stacked against walls where they'd soaked up the condensation that clung to the mud and stone. A thin trickle of water ran along the centre of the room where it had worn a deep channel into the stone slabs which were placed down before the first palace was built. Like Rams Keep back on Earth, this building had a network of tunnels and hidden rooms scattered beneath it. Locked and long forgotten they belonged to a different time, a different people.

Bray put the toe of his boot to the nearest chest meaning to nudge the lid open, but the crumbling timber gave beneath the pressure and his foot pushed through.

"Rotten, just like the others," Flek said, peering over Bray's shoulder.

Bray shook his boot free. "What did you expect? We can't be far from the river, so the mud from all these walls will be saturated."

This was the fourth room they had broken into and with the same results as before. Rot, decay and damp. Even the rats which they found in the higher levels of the catacombs had avoided these more sinister chambers.

Flek flexed his hands making his leather gloves creak under the pressure. "I'm sure we'll find something soon, maybe the next tunnel will be dryer."

Bray followed the Voice out of the chamber, not bothering to close the door behind him – the wood was swollen and warped and probably wouldn't shut anyway.

They followed the dark corridor as it led deeper under the palace, the lantern light playing along the dust coated cobwebs that clung to the ceiling so thickly that the beams and empty sconces were no more than grey mounds. Nobody had been down here for a long while, it may have been safer for the Emperor to order the entire warrens below the palace to be filled in and save the risk of the building collapsing into the mud.

Ducking beneath a fallen beam, Bray stopped outside another door, this one half buried beneath a rock which had sunk in a semi-landslide, but which appeared stable enough if left undisturbed.

"You might want to back off to a safe distance," Bray warned as he put his hands to the partially visible door and put pressure against the wood. At least this one seemed dry.

"We can skip this one, it may not be prudent to upset anything," Flek replied, eyeing the huge boulder.

"No rock left unturned, remember?" Bray replied.

Flek shook his head, "Bad choice of words."

The chords on the back of Bray's hand stretched as he gently applied pressure to the door, eyes firmly locked on the boulder for any indication it would shift. Beside him, Flek held his breath as the door suddenly jerked inwards.

Instinctively Bray dropped to his knees and was about to drag Flek out of the way, but the boulder held, only a trail of soil dislodged from its outer edge to spill to the floor.

"That was easier than I thought," Flek offered, mirroring Bray's thoughts as he grasped the lantern and crawled into the open doorway.

The chamber was larger than the previous ones they had searched and it was mercifully dryer. Cobwebs and dust coated everything, but there was no sign of damp.

"Interesting," Flek said as he approached a large object in the centre of the room, a grey sheet flung over it. He pulled it free, sending a shower of dust in the air and revealing a bust of a figure sat upon a short marble plinth; its face long ago worn and missing a nose.

"Emperor Delimal?" Bray asked, tapping the carved head.

Flek wiped his finger along its base, revealing old writing which had weathered no better than the rest of it. "I Don't think so. Why would it be down here and not locked in a vault above? It must be priceless. But I'm thinking it's from the time of the small gods."

"It looks old enough. So we're in the right area," Bray said as he studied the rest of the room.

He approached another object similar in size to the bust which was also covered in an old sheet. Removing the cover Bray revealed a large sphere made from the same dull marble as the bust, with an intricate pattern carved into it. He ran his finger along the grooves and ridges, bringing his lantern closer.

"It's a globe. Thea," stated Flek, excitedly. "Finally we've found something."

"Not Thea," replied Bray, pointing at the contours of a large continent. "See. On Earth this is Italy, you can make out the leg-like shape of the country as it reaches away from Europe. It's whole. On Thea, this part is under the sea. Remember, the people there had dug a channel severing the tip into a new country."

"Gosland," Flek said. "I could never understand why the king wanted to part his people from the mainland."

"Exactly. But they did and only after the great rift which parted the worlds."

The Voice nodded, "So if this is Earth, Where's Thea?"

They both scanned over the rest of the objects in the room, but there wasn't anything the same size and shape as the globe. Bray studied the stone walls, searching for clues while Flek pulled another sheet from a large frame that turned out to be a plain mirror. When he realised it was nothing special he joined Bray at examining the stonework.

"There has to be something here in this room," Bray said, determined to find whatever it was, although his mind kept wandering back to Elora.

He had watched her leave earlier. Observed her and Flek exchanging a few words beyond the walls before she departed out of sight. He had expected Flek to join her and was surprised that he returned to help him search the palace libraries and vaults. He was even more astonished when Flek explained that Elora had chosen Sibiet to accompany her in place of himself.

"Don't worry," Flek said.

Bray realised that he had paused in his search, his fingers held above a crack in the stonework while he stared off into another place.

"Don't worry?" repeated Bray. Easy for him to say, it wasn't his girlfriend; his love that had disappeared into the Shadowlands to kill a dragon. "Are you sure she didn't tell you anything before she walked away?"

Bray heard the desperate tone in his words but didn't care anymore. And he could trust Flek, he had known him since his days in the shades and he seemed to know about his relationship with Elora and appeared to be the only one not judging him for it.

Flek sighed, "What do you want me to say?" He placed a gloved hand on Bray's shoulder. "She knows what she's doing."

"And Sibiet? Do you believe what he says, what he's told the Emperor and the Supreme?"

Sibiet had returned a few hours after they departed. Dropped from the gate into the Shadowlands and left unconscious. A party of Shades found and returned him. When the Shadojak had awoken he told of how Elora had turned traitor and instead of killing Grycul, set her free. Elora rode the dragon to Earth to join the Dark Army and spread Chaos.

Bray had not believed a word of it until Sibiet explained that she had also taken his sword, his Soul Reaver and given it to the demon Zionbuss. That was when he began to worry and realised that the Shadojak was speaking the truth or a truth which he himself believed. But could it be possible? Could his Elora have done such a thing? Of course, there was no telling what devastation the daughter of Chaos would do if Elora couldn't control her.

"Argh, look!" Flek said, becoming animated as he brushed dust from the wall with his sleeve. "It's a circle."

Bray snapped out of his troubled thoughts and began to clean the stone. If he was to help Elora then he needed to find this weapon.

The circle was large and simple, below which were words and runes chiselled into the wall. Flek ran his finger over them.

"Chaos will unite us," he said.

Bray nodded, he recognised the runes from the older pieces of parchment they had found amongst the library.

"So where's the rest of it? Where's the other circle overlapping this?" Bray asked as he began to clean dust from the other walls.

Within a few moments the stonework was visible and a grey cloud hovered about the chamber. Bray waited for the dust to settle, yet it was clear that there were no more signs, shapes or runes anywhere. It was a mystery to where the other pieces of the puzzle were.

"Don't worry, we'll find it," Flek offered.

Bray took a deep breath and unclenched his fists. He felt desperate and it must have shown on his face.

"Don't worry," the Voice repeated. "We're getting close, rushing in like a bull-at-a-gate might make us overlook something."

Bray knew that his companion was right. He might destroy a vital clue in his haste to find the weapon before Elora did.

"Sit here and think, don't touch anything, just think," ordered Flek as he crossed the room. "I'll fetch us something to eat." He opened the door and paused, his grime-filled face turning serious for a moment.

"When I said goodbye to Elora, at the palace gates; she did say something, but insisted that I not say a word to you, but...I feel that you ought to know."

"What is it? What did she say?" Bray took another breath to stop himself from gripping the Voice by the arms and shaking it from him.

Flek sighed. "She said that the reason she didn't want you to accompany her was that she couldn't trust you and couldn't trust herself."

Bray didn't understand and was about to ask what she could have meant when Flek held up a hand to stop him; his face full of sympathy.

"She said that after killing the dragon she would carry on through the Shadowlands and reach Earth." Flek curled his fingers in his glove and tapped the door, his gaze falling to the floor. "And she wanted me to find her another Shaigun and send him to her."

Bray cleared the chamber in two strides, ready to slam Flek through the wall, but gained control in time to prevent the disaster. It wasn't the Voice's fault; he was just the messenger.

Flek lay his hand upon his arm, "Elora told me to explain things to you once this was all over. Once she had reset the balance. She told me to tell you that you are now free. You can choose to be anything that you want to be - Shaigun even, but not to her."

Bray's arms fell to his side, he felt giddy, nauseous. "It's not true."

Flek shook his head, "I'm sorry, my friend. Elora has taken the role of Shadojak seriously. Maybe you should too."

"Why tell me now?" Bray heard the resignation in his own voice, Flek had no reason to lie.

His companion stepped out into the corridor before he turned to offer him a sad smile. "Because I need you to focus. You need to be who you were before all this. You need to be Shaigun. If not…well like Elora said, you're free to go."

Flek ducked beneath the boulder and began to trudge away. "Use this time to think, Bray. I'll bring us something from the servant's kitchens; that is if the sugar sprites haven't run amok again."

Bray ran his fingers through his hair as he began to pace the room. Elora couldn't end things between them. She just couldn't leave without a word or an explanation.

Tears prickled the edges of his lashes as he forced his emotions back - he wouldn't cry. If he let the pain take hold of him he would be no use to anyone, least of all to Elora herself. Instead he concentrated on the Shaigun training, his abilities to master his emotions; love is only a chemical reaction in the brain. Yet his mind returned to Flek's words desperately seeking a new meaning from them, a hidden message that would give a hint to Elora's actions of why he may be doomed to spend the rest of his life alone.

Even the mention of the sugar sprites carried him back to a time in his youth, before he left the church of the Blessed Mother and joined the Imperial Guards. That was also a lonely time when his only friend was a sugar sprite which he had kept as a kind of pet. Bray let out a dry laugh at the memory. He'd absentmindedly swatted what he thought was an annoying fly and only realised it was a sprite when his gaze fell to its limp body on the desk he had been studying upon. Carefully he placed the tiny body in a jar and kept it by his bedside, guilt forcing him to gently nurse the small creature back to health. Within a week of feeding it sugar or honey that he had stolen from the church's stores, he witnessed the light and colour return to the sprites wings as it recovered. After another week had passed the sugar sprite was strong enough for him to release from the jar. Bray had fully expected the thimble-sized creature to fly away, to zip from harm and maybe disappear into the mirror it came from. But the sprite stayed and shocked him further by remaining by his side, no matter where he went. Neary, he had called her. She had been with him for over a year before one day, she simply flew off into a mirror never to return.

Bray rested his brow against the cold stone wall, taking deep breaths and trying to calm himself. Was life any easier for a creature of light that lived in the mirror world; only coming out for a nip of honey or a taste of sugar? No, they probably had their own sprite problems. He pulled away from the wall and stretched his neck, he needed to focus.

Dust flaked from his fingers as he traced the circle once again, searching for anything that would lead him on. The large sphere didn't offer anything else, other than the image of how Earth appeared a few thousand years ago – much the same as it did now, he expected. He lifted the sheets and roughly shook the years of grime from the grey material, thinking that maybe they were great canvasses with hidden meanings scrolled on them, but no. He let them drop to the floor as he began to pace again, keeping his mind in check as it attempted to wander back to Flek's painful words. Then his gaze settled on the simple mirror that was left propped against the wall.

Bray approached the wooden frame, standing almost as tall as himself he stared at his own reflection; something wasn't right.

Grey dust covered the entire chamber: it coated the walls, clung to the other objects and the old sheets, even sticking to himself, yet not one speck touched the glass of the mirror. Odd.

He leaned in close enough to blow his warm breath against it, yet the surface did not mist up and he felt a subtle draft play with the hairs on the back of his hand.

Was the mirror charmed? There were no etchings on the frame, no runes or binding symbols, yet Bray felt as though there was more to this object than it its appearance suggested.

He stepped away to study it and noticed the reflection of the other objects, the large globe sitting just off-centre to the circle on the wall. Could it be…?

Bray gripped the frame and shifted the mirror a foot to the left and angled it in such a way, that it placed the reflection of the sphere inside the image on the wall.

Now the globe appeared to dull and became a shade darker. Along the base of the marble, the shadows merged together to form ancient-styled writing.

He pulled his gaze away to glance behind him but everything was as it was before, the globe still the shade it was when they first revealed it and there was no writing at its base. When he returned his attention to the reflection he witnessed the changes once again; the globe overlapping the circle like the symbol of the twin worlds which they had found in scrolls, and scribbled by the Supreme and indeed the same insignia used by Silk. The writing at the bottom of the circle also paired with that on the base of the sphere – Chaos will unite us; Chaos will set us free.

Bray had found it. He had solved the puzzle, but what did it mean? Where was the weapon? He pushed his fingers through his hair as he debated whether to fetch Flek and show him what he had found, then his eyes picked up something else in the mirror. An object that wasn't in the room.

Nothing more than a smudge on the glass, the strange phenomenon began to take shape the more Bray focused on it until it became recognisable as a rock floating in mid-air, although only appearing on the image inside the mirror.

Stepping closer Bray reached out to grasp the rock but instead of his hand meeting resistance from the glass, his fingers passed through, then his hand and arm. The rock spread out before him and as his fingertips brushed against the solid matter he realised he'd found a hidden tunnel inside the mirror.

An excitement, pulsed through him as he retrieved his arm and flexed his fingers. It all felt and worked fine. Maybe the weapon was hidden inside.

He stooped to pick up the lantern and was about to leave the room to find Flek when he paused. There wasn't time, and he doubted the Voice would follow him into the strange mirror-land. Instead, Bray licked his finger and swiftly scribbled on the wall, leaving Flek the message of what he'd found and where he was going.

He thought about leaving the lantern for when his friend returned; better to see his message with, then decided he would most likely need it himself.

Pushing the strong emotions of betrayal aside, Bray gingerly placed his foot through the looking glass, found solid ground then stepped into the mirror-world.

Flek ducked under the boulder hanging precariously outside the door and stepped inside the room. Betrayal was consuming his mind and forced a smile upon his lips – this had been child's play. The plan flowed so smoothly that it just had to be the right course; it was as if the god's themselves had been guiding his hands – well, Neptula anyway.

He held his free hand up, the leather glove creaking as he flexed the unfamiliar fingers beneath. With his other hand he placed the lantern on the marble pillar beside the globe. He knew he would need it. Bray would have been a fool not to take his.

Flek's gaze fell on the wall where Bray had left him a message: found secret tunnel through mirror, have gone through – Bray.

Flek's smile grew wider as he wiped it clear, dislodging dust that floated to the floor. Well, it wasn't dust really. It was flour, stained grey with ash and scattered about the chamber to appear as dust that had built up over centuries. The truth was that Flek has spent many weeks in this very room. Hour upon hour deciphering the riddle.

He stepped lightly to the mirror that Bray had passed through only moments before, watching his reflection as it smiled back at him.

"Perfect," Flek told himself as he straightened his tunic and cloak.

Doubts had played in his mind for the past few days, the judgment had been the biggie, yet the old man had pulled through as intended. He felt relief after Elora was spared, she was the vital part to his plan, the key. It was the Emperor that kicked the cauldron over. Arranging a deal that put Elora back in danger; to kill Grycul no less. That was when he thought his months of planning had gone to ruin. Weeks spent in the dark and musty libraries and cellars, searching for clues to the hidden weapon and finally finding it. The endless hours given over to this room and then finally deciphering the puzzle that opened the tunnel – all that would have been for nothing should the girl die, should Bray die before the allotted time - but what could he do? Once the Emperor had made up his mind, it was made up.

It was by sheer luck that Elora chose to leave her Shaigun, sparing at least one of them. That was when he saw his opportunity to go with her. He could pretend to be an observer, then simply entice the daughter of Chaos out of her, that was all he needed to do then she would do the rest. When Elora chose to leave him also, his first thought was to refuse, to demand he be taken, but when she asked for Sibiet to go in his place he almost choked.

The southern Shadojak was a sure way to drag that demon bitch out of her and that was when he realised that that was her intention all along. If she had to kill Grycul, she would need to be that other her. So be it; but afterwards she wouldn't be able to gain control of herself again. Perfect. And then, when Sibiet returned to tell of how she didn't kill the dragon and that in fact she had rode Grycul to Earth, Flek could almost have kissed the old fool.

Flek laughed, his mirror-image chuckling with him.

He raised his right hand to the mirror and tapped the glass. A solid ring echoed inside the chamber, while his left passed through without meeting resistance. When he had gone through the looking glass to the hidden tunnel, some few weeks earlier, he had needed to remove his hand – apparently god-created metal couldn't pass the barrier. It was a small task to unscrew his five fingered weapon and he gladly shed his burden while he probed into the mirror realm, seeking the ancient machine. The object of which Bray will find by the morning and of which he will use, as long as Elora played her unknowing part.

"Oh, the trappings of love," Flek sang to himself.

It hadn't been hard to coax Bray into doing what he wanted him to do. A suggestion here, a tap in the right direction there, and then a few words to drive him on. Easy, so easy it was meant to happen. The last lies he told him were only an afterthought, but Bray took them like a greedy tiger trout after the wriggling maggot.

That face the Shaigun pulled after he had been told she no longer wanted him; priceless – that he was free to go, that she wouldn't see him again. For a moment Flek believed that Bray would strike him, but luckily he regained control.

Flek tapped his fingers against the glass a final time before curling his hand into a fist and striking the mirror.

It shattered, showering the floor with sharp shards and splinters, each reflecting Flek's grin.

Bray could never leave the tunnels, he would use the weapon and die with the effects of the machine.

"I am sorry, little half-breed," Flek said to the pile of glass at his feet. His past had intermingled with Bray's several times. They joined the Shades together, entered on the Shaigun path alongside each other and became friends. Bray had even helped him pass some of the tests and spent evenings practicing his swordsmanship; showing him a better way to dance between the blades. Things had been going well, right up until he had lost his thumb in a duel. His path to becoming Shaigun had been severed with his opposing digit.

Flek rubbed his new thumb, the hardened metal which flowed into the rest of his god-created hand which Neptula had gifted him with. That day he lost the duel, his new life began. It was tortuous at first, months spent grovelling and pleading with the Supreme to let him stay on in some kind of capacity at the garrison. He no longer possessed a whole hand to wield a sword, but the skills he had learned and the wisdom he'd acquired was worth something. The Supreme had given him the position as his Voice. He should have been grateful - he had been at first, but years of serving the 'great man', had worn him down. Time spent watching his friends become Shaiguns and a few even reaching the heights of becoming a Shadojak while he was little more than a servant, a lackey.

More likely than not another year would have seen him leave, to be free of the place as he sought his own path away from the garrison. But a final errand as the Voice had him crossing the open seas to Paqueet, on a peace-keeping mission for the Supreme. They had hit bad weather and the ship they sailed upon had sunk, although the reasons for the vessel's damage was more due to the sea witch Neptula, than the influence of the storm.

The vessel had gone down fast and every hand on deck had gone into the water. Within moments the men were pulled down into the inky depths, disappearing swiftly until only Flek remained.

He went cold as the memory touched his mind.

Neptula toyed with him at first, pulling him below the waves, then letting him surface before he passed out – a game that amused her while her children fed on the rest of the crew. He thought he would die that day. Eaten by the sea witch herself, yet the fates had intervened.

"Flek, I have a proposition for you," she had said, smiling at him and showing row upon row of tiny triangular teeth. "Don't look surprised, I don't attack ships randomly. I knew you were aboard."

Flek had struggled in her cold embrace, the sour breath of Neptula making him gag as her tentacles wrapped tighter around him. "The time of the small gods is returning, our day of freedom is coming to the worlds and you will be one of my pieces to play."

Caught between teeth, tentacles and the brine - Flek could hardly decline.

Now back in the room, he shook the memories of that day from his head and scattered the glass about the floor before leaving.

The plan so far, was perfect.

He straightened his gloves, brushed fragments of dust and glass from his clothes and took his lantern. His next task was to tell the Emperor of Bray's treason – this was the next part of the plan which he hoped would carry on in that smooth vein, in which the rest of it had.

The small gods were returning and he had the sweetest deal of any mortal; may the Blessed Mother smile down on you Neptula, although it would be the small gods who would be cutting the Mother's divine throat.

Betrayal – when you had nothing else to play, you could always put your trust in betrayal.

Chapter 20

Dark Wings

The fresh night air rushed over the contours of Grycul's head and slender neck. The current streaming over Elora's body and washing the last remnants of the Shadowlands from her hair as it billowed wildly behind her. The thrill of flying pulsed through her veins as the dragon's wings stretched out either side, like huge reptilian sails blanketing the sky.

Their minds were one. Elora could see through the dragon's eyes, observing the land from the predator's perspective and focusing on the horizon more keenly than that of any living creature. She caught glimpses of the deer and rabbits that darted along the fields and forest floors some few thousand feet below. Grycul also perceived her thoughts, changing direction as her master demanded, altering altitude at the slightest whim as if predicting her wishes.

No sooner did Elora's gaze fall on the black river of men snaking below, than the dragon banked to the side and dived at an aggressive angle. She swept level and glided mere feet above the body of the Dark Army as it marched onwards. Tendrils of new soldiers joining the ranks with every village and town they passed. The takwiches gaining bodies they possessed while the grumpkins and bulworgs herded the children; their faces full of fear and panic. The tears that made tracks down dirty faces caught the flames of the burning buildings they were forced from. The smoke rising high into the night to blend with the clouds and blot out the stars, only the moon hung visible, its ghostly halo partially revealing itself when there was a break in the haunting vapour.

Grycul ascended once again, her long tail twisting the air as it soared on thermals, the vast army stretching into the distance; to the horizon that lay beyond the beast's vision. However, Elora could see it all, her mind was not only linked to the dragon, but to those of the scraw-harpies that were scattered around Europe and Asia. Thousands of drones circling in the sky and sending images of the scenes below them; visions much like she was witnessing with her own crimson eyes. Pockets of fires; flames greedily feeding from the buildings, vehicles and sometimes bodies burning around the landmass to mark out the path of the Dark Army, laying waste to civilisation and spreading Chaos to all reaches and in all directions. Her father's legacy had arrived and now Elora would rule this darkening world, but first she had a machine to play with, a relic to dig up.

In the distance a city burned. The flames reaching so high that it dwarfed the carnage beneath. Elora steered the dragon towards the inferno like a moth attracted to a flame.

Smoke curled about them as they landed upon the steeple of a church, Grycul digging her claws into the spire and dislodging masonry which crashed onto the cobbled street below. Men who had been running towards the building had narrowly missed being crushed by the falling debris, but their momentary pause was long enough for the perusing bulworgs and takwich to catch up. The group's screams and snarls filled the night, a chorus which was soon joined by others around the city.

Elora eagerly grinned down at the scene unfolding, at the destruction and confusion; at the mass of takwiches which were flowing through the streets, staying to the darkness and shadows before crawling into houses and hideaways and re-emerging as warriors with newly possessed bodies. The bulworgs and men spread anarchy throughout the city, burning, destroying and finding and killing – and the grumpkins who danced in the roads amongst strings of children, tied together to be led away by grimbles and trolls.

Grycul spat flames into the air, her movements causing the tiles to loosen beneath her crushing weight. She gripped tighter with her talons, dislodging more masonry and toppling a gargoyle.

Elora tenderly stroked the dragon's head, her fingers rubbing along the fine scales which ridged down to her neck.

"Calm yourself, there'll be plenty of time for burning after," Elora said.

A door suddenly swung open on the spire beside them and a monk rushed onto the roof. A flame teased at the hem of his robes as he skidded to a halt, but he only had eyes for the dragon; his mouth silently working up and down as he took in the powerful creature and the greater power which sat upon her back.

As the smell of burning flesh tickled her nose, Elora watched fascinated as the monk yelped and attempted to swat at the flames on his robe which he had only that moment noticed. He spun on the spot, one hand flapping while gripping tightly to the bible with the other.

Giggling, Elora watched until the flames licked up the back of his clothes and the hood caught aflame. His frantic dancing and the thrashing of his limbs only making the fire spread faster.

"Enough," Elora whispered to the flames and they gutted out.

The monk glanced about his body, patting down his robes and wafting the smoke away. When the immediate threat of burning to death had ceased, his attention returned to them. He raised his bible before him as if it were a shield and began to recite a passage in Latin, over and over again. His singed eyebrows meeting together as he focused all his will on her.

Elora sighed as she patted Grycul, halting her from leaning down and sinking her teeth into the man.

When the monk realised his attempts at condemning them to hell had not worked, he franticly opened his bible and found another page before launching into new verses, darting glances down at the words to make sure he was saying them correctly.

"Really?" Elora asked sarcastically as she hung her head to one side. "Do you believe God will help?"

The monk paused his rantings to listen, a wet finger marking the page.

"The only god on this roof is me." Elora said, hearing a familiar sound tapping along the tiles of the lead roof – tak...tak...tak.

"And there is only one religion that I'm giving the worlds."

Tak...tak...tak.

The monk suddenly became aware of the insect as it began to scurry up his leg, his arms suddenly becoming more animated than they were when he was on fire. His bible forgotten, dropped to the sloping roof to slide into the gutter.

"And that is Chaos," Elora finished, as the man went rigid, his head thrown back and the chords of his neck tightened.

He began to violently shake, fitting to the point where his mouth began to froth. Then as abruptly as it began, he went still.

Elora opened her mouth, "Tak...tak...tak."

The monk rose to his feet and flexed his fingers before his face, which was now wearing a maniac's grin.

"Yes, my Queen," he said, bowing low before departing calmly through the door he had come through.

Elora patted Grycul once more and the beast crouched low before leaping into the sky, dislodging more masonry and crumpling the top of the steeple which now teetered over and fell crashing to the cobbled streets below.

Putting the burning city behind her, Elora glided back over the growing army and flew in the direction they were heading. It would be a long flight, following the snaking black river. Their destination was still half a continent away and buried in snow.

Before Elora had finished her thought, Grycul had tucked her wings into her body and crashed through the barrier into the Shadowlands. Her scales flashing red with the sudden brightness from the hot dusty air. Cold to hot, fresh to thin, the dragon could switch worlds on the slightest of whims, which was an advantageous tactic she was glad to use. Time was of no consequence here; they could fly hundreds of times around the world before morning arrived on Earth. Solarius had thought of everything when he plotted his attack. It was a shame he wasn't here to enjoy it. Elora grinned, but then she wouldn't be the one to rule if he was.

Long sweeping ranges of rock and flat plains passed below them, the cracks and fissures passing in a blur as Grycul picked up speed, no longer troubled by Earth's thicker atmosphere. Her shadow gracefully followed as they traversed the sky, their only companion in the vast lands. She had no inkling as to where Zionbuss was or what he was doing. Maybe he had gone to warn the Shadojaks of her plans or maybe he hadn't – she didn't care, the more bodies involved in the conflict the more chaos; and that was the whole purpose. There was plenty of Chaos for everybody.

Another flash as Grycul passed through the barrier again. It was the same night, the same minute as when they were last on Earth, although they were hundreds of miles further along the column of men. Checking they were heading in the right direction, Elora's mind fixed on the dragon's and then in another flash, they were flying once again in the red dust of the Shadowlands.

Excitement pulsed through Elora, the thrill of skipping worlds, of flying, of seeing everything through hundreds of minds and observing her darkness spread. This is what it was to be alive, to feel – to just simply be. She was the embodiment of darkness, the daughter of Chaos - a God.

Laughing with exhilaration, she willed the dragon on. Flash into night, searching for the marching line, then back into the sky of fire. Then flash through again some hundred spans later and witnessing another city aflame, then to pass once more through the barrier. Flash – night, flash – red, through the dark, through the dust and back to the blood and carnage of a suffering world.

They were close now, the river of men at the head of the snaking column thinning to a stream and then a trickle. She descended to the front, sweeping low over the platoon of men and bulworgs that paced through the snow, their gazes rising to watch them glide above and then land before them.

Elora dismounted the dragon to cheers and salutes from her army and as one, they knelt.

"Onwards!" she shouted, drawing her sword and pointing north. "Onwards to glory."

The men and beasts rose, setting their pace once again to a swifter march. Determination clenching their teeth and zeal narrowing their eyes. Bulworgs dropped to all fours and began to run, huge paws flicking snow as they bounded on. Rock trolls, grimbles and men sped to catch them as the ranks of her Dark Army surged forwards, the wave of the black river passing back down until the entire host became a stampede.

Suddenly she heard the rapid cracks of a machine gun.

Glancing above a ridge of snow that flanked the army, she saw a burst of fire erupting from several rifle barrels. A small militia hid themselves atop the roof of a building and were shooting at her dragon.

Grycul screamed in rage, spitting fireballs into the night, yet not one bullet could penetrate her thick scales.

"My Queen," said a soldier, kneeling before Elora and bowing his head low. "Give me the honour of sending my men to kill these defiers of Chaos."

He rose and bringing his sword to bear, he pointed the blade at the men firing from the building and was about to issue an order.

"No Captain. Chaos has no honour," she grinned, the expression mimicked by her subordinate. "Just kill them, unless there are any takwiches present?"

Gunfire erupted once more, the reflection glimmering upon the Captain's helmet as he shook his head.

"Then steel will do," she replied, remounting her dragon.

"Charge!" the soldier bellowed.

A platoon broke away from the main body and hurtled up the snow ridge; feet, hands and claws – they scrambled through the white powder to the base of the building.

Elora watched from a high vantage point on Grycul's neck, as the men firing switched their aim to the charging soldiers below them. Panic showing in their white teeth, white eyes and the white snow that began to fall from the passing clouds.

She suddenly felt a slither of guilt, an alien feeling from deep within the recesses of her mind. Guilt for the men that would soon die, guilt for the families they belonged to and anguish for the world in general.

Elora laughed, "You will not gain this body back, little girl," she said to the other being that fought to surface – you've had too much control over this body. This is my time, my reign.

The gunfire ceased as a bulworg gained purchase of the building top and began to tear through the militia. Men screamed as they were cut down, blood splattering the snow as their bodies were thrown to the ground and their guns taken.

There were six of them. None older than twenty and wearing torn and dirty clothes which once could have been military uniforms. Russians, Elora guessed from the hammer and sickle insignia they had on their fur hats. Had they been hiding and fighting for the past few weeks as Earth began to crumble? Such a long pointless struggle against an unstoppable tide. At least their end had been swift; bloody like they always were, but swift.

350

Elora snorted air through her nostrils, she had wasted enough time dawdling. Grycul picked up on her thoughts and bunching her legs, she jumped into the air; huge wings battering the ground and sending snow scattering about the fallen and covering them over with an icy blanket.

The vast plains of Siberia spread out before her. The Dark Army already advancing into the white wilderness. A darkness spreading into the pristine landscape.

The cold tore at her face, harsh winds battering against them as they flew above the clouds so the only thing higher was the moon and stars witnessing their graceful arc across the sky. Elora clung tightly to the dragon's neck, her teeth chattering against the chill; Grycul's scales feeling as hard and frozen as the weather but protecting her from the rough caresses of the wind. She debated whether to flash into the Shadowlands, let her thaw out and warm her aching bones, yet they were too close now and she didn't want to fly blindly passed their destination. It also gave strength to her army to see her flying above and leading them to victory.

The clouds soon began to fade as they descended. A long snow-capped mountain range jutting from the frozen wastelands below and flames burning brightly from one of the peaks. A small contingent of her men were already at the site, piles of loose rock lay about the edges of a large square hole the size of an olympic swimming pool, yet it was filled with snow.

Grycul came in close to the sheer cliff face of the mountain and glided vertically up the rock, wings almost brushing against the black surface. Spires of granite poked up from an outcrop carved into the peak and the dragon cut between them, her passing causing snow to blow from the tops.

Elora circled the site, observing the twenty soldiers gathered around a fire at its centre, hands out towards the flames while shovels and picks lay discarded at their feet. A lone child was tied to a stake in the ground. Dressed scantily, the little girl stared at the fire as if seeking comfort from the heat she was denied.

Grycul landed hard, the rock shaking with the impact and knocking a cauldron of steaming stew into the pit it was cooking above; dowsing the fire and hissing into the night. A grumpkin frantically began to right the iron bowl and save the stew but when his sunken eyes fell on his approaching Queen, he scrambled back and bowed low.

"My Qu…" began the grumpkin, his words being snatched away as Elora put her boot to his shoulder and kicked him onto his back.

All attention was on her now, the remainder of the advance party leaving the warmth of the fire to kneel before her, heads low and gazes fixed on the ground.

"Why are you not digging?" Elora asked, her voice eerily calm as she stepped around the body of men. "Have you found my machine?"

Men, bulworgs, and the grumpkin bowed their heads impossibly lower.

"Who is in charge?" She paused by the shivering child who could be no older than ten; blonde hair filthy as she hugged herself, scared eyes staring back into her own, swimming in tears.

"I am, my Queen," said the grumpkin as he approached her, a nervous laugh escaping his baggie face; yellow teeth showing through the paper-thin skin.

"You're in charge?" She stepped away from the girl and began to circle the shrivelled little man, his tattered clothes and hat matching his sallow flesh. His nose hung crookedly and had fallen out of place to hang drooping and twisted above thick lips. "And you gave the order to cease digging? You have found my machine?" Her voice still quiet and soft, a playful smile tickling the edges of her mouth.

"No, my Queen," he answered, twitching eyes following her as she circled like a shark. "But the snow – it keeps filling in the hole. This grumpkin is sorry..."

Elora leaned in close so her face was looming above that of the skin-takers, so close he needed to crane his head back and his hat fell off. She put an arm around his shoulder and guided his attention to the girl, who watched the exchange and shrank away from them as far as the rope she was tied to allowed.

"Yet it seems you have managed to organise yourself a gift." She sucked air in through her teeth. "It couldn't have been easy to carry her up this large rock."

The grumpkin cowed beneath her, mimicking the child. "This grumpkin's skin is getting too many baggies, will be needing new..."

"And so you thought you could pause the excavation." She led him closer to the pit, speaking quietly as if addressing a child who she was tenderly trying to explain right from wrong. One arm still resting against his bony shoulder while spreading her other over the large pit of snow. "You didn't think that perhaps you could dig a tunnel in the snow so you could reach the rock below and be sheltered from the weather."

"Ermm..."

"Did you expect the snow to stop in the next day or two and that it would melt away so you could happily carry on your work?" She stroked the top of his head, mussing up the yellow strands of rotting hair. "You are a silly billy."

"This…"

"Shhh, it's ok," Elora said warmly, shaking her head and placing her hand over her own heart. "Maybe I'm getting a bit soft, - of course I'll give you a second chance to prove yourself."

The grumpkin sank to the floor, kissing Elora's hand.

"Thank you, my Queen. Thank you." Then rising, he signalled for his men to gather their tools. But as they moved back to the pit, Elora halted them.

"No, not them. Just you my little grumpkin," Elora said, fondly. "You were in charge, so it should be you who puts it right, no?"

The grumpkin nodded, his baggy face jostling as a nervous smiled twitched at his loose lips.

"Go on, little man. Off you pop."

Elora watched the grumpkin pick up a shovel and slowly walk to the edge of the hole, everyone watching quietly as he began to dig.

"No, silly. You need to start from the middle," Elora said, waving him on.

Reluctantly he obeyed, stumbling over as his feet failed to find solid ground and sinking to his waist. Twice he floundered in the deep snow before reaching the centre of the huge pit. Glancing back to make sure he was in the right place, Elora nodded encouragingly.

Eyebrows raised, his mouth went slack as he began his work. But as the snow was so light and powdery he did little more than flick it around him, causing a small snow shower over himself. After flailing and angrily thrashing he did no more than sink himself to the chest, the snow resettling around him.

"It's no use," said the grumpkin, shrugging his shoulders as if to say, I told you so.

Elora chuckled, spreading her arms to include the entire group of men around them. "Difficult, isn't it?" she laughed and her men nervously laughed with her. Even the bulworg made a gruff rattling chortle from his huge lungs.

"Yes, my Queen," the grumpkin said, beginning to chuckle himself. "You sees; it was an impossible task for this grumpkin."

"Yeah, I do, I do indeed," Elora agreed, then her face hardened and she ceased to laugh.

The laughter also died around her and the smile quickly vanished from the old skin-stealer who was beginning to cower under Elora's glare once gain. His nervous fingers playing with his slipping nose.

"I hate failure; I will not tolerate it. And I especially hate grumpkins!" Elora shouted the last word and the twitching man at the centre of the pit toppled back, cursing himself in a high-pitched squeal.

Elora's mind was already portraying her intentions to Grycul, who stalked closer to the pit of snow; her tall neck craning high as it loomed over the floundering creature at its centre - his slack hands protectively waving above its head.

"This is how I deal with, failure," Elora said, eyeing each of the men about her, scolding them with her crimson glower.

She gave the dragon a single nod and Grycul opened her mouth wide, exposing her long teeth and sharp tongue. She pulled her head back, chest rising as she sucked in air. Then roared.

Blinding white fire ripped from her mouth devouring the grumpkin and melting the snow around him. Steam billowed up in great plumes from the bubbling liquid; a huge wall of scolding vapour that rose like a pillar into the night.

Elora grinned wickedly, witnessing the horror-filled faces of those around her. Impossibly the grumpkin at the centre of the broiling mass was still alive, his wailing screams sinking lower as the water left the pit.

Grycul's fiery breath was eventually spent, yet the liquid was so hot now, the clouds were continuing to rise until there was nothing but glistening rock angling down to a shallow pool. The scorched body of the grumpkin floating face down, his flesh bubbling and blistered.

"You," Elora shouted, pointing at the man closest to her. The soldier almost struck his head against his knee as he dropped to the floor, bowing low. "You are the Commander now."

The man gulped, his Adam's apple bobbing as he stared with large eyes.

"Yes, my Queen. I won't fail you."

"No, you won't," she nodded towards the dark pit now empty of snow. "Begin digging and don't stop until you reach my machine."

She didn't shout, she had no need to; the demonstration of what she did to failures worked well enough.

With a swift shake of his fist the men piled into the hole and within a moment the sound of picks striking rock echoed around the outcrop.

Elora sighed and shaking her head went to the small girl. The meagre child shuffled back, bringing her knees up to her chin and hiding her face. She was mumbling in a foreign language – probably Russian. Gazing above the safety of her knees she cowered back to the point where the rope around her neck began to strangle her. She was a little thing, barely enough flesh to keep her bones held together. Filthy, crying and terrified.

Elora hunkered down in front of her and drew her sword, letting the god-created metal ring against the scabbard. She put the tip of the blade against the rock, the pummel gripped between finger and thumb as she spun the blade idly, soaking up the girl's fear. Make it quick and end the suffering or draw it out and have some fun?

"What is your name?" Elora asked, offering the pathetic creature a sad smile.

The girl stared, her thin lips drawn tight as she bravely fought a wave of fresh tears. Then spoke several rushed words in her local dialect.

"Where did my men take you? Where's your home?"

Scratching a square shape in the rock Elora's blade cut the angle of a roof, a door and windows. Once done, she pointed at the house she had carved and then at the girl.

Wiping her nose with the back of her hand the girl glanced at the diagram and then back at Elora and shook her head.

Elora gripped her blade tighter, she was losing patience. Why was she talking to her anyway? Then she realised, it wasn't her talking, but that other her; the weak Elora who was as feeble as the girl at her feet.

Snorting disdainfully, Elora rose back to her feet to tower over the girl and drew her sword back, ready to thrust it into her. Their eyes locked for a moment and she thought she saw recognition in the other's face, an awareness of what was about to happen.

"Are you scared little girl? Do you think me a monster?" Elora laughed.

The girls fragile hand fell away from her face and grasped Elora's; small fingers wrapping around her thumb as she squeezed.

"Please, no," she pleaded, clenching her teeth as another tear snaked a track down a dirty cheek. It was the same shape her army made as it marched through the land.

A new emotion welled up in Elora. A heavy ache which formed in her belly and beat its way up to her throat. She dropped her gaze as water leaked from her crimson eyes. It ran down her face and dropped from her chin. The girl caught it on the tip of her finger.

"Cry," the girl said. Then tapped the picture of the house etched into the rock, then touched Elora's chest. "Home."

"Home?" Elora repeated, the word having to be forced through the lump in her throat. "No," she croaked. This wasn't her, this isn't what she does - she doesn't feel. Biting her tongue, she tasted blood and willed herself to turn away. Chaos has no mercy. But she knew, deep inside that she was already losing the battle.

Elora glanced at the sword, at the flames reflecting along its edge, at her dragon and listened to the darkness; their whispers pouring into her once again…kill…kill…Kill.

She snatched her hand away, gripped tightly to the rope tied around the girl's neck and yanked the child to her feet.

Then simply brought her sword down.

Elora turned away, hanging her head as the sound of the girls falling body reached her ears. She willed herself to push her sword into the smuggler's pouch and stepped away.

"We've found it," came the shouts of the digging men echoing up from the pit. The new leader came bounding over to her with a bulworg at his heels. "My Queen, we've found it," he repeated. His gaze falling on the scene she had left behind her, a frown creasing his brow.

"Good," Elora said. "Bring me the machine."

He returned his attention to her. "My Queen, it's not a machine. It is a mirror."

"A mirror?"

"Yes, set into the rock itself. And beside it is the carving of Thea. What would you have us do my Queen?"

"Nothing,"

"And what of this?" the leader asked, nodding at the floor behind her.

Elora slowly turned and gazed down at the girl and watched her smile back up at her while trying not to smile herself.

"Take her home," she said, stooping down to pick the girl up.

Elora ordered the bulworg to drop to all fours before placing the girl on his back.

"See to it she doesn't come to any harm and leave her where she'll be found by others of her kind."

Frowning at the girl, whose fingers were now holding tightly to the bulworg's fur, he nodded. "Yes, my Queen."

Elora removed her cloak and set it about the girl's shoulders. "I mean it. Not a hair is to be harmed on her head."

She watched them leave down the mountain trail, the girl wrapping the cloak about her body to protect herself from the harsh weather. Elora scowled as she shook her head. How could she rule a world of Chaos if she was weak and feeble? She wiped the fresh tears from her face as she strode purposefully to the pit. Grycul was watching her with a keen yellow gaze and Elora stiffened her face back into a grimace.

The granite walls of the pit glistened as the water which clung to it had already turned to ice and caught the glow from the lanterns which the men held. They parted as she neared, allowing her to descend the roughly carved slope which swept deep into the mountain. Nearing the bottom, she passed the body of the grumpkin floating face down in a rock pool. The top layer of the water freezing around his bloated skin. From hot to cold, from life to death. Elora pulled her gaze away, feeling sickened when she should have been experiencing joy at the destruction.

A rock troll stood beside the mouth of a cave, a lamp grasped in huge square fingers as he began to lead the way inside the rough opening.

"Stay here," she commanded, taking the lamp and venturing on alone. The last thing she needed was for the Dark Army to see her cry. Chaos rules without remorse and without emotion. That other weak Elora had saved one girl, but she wouldn't be able to save the worlds.

Once inside she gutted the lamp and allowed herself to be smothered by the darkness, giving herself back over to the whispers of death.

Kill...Kill...Elora...Kill - she breathed a sigh of relief as she regained control.

The darkness was all consuming, yet Elora's night vision was strong enough to find the mirror, its clean surface appearing ghostly silver in the dimness. She approached, seeing herself taking steps towards herself from the mirror land. Eyes glowing like hot coals, a grin curling her lips and a wickedness set into her countenance.

She folded her arms as she stared, finger and thumb stroking her chin and that other her mimicking her actions. How was she to use this? It wasn't what she was expecting. Not a machine or weapon of any kind, just a simple mirror. She caught the reflection of Thea, carved into the cave wall behind her and studied the dark grey etching against the black granite. It wasn't Thea, it was Earth.

She turned and glanced at the world once again, seeing that it had returned to being Thea, below which she noticed, ancient runes – 'Chaos will set us free'.

Another glimpse through the mirror showed that the writing said, 'Chaos will unite us'. Very clever, but what could she do with that?

Her anger began to rise as she paced about the cave, searching for clues as to where the real weapon was. Without the other her inside her head, fury was building and wanting to release itself. The whispers at the edge of her hearing taking up the chant to kill while she examined the walls, the symbol and the mirror yet found nothing.

Elora's temper rose, an angry storm welling to a cyclone as she sought an object to unleash it upon.

Frustration forced her to pivot on her feet and slam her fist into her reflection.

Her hand passed through the glass, the lunge taking her off balance as she almost fell through.

Taking a deep breath, she retrieved her fist, opened it and flexed her fingers.

"A hidden passage?" she said to herself, pushing her hand back through the mirror then stepping after it.

The walls inside the hidden passage were night black and glimmered with crystal flecks which shone in different colours like millions of tiny stars. She ran her finger along its rough surface, the tiny flecks sharper than diamonds cut into her skin. Flames erupted along the wounds as her blood touched the air to seal them closed. The brief flame-light flickering along the passage as the crystals passed it along in a haunting relay.

Smiling, she sauntered along the narrow passage, pausing now and again to run her hand over the walls and watch the effects flicker ahead of her. This was the mirror world; part of the domain that belonged to the sprites and other creatures of the light - if only Bray was here to experience this with her.

What was she thinking?

"Get a grip!" she scolded herself. Chaos had no place for love.

She trudged on, determined to find the mirror world's secrets before that other her took control. Inside here, she realised, the darkness couldn't follow her.

The gleaming starlit tunnel ascended, twisted, swept down and around, flattened out and dropped. Steps were carved in places, bright fungus growing from cracks, mushroom heads as large as her own head, radiating blue, pink and yellow. Other cucumber-shaped plants hung from the ceiling; deep purple stems with dayglow orange tendrils that floated in an invisible breeze. A warm smell of jasmine, lavender and cedar permeated the air she breathed, making her head feel light and her vision fuzzy at the edges. It wasn't an unpleasant feeling, but she had work to do – dark deeds to commit and waltzing around the mirror world in a dreaming stupor wouldn't bring Chaos to bear.

She dissolved to smoke and flew against the breeze. Her presence traveling in a long reaching tendril that wound through the passage, flowing over the hypnotic flowers and sweeping unhurt against the walls, watching the many bright colours flicker by from all angles as she raced on.

Eventually the passage ended in a circular chamber, light spilling down from the tall shaft above as if she was gazing up from the bottom of a deep well. Without pausing she floated up the shaft, the black burning tendril that she was washing over the walls.

Above her, suspended from the ceiling was a large circular mirror, angled so the light bounced down into the shaft. She flowed with the beam, bouncing herself from the mirror into a huge cavern. A light source burned blindingly from the centre.

Elora materialised as she passed over solid ground, her feet once again reforming as she walked towards the light, feeling the weight of the void-like cavern pressing down on her. It was vast.

She knew it had walls, it had to have, although because of the effect of the night-black rock and crystals, it gave the same effect you had of staring up at the night sky, only this was over the entire cavern.

363

Then the ground suddenly dropped away, forcing her to stop. A thin bridge reached out ahead of her, appearing to float impossibly towards the light at the caverns centre. It shimmered like the walls and ceiling, making her feel dizzy if she concentrated too long on it.

Gingerly she placed a foot on the bridge and tested her weight. The fragile looking structure didn't budge. She took another step, then another; holding her arms out to either side for balance. One ill-located foot and she would fall into space itself – although she could rely on becoming smoke once again, she somehow got the impression that she was supposed to walk the bridge as if it were a test; proof that she was worthy to reach the centre. Concentrating on the light ahead she strode purposefully, trying not to gaze at her surroundings.

A deep grinding sound suddenly reached her ears. It was like rock grating against rock, a deep heavy weight as it rolled over another, like the stone-grinding wheel inside a windmill, only much louder.

Her hair suddenly swished back as a large blue ball rushed around the outer wall. Elora instinctively ducked to the bridge floor, curling tight and making herself small as the strange phenomenon roared passed.

As big as an air balloon, it rolled around the wall, clinging to the surface as if gravity held it in place. Elora steadied her racing heart as she watched it go by. It was Earth; rolling so fast that she saw the vast continent of America in one breath before Europe spun over as she exhaled, each day on that rolling mass lasting no longer than a few seconds. It carried on its path of the cavern perimeter, rolling around the back of her and along the opposite wall. Then as it passed out of view behind the blinding light another world rolled into view – Thea.

Elora stayed rooted to the spot, watching the worlds rotate on opposite sides of the cavern, roaring around and never meeting. She gazed at the light at the centre of the cavern once again. So that must be the sun, or like the rotating worlds, a strange working model of a sun. Elora then realised that she must be inside the vast machine which she had been searching for, which her father and the Dark Army had been searching for.

A giddiness threatened to topple her from the bridge as she rose to her feet and began to take steady steps. She set her teeth in grim determination and concentrated on the bright orb, if she attempted to look elsewhere, especially down, a strange sense of vertigo tugged at her, willing her to fall into the void.

Elora thought her precarious walk would never end as she crossed the cavern. Feeling the temptation to dissolve to smoke and drift, but gravity worked oddly here, her hair floating towards the whirling mass of the worlds, proved it. If she became smoke she might not be able to control where she went and end up being sucked into the rolling planets to be crushed and spread out too far for her to regain her body. But mercifully she arrived at the central sun; the bright ball radiating a blinding white light, yet no heat.

Squinting, she noticed that a narrow walkway clung to the perimeter of the sphere, made from pale green metal. Most probably god-created like the rest of the machine. Elora stepped carefully around the sun, tapping it with her knuckle and feeling a static prickle along her nerves making her tongue fizz and teeth itch. Immediately she withdrew her hand, not wanting to repeat the unpleasant experience.

Further around the huge glowing ball she spotted a ladder created from the same metal as the walkway that reached over the top.

The whirling worlds groaned about her as she climbed above the sun, feeling the pull of the starlit void drawing her in. She fought hard against the urge to look down and studied the rungs in front of her. Reaching one hand over the other as she ascended over the orb to reach the top.

The ladder flattened out as it went over the sphere, then dropped into a circular hole at the sun's northern pole.

So, it was hollow then.

Traversing over the glowing orb she gripped tightly to the rungs, willing herself to gaze at the worlds as she shifted her body around and began to climb down the ladder into the sun itself.

Elora dropped the last few rungs onto a circular platform, careful not to touch any of the spinning gears and cogs that surrounded the interior of the sphere.

Wheels of green metal rotated around golden chains which linked to various cogs at right angles. Bronze rods connecting thousands of gears spun around, interlaced to the teeth of silver cogs. A network of long thin pipes interworked between the revolving wheels, hissing steam from flute-holes as the entire machine hummed.

The mechanics of the contraption were so complex and intricate that Elora didn't know where to look, where to rest her eyes to stop herself feeling dizzy. If there was truly a machine that could spread Chaos through the worlds, then surely this was it. She caught her own reflection in the highly polished metalwork, her crimson gaze opening to large circles as she absorbed the ingenious of her surroundings. This whole machine had to be god-created, but how would she use it, there was no obvious on or off button.

Breathing deeply to steady her nerves she paced about the platform, studying the machinery, pieces at a time. Her gaze couldn't settle on any large block so she kept her stare on small patches.

Gold, silver, bronze and copper cylinders fed into glass vials which pumped a blue liquid into a pneumatic piston. This cranked about a thick shaft of steel which in turn spun dials of a clock; the six hands all spinning at different rates. Should she try to turn one of these? Her hand was almost upon one of them when steam suddenly hissed from a flute behind her, making her jump.

She snapped her hand back, her nerve to alter the clock's course evaporating with the vapour. It was then that she noticed a large lever rising out of a green slot beside her.

No bigger than her forearm, the lever was brass in colour with a black stone screwed into the top. At the base of the lever was a large silver disk; two circles ingraved, one over the other. The twin world symbol.

Was it that simple?

Before she'd realised that her feet had carried her to the lever, her hand was upon the black ball. Fingers curling tight as she applied pressure.

It didn't budge. She tried again, pulling with all her might yet it still didn't move. It was locked somehow. She searched carefully around the switch and found a square plaque with a picture etched upon it.

The picture was a diagram of the two worlds and the sun in between them. Inside the sun were two figures standing side by side holding hands.

Elora felt herself scowling. Did it mean she would need another to help her use the machine? It would have been too easy for her to simply use the contraption by herself and judging by the figures in the diagram she would need to find somebody from Thea to help pull the lever.

It was then that she heard somebody outside the sphere, feet making metallic clicks as they climbed the ladder.

Instinctively she let go of the lever and reduced herself to smoke.

Chapter 21

Prices

Flek found it hard dropping the grin that had been perpetually fixed upon his face since he left the tunnels. The damp warren of catacombs and crypts beneath the palace had been almost a second home to him for the past few months and now with Bray firmly fixed in the mirror world, he need never go back. But lose the smile he must. He had grave tidings for the Emperor and grave tidings needed a grave face.

Grasping the lantern, he ascended the spiral staircase leaving the chill air which he had endured overnight as he waited patiently for Bray to progress through to the machine. It had taken himself two days to find the vast cavern which held the rolling worlds. Two entire days walking through the star-lit tunnel, cutting his remaining hand to shreds along the diamond-filled walls.

He trailed a gloved hand along the stonework of the staircase, its ancient surface worn smooth by the years of use; the opposite of the cruel surface of the mirror world. Thankfully he had a reason to wear gloves and so he wasn't questioned over the network of scars that he now wore on that hand. He surmised Bray wouldn't be as slow as he was. Two days slowly investigating, pausing to rest and sleep – luxuries which the Shaigun wouldn't have. That was why he waited in a dry chamber by the tunnel entrance; allowing Bray a full day to reach his goal.

As Flek arrived at the top of the stairs he paused once again, checking that nobody was watching – nobody to witness what he was about to do.

He took a deep breath and held it, then blew the candle out. There were prices to pay if you wanted to reach what you desired. Pain to endure and sacrifices to be made.

Placing the extinguished lamp on the floor, he pulled a knife from his belt - one he had ceremoniously cleaned with sterile water, and roughly pulled his shirt open. Clenching his teeth, he drew the sharp blade across his bare chest, blood already running freely down his torso before he wiped the knife clean and placed it away.

Flek hissed through his teeth, the wound burning more than he thought it would. He winced as he tugged his cloak off and began to muss his hair out of the tidy centre parting.

Making sure nobody was watching he approached the wall, placing his hands against its cold surface. "Prices," he repeated, then drove his forehead into the brick.

White dots exploded at the corners of his vision as he stumbled back, his arms flying wildly to keep himself upright before he dropped to the floor.

Blood ran over his cheekbone and down the side of his face. Flek shook the giddiness away and probed his teeth with his tongue – none were loose, thank the Blessed Mother; or should that be Neptula, his new God.

Dragging himself to his feet, Flek touched the injury on his head. His fingers came away sticky. Prices indeed. He smeared blood over his nose and chin, then tore an arm from his shirt and rubbed his bare forearm over his chest wound.

Approaching his refection from a suit of armour, standing sentry in an alcove, Flek glanced over himself. He readjusted his belt, dabbed more blood in his blonde hair and grinned. Now for the performance.

Stepping away from the suit of armour, he fell to the floor and screamed.

"Guards! Guards!"

He crawled along the floor in the direction of the rushing feet, leaving bloody hand prints in the stone.

"Guards!" Flek repeated, shouting at the top of his lungs.

He saw the shining metal toe-caps of the first guard to reach him, then felt strong arms lift him into a sitting position.

"What is it?" demanded his rescuer, setting him against the wall as wild eyes glanced down the corridor seeking the threat.

"It's the Shaigun," Flek pleaded, gripping the guard at his elbow. "He's...he's, turned traitor."

Before he spoke the last word another two men rushed to his side, swords drawn and glaring in all directions.

"What?" exclaimed one of the new arrivals.

"Traitor. The Shaigun Bray has turned against his Emperor and has joined his lover, Elora," Flek said, putting every ounce of misery he could muster into his voice.

Scowling, the guard spat, "Solarius's daughter. I knew she couldn't be trusted."

Flek almost laughed and turned the sound into a painful cough. News of what Elora had done had spread like wildfire. Within the hour of Sibiet returning, the entire palace had known.

"It's true, I blame myself for not seeing it." Flek touched his chest wound and groaned. "For not stopping him."

"He did this to you?"

Flek nodded. "And worse. I tried to stop him. But I was unarmed and he's a Shaigun, I…" The nod turned to a shake as he whimpered out the next words. "Bray left me for dead and disappeared into the mirror world."

"Mirror world?"

Flek sighed, his breath turning into a sob. "The machine. The weapon which we've been searching for is hidden there and Bray has found it and will use it against us - against this city and the Emperor." He gripped the guard's elbow tighter and dragged him closer. "We must abandon the city and get the Empire to safety before it's too late."

Shocked expressions hung silently from the men. Too stunned to speak, they gawped open-mouthed. Flek took several deep breaths before clenching his teeth. He needed to rally these idiots into action. Why was he always surrounded by fools?

"You!" Flek snapped his fingers at the smaller of the three. "Raise the alarm, let the palace know." The guard nodded and set off at a run, shouting for other guards around the corridors. "And you," he pointed at the other, "will send a message to the Supreme. I want him and every Shadojak in the garrison here." Flek raised an eyebrow at the guard who stood rooted to the spot. "Now!" he shouted, infusing the man into action. He took off at a sprint, crashing into a decorative urn that was in the corner, it rolled on its base for several seconds before settling back.

"And you," Flek continued, using the guard's arms as he pulled himself to his feet. "Will see me to the Emperor's quarters, at once."

Twice Flek dropped to his knees as they made their way through the many levels and corridors of the palace. Oh the drama – a winning act, fit for the city theatre. By the time they paused outside the Emperor's throne room the guard was red faced and sweating from supporting Flek's weight. When they entered, Flek stumbled over his own feet in his haste to reach the throne, falling in a heap at the Emperor's feet.

"I regret to inform his Excellency, that the Shaigun Bray has turned against you." Flek paused for effect, letting the leader of the Empire soak up his words and his dramatic appearance. "He's aiding his Shadojak, his mistress and is going after the weapon."

The Emperor shifted uncomfortably on the throne; the hand supporting his wine beginning to tremble. Behind him, his personal guards, Quantico and his brother Quantala, drew their swords, keen eyes scanning the doorway and balcony.

"How?" The Emperor asked, waving a hand for his manservant to take his glass.

"We found clues that led to a chamber inside the catacombs. It had the bust of the small god Zalibut stored along with an old wooden globe and a mirror."

"Zalibut the god of inventions?"

Flek bowed. "Your Excellency is well educated in Thea's history. Yes, Zalibut invented and created the machine which caused the great rift and separated Earth and Thea. We only exist on different plains because of it. Also inside that chamber we found a secret passage into the mirror world. That's where the machine is hidden and that is where Bray fled to."

"And the Shaigun will destroy this machine?" The Emperor asked, waving the servant over to return the glass of wine.

"Not by himself. The scrolls we had been researching led us to believe that the machine would need two people to use it. One to enter from Thea and another from Earth."

The Emperor swallowed the wine down in one go and held it out for a refill.

"So if Bray has already entered," Quantala said softly, staring down at Flek.

"And Elora is searching for the mirror on Earth," finished his brother.

Flek dropped his head, "Has found. The Dark Army had been digging for the mirror ever since Solarius had been freed. With the help of Grycul she could have flown to that site within hours. She's probably already there."

The sound of shattering glass echoed around the throne room as the Emperor dropped his wine on the marble floor; red stains spreading out in a gruesome pattern.

"Then we are too late?" exclaimed the Emperor, his hands turning white upon the arms of the throne.

"I tried to stop him, your excellency." Flek opened his arms to show his injuries, the wounds still wet and glistening. "But by the time I regained consciousness he had passed over to the mirror world and smashed the entrance so I was unable to follow. I'm afraid the outcome is now inevitable."

"Bastard traitor," growled, Quantico, pounding a hand down on the back of the throne, then gave the Emperor an apologetic shrug.

"And what will happen when the machine is used or stopped?" The Emperor asked, loosening his collar with a neatly manicured finger. "Are we safe?"

Flek breathed in deeply, shaking his head. "The worlds will collide. Thea and Earth will become one, once again."

The Emperor bit his lip, his arms gesturing to say something, then he paused as if the trail of thought had suddenly withered.

Quantala placed a hand on the Emperor's shoulder. "Your Excellency, we must take you somewhere safe."

"Safe? Where is safe if the worlds are to collide? It will wrench us all out of existence."

"They will collide, that is true, but I don't believe we are all doomed. The plains will merge back to how they were. The continents, countries, mountains and islands will remain the same. The coastline only having being altered subtly over the years since the rift. Maybe rivers have changed course, but the lands will roughly fit back to how they were."

"And everything else? The cities, the palace - my people?"

Flek shook his head and blew air through pursed lips. "I don't know, I'm only theorising. But say, if we suddenly merged with Earth while still inside the palace." Flek held his arms out to the surroundings. "And on this precise location on the other world was a forest: the trees would suddenly appear inside these walls, in this very hall."

Wild eyes darted about as if the Emperor suddenly expected a forest to appear inside his throne room.

"The Palace would collapse under the strain of all that wood breaking through the masonry and upsetting the foundations. But it might not be a forest. It could just as easily be another building, another city. I've studied the maps and atlases of Earth and where Rona is located on Thea, a large city called Rome exists on Earth."

"So a city merging with another would be…" the Emperor trailed off, his gaze settling on the balcony.

"Not good," finished the twins together.

"And if a person was to take up the same space as say, a rock or wall or tree on the other world: then they will most certainly die, horribly."

"Crushed to nothing," Quantala offered, closing his fist and staring at it.

"It would throw both worlds into…" Quantico began, then scratched his head as he sought the word he was searching for.

"Chaos," Flek said, then rising to his feet he gestured to the balcony. "Your excellency, the only safe place is the sky. You will board your airship."

"No," The Emperor replied, "my place is here. Send my guards out to warn the people. They must abandon Rona."

"Your Excellency, there isn't time. The worlds could collide at any moment and if the city is in a wild panic they would make the catastrophe worse."

"Worse how?"

"There are thousands upon thousands of people, families. If they were to panic and try to rush all at once, then the streets would be filled, a mass of people in any one part of the city, crushing to leave through the gates would be mayhem. Bring the pressure of another world arriving on their doorstep, buildings and trees appearing where only moments before there was empty space and you will have nothing more than a city-sized burial site. At least left un-warned they'll be spread out and offered the better chance of survival." Flek lay a hand on the Emperor's. "Your Excellency is truly a great and honoured man to wish to remain and suffer the same fate as his people. But after the collision, the merger – the world will need rebuilding afresh and it will need a great leader to bring it all together. I know the burden lays heavy with you, but Rona – Thea, has a better future with you in it."

Flek fought to hide the rising smirk. This pathetic man was so easily played. He could almost hear the royal brain working behind that pampered face.

"I am afraid I must insist, your Excellency. As the Voice, I do hold certain powers in time of great peril." Flek shook his head sadly, holding a limp wrist against his brow. "And as the Supreme isn't here yet, I will take command of this situation and order you to your airship. Immediately!"

Flek looked to the twins for help, "Please escort him at once. It is paramount that the Emperor survives."

Both brothers nodded, then taking an arm each pulled the Emperor to his feet.

"Excuse us your Excellency, but the Voice is right," said Quantico as they led him across the throne room.

The Emperor appeared like a lost sheep being herded away from a cliff-edge. He gathered his thoughts after a brief hesitation and gestured for his servant to follow on.

"And you?" asked Quantala pausing at the door.

Flek sighed heavily. "I will wait for the Supreme to arrive. I've sent word already; for him and the remaining Shadojaks. After the collision, the new world will need every high power we can muster."

The northern Shadojak nodded, then followed his brother and the Emperor from the room.

Now alone Flek allowed his smile to emerge.

He crossed to the Emperor's decanter of wine and poured himself a measure into the crystal glass. Bringing it to his nose he swished the red liquid around and inhaled.

"Hmm, prices," he chuckled as he dropped heavily into the throne and threw a leg over the polished golden arm. "Prices indeed."

The wine melted on his tongue and he savoured the divine vintage. He'd tasted none better, a spirit fit for an Emperor. Flek chuckled as he finished the glass and let it fall from his fingers. It shattered on the marble floor, the fragments mixing with the shards from the glass which the Emperor had dropped.

He precariously stepped over the mess as he sauntered out of the room – there will be a lot more broken glass before the day is out. Broken furniture, broken walls and buildings, broken cities and broken people. Flek's chuckle turned into a throaty laugh; the worlds will be broken and he would be watching with a bird's-eye view. But first he had a final theatrical act to perform.

The sun shone above the monolith casting its long shadow across the palace grounds and the approaching stagecoach. It rolled to a stop outside the front gates, its springs squeaking as several men climbed out. Flek clicked the joints in his hand, then stumbled down the steps to meet the Supreme and his contingent of Shadojaks.

"What is this about?" demanded the Supreme on seeing Flek's approach. In his hand he held a scrap of paper; the message he had told the guard to send.

"It is all true, Supreme. Bray, like Elora, has turned traitor. They have the weapon or machine in their hands and..." Flek stared away, putting on an expression of anguish. "And they will use it. Anytime now the worlds will collide."

The four Shadojaks gasped, each glaring around as if expecting to find Earth already merging into the palace.

"We cannot delay, Supreme. I have ordered the Emperor to board his airship. I suggest we do the same."

The Supreme turned to his men, gesturing with his arm. "We will not abandon the people. There is still time to evacuate..."

"It has been taken care of," Flek lied. "I've dispatched runners to the three gates of the city, ordering them to stay open and have arranged for every guard, manservant, cook and sweep to spread the word to Rona's populace. It's not a lot, but it is all we can do."

The Supreme gazed up at the airship silhouetted above the monolith.

"How many can we fit in that contraption?" he asked, pointing a shaky finger into the sky.

"Not many. The Emperor has taken many of his contingent and the northern brothers are already aboard." Flek sighed heavily. "We need to make haste if we are to survive. We are the only ones who can stop this daughter of Chaos, but only if we live through the collision."

Flek saw the turmoil in the Supreme's expression, it mimicked those of the Shadojaks' faces. They wanted to

379

stay and help the people escape the coming disasters, but they knew that his words spoke the truth.

"How much time do we have?" Hashim asked, standing as tall and as still as his god-created spear.

Flek shook his head as he began to walk back to the palace entrance, gesturing for them to follow.

"None. The machine will be used imminently."

The swift pace they took through the palace left Flek with just enough time to explain all that had happened: the finding of the scrolls and the description of Zalibut's machine, the chamber and mirror. The way Bray had turned traitor and tried to kill him. He filled the conversation all the way up the many staircases and bridges that led to the top of the monolith and gave no room for questions. They would get all the answers once they were on the airship – and Flek had a feeling they were going to enjoy the answers least of all.

The wind tugged at Flek's hair as they ventured onto the flat platform of the towering monolith, teasing at the scab that had begun to form over his injury. If he had known how easily his lies were taken by the Emperor and the Supreme, he wouldn't have head-butted that wall so hard. But it was done now, much like the rest of the plan. All he need do now was see it through.

The airship hovered a few feet above them. Its long grey balloon filled with an expensive charmed gas and appeared like a giant bloated silkworm wriggling inside its chrysalis, yet it was strong enough to float the huge vessel. Thick ropes secured the craft to anchor supports bolted into the platform itself; red silk sails spreading out to either side, bigger than those of any seafaring galley. This was the closest Flek had ever been to the airship. It hadn't looked so grand from a distance but up close it was as imposing as it was magnificent. Probably equal in size to the Necrolosis, but where that ship had bones, teeth and skin, this had polished oak, mahogany and gold. Even the studs which held the luxurious wood together were made from brass, gleaming in the daylight.

Magnificent – and it would soon be his.

Guards met them at a mechanical lift. The circular device worked much like a corkscrew, but on a much larger scale. The group stood upon a raised dais with a rope barrier around the perimeter to stop a person from falling. Once secure, two guards began to turn a large wheel and the dais rose up the bevelled rod that was at its centre.

Quantico and Quantala were waiting for them as they stepped aboard.

"The Emperor is asking for you on the foredeck," Quantala said, gesturing for the group to follow.

Once the dais was lowered Quantico ordered the anchor ropes to be released. Flek wasn't prepared for the sudden lift as the airship rose and he almost stumbled into the back of Yaul-tis-munjib, his hammer held tightly in both hands. It was Gunwahl who steadied him, roughly taking his arms and pushing him on. Flek wouldn't expect anything else from the Shadojaks; friendliness was something they shed many years ago. But not to worry, Flek had his own share of roughness to pass around soon.

The steam-engine began to hiss as the water boiled, liquid fire feeding into the steel bulk through pressured pipes. The engine turned the large propellers fixed at the rear of the ship and gave thrust to the vessel.

"Supreme," came the Emperor's weak voice from the front of the ship. His robed form leaning out over the bow as he studied Rona below him. Flek heard a thickness, full of emotion in the old man's throat. "Is there anything we can do?" He slowly turned and pointed down at the city. "Is there any way of saving my people?"

Tears were running down the Emperor's face as his lip quivered. Pathetic, thought Flek – and this man was the glorious leader of the Empire?

"No, your Excellency. Not if what Flek has told me is the truth."

He joined the Emperor at the bow and together they stared down; two weak pathetic men, crying over the unstoppable, the inevitable. He should throw the pair of them over and see what good their tears did for Rona. Weak leaders produced a weak Empire – well things would change.

"Maybe it won't come to be," Hashim said, leaning against his spear and staring wistfully into the big blue. "I didn't take Bray for a traitor. Nor Elora."

"We were warned. Sibiet spelled it out plainly enough at her judgement," Gunwahl put in. "I'll put them both beneath my blade before I die." He spat out over the rail and watched it arc out of view. "I knew the half-breed couldn't be trusted."

"Half-breed has nothing to do with it," Quantico, argued. "We trained with Bray, he wouldn't do this of his own free will."

"But he would for his lover." This from the dwarf Dwenal, his stubby fingers working through his Mohican.

They stood for a moment in silence, each to their own thoughts. Flek stared over the rail and down at the city. Strange how small people were from this height - like insignificant ants, busying about the labyrinth of soap-stone walls and buildings, hiding beneath thousands of sloping roofs, verandas and terraces; working, relaxing, playing and living. All that would change any moment from now.

"Flek, you told me that the guards were instructed to open the gates," said the Supreme, turning his gaze on him. "That the people were to evacuate the city." The old man pointed down. "The east gate is clearly closed and nobody is leaving. Even the train is running as normal."

-And so the façade is over, thought Flek, letting go a heavy sigh. Then again, relying on lies alone wouldn't bring him his goal. That's why he had a 'plan B'.

"You're right," Flek said, stretching his neck first one way then the other. He took a few cautious steps back, putting the entire group in front of him; only Quantico and Quantala remained behind him and out of sight, but he knew they were there. "You are always right, Supreme."

The Shadojaks shifted uncomfortably, Dwenal even going so far as to draw out his axe. Flek felt the tension aboard the airship suddenly rise, faster than the vessel itself.

"What lunacy is this?" growled the Supreme, slamming both his withered hands together.

Flek chuckled, "Lunacy? Lunacy was serving beneath you. I had skills, real skills until I lost my thumb. I would have been a great Shadojak, the best." He glanced down at his right hand, flexing his gloved fingers. "But it was never to be," With his left hand he subtly brushed the bulge beneath his shirt, reassuring himself that 'plan B' was there. "And so I have taken what should be mine. I will rise to the high rank of Shadojak and I will go even higher still."

The group or warriors before him remained still in utter confusion until the giant rolled his huge shoulders and bared his large square teeth.

"Madness," Yaul-tis-munjib said. "Did Bray break your brain when he walloped you?"

"No, madness has been a close friend while I served in the garrison. But I've been serving another for some time. Another who has seen my worth and given me my own god-created metal, worthy of any Shadojak blade."

Flek slowly removed his glove from his right hand and held it out for all to see.

His given gift glimmered in the sun, shimmering along the intricately carved fingers and knuckles, sparkling from the working tendons and wrist joint. He turned it over so they could see the back, where the sigil of the eye and octopus was.

"Neptula?" the Supreme, asked, incredulously.

"Neptula," Flek repeated. "My saviour of the sea, my God and my vanquisher." He stretched his hand flat and the fingernails suddenly flicked out. Five, inch-long blades sharper than the claws of any animal.

The Supreme drew his own blade, holding the sword with a steady hand that belied his age.

"The sinking of the ship on its way to Paqueet?" he asked, anger drawing his grey brows together.

Flek grinned. "The Sea witch's doing. She saved more than my life that day – she gave me hope. Gave me the means to fulfil my dreams. She gave me the Empire."

"My Empire?"

The Emperor left the bow to stand beside the Supreme. "You tricked us, you and the sea whore have been plotting…"

"Pipe it you, old wind bag," Flek spat, his irritation rising the longer the situation dragged out. He felt satisfaction at watching the Emperor open his painted lips to speak, but unused to being spoken down to had nothing to say. "Yes, I've been plotting, a lot of us have. We're sick of taking orders, of doing menial tasks for pompous arses like yourselves." Flek's knowing smile returned. "And it was so easy. Easy to manipulate, to goad, to press, to push all of the key people needed. Even you Supreme. Thinking yourself going mad as you went into those trances of yours and making symbols and writing on paper – all those scribbles about Chaos uniting us and Chaos will set us free." Flek laughed, the Supreme's face was priceless.

"You poisoned my tea?" the old man whispered, his sword beginning to tremble.

"Yes, the tea. And when I replaced Elora's name with that of Chaos, it had you all intrigued. Neptula is many things – but a fool she is not."

"And the machine? The collision will still happen?"

Flek nodded, "The planning has been years in the making. Although Neptula planned for Solarius to have merged the worlds. His daughter put ruin to that when she destroyed him."

The Supreme raised his arm, the blade catching the glare of the sun along its razor's edge. "And so you used his daughter?"

Flek shrugged, "It turns out she was just as willing as her father was to spread Chaos, she just needed a little needling." His eyes passed over the men before him:

385

Supreme, Shadojaks - swords, spear, hammer and axe – so much god-created metal; extremely sharp and pointing at him. What a predicament he found himself in.

"Flek, former Voice of the league of Shadojaks, I judge you guilty of high treason," the Supreme said, his teeth grinding out each word with wrath. "I sentence you to death."

A quietness descended on the airship, the engine gently humming above the breeze which kept the sails taught was the only sound, until the Supreme lowered his sword.

"Do you yield?"

Flek chuckled, "Does anyone actually yield? I find the question as pointless as it is useless."

He sensed movement behind him and realised that the twins were drawing their weapons out.

Flek reached inside his shirt and pulled out 'plan B'. "I'd offer you the same question," he said, levelling the army issue Browning 9mm at the Supreme. "Although…."

Flek squeezed the trigger, the light kick forcing his hand to twitch. "You'd only refuse."

He watched the Supreme topple. A pathetically small hole in the middle of his forehead, leaking a single bead of blood. But when his body struck the wooden floor, he caught a glimpse of the large chunk missing from the back of his head; fragments of white bone glistening amongst the grey veiny matter. Dwenal stepped clear of the body, spots of red dotting his astonished face.

Time froze for a moment, all gazes locked on the dead Supreme, his sword slowly spinning atop the polished surface until Flek lay his foot on top of the blade.

"Bastard traitor!" Gunwahl spat as his broadsword cut an arc across the space between them, forcing a thwacking sound from the air. "Your little hand-cannon won't kill us all."

Flek smirked. Gunwahl was right of course, but then, 'plan B' wasn't just about himself.

Two flashes erupted either side of his vision followed by sharp bangs that echoed into the empty sky. Gunwahl abruptly spun backwards, arms flinging wide as his chest filled with bullets; small splashes of blood spattering out with each impact. Before his body hit the ground, Dwenal's head rocked back, his tiny body slamming into the gunnel and Yaul-tis-munjib only had time to raise his hammer before Flek put a bullet in his throat. The giant stumbled to the bow, his hands wrapping around his wound as blood leaked between huge fingers. He hit the rail and kept going, his body suddenly dropping from view over the side, but not before flinging an arm wide and grasping Hashim's cloak. The tall spear-wielding Shadojak's eyes suddenly widened as he was pulled off the airship.

Flek watched his departure with worry, he didn't want Hashim to drop without confirming his death. Although, the fall would more than likely end him. He slowly turned and watched both twins draw their guns up to their mouths and blow smoke from the barrels.

"I don't know. Kind of feels like cheating," Quantico said, raising an eyebrow.

Quantala nodded, "Yet it's a lot more efficient."

They both placed their guns away in the holsters hidden beneath armpits, then whistled for the contingent of warriors hidden below deck to come up and clean the mess.

387

Thirty burly men, all seasoned fighters, had been smuggled aboard under the direction of the twins, even the crew who manned the airship were of their choosing. The pair of them had been easy for Flek to win over to his cause – they hated their babysitting duties and because he had grown up with them along the Shaigun path, they had always remained friends.

"And what about him?" Quantico asked, pointing at a cowering figure tucked up in the corner of the bow and trying to make himself small while he gazed about the carnage.

Flek approached the Emperor, stepping over the bodies of the Supreme and Dwenal, careful not to get blood on his boots. He hunkered down before the quivering man.

"You c...can't do this," stuttered the Emperor, his gaze following the body of Gunwahl as it was thrown unceremoniously over the rail, followed by Dwenal's.

"I think you will find that I just have," Flek replied, as he tapped the gunnel with his metal hand, digging the nail blades into the soft wood.

The Supreme's body was hauled over last, his already damaged head smacking against a sail arm, his jaw cracking together as if he'd had enough of talking and that was that. Flek watched his body disappear, his limbs moving against the wind as gravity took him crashing through a tiled roof, hundreds of feet below.

"What do you want? I'll give you anything, anything," pleaded the Emperor, his manicured hands twisting Flek's shirtsleeve, desperation leaching from every pore.

Flek laughed as he snatched his arms away. "What can you give me?" he asked, opening his arms over the city.

"The Empire, I'll give you the Empire. Just let me live."

"Can you believe we served under that blubbering weakling," Quantala offered, snarling in disdain over the wretched man at their feet.

Flek grabbed the fine silk robe about the collar and dragged the Emperor to his feet.

"The Empire is no longer yours to give," he said and drove his hand into the old man's chest. His blade finger nails parted ribs and entered the heart. "It is mine."

Flek felt the soul of the former Emperor glide up the metal fingers and absorb into his hand, a faint flicker as the green flame disappeared. Then the body collapsed and Flek let it fall to the floor. The brothers grabbed either end of the man they had been ordered to protect and threw him overboard.

"Anyone on the ground will think it's raining men," Quantala smiled.

"They won't look like men when they meet the ground," chuckled Quantico.

Flek couldn't help but laugh, his hand throbbed as the trapped soul inside him worked its memories into the metal. It ached like a sore tooth there was no getting away from, but that was the price of taking an Empire.

"What now, your Excellency?" asked Quantala mockingly, as the three of them leaned over the bow.

"We wait. The merger of worlds will happen any moment, the sights we'll see will be breathtaking." Flek gazed at the city below; so tranquil with the train racing around the walls, the river sparkling, the sun shining and the people going about their day not knowing that their lives would change drastically any second now. "Then we start again. A new world, a new empire."

"A new Emperor," finished Quantala. "And what will this new world be called?"

Flek scratched at the scab forming on his head. "Thea and Earth - Thearth, Rearth?"

"How about Ethea?" Quantico offered.

"Ethea," Flek said, trying the word on his lips and finding he liked it.

"Ethea will do nicely."

Chapter 22

Stolen Kiss

Bray's fingers reached the top of the ledge, blood leaking through the makeshift bandages as he struggled to pull himself out of the shaft. He scraped his chest against the sharp wall as he struggled over. He rolled onto his back and stared up into the dark cavern, panting with exhaustion. That had been one of the hardest climbs in his life. His body spent, he could do no more than lie where he was, arms, legs and back screaming with fatigue while the rest of him burned from pain. He was hungry, thirsty and his skin had been cut and scraped by raw diamonds imbedded in every surface. The mirror world was a domain for sprites and creatures of the light, not living breathing flesh.

Falling into a semi-state of consciousness, Bray let his eyes close just for a moment – he wouldn't doze, he needed to find the weapon, needed to find Elora. He felt himself slipping deeper into sleep, unable to find the strength to push on.

Bray snapped his eyes open as something heavy whooshed by. Staring into the darkness he saw nothing but the twinkling of the diamonds cast along the roof and wall of the cavern. Then, when his head slumped to the side he saw a bright globe shining from the middle of the gigantic cave; its light bouncing from the mirror set above the shaft and beaming down. He forced himself into a sitting position, his body shouting at him in protest as he shuffled back and rested against the cavern wall, his sore hands limp in his lap.

Bray guessed he had spent an entire day and night in the mirror world. Working through the long passage at mostly a run, only slowing for steps and rocks which crossed his path. His lamp had gutted out hours ago leaving him in darkness. Yet as his eyes grew accustomed to the lack of light he noticed that the wall of the passage glimmered with tiny crystals lighting the way. Even the mushrooms which grew from the strange surfaces glowed and the odd plants which hung from the ceiling, radiated coloured light which he hadn't noticed while his lamp was shining. If it wasn't for him constantly cutting his hands as they brushed against the walls or tearing his clothes, he might have appreciated the haunting beauty – but like the foreboding feeling that twisted in is guts, he had to press on.

By the time he reached the bottom of the shaft, his hands, arms and shoulders were bloody; his shirt torn and his body lacked the strength to keep going at the punishing pace. Only thoughts of Elora compelled him on. Climbing the sheer walls of the shaft had been a gruelling endeavour. Using his sword to slice his cloak into bandage strips, he wrapped the material around his hands, elbows and knees. He stared down at them, the wrapping coming undone and trailing down to the floor. It was a mess; he was a mess.

Whoosh.

That sound again. This time Bray caught a glimpse of a passing object. Huge and round it rolled around the perimeter of the cavern, the sound of rock grating against rock grinding after it. The wind it brought played with the hairs on Bray's bare forearms and tussled at the trailing strip of bandage.

Struggling to muster the energy, Bray tipped his head to the side to follow the progress of the large ball. It was Earth or Thea. It went out of sight before he focused on it. After several moments staring into the black void of twinkling stars another world whirled across his vision.

The two planets were orbiting the sun at the centre of the cave, each locked in a gravitational pull of the other – were they the representatives of the original worlds? A minute glimmer of hope sparkled from the pit of Bray's stomach. He had found the machine.

He rose on shaky legs. His thighs and calves screaming at him to stop as he took a tentative step into the cavern and then another. Sweat and blood soaked into his torn shirt, sticking to him like another skin, his arms dangling loose as he willed himself on.

Before him the cavern opened up like a small universe, stretching out of sight beyond the glowing sun. The twin worlds rolled passed, sucking at his aching body and forcing him to sway like a new sailor riding the waves on his first voyage. He tried not to stare at the imposing masses as he pushed his feet on, taking a third step and then a fourth. Then his foot met empty space.

An abyss opened up as he stared down.

Bray felt himself tipping over into nothing. Teetering on the edge of existence as Earth rolled towards him. He could do no more than tip his head back and let his body collapse, praying to the Blessed Mother that he hit solid ground and not empty nothing.

He crumpled on the rock, legs dangling over the ledge, staring as the world passed over him. Bray didn't want to move but knew he must – Elora needed him, the worlds needed him to see this through.

With grim determination, Bray rolled onto his knees and rose once again. He scanned the ledge he was on for a possible means to reach the centre of the machine, his eyes fell on a bridge. It was more of a thin connection which linked this ledge with the bright orb in the middle. Yet it seemed the only way across. Maybe he should wait for Elora to turn up, he didn't like the thought of her crossing that alone. Or maybe she had attempted it already and had fallen and now lay in a crushed heap at the bottom of the colossus machine. No, if she was dead he would know.

What if she was already across and about to use the machine? He failed to see how it could be used as a weapon, but it had been built for something and from the size of it, that something would be catastrophic. That thought drove him on.

The bridge or sky-link, didn't budge as he put his weight on it. Taking small shuffling steps at first he focused on the centre, knowing that he might lose his balance should he glance down. The bridge was so narrow he needed to place one foot directly in front of the other.

He paused as the worlds passed, feeling that pull towards them; an attraction that could very easily suck him off the link to plunge into the bowels of the cavern, unless the gravity the planets produced was strong enough to draw him into their orbit and then grind him into nothing. Bray didn't fancy either and so halted his progress when either Earth or Thea advanced by.

Slow steps, easy and steady; counting to ten before pausing, then another ten. Taking a breath and releasing. Feeling his cuts, his grazes and bruises as they gently began to heal. When he was halfway across he unwound the bandages from his hands and elbows. Blood soaked, they momentarily stuck to his fingers before he let them fall, the thin strips uncoiling like phantom snakes as they vanished from view. He began to feel a little better, his elf genes working to replenish and repair yet his fatigue increased. The body needing to pull energy from somewhere, although his pains settled into an ache.

Bray's mind wandered as he progressed. No matter how hard he tried to push the thoughts away they always returned to Elora and of her departing words to Flek. He didn't know which scared him the most – the thought of the weapon being released and devastating the worlds or of never seeing Elora again. He willed himself to push them away, what was the point of mulling over what was out of his control? If she didn't want him, how could he persuade her otherwise. She was a Shadojak.

Clenching his teeth, he used his painful reflections to spur him on. Growling as he turned the steady shuffling into a walk and then a jog. By the time the worlds had done another circuit of the cavern wall he was doing an all-out sprint, only ducking low to the bridge as they went by. A brief lapse in concentration now and he would disappear forever - reckless he knew, but at that moment that was just what he was feeling - reckless.

Before he knew it he was upon the sun, flinging his arms in front to stop himself as he slammed into the massive glowing orb. Static, sizzled along his palms on contact, vibrating through his chest, setting his teeth to itching. He let go and instantly the feeling passed. The machine was god-created; he didn't expect anything less.

There was a platform that surrounded the sun. No wider than the bridge he had crossed, it was metal and made a clanging noise as he stepped along it, searching for a way inside the heart of the machine - which he guessed was what the sun really was.

He found a curved ladder that reached over the top of the throbbing sphere and began to climb, the sound of humming and hissing coming from inside. At the top he discovered a hole where the ladder went vertically down. Twisting his grip, he descended into the machine.

Bray's feet touched down on a solid metal platform, although thick black smoke coalesced around his ankles hiding his feet from view. The smoke was scentless but felt warm, hot embers curling about as they tumbled in the dark cloud, flowing about the bottom of the machine but never rising above his knee. Bray thought it was the fumes belched out by the engine or whatever it was he was staring transfixed at.

The surrounding circular wall was a mass of kaleidoscopic movement. No single piece of surface was stationary. Wheels, cogs, rods, and cylinders revolved, twisted, gyrated and spun. Tall flutes whistled out steam while coloured liquid was pumped into vials to work cranks and pistons. It was a wonder of engineering. Then a realisation hit him. This was the invention created by the god Zalibut. It could be no other, which made this the machine that caused the great rift that split the worlds. Was it Elora's intention to shut it off and crash the worlds together once again? That would be Chaos.

His eyes picked out a single lever with a black rock on the end, rising from a slot surrounded by a polished disk. Engraved on the disk was the twin world symbol and a plaque with a diagram of two figures holding hands inside the sun. Bray glanced back at the lever, all Elora need do was to pull and Earth and Thea would collide.

He would need to find a way to prevent her from reaching this far.

Bray's mind was working out a plan to destroy the bridge when the smoke at his feet began to rise. A warmth spread up his legs as long stems of the vapour coiled around his thighs; thick shoots wrapping around and around as if caressing him. He waved his hand through it but it didn't disperse as smoke should, only flowing over his arm to carry on its upwards spiral. Thick vines weaving over his stomach and tenderly brushing across his chest. When he tried to step away from it he found that his legs wouldn't move, the black fumes somehow holding him tight in a hot embrace. Then as the smoke drifted over his shoulder he felt a kiss lightly placed on the nape of his neck. A warm gentle kiss, which he thought was crazy until he felt another.

A tendril of smoke across his stomach thickened and became a pale arm; dark wisps solidifying into smooth flawless fingers as they pressed against his shirt, probing inside the rips to stroke his skin. What was happening?

Bray sensed a solid presence behind him, a body holding against his. Then another arm folded around his chest and he felt lips once more upon his neck, felt long hair tickling his shoulder and then the soft wetness of a tongue licking his ear and sending a wave of pleasure though him before teeth painfully sunk in.

The sudden pain gave him strength to twist out of the embrace. Bray spun on his heel. No longer trapped by the smoke he slipped his sword free as he went and brought it across him.

The blade stopped and inch from his attacker's chest. His mind raced to understand what he was seeing and he fought to stop his legs from buckling under the shock.

"Elora?"

Elora smiled, crimson eyes sparkling with mischief as they hungrily inspected his body. She placed a hand against his sword and pushed it away.

"Want to play?" she asked, her voice sounding throaty as her tongue played across her teeth.

Bray let his arm drop and he clumsily shoved the sword into the smuggler's pouch. Before he had chance to do anything else, Elora's hands were pressing against his chest.

"Weak and pathetic she may be, but she has a fine taste in men," Elora said.

A hand wrapped around the back of his head and pulled him down for a kiss. Their lips crushed together and Bray gave up on thinking, gave up trying to work out what was going on. He let himself get lost in that moment as he put both arms around her and pulled her closer. Feeling her warmth and desperate passion. Feeling the growl that thrummed from inside her chest like a wildcat purring.

Her hand left his head and trailed down his back, nails digging into his already torn shirt and ripping it further, then raking over his skin hard enough to draw blood.

Bray attempted to pull away from the kiss, he wanted to see that face once again, his Elora, his love. But she wouldn't let him. Gripping him tighter, her mouth locked to his stronger than a spider feeding from its prey. Her hand drifted lower and he suddenly found the strength to push her off.

Arching his bare back, he forced her at arm's length.

They were both out of breath, both panting, both lost amongst the heat of the moment. Her chest rose and fell as she stepped closer, taking what was left of his shirt, which wasn't a lot and tearing it off. Bray watched as her red gaze hungrily searched over his torso, going wide with an animal hunger bordering on desperation. He held her at bay, having to lock his elbows to halt her advance. She was unmeasurably strong.

"Slow down," Bray said once he gained control of his breathing. "We need to talk." He knew he was talking to the daughter of Chaos; the other Elora who had tried to kill him before.

Elora brought her gaze away from his body to regard his face, anger creeping into her greedy expression. "Talk? What is there to discuss when we are at the centre of things?" She threw her arms out to either side as she spun on the spot. "The centre of this machine, the centre of the axis between both worlds and on the verge of releasing Chaos. This is where it begins." She sounded as giddy as a schoolgirl.

"No, Elora. The worlds need to stay as they are. They need to be equilibrium."

Elora laughed, "Why?" She traced a finger along a wheel, then down a long rotating rod, her eyes never leaving his. "This machine is supposed to mould the worlds together, why else would the creator make this lever? Her hand played along the shaft of the switch and over the black rod that sat atop it."

"Don't do it," snapped Bray as he approached, readying to fling himself at her. Panic ripped through him as he saw her fingers tighten and begin to pull the lever down.

Her lips curled into a smirk. "It won't budge. Not by my hands alone, I've already tried. But if you place your hand atop mine we can pull this down together."

"No, Elora. Think of all those lives you'll end."

"Think of all the Chaos I'll spread."

Bray slowly drew out his sword and held it slack in one hand, the tip of the blade brushing the metal platform at his feet. He struggled to control his emotions; the core of his Shaigun training, but failed. This was the very reason why love was forbidden.

"I made you a promise some time ago," Bray said, forcing himself to sound hard while he felt anything but. "That if you were to ever to turn into the daughter of Chaos, that if you were about to hurt someone, I would kill you."

Elora cocked her head to the side, her bottom lip pouting in a mocking gesture of sympathy. Bray hated her for making him do this, for using Elora's body and making those facial expressions which looked wrong on her. He shared some of that hate for himself, for falling in love with her in the first place. He sensed she knew what he was feeling when she began to laugh.

"So kill me." Elora let her hands drop as she stepped closer, her crimson gaze narrowing as she slipped out her Soul Reaver; the blade catching fire as it sang free of its invisible scabbard.

Bray barely had a chance to set his feet solidly before Elora's sword was cutting an arc through the air. He ducked beneath the blow and spun away, dancing into a defensive stance.

She came back at him, her sword held with both hands as she pressed her attack.

Their blades met before them, sparks spitting from Bray's inferior steel as he countered and parried each ringing blow. Flames from Elora's sword singeing the hairs on his arm, his naked torso feeling wave after wave of the scorching heat. She meant to kill him, yet he couldn't commit himself to force an attacking move.

Elora had him pinned momentarily against the wall, cogs spinning against his back, their teeth biting into his skin. Bray counter-blocked an overhead swing, caught the blade and shoved her off him. He swiftly rolled out of the way as Elora swung again and her blade cut deep into the working mechanism of the machine, severing a pipe and cracking a long cylinder. Red steam and fluid gushed onto the floor as she wrenched her blade free with a scream.

Bray prepared himself as Elora sprang at him, venom grinding her teeth. He dodged the first swing, parried a slice to the midriff and was about to block a lunge when she instantly reduced to smoke, his body carrying him off balance.

She reappeared behind and he felt an explosion of pain erupt from the back of his skull. His body crumpled to the platform, his vision clearing in time to see her falling body above his, blade poised above his chest.

Bray rolled to the side and flipped into the air as her sword cut a deep rift into the metal floor. But he no sooner landed when she disappeared and rematerialised directly before him, her fist driving into his sternum and knocking the wind out of him as he slammed back into a column of flutes. When he tried to stand, several ribs made a grating sound, pain snatching what air was left in his lungs.

"You're not very good at keeping your promise," barked Elora, swinging the hilt of her sword against his jaw.

Teeth smacked together as his head whipped to the side and he instantly felt a vice-like grip on his sword-wielding wrist. Fire suddenly engulfed his hand and he dropped his blade.

It made a clatter as it struck the metal platform, followed by himself.

Bray knelt on the floor, head hung low and feeling broken. The wrist of his injured arm was charred black, blood leaking through the cracked and blistered skin. He knew he couldn't kill her; he didn't even attempt to attack her. If he was being truthful with himself, he realised when he first drew his sword that he wouldn't see it through. Even if he could have bested her, which he doubted.

Bray watched as Elora kicked his sword away, then felt her fingers lift his chin; her contact sending another shock of pain from his jaw. He didn't fight against her, he lacked the strength and the will as she raised his head to glare into his eyes and he stared back into Chaos.

The long shadow of her arm extended out to the side, sword poised ready to unburden his body with its head. Bray waited for death to take him. Then he saw a flash of violet; brief as a heartbeat but it was there, softening the red haze of her iris before it disappeared.

Elora smiled down at the mortal at her feet. He didn't cringe away from her and wasn't grovelling for his life - yet he was broken. She held her arm out steady, his life balanced in her grasp, in her very hand. She squeezed the fingers that held his chin, forcing his lips to bunch together as if they were primed for a kiss. His green eyes stared up into her own, full of sadness – she felt a sudden flicker of doubt, a tinge of pity and care over him. Like the girl on the mountain top she had let go, only stronger.

She took a deep breath and swallowed the emotion down into the pit of her stomach.

The flames licked along her blade briefly before they guttered out as she slid it away. She had no intention of killing the boy, although death would come on swift heels after she'd used him.

Confusion wrinkled his brow as she took hold of his injured hand and yanked him to his feet.

"Now that I've softened you up, you may be more willing to participate," she said, dragging his body over to the lever. She was surprised to find that he came without protest, like an innocent lamb being led into the slaughter house. Only this slaughter house was on a global scale.

She held firm to his hand, turning so his body was behind her and placed it down upon the lever. She put her other hand atop his and the black rock beneath began to crackle with static.

Elora let out a wild laugh. The machine was working, all she need do is pull the lever and the worlds would merge into one. Chaos will unite them.

Her knuckles tuned white as she applied pressure to the boy's hand beneath hers and the lever began to fall. Elora felt a wave of euphoria pulse through her being, this was it – she had done it. Then she sensed her hair being brushed to the side and soft lips settle on the nape of her neck.

The new sensation sent a jolt through her. The feeling so sudden that it forced a moan from her mouth. Her teeth bit into her bottom lip as she sensed his mouth move along bare skin to the tender area beneath her ear. Each touch of his lips gentle, caressing and sensual. The contact caused goosebumps to form on her forearms. She watched them rise as his blood stained hand upon the lever flexed, slowly turned over and his fingers interlaced with her own.

The boy's other hand drifted down her side, slipping under her arm to slide over her stomach, his thumb moving in gentle circles beneath her shirt, stroking her skin and sending a tingling sensation directly to her core.

His lips increased pressure, kissing more urgently as he pulled her against him. She sensed the heat of his bare chest rising and falling and when his tongue darted out to trace a line along her neck, she experienced a heat radiate from deep within, filling her veins with fire - with pleasure.

Elora spun around, hands pressing into his pectorals and abdomen as they greedily quested over his toned body, the many ridges and lines which formed it and the sweat and blood which clung to him. She leaned towards his face, desperately wanting to taste his kiss as his hands settled on her hips. Reaching up on tiptoes she was startled as his foot hooked around her ankle and he pivoted back. The vision of the machine room was a blur as she slammed onto the floor, her back striking the metal as Bray pressed his body above hers.

The shock at being manoeuvred below him soon passed as Elora wrapped her legs around his waist and ground him tighter against her. She put her arms around his neck and lifted herself up to his face, pressing her lips against his, her tongue probing his mouth as he kissed her back.

She wanted him. Everything else was dust as she raked her nails down his naked back, then trailed them over his wide shoulders and down his arms; thick triceps and bulging biceps trembling as he held her in place.

Bray's kiss became more passionate, his deep moan escaping with her own as she let go of every other sense of who she was, letting go of all but this one place, this single incredible experience.

Their lips parted and she took a deeper breath, feeling a dizzying concoction as her hands sought lower down his body, rising and falling with the contours of muscles, stroking down his abdomen until they reached his belt. Her fingers tore at the buckle, a frenzied movement that she couldn't control.

Bray leaned close to her ear, nibbled at the lobe; his hot breath whispering her name.

"I love you," he said.

And in those three small words she came crashing back down into herself. Her fingers lost to their frantic job, softened and settled once again over his head, her legs relaxing as she stared up into his moss-green gaze.

"I love you too, Elf boy."

Elora slowed her breathing in an attempt to calm her thumping heart. It had taken her days to break through the impenetrable barrier inside her mind. Struggling against herself, against the daughter of Chaos that willed her body to do terrible things. She remembered them all with stark clarity, re-lived them in her memories and knew that they would plague her for the rest of her life.

"Are you, you?" Bray asked, rolling off her and sitting up on a metal step. He pulled her into his arms and held her as if his life depended on it.

"I'm me," Elora replied, leaning into him. Only moments ago she had been beating him senseless, attacking him with her sword and burning his flesh. She stared down at the charred wrist and winced. She lifted his hand and delicately kissed the injury. "I'm so sorry."

405

"It'll heal. I'm just glad you're back."

He put his arms around her and she put her face to his chest to hide the tears – she had tried to kill him.

They were quiet for a time, the rhythmic humming of the machine and the whooshing worlds echoing around the cavern filling the silence. Until Bray spoke again, his voice thick with emotion.

"Flek told me that you were not coming back. That you were going to Earth alone. He said that you wanted another Shaigun and that I was free to do as I pleased."

The words played over in Elora's mind as she sought the truth of it.

"I didn't say those things."

Bray cleared his throat. "When he said goodbye to you outside the palace. You told him that he was to send you a replacement Shaigun. I didn't want to believe him, but you had been so cold with me after your judgment."

Elora squeezed his hand as fresh tears tracked down her cheeks.

"I was cold with you because my biggest fear was that the Supreme or Sibiet or any other of the Shadojaks would insist on us staying apart – I couldn't bear the thought of not seeing you. Then when the Emperor ordered me to kill the dragon, I knew the only way was for me to become…her…then I couldn't stand the thought of you being near me. But I never said those words to Flek." She turned to face him and planted another kiss, this one on the lips. "I swear here and now, that I want to be with you forever."

Bray's grin stretched his face, seeming all the more gorgeous for the cuts and the tears.

"Me too. Only…what do we do now?" Bray stroked her hand as he spoke, bringing it to his lips to kiss. "We can't go back to Thea; you've been marked as a traitor. And the Dark Army awaits us on Earth."

"Maybe they'll still take my orders. We've still got a chance to save the worlds."

"Or maybe we'll die trying." He gave her a lopsided smile. "Then again, those are the odds I've been used to and as long as we're together, it doesn't matter. At least you didn't merge the worlds." He gestured to the room and machinery. "That would have been Chaos on a scale nobody could save."

"At least there's that," she said, pulling him to his feet. "Back to Earth then?"

"Back to Earth."

Elora was smiling now. The thought of returning to Rams Keep, to Ejan, Norgie and Gurple was a happy one. Rams Keep inn felt like home.

She interlaced her fingers within Bray's, grasped them tight and planted a kiss upon the back of his hand.

Then in a single, almost lazy movement set their hands upon the machine's lever and pressed it all the way down.

Static crackled and hissed below her hands and she realised what she had just done.

-no!

They stood there motionless, Elora not believing what had just happened. She blinked, focusing on the fallen lever and the sparkling rock. The sickening sound of laughter dwindling in her mind. The daughter of Chaos had won.

"No," she groaned as she let go of Bray's hand and attempted to push the lever back into the up position. It wouldn't budge, not even with Bray's strength adding to her own.

"What have you done?" he growled as he put everything into lifting the switch. There was a sudden snap and he fell against the wall, the broken lever clenched in his fist.

"She...she did it," Elora murmured as steam vented from every flute all at once. The cogs stopped turning, the wheels paused mid-spin and the fluid in the cylinders ceased to rise.

They both stood gaping as the entire machine slowed then stopped entirely. The humming of the working mechanism quieted until only the sound of the worlds whooshing in the cavern could be heard.

"How do we get it going again?" Elora asked, desperately touching random parts of the apparatus yet it already felt cold and lifeless. As if it had suddenly died.

Bray dropped the useless lever and it clattered to the platform. The metallic clang echoing around them and sounding very much like the death tolls of a bell.

"We can't."

"But there must be something we can do. We cannot let the worlds collide." Yet she saw the resignation in Bray's face, in the forbearance of his battered body at his slumped shoulders.

Outside the quiet room the worlds began to take on a different sound. They no longer whooshed, instead the grinding sounds became deeper as they slowed.

Bray was the first to climb up the ladder to the top of the sphere they were in, offering her his hand as she followed.

From above she noticed that the sun no longer shone, its surface now dulling to a dark grey; the colour of dust.

With no light to brighten the cavern, she could just make out the large worlds as huge black globes. Neither following the same path as they had for the last tens of thousands of years, but making sweeps of the domed cave. Weaving up then down as they danced around each other, narrowly missing collision but growing closer as they settled towards the bottom. As they rolled passed the bridges, they bowled through them as if they were made of sugar glass, shattering the thin structures on impact. Elora gazed at both the exits that they were now cut off from. She felt Bray's arm around her shoulder as he hugged her tight – it seemed he had just realised that fact too.

They stared as the twin worlds passed within a hair's breadth of each other, then roll away in opposite directions up the cavern wall before they began to roll back.

"This is it," Bray said, planting a kiss on the top of her head. "I love you."

Elora sighed, leaning back into him as she watched the blackened globe of Earth collide with Thea. "I love you too."

She was expecting an explosion, the shattering of rock as the two came together. But instead the one world absorbed the other becoming a single globe that rolled by itself. The huge spherical mass weaved lower until it went out of sight, yet Elora could still hear its weight grinding against rock.

The explosion happened below them. A tortured groan as rock crushed through metal.

The sun globe they were on was supported by a long stem that connected with the floor of the cavern. That stem had just been broken by the world bowling through it, the impact throwing both herself and Bray to the platform which surrounded the sphere. She held on to the ladder, as did Bray but the notion was futile as the sun and what was left of the stem began to teeter over; falling into the void.

Blackness opened up before them as they tipped over at an acute angle, hurtling towards the diamond imbedded rocks. Bray slid off the platform first, his fingers gripping the bottom rung of the ladder at the last moment. With his other hand he caught hold of Elora's arm and pulled her up into an embrace. Most probably her last, but she wouldn't be anywhere else.

"Go," Bray shouted above the screeching metal and crumbling rocks. "You can turn to smoke and leave this place."

"I won't leave you." She held him tighter, burying her head against his chest.

Rocks began to rain down from the ceiling. Sharp stalactites as tall as trees amongst them.

"You have to, you're the only one who can unite the worlds, remember?"

She shook her head, "I did that already. Chaos is all that is left."

"Then rid the world of Chaos. That is what you're supposed to do. Elora will unite the worlds and Elora will set us free," Bray quoted.

The ground raced up to meet them, the large black globe still rolling partially up the concave slope as it spun before it began its downwards arc. It was heading straight for them.

Killed by the impact against the rocks, obliterated by the falling cave and then crushed beneath a rolling black world. They were three times dead.

"Go!" Bray repeated then released his arms. "Go now, before it's too late."

Elora faced up into his moss-green eyes as she fell, fighting the temptation to turn to smoke. How could she live without him? How much fight did she have left to carry on once he was gone? This wasn't fair.

Anger ripped through her chest. It burned from her heart and seared her veins. She closed her eyes and roared in frustration. She felt a building fury well up from deep within her stomach, it engulfed her, rupturing through every cell, every fibre of her being. Elora glared at Bray, at the crumbling cavern and at the rolling black death and grinned.

Flames ripped from her back. They unfurled and spread out like the burning wings of a phoenix, like her father's wings, spanning out like the angel of death.

She wafted them, testing their power; flames burning in the shapes of feathers as they curled and flickered. The brightness lit up Bray's face as she ascended, taking hold of him around the waist as she rose.

His extra weight pulled her down and they began to fall once again until she beat her wings harder and faster.

"I'm too heavy," Bray shouted, as she dragged them out of the way of the falling platform; the sun impacted with the ground and broke apart in a thousand pieces. She gave a final wrench with her new limbs and they cleared the huge world which crushed the sun, sending the sharp pieces of metal scattering in all directions.

More of the ceiling broke away and larger chunks of the diamond rocks came tumbling down. Elora witnessed their lethal fragments and pushed on, an intense determination fuelling her body as she scanned for a means of escape.

Her eyes found the tunnel entrance that led to the shaft and the way back to the mirror – or was it the way which Bray came? The way back to Rona.

Screaming with the effort, Elora flew towards the entrance having to dodge and weave between the raining rocks and stalactites. She sensed the huge mass of the rolling world as it followed their path, the natural flow of the basin-like cavern guiding it.

With a final dip of her wings she ducked her head and dived into the shaft, feeling the impact of the world as it collided with the wall.

She flew head first down the well-like shaft, pulling up at the last moment before hitting the ground and glided along the tunnel so fast that her surroundings passed in a blur.

Elora glanced down at Bray for the briefest of moments, not wanting to take her eyes off the way ahead, but it was long enough to see that he was unconscious; a deep gash had opened up on his temple where he must have been hit.

Elora couldn't think about that now, all her concentration was on getting them out alive – and to make matters worse, she realised that the tunnel itself was collapsing.

The walls and ceiling were crumbling before her, the glowing plant-life fading and dropping lifeless in their wake. She pulled Bray's body tighter against her own and willed her wings to go faster but in the tight confines she was already striking the walls with flames. It was then that she noticed this wasn't the same tunnel in which she had entered the mirror-world. It must have been the way Bray had come – she just hoped the mirror he stepped through wasn't too far.

Black chippings showered against the diamonds as they pushed on, the entire tunnel disintegrating and becoming no more than a thick haze of sharp dust. If her wings had not been flames that could harmlessly pass through, she would have been shredded a while ago.

Ahead she caught a glimpse of what she thought was the mirror, although it looked wrong – like a hundred different little mirrors, broken into small shards and splinters; none big enough for them to fit through, none large enough for her to squeeze her fist through.

Elora suddenly felt the crumbling walls and ceiling begin to gather around her trailing feet as it closed up. She had only one choice left that wouldn't leave them buried in the mirror-world – she just hoped Bray would survive.

She aimed for the biggest shard of broken mirror, folded her scorching wings protectively around Bray and reduced herself to smoke.

Chapter 23

Twin Worlds Merge

It started with a subtle shift in the air. No more than an awareness; a perception that something had changed, had altered – had added. Like the heavy feeling of an approaching weather front although this came from all directions including from the inside out.

The birds were the first to sense the shift. Flocks of every kind, the worlds over suddenly taking flight and those that were already in the air darted in a different direction. Wild animals paused, sniffed and tasted an unfamiliar scent. Hackles rose, claws protracted, eyes narrowed and in a flash of bared teeth every creature ran, sprang, slithered or burrowed to safety. Cattle raised heads to regard their surroundings, sheep stared at each other ready to follow whoever ran first and the pigs stopped wallowing in the mud and began to twist their snouts deeper into the mire.

Lightening forked across the sky, scorching the thickening atmosphere while thunder ripped the heavens apart. A gloom enveloped the new planet as Earth merged with Thea and a darkness shrouded the new world as Thea merged with Earth, the two becoming one.

A stagecoach bounced down the cobbled road towards Rona, the occupants, being jostled by the bumpy road began to tap on the roof to get the driver's attention. Smiling to himself the driver ignored them and carried on his merry whistling – when would the city folk realise that you cannot cross cobbles smoothly? The city lay before him, the day was warm and the sun shimmered off the Imperial Monolith. This route was one of the driver's more enjoyable journeys and he wasn't going to let his passengers spoil it.

A dark shroud passed above, dimming the drivers view – his whistling died on his lips as he sought the clouds that blotted out the sun, but there were none. Suddenly a wind picked up from nowhere, thrashing at him from several directions as lightening lit up the sky. His team of four horses startled and began to gather speed in their haste to be elsewhere.

Disregarding his tapping passengers, who were now banging harshly against his roof, the driver fought to hold tight to the reins while hanging on to the floundering coach.

Still wild-eyed, the horses slowed to a steady trot, their nostrils flaring as they chomped against their bits. The driver breathed a sigh of relief as he relaxed his grip on the lantern bracket. Then his mouth fell open at what he was witnessing.

Ahead of them, thick trees suddenly appeared causing his already panicked team to rear up; hooves thrashing at the giant oaks that blinked into existence as if they had always been there. The square cobbles that were at the base of the trunks exploded, the space they shared with the trees uncompromising between wood and stone.

The driver heard shouts from the men within the coach, but what could the driver do? He glared about, open-mouthed as they were no longer on the straight road through open farmland, but in the middle of a forest. The trees so close together that he wouldn't be able to drive his couch between two of them. Glancing behind him, he saw that the way they had come was equally as wooded,

415

the road torn and missing as it passed through trunks and the wind blowing so fiercely, that he was being constantly slapped by the shedding leaves.

His mind was a mess as to what had happened, as was those of his passengers who stumbled out of the now immobile coach.

"By the blessed Mother…" began one of them as he took in the surroundings. "I thought it was a bumpy ride but…" He opened his arms out to the forest. "Where are we? Rona was only over the next rise."

"It still is," said one of his companions, pointing a shaking finger along the broken road.

"By the blessed Mother…" repeated the first.

The driver's mouth fell open as he stared through the canvas of the trees and recognised the tall monolith of the city. Then he too was praying to the Blessed Mother as he watched the tall structure begin to fall.

A platoon of soldiers loyal to the Dark Army and the daughter of Chaos, paused beneath a large building by the River Thames near the centre of London. Two takwiches talked together as they stared up at the imposing tower, a large clock face on each of its four sides.

"Big Ben," said one of them, scratching at the beard that had sprouted from his new body. It was something that none of the takwiches had gotten used to: that and the way they stumble upon pointless facts that had been lodged in the minds of those they had snatched them from.

"No," replied the other as he kicked at the bulworg who was sniffing around at his feet. "Big Ben's the name of the bell inside the clock tower, not the building itself. Them's the Houses of Parliament."

"Are you sure?" asked the first, leaning against the shell of a car. Its doors and bonnet had already been taken to be melted down to forge into weapons.

"Yep. A lot of people mistake the tower itself as being Big...Ouch!"

A grumpkin had sneaked up on them and cuffed the takwich around the back of the head, knocking his dented helmet askew.

"No time for talky talkies," the grumpkin said, his long bony fingers holding his face in position. "We needs to find those rebels."

"They're not rebels, just people who haven't been caught yet. And most likely children at that." The speaker earned himself another cuff.

"Yes, and I needs a child for a fresh skin. This one has blown: too many baggies, holey pokes through skin shins and the flies have made a fine feast of the rest." He stared at them below a drooping forehead that hung fat and low as if his head was mad of wax that had become too warm. "You sees?"

The grumpkin poked a finger through a hole in his cheek and wiggled it around causing the takwich to wrinkle his nose in disgust. He had already sewn his leader's skin closed more than a few times in the last week. Then, when the skin became too soft to hold the thread, he used gaffer tape. That seemed to work until the grumpkin tripped over a rotting corpse and ripped his skin. Now he was so covered in patches and strips of the gaffer tape that his movements became as stiff as a rock troll's. He only wanted to find the children so he could carve himself a fresh hide.

417

"Now stops talky talking about stupid towers called Big Bensies and gets to searching."

"No not the tower, the bell…" The takwich fell silent when the leader glared at him.

They were about to begin hunting along the building when the sky suddenly darkened. No, not just the sky, but everything as if the very city they were in, dimmed considerably. Birds broke from the roof of the tower and circled, unsure of which direction to fly. Then lighting flickered somewhere in the distance but the thunder it brought erupted directly above, the force shaking the ground.

The two takwiches fell to the floor and scuttled inside the shell of the car as the sound of explosions and earthquakes roared around them.

Everything shook. The tall structures before them seemed to vibrate, masonry coming loose and raining down, shattering as it hit the path or road or in one case, a soldier.

The takwiches stared on as a large crack ripped up the one side of the clock tower, its jagged path taking it from the floor up vertically to split the clock face.

"We needs to be runny runningsies," screamed the grumpkin as he dashed along the shaking road, one hand holding his face together while his other hand flopped uselessly from his wasting arm.

The takwiches paid him no heed as their attention was on the cracked building which widened and a thick green limb of a tree forced its way out. From the roof more branches sprouted; spewing bricks as they fought for space with the building. Inside, came the torturing sounds of crushing stone, the wrenching of steel and another explosive crack.

One side of the tower crumbled completely, falling away to reveal the inside. It reminded one of the takwiches of a dolls house with the front open – although the dainty furniture and decor that his mind's memory showed seemed vastly different from the sight before him with its broken floors, hollow rooms and twisted staircases. The colossus tree that was still forcing its way through the structure took up all the space as if a god couldn't decide whether to place the building or the tree in that exact spot, so attempted to place them both.

As it tore through the clock room there was a deep ding sound and a large clumsy object blasted through the remains of the clock face.

The takwiches watched the progress of this big metal projectile as it tumbled through the air, its steel clanger banging a dull chime before it fell.

Big Ben's arc brought it down on top of the fleeing grumpkin, his tiny body disappearing beneath the giant bell. As the momentum carried it over it clanged once again. An ominous toll for the destruction, for the death and the ugly red smear it left in its wake.

"Think he has more problems than just baggies," sniggered one of the takwiches.

"Yep – and gaffer tape isn't going to fix that mess," laughed the other. "And I was right, that is Big B…"

A second bell fell onto the vehicle they were hiding in, followed by three more, snatching his words as they crushed the car flat. Big Ben had four little brothers. The quarter bells made a clatter as they bounced then settled against the trees that had appeared, making a forest amongst the buildings of Westminster.

Captain Brindle halted his men outside the perimeter of the warehouse on the edge of Brecon town. Slater was providing over-watch from the roof of a building opposite, the barrel of his sniper rifle trained on the compound they were about to search. Scott and two other soldiers were spread out on each corner while Pudding sat on the cart, the horse reins in one hand and a slice of Ejan's cake in the other.

They were on a routine operation: to find supplies to add to the large stockpile of food they already had at Rams Keep. Winter was almost upon them and with more people being found every few days, they would need all they could find.

Scott cut the chain on the gates and swung them open. He turned to Brindle for the signal to go ahead. Brindle glanced up at Slater who cocked his head over the edge of the roof and nodded – the coast was clear.

Brindle gave the signal and they entered.

The concrete yard was empty and quiet. An old newspaper blew about in circles before falling to the ground where it settled amongst many months' worth of rubbish that the wind had brought in. Brindle closed his hand into a fist and pointed to the large roller-doors set into the brick building and his men darted to either side, rifles trained on the dust-coated window above.

Using bolt cutters, Scott cut the padlock and pushed up the door. It squeaked and groaned as it opened to reveal a large folklift truck blocking the way in. Brindle approached and slammed the butt of his rifle into the back window of the forklift truck; the sound of smashing glass filling the empty silence. He cleared the broken fragments from the frame and climbed inside, opened the driver's door and stepped into the tall warehouse. The

420

rest of his men followed and began to filter through the stacked shelving, scanning into shadows and dark corners, fingers resting upon triggers.

They had not seen a takwich, grumpkin nor bulworg in days. Nothing since before Elora and the others had left Rams Keep, but it always paid to be cautious.

"Clear," Brindle said when they had reached the other side of the room. His men slung their rifles on their backs and began to root through the shelving, bringing out bags from pockets to fill with the tins of food. The warehouse was part of a factory that canned tuna and salmon. The fish inside would last for months.

Brindle crossed back to the entrance, his rifle remaining in his hands, cocked and ready as he remained vigilant. He glanced out at Pudding, his cheeks coated in cream and then up at Slater, the coast was still clear. He was about to return his attention back to the men gathering tins when a darkness suddenly fell over the sky. A shadow passed over them, dulling his vision as if night had suddenly crept on – something didn't feel right.

The hairs on the back of his hand rose and he got a tingling sensation down his spine.

"Stand-to!" Brindle bellowed to his men as he instinctively adopted a defensive stance against the forklift truck, resting his gun out of the broken window but not understanding what he should be aiming at, just that he felt an imminent threat. Behind him he heard his men cock their rifles and join him at the door.

Lightening flashed across his vision. It struck the roof beside Slater, shattering tiles and forcing the sniper to jump onto the neighbouring building. The sniper scrambled down the drain pipe and joined Pudding on the cart as thunder boomed, shaking the ground and reverberating in Brindle's chest.

The ground kept on shaking and the warehouse joined in. Tins fell from the rocking shelving, striking the floor and rolling in every direction as the entire warehouse swayed.

"Earthquake?" asked Scott above the noise.

Brindle shrugged. "Has to be," he said, then was knocked off his feet.

The force slammed him into Scott and the pair of them fell into the compound, the folklift truck passed them as it tumbled across the concrete and crashed through the far wall. Brindle stared after it wondering what had just happened. When he turned to check on the rest of his men he saw that a stone wall had appeared where the truck had just been.

Thick square blocks of stone reached across the entire warehouse and poked above the falling roof. His men jumped clear as the original brick wall of the factory folded over and shattered on the ground.

Giving the signal for them to fall-back, they ran to the cart to join Slater and Pudding.

The ground was still shaking as Brindle tried to calm the panicked horse as the mare whinnied and stamped her hooves.

"Where the hell did that come from?" he heard Slater ask.

Brindle cast his eyes back to the stone building that appeared inside the warehouse. Now he was further away he saw how big it actually was. Large turrets ran along the top of the stonework, stretching between two tall towers; like a fort or small castle from the middle-ages. A remaining wall from the original warehouse struck out down one side of the tower and as he watched, that entire side of the grey fort fell away.

Huge blocks of the stone masonry collided with the red brick as it fell. It crashed to the already shaking ground, kicking up a cloud of dust.

Brindle gaped inside the crumbling castle. Sat along a table were men dressed in shining armour, like knights or Roman centurions. They stared about themselves, eyes wide and disbelieving as broken shelving collapsed around the cramped room, showering them in tins of tuna and salmon. Then he felt the gaze of a centurion fall on himself, the goblet in his hand dropped as he pointed at him and shouted something in a foreign language. The rest of the knights around the table rose and climbed over the mess as they gathered up swords and spears.

"Is this real?" Scott asked as he watched the scene unfold, keeping his arms out as the ground still shook.

The armoured men rushed out into the cluttered compound which was now sprinkled with bushes and strange plants. The concrete yard was full of cracks and became broken rubble around an apple tree that stood in the middle as if it had always been there.

Thunder continued to tear at the sky while a vicious wind picked up and buffeted the cart while tussling the red cloaks of the approaching soldiers.

They halted on the other side of the broken gate and pointed swords, spears and levelled two crossbows on them. The tallest, who had gold inlaid into his breastplate began to shout at them in that same strange language.

Pudding yanked the cocking lever back on his machine gun and slid a bullet into the chamber.

"Don't they see that we've got rifles?" he asked, lowering his barrel on the line of centurions who didn't react to the weapons pointed against them.

"I don't think they've seen guns before," Brindle replied. "But keep that GPMG trained on those crossbows..."

He took a cautious step towards the armoured men, raising an arm before him, hoping that it was taken as a friendly gesture and that he wouldn't attract a crossbow bolt in the gut.

"British Army, lay down your weapons or we'll shoot," Brindle shouted.

The leader thumped his chest and his men advanced a step, those with spears cocked them back while the crossbowmen took aim.

"Damn it, man!" shouted Brindle, bringing his own rifle to bear. "Lay down your arms." It was as if these fools were from another world entirely.

Captain Jalothorn glared at the man before him. The fool dressed in the strange clothes was still approaching and still shouting in a foreign tongue - didn't he see that he had spears and crossbows aimed at him? It was as if they were from another world altogether.

"In the name of the Emperor I order you to halt!" Jalothorn shouted once again and then held his fist to his chest. Striking his fist away would give the command to kill.

Jalothorn sighed. Six years he had spent at this fort, one of the outer gates of the Empire. There were a few more scattered further north but he'd always like this posting. It was quiet, peaceful and he'd had no need to draw his sword in all the time he commanded this post.

He spared a glance at the devastation behind him. The second tower began to crumble and fall, crashing against this strange grey stone that was covering the ground. He kicked it with his toe. It was like lava after it had dried, only this was dull grey in colour and much stronger.

The approaching man shouted once again and raised the pipe-device he held in his arms. It reminded Jalothorn of a kind of instrument played in the highlands, although this had no coloured bladder and it didn't appear as if the fool was going to place the pipe end of the thing in his mouth. - why wasn't he halting? They didn't seem like Norsemen. The Vikings were the only people who dared attack the Imperial guard.

"Give him a warning shot," Jalothorn ordered the bowman beside him.

The bowman complied and shot a bolt into the grey lava rock at the fool's feet. It hit the strange material and harmlessly skittered away.

Bloody strange stuff that; flowing grey rock, he thought and then a loud bang erupted before him and he witnessed the sparks of blue and white flame flash from the end of the fool's pipe device.

Jalothorn felt a thud at his feet and when he glanced down he noticed that a chunk of the grey lava was reduced to crumbling chippings. He glared up at the pipe device – not a musical instrument then. He scanned the rest of the foreign party and took particular notice of all the other pipes pointing at him and his men, especially the big one with the chain of metal points feeding into it the huge pipe the overweight man held.

Then his gaze fell on a foreigner who had a fish painted on his arm; his pipe was longer with a larger hole in the end. He stared at the man wielding it and death stared right back at him.

Slowly Jalothorn opened his fist and signalled for his men to lower their weapons. They did so reluctantly, but what choice did they have? His tension eased as the men before them also began to lower their pipe weapons.

The approaching man smiled. Jalothorn recognised his gait and the way he carried himself – they were military men of some kind. At least they had a common footing.

Pablo supported the old man as they climbed the great hill, the statue of Christ the Redeemer looming high above them; his arm outstretched over Rio de Janeiro.

"The Blessed Mother," the old man grunted, his watery eyes never straying from the wondrous statue.

Pablo shook he head as he guided his companion up the steep steps. "No, he is Jesus. How many more times must I tell you?"

"Blessed Mother," insisted the old man, sweat dampening his strange triangular hat.

Pablo had met the old hermit weeks ago, after the electricity vanished and the lights went out. He had been peddling his rickshaw towards home after a day spent fishing, when the old man stumbled into his path. Pablo hadn't had time to react and crashed into him, knocking him unconscious. They were alone as the streets and town were empty, the people having gone to ground or hiding from looters and thieves which patrolled the now lawless Rio. Pablo had lifted the frail body into his rickshaw and peddled home to his mother. The hermit was a strange character: dressed in odd clothes and didn't speak Portuguese, English or any language which they had heard before. His mother was reluctant to let him stay, but knew that the weak old man wouldn't survive by himself in this new Brazil that had become hostile. After a few weeks spent with them he began to learn a few words of English, yet still was unable to communicate any sense other than repeating 'this not Paqueet, this not Thea,' while gesturing to the world in general.

Then one morning he began to say, 'Blessed Mother' and pointed to a large rock that jutted out from the coast; Christ the Redeemer standing tall above it. 'Blessed Mother, Blessed Mother,' he repeated again and again until his mother was so sick of hearing it that she told Pablo to take him up to the statue to shut him up.

"Blessed Mother."

Pablo blew air through pursed lips, maybe he should leave the hermit up there and let Christ himself watch over him – that is if he made it still alive to the top.

They rounded a bend in the steps, the back of the Redeemer's soapstone robe was coming into view, when the rock they were climbing up suddenly dulled in colour. A darkness descended over them and when Pablo paused to stare down he noticed that a black veil had spread over Rio and the harbour below.

There was a bright flash that lit up the sky as lightening forked across from nowhere, even though there was not a single cloud. A harsh wind picked up, first blowing Pablo and his ward into the steps and then changing direction to push them the way they'd come.

The hermit gripped tight to Pablo's arm.

"Blessed Mother, Blessed Mother," he babbled as the wind stole his hat and tossed it out over the cliff.

Thunder roared once again as Pablo dragged the man up the remaining steps, he knew that there would be shelter from the wind, behind the large statue.

Suddenly something heavy crashed onto the ground as they reached the final steps. The impact was so great that it knocked the pair of them off their feet.

Rocks and chunks of stone began to rain down, smashing and bouncing against one another. Pablo dragged the hermit beneath a tourist bench before they were stoned to death. Once they were safely beneath he spared a glance at the rocks and realised that they were parts of Christ the Redeemer. Great white chunks still falling from the statue. He watched in horror as the head of Christ dipped away from them, making a terrible cracking sound as it toppled over the cliff, leaving a decapitated form.

"Jesus..." Pablo hissed between his teeth.

"Blessed Mother..." wailed the hermit.

Then as he continued to watch he noticed that the head of the statue hadn't gone at all. It was still upon the holy shoulders, although his hair appeared very different. No longer was their carved straight lines but long intricate plaits.

"Blessed Mother,"

The ground continued to shake but the rocks had stopped falling and so Pablo crawled from under his hiding place and ran to the front of the statue, careful not to trip over the cluttered floor.

He had lived in Rio for his entire life – all sixteen years of it with Christ the Redeemer standing vigil over him; a constant that had always been there. Almost to the point where it was no longer a wonder, just a large piece of the landscape. But now when he gazed up at the holy statue before him his mouth fell open. It was no longer Jesus. It wasn't even a man, but the image of a beautiful woman, her brows brought together in a frown. Gone was the bible held in Jesus's arm, replaced by this imposter's globe and upon the holy chest were breasts.

"Blessed Mother," sobbed the hermit as he fell before the statue and began to pray in that strange foreign language.

Pablo could only stare at the new image that had replaced the Redeemer. It was as if the divine statues had fought for the same place and the lady had won. Although she now had an extra limb jutting from her shoulder. It appeared that Jesus had left her his papal arm.

Zilabeth stepped away from her flying machine; something wasn't right. She folded her arms and rubbed her chin as she inspected the bird-shaped craft. This was her latest invention. Three years spent designing and two years creating it. She ran her fingers over a silver wing which she had crafted from a metal alloy that she'd dreamt up herself. It was thin, flexible and strong enough for the job. But more importantly, light. Finding the perfect mix of metal was probably a bigger achievement than flight itself, although that was her aim and she didn't dwell much on her achievements – she had so many. That's what you got from being a fortieth generation metalsmith, not to mention that she was a direct descendant of Zalibut - the God of Inventions himself.

The front of the machine was cone-shaped; an oak propeller mounted on the front. Inside the cone sat the steam engine fed from twin pipes that ran down either side of the long cylindrical body. The pipes fed from two small barrels, one containing pressured water and the other liquid fire, which she had bought at an extortionate rate. Inside the body of the craft were two seats, one for herself as the pilot and the other situated behind for Teaselberry.

She tapped the tail wings and rudder, it all appeared fine. Yet something still niggled at her and she didn't like the little niggles – they always turned out to be big disastrous niggles and she didn't want to find one while flying hundreds of feet up.

Then she noticed a rivet sticking loose from a side panel. Zilabeth felt along her utility belt, which she always wore, her hands searching for the tool she needed. It wasn't there.

"Teaselberry?" Zilabeth shouted.

The sound of light feet came hurriedly from the other side of the flying machine and a light brown wood troll, full of excitement, stood before her; leather flying cap and goggles sitting skew-whiff upon her head.

"Hammer?" Zilabeth asked.

Teaselberry pushed her goggles and hat straight, large pointy ears flapping to accommodate the straps. "Mammer," she growled enthusiastically as she patted her own utility belt, exactly the same as Zilabeth's only the tools and pockets were on a smaller scale. Her tongue stuck out as she concentrated in wriggling the hammer free with her tiny paws.

"Mammer," Teaselberry repeated when she had finally gotten the tool free.

Zilabeth took the hammer, held it poised above the rogue rivet, then with one delicate tap knocked it into place.

"There." She handed the hammer back to Teaselberry and gave the flying machine another cursory glance. "I think we're ready now." She looked up into the empty blue sky. Not a cloud was in sight. "Are you ready Tease?"

The wood troll nodded excitedly then clambered into the seat behind the pilot's, adjusting her hat; wide mouth set in a toothy grin as her large brown eyes filled the goggles.

"I take that as a yes then," Zilabeth chuckled as she put her own helmet and goggles on, tucking a loose strand of dark hair behind her ear. She scanned down the hill, a final check for any stones or rocks protruding from the freshly cut grass. She would need as much speed as possible to give her craft lift.

Satisfied, she clapped her hands together and approached the machine, the long tails of her leather flying jacket catching a gentle breeze. She was about to fire up the engine when the sky suddenly dulled.

There came a violent clap of thunder which shook the ground and lightning spat across the land, flickering out into the distance as far as she could see.

Slowly she pushed her goggles up onto her forehead as she signalled for Teaselberry to climb back out of the machine – they wouldn't be flying today. Not when this strange phenomenon was searing the heavens.

The wood troll's eager smile faltered as another blast of thunder boomed over the hill, this time bringing a wind that whipped at her from all directions and rocked the flying craft with enough force to knock Teaselberry back into her seat. Zilabeth rushed to help when something struck her.

She was thrown back, seeing the sky then the ground tumble around her vision until she struck the earth.

When her head stopped reeling, Zilabeth sat up, pain pounding from the back of her head as she tried to come to terms with what had just happened and what she was now looking at.

A tall steel frame towered above her, reaching high in the sky with thick cables that linked it to another frame further down the hill. Her eyes followed the cables as they ran to more frames, each the same distance apart, flowing a single line over the countryside. The towers shook and the cables swung with the moving ground as an earthquake rippled around her. The closest tower tilted so far one way that the cables snapped and the entire frame fell onto her machine.

"Tease!" Zilabeth screamed as she rushed to the crushed craft.

The steel had struck her invention with enough weight to snap both wings and sink the body into the grass. Flames suddenly burst from the barrel containing the liquid fire, spreading quickly along the entire craft.

"Tease!" She climbed over the steel frame of the fallen tower and watched with horror as the light panelling of the body sunk lower, twisting out of shape and the seat the wood troll had been sat in was completely folded flat.

Her hands moved with the swiftness of years practiced with tools, reaching for the sharp snips and screwdriver in her utility belt. She sunk to her knees and drove the screwdriver between the rivets of a panel and levered it open, making a crack large enough to set the snips in. With an urgency married with skill she cut along the thin steel to the length of her arm then cut vertically down.

Once she reached the ground she dropped her tools and using both hands peeled the panel away.

Teaselberry's paw reached out of the hole and Zilabeth grasped it. She sat on the ground and pulled, straining her back as she watched the crushed machine sink further.

The wood troll's head appeared next still wearing her helmet and goggles; large eyes bulging with terror, then her other arm, but her belt caught between the frame and the ground.

"Come on, Tease, wriggle," Zilabeth shouted through clenched teeth, frightened that the weight of all that metal would press her friend into the earth.

Releasing a roar of her own to add to the ripping thunder, Zilabeth yanked back and mercifully Teaselberry came with her. A heartbeat later and the body of her flying machine crumpled flat.

They both climbed over the steel tower and fell to the floor, panting with the excursion and relieved at being alive.

Zilabeth stared at her beautiful flying machine; twisted, mangled and crushed. Five years spent creating her through sweat, blood and tears, through countless sleepless nights and through the failures and triumphs to reach the perfect end product. Teaselberry's sad expression matched her own as they both gazed on.

The wood troll pulled something out of her utility belt and handed it to Zilabeth.

"Mammer?"

Zilabeth chuckled and patted the troll's paw, "I don't think that will help this time."

A large groan and the sound of splintering wood came from behind them. They both turned and watched in horror as their home began to cave in.

The earthquake had done more than merely shake the foundations of the wheelhouse. It seemed to Zilabeth that the river itself had shifted directly beneath their home. Impossible! The river had altered its course by at least twenty feet.

She rose on unsteady legs and watched helplessly as it tilted into the fast flowing water, sinking beneath the rushing waves that engulfed their home until only the top of the chimney stack remained above.

Zilabeth felt Teaselberry's paw slip into her hand as she squeezed it. That home had been in the family for hundreds of years. It had been perfect, a work of art even. The wheel that spun upon the river drove the cogs inside, which she could attach an array of tools to - from a saw to sander, from a grinder to the bellows. Now that huge wheel floated away, along with a lifetime of work; generations of lifetimes of work. She bit her lip to stop the tears from coming. How many memories did she have locked in that home which now resided below the river it'd worked from? The hours, day and weeks spent at one of the three forges, smelting, melting and shaping. How long had she toiled at the many benches, soldering copper disks, tinkering with brass rivets or hammering or engraving, cutting and bleeding?

"Oh Tease," Zilabeth sighed as she stared at that lone chimney stack poking above the water – a fitting gravestone to all those memories and all her possessions. "What has happened to the world?"

She shook her head as she pulled her gaze from the watery grave to consider the strange steel frame that had suddenly appeared with its line of siblings to blot the landscape. They still shook but with less ferocity as the earthquake had begun to subside.

She approached the fallen tower once again and studied the metal it was made from. Taking the hammer from Teaselberry she tapped the thick steel and made a dull clang.

"It's good quality – seems to be galvanised with other steels too," Zilabeth said, taking a micrometer from her belt and set it to a large bolt. She measured it, then gauged the next bolt along and then another. "Impressive, they're all exactly the same size. They must have been forged by a master metalsmith." She glanced at the rest of the tower and then followed the line of them as they disappeared over the horizon. "Or by machines, but nothing which I've ever heard of on Thea. Unless…"

Zilabeth walked out onto the crest of the hill and studied the land around her. There were large trees standing tall and proud where there hadn't been before the lightning and thunder. There was a new stream that fed into the river where there wasn't one at all before the earthquake – and in the distance she could see the spires of a large cathedral and the rooftops of several tall square buildings; still shaking with the unstable earth. She pointed it out to Teaselberry. "That city was a tiny village this morning. It's as if another world has been dropped on our own."

The wood troll nodded in agreement as she lifted her flying cap to scratch absently at her ear.

"That's it!" Zilabeth exclaimed, clapping her hands together. "That is exactly it. It is Earth. Zalibut's god-created machine had finally failed or somebody had turned it off or destroyed it." It didn't matter how but she knew that the worlds had just merged.

She struck the steel frame excitedly. "Pack the cart and tether the horses, Tease. We're going on a journey."

Zilabeth shoved the hammer away and made off for the stables when a blinding flash rooted her to the spot.

Pain suddenly erupted in her brain. A blind stabbing scream that gripped her behind the eyeballs and she fell to her knees. By the time her hands were squeezing against her temples the pain had evaporated. She shook the dazed feeling from her mind and had a sudden vision of purple – no, not purple, violet. In her mind's eye she pictured a girl with black hair and violet eyes. She had flaming wings that sprouted from her back and held tightly to a large burning sword.

Zilabeth didn't know the girl and had never seen her before but had an overwhelming urge to find her – whoever she was.

With the help of Teaselberry she clambered back to her feet. "We need to go west," she told the wood troll. "And we'll need to bring as many tools as we can load onto the cart, we've got a job to do."

Ben wiped the dust from the Molly's window with the sleeve of his coat. The Dutch barge had eventually stopped rocking and become still once again. Now that the strange thunder storm and earthquake had passed, he stared outside to assess the damage.

"Well?" his girlfriend asked, nursing his newborn son on her lap. "What do you see?"

Ben scowled as he took in the view through the window. "It's different. It's the same, but…different." He scratched his head and shrugged. "The barge hasn't moved, we're in the same spot, I recognised that large tree with the broken branch and the overgrown cornfield, but there are more trees, a lot more and some in the cornfield which is daft."

"None of those monsters and creepy crawlies?"

Ben shook his head and came to sit beside her on the borrowed bed. Elora's he guessed. They had spent the past few weeks on the Molly, hiding from the looters and gangs that were roaming Gloucester. They left the city not long after the electricity cut out, seeking safety in the countryside. They had found the Molly purely by chance, moored up on the canal bank and abandoned. When he realised that Elora or her uncle were not aboard they waited for a time, expecting them to turn up. It was then that Nelly went into labour and she'd almost pushed him into the canal as she boarded the barge. A few excruciating hours later and their baby was born.

Ben stroked the blonde tuft of his son's hair as he slept in Nelly's arms – they had yet to name him. His gaze fell on his battered guitar leaning in the doorway. Funny how it had come in handy so many times in the passing weeks and none of its uses had been musical. After they spotted the monsters they untied the barge from the canal and he'd used his guitar as a paddle to reach the middle of the water, away from the huge wolves, trolls and ugly little men with saggy faces. They all glanced at the barge as they passed but none bothered to swim out to check. One of them had thrown a large spider from the bank. It landed on the deck and made horrible clacking sounds as it crawled into the boat. Ben had used the guitar to crush it, striking the insect over and over until it stopped moving. Later when they had spent a week on the Molly without once venturing to either bank in fear of the monsters return, he had unstrung the guitar and used the strings to make a noose to catch ducks, moorhens and in one case, a swan, but Nelly made him release that one. The swan was far too big to cook and it did seem wrong to eat such a beautiful bird.

Now he thought of his guitar as a lucky tool, weapon and silent companion all in one.

"He'll need feeding soon, and fresh water," Nelly told Ben as she gently rocked the newborn.

Ben nodded, he grasped his trusted tool and stepped out of the borrowed room and onto the deck, wondering what had happened to Elora and her uncle. They'd never returned to the Molly and after the panic of his son being born had passed, he noticed that there were signs of a struggle. The door to Elora's bedroom was smashed, a lamp was broken in the main room and a bullet hole was in the sofa. He hoped that where ever she was she was safe, but he guessed she had succumbed to the monsters.

Outside everything seemed calm. The opposite of what it had been an hour ago when the whole world was shaking, thunder and lightning ruled the sky and the Molly was thrown around in the canal like a toy boat. Then as he glanced over the side of the barge he almost dropped his guitar.

The canal had gone. The entire body of water had vanished and in its place was mud; dark thick and wet; blades of grass poking in random tufts up and down the stretch where the canal should be.

Confused, Ben climbed onto the outer ledge, lowered himself down and placed a foot on the new ground. His foot sunk into the mud and disappeared. There was a soggy galumph sound as he pulled it back out, minus his shoe – what had happened?

Grasping his guitar by the neck he pushed the rounded body into the shoe stealing muck and watched as it slowly submerged. When he had shoved it far enough for the mud to reach the guitars bridge he decided to pull it back out. But it stuck fast and when he heaved back, the head broke from the guitar and he landed hard on his rump.

"Is everything ok?" asked Nelly as she joined him on the small deck.

"No," Ben replied as he pointed at his guitar that was sticking out of the mud like a spoon in thick porridge. Then he watched as his battered pride and joy began to sink. "I can't swim across, not like the last time. I'll get sucked under."

He stared at the mud that surrounded them on all sides, trapping them like prisoners. It was as if something filled in the canal with earth, forcing mud and grass to mix with the water to form this sinking muck. His heart also began to sink as he realised that the Molly itself was being slowly pulled under.

Ben scanned around for inspiration or anything that he could make a bridge out of but he found nothing that could be used. "Maybe if I break the beds apart and use the slats to make a raft or…"

"No," Nelly said firmly. "If your building skills are anything like your singing, you'd sink us before…"

"Nothing wrong with my singing," Ben snapped back, then hushed his voice as the baby began to wake. "Look, it's worth a try."

Nelly was about to protest when her gaze fell on something behind him. When he turned he saw an old wooden cart being pulled by two heavy-set horses. The driver was a woman in a thick leather jacket and beside her sat a child in what appeared to be a bear suit.

Ben was about to grasp Nelly and pull them out of sight, but before he had chance the baby began to cry. He cringed as he realised the woman on the cart had seen them.

"Don't come any closer," he shouted, raising his hands before him. "Stop there!"

The woman pulled on the reins and the horses halted. She climbed from the cart, along with the child in the bear suit and gingerly approached them.

"Careful," Ben said. "The canal's turned to quick mud."

He made a pushing motion with his arms as if he was forcing them back. He thought she got the message as she pulled a bulrush stem from a nearby plant and pressed it into the muck. When it stuck up by itself and slowly sank she nodded to herself and spoke to the child.

"Can you help us?" Nelly shouted as she rocked the crying baby. Ben put his arm around her and looked pleadingly at the strange woman. She shouted back, but it was in a language he didn't understand.

The child stood on tiptoes to speak with the woman and pointed to them. The woman nodded and tried to speak to them once more before turning to her cart and rummaging in the back. When she returned she had a length of rope. The bear-child took one end and swiftly tied it to the rear of the cart while the woman threw the other end to them. Ben gratefully caught it and tied it to the rail – please let this work, he prayed as he joined his girlfriend and son.

The child climbed into the driving seat of the cart and taking control of the reins, worked the horses until the rope pulled taught, muddy water dripping from the length as it rose from the muck.

Nothing happened at first, the Molly remained stuck in place and he could hear the creaking of the stressed wood on the cart. But little by little as the horses strained; the barge moved. Inch by agonising inch they grew closer to safety until the bow of the barge nudged against solid ground.

Ben jumped from the barge and Nelly passed him the baby. He looked for a place to set his son down so he could help Nelly, when the child in the bear suit hopped from the cart and opened its arms out to take him.

Glad for the help, Ben passed his son over to the child then reached up to help Nelly down. It was then that his mind had worked out that something was very odd about the person he'd just given his baby to.

Horror struck him to the core when his eyes roved over the child. It was a monster. Without thinking he snatched his son out of the beast's arms and stepped away. Then he yelped as the woman grasped his shoulder, a stern look on her face. She spoke to him harshly, but he didn't understand her.

"Please, don't hurt us," Nelly said as she took the baby back and Ben stepped between her and the strangers.

The creature was like nothing he had seen before. It was the size of a small child and covered in a light brown fur. It had overly large ears and a head which reminded him of a pug, albeit a pug that stood on two legs. It stared up at him, big bulbous eyes sparkling as its mouth formed a large crescent full of teeth as it attempted an almost comical smile.

Ben backed away from it, ushering Nelly behind him, although there was nowhere to move to without climbing back on the Molly. He wasn't sure if the creature was a bear, a dog or a kind of hybrid creature created in a lab by a mad scientist.

The woman continued to speak in that strange language as she rummaged once again in the back of the cart. When she returned she gave Ben a small peculiar device. It was a small disk attached by a fine chain to a cylindrical clasp. Ben didn't understand what it was until he watched the woman place a similar object to her ear, securing the clasp to the top so the disk hung over her lobe. She then gestured for him to do the same.

Unsure what it was supposed to do, Ben slowly clipped it on his own ear and was unprepared for it beginning to buzz.

The woman began to speak once again and when the buzzing softened it produced words he understood.

"Don't be scared, we mean you no harm," said the woman, offering him a reassuring smile. "My name's Zilabeth and this is my friend Teaselberry."

Ben gazed from the woman to the bear-dog who had begun to pick her own nose with her long fat tongue and swallowed the findings.

"How can I understand you?" Ben asked, doubting the woman could comprehend his question.

Zilabeth touched the device on her ear, "They're tinker's tongue charms. They change my words into those that you will understand and the same goes for me."

Ben found it hard to believe, how was it even possible? But the proof was ringing in his ears.

442

"Magic?"

The woman called Zilabeth nodded, "Spell-cast and spell-bound."

"And the…" Ben pointed to the bear-dog, "Teaselberry?"

"She's a wood troll and a friend."

Ben shook his head in disbelief, "Trolls, magic…" He flung his arms out to the world. "Monsters and the strange weather – what has happened?"

Zilabeth sighed. "It will be a long tale to tell, especially when there is one so young that is hungry," she smiled at the baby in Nelly's arms.

"I was about to go on a hunt for food and fresh water, but," he directed his head towards the sinking barge. "We had problems."

"So I see. Listen, I have water you may have, but where will you go now that your home is sinking?"

"We have nowhere to go, nowhere is safe – not with a baby. Where are you heading?"

"West. I'm searching for somebody."

"Who?"

"I don't know her name, just what she looks like."

"Have you a photograph?"

Zilabeth's eyebrows drew together. "What's a photograph?"

Ben grinned, "Really? You don't know what a photograph is? How will you recognise her?"

"There can't be many people with flaming wings and violet eyes."

Ben scratched his bristled chin, "Elora has violet eyes. The girl who owned the barge we were on."

The woman nodded, "Elora," she repeated as if testing the name on her lips. "Yes, Elora – that's who it is I'm supposed to find. That's why I was drawn here first."

Ben stared at the woman, then at Nelly and his son before settling on the Molly; the gloopy mud beginning to rise above the deck and seep into the open door. "Will you take us with you?" he asked, thinking that Elora maybe somewhere safe and it would be good to see a friendly face after the rest of the world had gone mad.

Zilabeth turned to the wood troll. "What do you think Tease? Have we room for three more?"

Ben's eyes fell on the small creature, Its mouth curling into a large toothy grin as it nodded enthusiastically.

"Then you may join us," said Zilabeth. "And we shall share some stories on the way. You've a world of knowledge that I want from you and I most probably have a different knowledge you may want to know."

Ben felt so grateful he could have kissed the woman, but it was the Teaselberry troll that prevented him by wrapping her strong arms around his legs in a hug.

Chapter 24

Ethea

Rona was in chaos. Flek smiled as he watched the city crumbling several hundred feet below him. Buildings toppled, bricks exploded, trees fell and people ran in all directions. The church to the Blessed Mother collapsed as another building merged with it. Both brick and slate, wood and plaster, crushed together - each fighting for the same space as Earth-made steel twisted around the Thea-sculptured soapstone. The merged mess of masonry became detritus, death and the tomb that sealed over the bodies below it. Carnage on a city-scale - on a world-scale.

The monolith was the last object visible above the dust which engulfed Rona, reaching out of the grey cloud it stood tall and proud above the Imperial Palace, like a square podium declaring itself the victor. Then it too succumbed to the devastation. It began to sway then slowly sink. Tipping to one side as it began a downwards arc.

"Wouldn't like to be under that," remarked Quantala as he joined Flek at the bow of the airship. Quantico stood to the other side of him, sandwiching the new Emperor between them.

"I imagine it might chafe," his brother replied.

Flek suddenly became aware how close they were to him, their hands near the guns that they now wore in holsters on the outside of their uniforms.

The monolith vanished leaving just the grey cloud of dust and the blue sky; the distant sound of thunder echoing up from below as the colossal structure crashed on top of the already ruined city.

"My brother and I have been thinking," began Quantico, his thumb fiddling with the hammer of his gun. "About what we should do next."

"You'll do as I've ordered," Flek replied, a feeling of trepidation sinking into him more ominous then that of the sinking monolith. "As your Emperor has ordered."

Quantala cleared his throat. "Yeah, about that. You see, metaphorically speaking, we were wondering how to better place ourselves."

"Or what would be the better place for ourselves, metaphorically speaking," continued his twin.

"What are you getting at?" Flek asked, but he'd known the brothers for a long time and knew how they thought, how they always wanted the next thing - the bigger thing.

"The Empire," they said in unison.

"The real Emperor is dead," said Quantico.

"And so too is the Supreme and the rest of the Shadojaks. So, metaphorically speaking…" shrugged Quantala.

"You are the only one standing between us and the Imperial throne."

Flek sighed heavily, he was expecting this. They were ambitious, that was why he was able to bring them to his side in the first place. Apart from himself, they were the highest ranking people in all of the new world, in all of Ethea.

"And so killing me now would automatically propel you both to being twin Emperors," Flek said, putting on the cockiest grin he could muster; his life depended on this act. "Possible, metaphorically speaking of course."

"Of course," the twins said together.

Flek laughed, although his insides felt as far from humour as was possible. "And how long before you would be fighting each other? Not long is my guess. Things that always start metaphorically have a knack of bringing about a speedy consequence. So, you both throw me overboard, then who will be next? There can't be two Emperors." He felt a little easier as he caught them glancing at each other out of the corner of their eyes. "Besides, I've always got a 'plan C' should things go...other than the way I want!" He raised his voice with the last word and gave them his coldest stare he could.

"I told you he would have a 'plan C,'" Quantico said, slapping his brother on the back.

"You did, that's exactly what you said. Good job it was all metaphorically spoken, aye?"

Flek watched them grin at each other, the threat of being usurped forgotten by them, but not by himself. He would need to watch them closely and finish them off once everything had calmed. He didn't have a 'plan C' just yet, but soon he would need to acquire one, 'a plan D' and 'E' might also be prudent.

The airship swayed in the wind as they waited for the dust to settle, a far cry from the gales that bombarded them as the two worlds merged. Flek had never see so much lightening flash, one after the other as the dry storm scorched the sky. There were several instances where he thought his life would end above Rona and that being in a such a delicate vessel at the mercy of the elements, wasn't such a safe place after all. Luckily, the storm had abated in the sky while a storm of a very different kind wreaked havoc on the populace below. He mused that he should feel guilty, sense some kind of injustice and accept the responsibility for the lives that had been lost, that were being lost at this very moment - after all he was the Emperor and it was his Empire and his people that were suffering, but he didn't feel a mote of any of those things. He merely felt…empty. Perhaps when he was on the throne with Ethea at his feet he would begin to enjoy life.

The sun glinted on his god-created hand as he scratched at an itch on the metal that was more in his head than in the end of his limb. He was becoming irritable with waiting. When the dust cloud began to dissolve he cleared his throat.

"Take us down," he bellowed to the airship's Captain.

The craft descended into the vast city which was now an immense pile of rubble, stretching in every direction. Fires were burning in many places, thick black smoke rising above the disorder. There were few buildings still intact, standing tall amongst the debris. People gathered around them, coughing, bleeding and dying. Flek could see that Rona had few survivors.

Parts of the train-track poked above the fallen station, the train itself was lost amongst the mess somewhere, never to roll again. The driver and passengers most probably buried with it.

"Where shall I set us down, your Excellency?" asked the Captain, his face paling as he absorbed the scenes below.

"As close to the palace as possible," Flek replied. All those that were loyal to the former Emperor would flock to the Imperial home. They would be the first to bend the knee to their new leader – if not, they could perish with the rest of the city.

The hull of the ship rocked against the remains of a lone palace tower that was still partially erect. Two of the crew leapt onto the battlements to secure the ship while two more hastily disappeared down the tower itself, creating a path for them to reach the ground. Once the lines were tied in place a rope ladder was rolled over the gunnel and Flek climbed down, followed by the twins. The pair flanked him as he made his way down the spiral staircase of the tower, having to lean inwards to compensate for the angle the structure was leaning at.

Their boots crunched over the rubble of the palace grounds. Soapstone broken over the concrete that was cracked and damaged; the white lines of road markings still visible and the shell of a car flattened beneath a fallen wall.

"What's that?" Quantala asked, nodding towards the vehicle.

"It's a car, like a carriage which uses a kind of combustion engine instead of horses," Flek replied.

"Car?" Quantico said, eyeing the machine suspiciously. "And that?" he asked, pointing to a white coffin-sized box; its lid open and revealing rotting food and plastic containers. The house that it once belonged to now sitting amid bricks and plasterboard.

"I think it's a device for keeping food fresh, none of them work now because they needed electricity and that has vanished from the worlds." Flek saw that Quantala was about to ask another question and stopped him before he spoke. "They'll be plenty of things you've never seen before, but forget them for now. There's time for exploring when we begin to rebuild the new world."

Street lamps, protruded from the mess; twisted out of shape like damaged fingers reaching from a disturbed grave. The twins stopped, as one had bent in the middle and was now blocking the path. They put their meaty hands to it and together pushed it out of the way.

The movement disturbed the loose ground and an arm fell out into the open. Bleeding and battered, the skin scraped from the knuckles, the hand clenched into a weak fist and the body it belonged to, was still buried. Flek sighed, should he help? He ought to, how else was he to build a new world.

The platoon of men that were with them in the airship were trailing behind, Flek glared at them before nodding towards the single limb, its movements becoming slower.

"Don't just stand there gawping, dig him out," he yelled.

Flek stood aside as the men began to scramble about the debris, lifting chunks of rock and masonry from the pile to reach the unfortunate person. When he was dragged free, Flek realised that the man before him was an Earth-born. Dressed in a flannel shirt and jeans he could barely keep his head from flopping, his tongue poking from his mouth and licking the dust from bloody lips as he attempted to speak.

"I don't understand you," Flek said, guessing that the man was speaking in a foreign language. "Can you speak English?" he asked, the only Earth-born language he knew.

"My wife…" the man struggled to say, eyes rolling back to the rubble he was dragged from. "Children, they're still under there."

Flek clicked his fingers at his men and pointed to the mess before him, while translating the survivor's words. "His family are still buried, find them."

He watched as his men began to heave great rocks and lift timber out of the way. "Careful, don't disturb anything too heavy." He gestured for the Earth-born to sit down before he fell and asked Quantala to give him some water.

"What are you doing?" the Shadojak whispered as he passed the man a flask.

Flek offered him a smile. "Hearts and minds. We're not going to win over the Earth-born population of Ethea by words and violence alone. It will be acts of kindness that will bring them to our way of life."

A woman's scream issued from under a fallen wall as it was heaved aside. The man dropped his water flask as he attempted to get towards the source of the sound but Quantico held him in place.

"Steady," he said, although Flek realised that the Shadojak's words were probably not understood.

The woman's scream was joined by the crying of children as more bricks and a large support beam were shoved out of the way. His men worked delicately as they pulled the man's family from the rubble; beaten, dust-coated but alive.

Quantico couldn't hold the man back and shrugged as he darted passed them to be with his wife and children. After they had embraced and he kissed the tops of their heads the man smiled back at them, mouthing the words thank you, tears making tracks down his dust covered cheeks.

"Hearts and minds," Quantala said, "might be there's something in that."

Flek pulled his attention from the family reunion as a tremor shook the ground. Everyone stood frozen to the spot as the sound of more crashing buildings echoed

451

around the ruined city. The palace walls and archways which were still standing wobbled from side to side dislodging loose bricks and forming cracks. It was then that he noticed another large building, its ancient stone construction rising from the rubble and its circular structure curving partially in the palace and out. Its many thick pillars seeming to merge with the other material of the Emperor's former residence.

"I thought we were close to Rome," Flek said, nodding towards the huge buildings that had joined together. "That's the Colosseum."

He left the twins gawping at the strange marriage between the palace and the earthly tourist haunt while he picked his way over the debris. They caught him up as he climbed onto a fallen wall that was leaning at an acute angle against a marble staircase; the body of an Imperial Guard lying still and crushed under a collapsed pillar. From his new vantage point, Flek witnessed other people emerging from the ruins, shocked faces, Earth-born or not, staring wide-eyed. They rose with grunts, wails and with one former serving girl from the palace, a scream as her legs were trapped. Flek pushed aside a large stone beam that was pinning her and realised that she had partially merged with a brick wall, her knees disappearing into the masonry itself. Flesh and stone becoming one.

"I'm sorry," he whispered as he held her head in his arms and slid a blade finger nail into the back of her skull. Her scream cut off suddenly as he withdrew his hand and he lowered the body; the girl's face slackening as if she simply fell asleep. Flek knew there would be hundreds more like this, thousands who were unfortunate enough to be in the wrong place as the worlds came together. But nothing could be done. Flesh was never meant to merge with anything other than itself.

"Sir?" shouted a Shade soldier as he came scrambling up the fallen staircase and knelt before them, slamming his fist against his dust coated breastplate. When he rose again Flek recognised him as a Colonel from the Rona Garrison. "Voice…"

"Emperor," corrected Quantala, sharing an amused smile with his brother.

"That is, Colonel," interceded Flek, seeing the confusion on the soldier's face. "Temporary or for the foreseeable future anyway. The Emperor is dead. Killed by the rogue ShadojakElora and her Shaigun Bray. They did all this." Flek opened his arms to the broken city. "They merged the worlds together, Earth and Thea."

"And the Supreme?" The Colonel asked, removing his helmet as he sat beside the body of the serving girl.

"Murdered by the same evil pair." Flek shook his head as he laid a hand upon the Shade's shoulder. "They slaughtered the Supreme and every Shadojak that stood in their way. It was a slaughter, it was Chaos. But then, she is the daughter of Solarius." Flek paused as he let his words sink in. "As the Voice I have taken charge, I will sit upon the throne - once it is found and restore order to the new world."

"New world?"

"Yes Colonel. The twin worlds are now just one. Earth and Thea have merged to become Ethea."

Flek nodded towards the gathering people who were arriving at the fallen palace in their droves. Men, women and children, either Earth-born or from Thea. Dressed in the fine silks and cottons of Rona or everyday civilian clothes of Rome. They came together like lost sheep

453

attracted to the bigger crowd, a safer crowd – united in the disaster. Other soldiers were arriving. More Shades from the garrison or Imperial Guards either returning from patrols or simply climbing from the rubble itself.

"But…what shall we…" floundered the Colonel.

"Pull yourself together. You're a Shade," snapped Quantico. The words had an effect on the soldier and he immediately stood to attention and pushed his helmet back on.

"Collect as many men as you can. Soldiers, Shades or guards and civilians - it doesn't matter," Flek said. "I want all able hands pulling this city apart searching for survivors. While you're taking command of this send a separate team of riders out to every garrison to spread the news of the Emperor's passing and that I have assumed charge. Every garrison leader is to take control of the cities and towns of their districts. Take control by any means and arrest anyone showing signs of resistance. There will be martial law in place until further notice. Do you understand Colonel?"

"Yes Sir."

"Emperor," corrected Quantala."

The Colonel cleared his throat. "Yes, your Excellency."

"Good, now go. Time is against us."

Flek fought to hide the rising grin that teased along his mouth. He watched the Shade climb down the fallen wall as he made his way from the palace grounds, snapping his fingers at the men he passed and indicating for them to follow.

Flek's gaze then fell on the remainder of the gathering crowd. "We're going to need to provide shelter, food and protection."

454

"Good luck with that, your Excellency," Quantico said while folding his arms and scowling at the growing mass. "They'll be fighting amongst themselves shortly."

Flek's grin swiftly vanished as he recognised the desperate glances the people were giving each other. Especially the Earth-born. They'd already had weeks with no electricity and the Dark Army tearing through their lands.

"Then see to it that it doesn't happen," Flek snapped, wondering if being back on the airship was a better idea.

"How?" asked Quantal, folding his arms and mimicking his brother's stance.

"You're Shadojaks. Anybody steps out of line, make an example of them. Do your job and judge."

Flek felt the anger rising in the pair and wondered if he'd pushed them too much as their hands drifted closer to their holsters.

A sudden shout from inside the Colosseum was a welcome distraction. When he glanced in the direction it came from he watched as one of his crew came bounding over, his face full of excitement.

"We have them, your Excellency," said the soldier as he caught his breath.

"Have who?" Flek asked, feeling a growing agitation. He didn't like surprises.

"The traitors. Elora and Bray both."

The words hit Flek like a bullet in the gut. "Alive?"

The soldier nodded, "The Shadojak is unconscious. But the Shaigun," he shrugged his shoulders. "He isn't moving."

"Lead the way," ordered Flek as he drew his gun and followed. From either side of him he heard the brothers drawing their own guns. Could it be possible that Elora

455

and Bray survived? Neptula assured him they would perish with the destruction of the machine.

They climbed an arch and ducked under a cracked beam before finding themselves inside the ancient Roman structure; pieces of masonry still falling in places as the entire circular building remained unstable. Flek needed help scaling a fallen soapstone staircase that lay in a haphazard zig-zag blocking their path. Once over his eyes fell on two bodies lying still above the rubble and he almost dropped his gun. It was them.

Bray lay face down, an arm bent back at a wrong angle and a large gash open on the side of his temple; dried blood and dust mixing with his hair. He was shirtless and covered in cuts and scratches to suggest he'd been dragged through demon thorns. Elora on the other hand appeared unharmed. She lay on her back, face catching the rays of the sun as if she was simply enjoying a light afternoon nap. Her clothes were torn in places but her skin remained unblemished and vibrant. Even her dark hair and unruly blonde lock shined in the light.

How was it they came to be here? Had they found a way back through from the mirror world? He had heard talks of Elora being able to reduce herself to smoke, perhaps she could have drifted through a fragment of the mirror he had smashed. The presence of Bray's body was an utter mystery though.

Flek cautiously approached, training his gun on the girl while he signalled for the brothers to take a closer look.

They both drew their swords, holding them in one hand while keeping their guns levelled. Quantala nudged Bray with the toe of his boot. Bray's body rocked before becoming still once again. Unsatisfied, Quantala gingerly lowered himself beside the unconscious Shaigun and placed the back of his hand against his cheek.

"He's still warm, I think he's alive," Quantala said as he pressed the tip of his sword into Brays' back. "It's a shame, I liked him."

Flek thoughtfully nodded. He also liked Bray, they had been friends since the beginning of the Shaigun path all those years ago. And he would have chosen Bray's help over the twins. Even though they came as a pair they were no match for him. But his old friend would never have agreed to such a scheme, he was far too honourable.

"Carry them both out to the raised ground," Flek ordered. "These judgments need performing in front of the crowd. Witnesses to the deaths of the traitors."

The twins easily slung the bodies over their wide shoulders and carried them back the way they had come. Flek followed, his gun held before him and flicking between the unconscious pair, ready for any sign of waking.

The crowd had grown thicker in the few moments they had been gone. More people arriving and jostling for space as all the attention turned to them. Flek climbed upon the fallen wall once again; raised high above the gathering and in clear sight for all to see. There will be no mistake, he thought as he indicated for the bodies of Bray and Elora to be placed down.

The twins lowered the unconscious Shadojak and her Shaigun and stood before them, swords poised above their hearts ready to take the souls of the traitors. No room for disagreement - for protest. This would be an example of how things will be done from now on. Let the deaths of his former friends serve as a warning to others.

It was so simple, the two lives here for the taking with nobody about to rescue them, no one to come running to their defence. Flek chuckled to himself, he would make it as swift as he could in memory of his friendship with Bray if for nothing else. But first he would use the full potential of this gift.

"People of Rona, of Rome - of the new world Ethea," Flek shouted, then waited for the crowds to quiet. "The Emperor is dead."

Gasps of shock echoed around the ruins.

"He was betrayed and murdered by the ShadojakElora," he pointed at her body lying below Quantico's blade. "And her Shaigun Bray."

Emotions ran high amongst the throng as people began to weep, openly cry or hiss with hatred. Some of the men even going as far as to pick up bricks and rocks and take steps towards them. Flek raised his arms to placate them before the crowd became a mob.

"Calm yourselves. Justice will be done, they will be judged," Flek said, softening his tones and making them listen. After all, he was the Voice – this had been his job. "We will need what energies we have to rebuild. To restore the Empire to what it was. And we have new friends to bond with, to accept and help. We are two different peoples that have suffered the same injustice, yet this disaster, this peril we have been forced to endure will unite us and as one we must go on." He paused, allowing his words to sway the men with weapons in their hands and vengeance in their hearts. He waited for the tempers to cool before proceeding. It was blood they wanted, someone to blame, someone to kill and he had them eating out of his hands.

"The Supreme is dead and so too are the Shadojaks. Only Quantico and Quantala remain. I will take the responsibility as the overseer until another Emperor is chosen."

Of course, no other would be chosen and he would kill any that attempted to take the throne, but his thoughts were best kept to himself.

Flek stepped back, allowing the main spectacle be the deaths of the traitors. The twins each grasping their hilts in both meaty fists, ready to plunge their blades down – so easy it was as if the Gods themselves were guiding his hands. His plans had gone so perfectly that there was no room for a flicker of doubt.

"With these deaths," he bellowed to his people. "We will mark the birth of the new world, our world. Ethea!"

Flek turned to the brothers, feeling a rush of excitement pass through him as he nodded for them to take the lives of his friend and his friend's lover. Both bodies seemed at peace with their faces turned up to the sun, how lucky they were to simply pass through the final door while asleep. It's what they would have wanted, he told himself, to die together.

Grim determination creased the faces of the twins as they leaned into the grisly task; knuckles turning white, eyes cast down as they were about to drive the blades home.

Suddenly an ear splitting screech ripped through the sky. It came from nowhere, searing fear into Flek's own heart as if it was beating for the final time.

A black shape dropped from the air, momentarily blotting out the sun before crashing into the Colosseum with enough force to shake the ground.

459

The tremor flowed through the ruined palace, toppling any walls still standing and making the crowd run in terror.

Grycul flexed her wings out before tucking them into her sleek body and roared, her claws crushing the Roman building beneath her as she gripped the stonework.

The dragon roared again and fire filled the ruins. White and orange flames scorched the broken rocks and brick, scaring the fleeing people as they scrabbled in their haste to get away. Another ball of flame was spat towards Flek and he and the brothers barely had time to dive from the platform before it hit the lone pillar behind, the impact breaking it in two. The soapstone along the seared edge ran like hot wax down a candle stick.

Flek hit the rubble beside the serving girl he had killed earlier. The brothers were nowhere to be seen and a gut-wrenching feeling of being alone loosened his bowels. Carefully he crawled to the girl's body and squeezed beneath her, pretending to be dead.

He watched through the narrow slits of his eyelids as the dragon left her perch and glided to the platform, screaming as she came. Without landing she opened her talons and grasped the bodies of Elora and Bray, then took once more to the sky.

Flek watched as Grycul banked high, turned and simply vanished into thin air.

Moments passed before he dared move, fearing the dragon may return. He shoved the dead girl off him and clambered to his feet as the people slowly returned to the ruined palace grounds now the threat of the dragon had gone.

"We should have killed them when we had the chance," Quantala grumbled as he swiped dust from his shoulders. His brother likewise brushing brick powder from his knees.

Flek couldn't agree more with that sentiment. Dread pooled within his core as he realised the full potential of his error. Would Elora come back and seek vengeance? Would she ride that fire breathing dragon as she hunted him down?

"It's not a happy thought, having Grycul flying around at will," Quantico said, his gaze casting about the sky.

Flek nodded but set a grin on his face. If you couldn't be brave, then the least you could do was act like you were. "Grycul is only one. There are plenty of other dragons, other beasts that are under Neptula's power," Flek patted the brothers reassuringly on the shoulder. "Elora and her boyfriend are mere specks compared to the Empire."

"And the Dark Army?" Quantala asked raising an eyebrow. "Does she not control that?"

Flek chuckled, his confidence slowly returning. "What's left of them will be crushed. They have no order, no discipline and no commander. We'll make an example of them, a demonstration for the world to bear witness to."

Flek turned his attention on the crowd which was slowly returning to the mass that was there before.

"You see?" he bellowed at them as he pointed at the air where Grycul had disappeared. "You see the power the traitor Elora has?" He let his gaze fall on them, judging their worth as he continued. "Without a united Empire she will conquer, without the Empire we will all perish and Chaos will triumph. But the Empire is nothing without its people."

461

Flek drew the sword he had taken from the Supreme and held it aloft. He didn't understand the impulse that drove him to do it, yet he felt that the crowd before him would appreciate the gesture. Any speech was always made stronger with steel thrust in the air.

"Death to Chaos," he continued. "Death to the Dark Army and death to Elora!"

Flek felt dizzy, partly due to the loud words wrenched from his tired lungs but the rest was elation at hearing the crowds cheer his name.

"The Voice, the Voice," some chanted. "Flek, Flek," others sang. But as the twins kneeled before him, offering up their swords, the shouts from the crowds became one word.

"Emperor, Emperor!"

Flek didn't attempt to hide the grin which curled his lips.

"Emperor, Emperor."

Not bad for a day's work. Wake up as nothing more than a glorified manservant, a valet and by the afternoon an Emperor of the largest Empire that ever existed. Not bad at all.

Chapter 25

Small Gods

Swish swish.

Elora sliced the scythe through the grain crops, swinging her upper body with the reaping tool and cutting the golden stems. She ignored her aching back and the blisters on her hands which were raw from the weeks of toil she endured as she harvested the fields at Rams Keep. Attempting to bring it all home before winter set in. October was already upon them.

Swish swish.

If she had the desire she could become smoke and sweep through the fields with her Soul Reaver and cut the entire crop within minutes; healing her aching back and tender hands as she became solid once again – if she had the desire to, which she hadn't.

Swish...

She let the blade of the tool fall and leaned against the staff, shielding her face and hiding her tears from the men working in the next field. An entire month had passed since the merge, since she had awoken in the Shadowlands on the Necrolosis and since she had opened her eyes and cast them on Bray, whose eyes had never opened again.

Elora inhaled deeply, forcing the lump down that was forming in her throat and began to swing the scythe once more.

Swish swish.

Her jaw clenched as she put everything into her work, taking her mind from the path her thoughts were leading down.

An entire month? She missed him so much.

"That'll do Elora," came Norgie's voice as he approached from the lane leading back to the inn. He leaned against the fence, his hand shading his gaze from the setting sun. "It's getting late and Ejan will have the table set for supper."

"Not yet, I want to finish," Elora replied, turning her back on him and willing him to go away.

"Come on now lass, the others should have stopped working hours ago."

"They can stop if they want. I'd prefer to be alone."

The fence groaned as Norgie climbed over it. A moment later and Elora felt his arm slip over her shoulder. "You know they'll carry on working as long as you do."

"I...I..."

More tears came then and choked off the rest of her words. Elora dropped the reaping tool and buried her face in Norgie's chest. She couldn't suppress her emotions anymore.

Norgie held her, his arm waving for the rest of the men to finish and head back to the keep for the night. Elora sobbed, her chest heaving with each shuddering breath.

"A death of a loved one is hard," Norgie said softly. "Especially one so close and dear..."

"Don't," Elora snapped, not wanting to hear his words. She felt a pang of guilt for being so selfish to shed tears over her own losses after so many people must have died at her hands. She destroyed the great machine, she brought the worlds colliding together and she was the one to blame for…Bray.

Elora slumped against Norgie as he guided them home. Her gaze downcast as their footsteps followed the narrow lane, not wanting to see the large willow by the lake or what was buried beside it. Yet as they neared the stone well she paused, allowing Norgie to walk a few steps ahead. He turned when he realised she wasn't following.

"I just need a moment alone," Elora said.

Norgie nodded, offering her a sad smile. "I'll be inside if you need me," he said and made his way towards the inn.

Elora waited until he was inside and the door was closed before walking to the willow and sat on the grass beside the fresh mound of earth.

She curled into a ball, bringing her knees up to her chin and rested her hand against the cold gravestone.

"I'm sorry," she whispered.

When Grycul had rescued them from Flek's judgment she had flown into the Shadowlands and delivered them into the care of Zionbuss. Elora had awoken hours later and waited patiently for Bray to slip out of his coma-like state. She had bathed him and cleaned his wounds the best she could but he wouldn't wake. They had spent a long time on the Necrolosis, maybe too long as time worked differently there. Elora thought that bringing him back to Rams Keep would help. But his condition only worsened as his body began to waste, his cheeks sunk and he had long periods where his breathing became so laboured that she thought he was on the edge of dying.

Grendal did what she could, which wasn't a great deal as his body had gone through so much. The hedge witch could only guess that when Elora had reduced them both to smoke to escape the mirror-world, his mind had not returned to his body when they materialised.

Elora felt angry with herself. A hatred for who she was and what she had done, at what the other her had done when she pulled the lever to spread Chaos.

She had been by Bray's side night and day for the first week, dripping water between his parched lips and moving his limbs to keep his muscles from seizing. But the longer he lay in bed, the worse his condition became until Elora couldn't stand it anymore. She left him in the care of Grendal who was a better healer than herself. She had first planned on revenge, to seek Flek and kill him. Even riding Grycul across the new broken world to find him, but as she soared high above the ruined cities and the wreck the merge had caused she realised that her energies would be better spent helping others.

Her first task was to regain control of the Dark Army and order them back into the Shadowlands. Most complied although she believed some men, grumpkins and grimbles went their own way, forming rogue bands of bandits she would need to deal with on a later date. The takwiches being god-created were easier to control. She forced them to return to the places where they had first possessed their bodies and release them. Some of which had already travelled across countries and continents to reach where they were. It would take them weeks to return, but day by day more people arrived and some of the children from the keep had already been reunited with their lost parents.

Elora then flew to Aslania to find her mother and uncle. The town, being situated high up in the God Peaks Mountains were little effected by the merge. The

466

Minuans were happy to be left alone although both her mother and uncle returned to the keep, along with Otholo who had outstayed his welcome with the people of Aslania.

The sun had finally dropped behind the tree line, casting a red glow in the sky and creating a long shadow from the willow which stretched to the well. Elora kissed her fingers and pressed them to the gravestone then clambered to her feet.

She stood for a while in the dimming light, gazing at the mound and trying not to think of the person beneath when an arm slipped around her stomach. A solid chest pressed into her back as she was pulled into an embrace.

"I'm sorry about your uncle," Bray said, kissing the top of her head as she relaxed into him. She held his arm in both of her hands, lacing her fingers into his. Both of them stared at the grave she had dug only a few days before.

"It was his time," Elora replied. "His heart was weakening and he died peacefully in his sleep amidst family and friends. And he lived long enough to see you stir."

Bray had begun to murmur in his dream-state the same evening Nathaniel had gone to bed never to wake. Elora had wondered if somehow her uncle had given something of himself in order for Bray to live.

"I missed you," Elora admitted leaning her head back and resting it against his shoulder. This was the first time she'd seen him up and about. It had taken days as Elora's mother, Grendal and Ejan had stayed by him, forcing him to sip soup and drink water. Elora wanted to help but she only made matters worse and got in the way so was forced to find other things to do. That was when she started on the harvest. She had known he was improving a little at a time and so trusted her mother and friends to restore her boyfriend to health.

"Missed you too," Bray said, kissing her again. "Norgie told me about Nat. Seems I've been out of it for some time."

Elora glanced up into his face, worried that he would still be gaunt and weak. But as his gorgeous smile lit up his face and his moss-green eyes sparkled brightly she knew he was fully healed, thanks to his elf genes.

"So, the worlds have merged?" Bray asked.

Elora offered him a wary smile. "Yeah, and Flek is the new Emperor. Quantala and Quantico at his side."

Bray raised an eyebrow. "They were always ambitious."

"That's not all," Elora said, taking his hand as she led him away from Nat's grave back towards the inn. "Flek tried to kill us and now has a huge bounty on our heads."

"We're outlaws?"

"Yes, and he knows where to find us. I'm just guessing that he's biding his time, keeping busy with re-building this new world Ethea. Then when he's ready he will come for us."

"And the Supreme and the other Shadojaks?" Bray asked, a frown creasing his brow.

"Dead. Apparently we killed them along with the Emperor, before colliding the worlds together."

Bray paused outside the inn door. "Has Flek and the twins turned against us?"

Elora shrugged, "You tell me, you knew them better. But so far everything is telling me they have." She stood on tiptoes to kiss his cheek. "Let's not talk about that now, let me enjoy just one night with my Elf boy before we decide what we're going to do."

Bray grinned as he took her hand and opened the door. "You'll have no argument from me there."

They were greeted with the smell of freshly roasted venison and the sounds of Otholo singing a merry tune about a piebald duck while playing on his lute. The large room was full, the meal laid out and waiting for them and almost every chair around the huge table was occupied.

"About time," Ejan said, ruefully. She gave them a wink before beginning to carve the roasted meat.

Norgie pointed to two spare chairs sandwiched between Gurple and Cathy who was gently rocking baby Genella. Bray held Elora's seat out for her to sit and then sat himself and began to pour out two tankards of ale.

"You seem brighter," Melvin offered from across the table, bouncing a small boy on his lap.

"I am now," replied Bray as he drank deeply from the tankard and squeezed Elora's hand. "Hungry though."

There were several conversations taking place around the table as they ate dinner. Captain Brindle was heavily engaged with Scott and Smudge, talking about the keep's defences while Jaygen was laughing with Grendal's son, Darrion. Elora was glad to see that a few of the older children were sat on the floor with Weakest by the open fire while Otholo sat on a chair beside them, legs propped up on the table as he plucked at his lute. Her mother, Athena, was talking to Norgie and Cathy about the babies that were still to be returned to their families and how they would get them there. The only person not in conversation with anyone was Ejan, her face forlorn as she stared at her late husband's hammer hanging from the wall. Elora left Bray's side and joined the Norsewoman.

"He would have loved this," Ejan offered as she drank deeply from a cup. "Raggie was the heart and soul of any large gathering."

Elora could only nod, her gaze falling back on Bray momentarily and wondering how she would have felt if he had died. It would have killed her.

"I'm sorry," Elora said.

"Don't be. Ragna died how he wanted to. He died like a Viking."

Elora nodded and sipped from her tankard of ale. They remained quiet after that, listening to the other conversations without contributing themselves.

Suddenly, the door swung open slamming hard against the wall. A harsh wind carried around the room causing some of the lamps to flicker out and the fire in the hearth to burn brighter. Otholo stopped playing and all voices went quiet. Stares locked on the open door as a small hooded figure walked in pulling a huge bear that walked upright, its front paws bound by string as it was tugged along. No, not a bear but a large man, Elora realised. His long greasy hair hanging low over his face so only his black eyes stared through the wet strands. He wore a thick fur coat over wide shoulders that ran to the floor, only his hands were visible, the string wrapped several times around his wrists as he took small shuffling steps into the room.

The smaller creature approached the table and threw back its hood. Elora recognised her as the little girl she had saved at the excavation site. The same child she had sat upon the bulworg's back and tied her cloak around with instructions that she be taken safely home. But how

470

did she get here when that happened hundreds of miles away in Russia? She was even wearing the same cloak, the same clothes although her skin glowed warmly and her golden hair shone as if the sun was bathing her.

"Greetings Elora," the girl said, a smile playing on her lips after she spoke.

Ejan rose, a knife already in her hand. "Who are you?" she asked, her gaze tracking the bulky man behind the girl who stood with his head stooped low, his face still hidden beneath the veil of dark hair.

"I am known by other names and have other forms but most call me Minu," the girl replied.

Elora heard her mother gasp as her glass shattered on the floor.

"The Goddess Minu?" Elora asked as her mother pushed away from the table and knelt. "But I almost killed you, almost ended your life on that mountain."

"There is only one, my child," the girl said, the fire from the lamps reflecting in her bright intelligent eyes. "And I was only testing you when we last met. I was judging your worthiness, seeing for myself if you were truly the daughter of my brother – a pure offspring of Chaos or if there was more to you, a piece of goodness."

"And if I didn't let you go, you would have killed me?"

The girl smiled. "I had full faith in you, as I do now. And I bring you a message."

"Message?" Elora repeated, finding it hard to come to terms with the fact she was speaking to a Goddess.

"There is a war coming, Elora – and you are the key to bringing peace."

"Flek is now the Emperor of this new world. He wants me dead. The only peace I could bring is more war,"

471

Elora replied, her gaze flicking to the man bound at the wrist as he slowly turned to gaze up at the Fist of the North hanging on the wall.

"Flek is a puppet, the master is Neptula who controls him from the seas," Minu continued.

The Goddess lifted her head as she raised her hands and a large image of the world hovered above them, like a ghostly apparition slowly spinning in place so all the counties and continents could be seen in vivid greens and browns with the blues of the oceans in between.

"Ethea, as it is now. A world of war, of famine and destruction. A world where Flek will bend its people to bow down to him. And a world the Blessed Mother will not accept.

This is what Neptula and a few of the small gods had planned. They want the world to return to how it was in the beginning. They want to once more rule the lands." She flicked her hands across the image and the world turned completely blue. "This is Neptula's aim. A world entirely under water, a planet made of one big ocean which she can rule."

Bray came to stand by Elora, his hand brushing hers as he stared up at the hovering blue sphere.

"How is that even possible?" he asked. "As powerful as Neptula is, she couldn't make the sea rise to conquer all the landmasses around the world."

Minu smiled as if she was explaining something to a child. "Neptula isn't working alone. She has friends who desire the same outcome. Hadis for one, Valcateous for another. They have the power to align and form volcanoes under both poles of Ethea. They will melt the ice caps and flood the world."

"And Flek?" Elora asked. "Why would Neptula involve him if she wished to drown everyone?"

"Just a means to an end. He's there to cause Chaos and force the other small gods into war. Luckily some wish to oppose the sea witch. The God of inventions, Zalibut, for instance wishes to aid you. He's sending you a descendant of his – a token of help to fight this war. The green man has also aligned himself with you – what form his token comes in I don't know, but suffice to say he doesn't want a world of water either. Even Death himself will be watching and gloating. Although he wins either way; you've sent more than a few souls to him lately."

"And what of my God, what of Odin?" whispered Ejan, her knife now laying abandoned by her hands.

"Odin," Minu said, handing Ejan the string which was tied about the huge man's wrists. "Odin wanted me to give you this."

Ejan grasped the string and rubbed it between her finger and thumb, a deep frown creasing her brow.

"And you?" Elora asked the Goddess. "Are you here to help?"

Minu offered Elora a smile as she lifted her hood back over her head. "No, my child. I am only a messenger. This war is for mortals and the small gods. But I will give you one piece of advice."

Elora fought against following the Goddess in a girl's form across the room as she stepped towards the open door.

"You will need to use all that you have and more to win. The war of the small gods is coming Elora. Mortal man's days are numbered, so make the most of what time you have. Make time an asset to use against them."

"Time? But how?" Elora asked but she realised her question would go unanswered as Minu stepped through the door, her body vanishing like a ghost before she had passed over the threshold.

Ejan suddenly grasped her wrist, drawing Elora's attention to the string in the Viking's hands.

"This is my hair," she said, her blue eyes following the golden strands to the huge grisly man who still stood in the centre of the room, his head hanging low. "Part of the plait I gave to..."

Ejan wound the hair through her hands as she stood up and climbed onto the table, crawling over the top and scattering plates and cups aside in her haste to reach the large man.

"Raggie?" she asked, her bottom lip beginning to quiver as tears ran down her face. "Raggie?"

Elora focused on the stranger. The dishevelled figure, who although he stared at the floor with slouching shoulders, was easily the biggest person in the room. Was it Ejan's late husband? Could it be Ragna brought back from the dead?

She watched as the Norsewoman raised shaking hands to the man and pushed his hair aside to reveal the face.

"Raggie!" Ejan cried as she threw her arms around his great bulk and buried her head in his thick coat.

Elora recognised the huge Viking now that his face was revealed although he appeared dazed, as if he didn't really know where he was. Confusion bringing his huge eyebrows together. Then slowly his hazel eyes focused on the person hugging him and his thick beard cracked to form a smile.

"Wench," he whispered through a parched throat and drew his wide arms around his wife.

474

Jaygen approached him next, slowly as if unsure then rushed at him all at once and embraced his father.

"Da," he laughed, tears swimming in his eyes.

Elora wiped her own tears away as Bray put an arm around her. They watched the reunited Vikings as they hugged each other tightly as if they daren't let go should their lost one disappear once again.

Ragna breathed deeply, stretching out his huge chest and shoulders as he reached for the war hammer on the wall and lifted it down. Jaygen stepped away while his father gave the Fist of the North a practiced swing. His gaze then fell on Elora.

"I hear there's a war coming," Ragna said, colour returning to his cheeks. Then he swung the mighty hammer towards Otholo and levelled the head inches from the bard's face. "And you owe me a song."

A string on Otholo's lute twanged and snapped.

Ragna tipped his head back and laughed, his eyes sparkling with mischief; just how Elora remembered them. She rushed to him, as did Bray and they all embraced.

A war was coming, but for tonight - just tonight, Elora would not think of such things.

The end

Acknowledgements

First of all, I would like to thank Paul Manning for the design and creation of the front cover. He has a wealth of knowledge and helped guide me in the right direction and has become a good friend.

Thanks also to my editor, Elizabeth Watkins (the Typo sniper), for having a keen eye and helping to spot the typos which had somehow slipped through.

To Genella Stephens for reading through Eversong, (several times) and has been there since the journey began.

To my children who gave me the inspiration, and my loving wife who had great ideas of her own and has kept me going on her home cooking.

And finally to the reader, for taking the time to read Eversong.

Printed in Great Britain
by Amazon